HE ATTRACTED HER
AS NO MAN HAD IN YEARS . . .

. . . which was exactly the reason Lane had tried to stay away from him. Now she fought an urge to take the next flight home to L.A.

Instead she looked up at him and smiled. "Dylan. It's good to see you."

She could feel his eyes on her, as blue as the sky, skimming over her beige slacks and peach knit sweater, subtly assessing her curves. There was something about him, something that made him seem dark and forbidding, like eating chocolate at midnight.

He stared at her so long she thought he was going to kiss her. Her breathing hitched and she realized she wanted exactly that.

Dylan wondered if Lane's tension came from the journey ahead or just standing next to him.

She'd been wary of him since the moment he had introduced himself in L.A. She'd refused to go out with him, told him in no uncertain terms she just wasn't interested. Not in him, or the job he offered.

For reasons he had yet to fathom, he had phoned her again when he got back to Alaska, offered her way more money than the job was worth. Since then, he had called himself a fool a hundred times, been thinking it right up to the moment he had seen her and felt that same punch in the gut he'd felt in L.A.

Now she was here, and he wanted her as much as he had then. Dylan was a man who went after what he wanted.

Books by Kat Martin

AGAINST THE WILD

KAT MARTIN

ZEBRA BOOKS
KENSINGTON PUBLISHING CORP.
http://www.kensingtonbooks.com

ZEBRA BOOKS are published by

Kensington Publishing Corp.
119 West 40th Street
New York, NY 10018

All Kensington titles, imprints, and distributed lines are available at special quantity discounts for bulk purchases for sales promotion, premiums, fund-raising, educational, or institutional use.

Special book excerpts or customized printings can also be created to fit specific needs. For details, write or phone the office of the Kensington Sales Manager: Attn.: Sales Department. Kensington Publishing Corp., 119 West 40th Street, New York, NY 10018. Phone: 1-800-221-2647.

Zebra and the Z logo Reg. U.S. Pat. & TM Off.

First Printing: June 2014
ISBN-13: 978-1-4201-4995-1
ISBN-10: 1-4201-4995-4

ISBN-13: 978-1-4201-3383-7 (eBook)
ISBN-10: 1-4201-3383-7 (eBook)

10 9 8 7 6 5

Printed in the United States of America

To my dear friends Sky and Linda Sylvers.
And in memory of their beloved cat, Alex.
Love you guys!

Chapter One

The low moaning of the wind awakened him. The old fishing lodge, constructed in the thirties, was built of hand-hewn logs, the chinking between them worn by time and weather, leaving spaces for the air to blow through. An eerie keening echoed inside the house, a chilling sound that sent shivers down Dylan's spine.

Just the wind, he reminded himself. Nothing to do with stories of ghosts and hauntings. Just an inconvenience, nothing more.

Still, he had Emily to think of. Dylan Brodie swung his long legs to the side of the bed, shrugged into his heavy flannel robe, and padded barefoot down the hall toward his daughter's bedroom.

The lodge he'd purchased earlier in the spring was big and sprawling, two stories high, with a separate family wing for the owner, another for the prestigious guests it had once hosted, back in its heyday in the thirties. The living room was big and open, exposing fourteen-inch logs in the ceiling. A massive river-rock fireplace climbed one wall; a second, smaller version warmed the sitting room in the master suite.

Dylan had fallen in love with the place the moment he had seen it, perched on Eagle Bay like a guardian of the two hundred forested acres around it.

Old legends be damned. He didn't believe in ghosts or any of the Indian myths he had heard. He'd waited years to find the perfect spot for his guided fishing and family vacation business, and this was the place.

The wind picked up as he moved down the hall, the air sliding over rough wood, whistling through the eves, the branches on the trees shifting eerily against the window-panes. Dylan picked up his pace, worried the noise would frighten Emily, though so far his eight-year-old daughter seemed more at ease in the lodge than he was.

Frosted-glass wall sconces dimly lit the passage as he walked along, original, not part of a remodel of the residential wing done a few years back, before the last owner moved out and left the area.

The four bedrooms and bathrooms upstairs on this side of the building weren't fancy, but they were livable while he worked on the rest of the lodge. The master suite had been updated, but it wasn't the way he wanted it yet. Eventually, he would rebuild this section, as well, bring it all up to the four-star standard he'd had in mind when he had purchased the property.

Dylan paused at the door to Emily's room, quietly turned the knob, and eased it open. His daughter lay beneath the quilt his housekeeper, Winifred Henry, had made for her as a Christmas gift. It had princesses and unicorns embroidered in puffy little pink and white squares, all hand-stitched to fit her youth-size four-poster bed.

His gaze went to the child. Emily had the dark hair and blue eyes that marked her a Brodie, but her complexion was as pale as her mother's. Unlike Mariah's perfect patrician features, Emily's mouth was a little too wide, her small nose freckled across the bridge.

She was awake, he saw, her eyes fixed on the antique rocker near the window. It was just her size, fashioned of oak and intricately carved. She loved the old chair that had been in the lodge when he'd bought it.

Emily never sat in it, but she was fascinated by the way the wind made it rock on its own. Dylan found it slightly eerie, the way it moved back and forth as if some invisible occupant sat in the little chair. She was watching it now, her lips curved in the faintest of smiles. She mumbled something he couldn't quite hear, and Dylan's chest clamped down.

It hurt to watch his little girl, see her in the make-believe world she now lived in, forming silent phrases, nothing he could actually hear.

Emily hadn't spoken a single audible phrase since her mother had abandoned her three years ago. Not a meaningful word since the night Mariah Brodie had run off with another man.

Dylan's hand unconsciously fisted. Maybe he hadn't been the husband Mariah wanted. Maybe he'd been too wrapped up in trying to make a life in the harsh Alaskan wilderness he loved. Maybe he hadn't paid her enough attention.

Maybe he just hadn't loved her enough.

Guilt slipped through him. He never should have married her. He should have known she would never be able to adjust to the life he lived here. Still, it didn't excuse her cruel abandonment of their daughter. An abandonment Emily had not been able to cope with.

Dylan forced himself to walk into the bedroom. Emily's

eyes swung to his, but she didn't smile, just stared at him in that penetrating way that made his stomach churn.

"Em, honey, are you okay?" She didn't answer, as he had known she wouldn't. "It's just the wind. The lodge is old. There's nothing to be afraid of."

Emily's gaze went to the window, where a lone pine branch shifted restlessly against the sill. Ignoring him as if he weren't there, she snuggled back into her pillow and closed her eyes. She blamed him for the loss of her mother, he knew. It was the only explanation for why she had withdrawn from him so completely.

Tucking the quilt a little closer beneath her chin, he leaned down and kissed her cheek. The wind picked up as he walked out of the bedroom and eased the door closed. Emily was his to watch over and protect, his to care for and comfort. But he had lost his daughter three years ago.

When he had driven her mother away.

Lane Bishop stepped off the Alaska Airlines flight at the Ketchikan International Airport. When she had finally agreed to make the trip from L.A., she'd been surprised to discover that the journey—two and a half hours to Seattle, then two hours on to Ketchikan—was shorter than a flight to New York.

Alaska had always seemed so far away, so remote. And yet she had always wanted to see it.

Of course, she had never imagined she would accept Dylan Brodie's offer and take a job helping him remodel the old fishing lodge he had purchased in the middle of God-only-knew-where, Alaska—even if it was a challenge she found hard to resist.

As the owner of Modern Design, an interior design

studio in Beverly Hills, Lane had done a number of log homes, ski chalets, and exclusive rural getaways for the rich and famous. But a handcrafted nineteen-thirties fishing lodge on a bay in the Inland Passage pushed every hot button she had.

But then so did the lodge's incredibly sexy owner.

Which was the reason she had been determined to stay away.

She still wasn't completely sure why, after half a dozen refusals, she had changed her mind and agreed to take the job. Perhaps it was the debt she owed Dylan for saving her life—and getting himself shot in the process.

They'd only just been introduced, both simply guests at the wedding of a mutual friend, when gunfire had erupted. She hadn't been the target and neither had he, but Dylan had shoved her to the ground and been grazed by a bullet while trying to protect her.

Gratitude for the near stranger who had come to her rescue accounted for at least some of her motivation.

The rest had to do with the attraction she'd felt for him from the first moment she had met him.

She spotted him walking toward her, as tall as she remembered, at least six-two, and even more imposing. Her mouth went dry and her insides quivered. He was wearing a red plaid flannel shirt, the sleeves rolled up over sinewy forearms. His rugged features were chiseled, his face darkly tanned, and in a hard, masculine way, he was amazingly handsome.

He'd attracted her as no man had in years, and seeing him now, Lane felt the same jolt of heat she had felt back then. It was exactly the reason she had tried to stay away from him, and she now fought an urge to run back to the plane, take the next flight home to L.A.

Instead, she forced herself to look up at him and smile. "Dylan. It's good to see you."

She could feel his eyes on her, as blue as the sky, skimming over her beige slacks and peach knit sweater, subtly assessing her curves. There was something about him, something that made him seem dark and forbidding, like eating chocolate at midnight.

He stared at her so long she thought he was going to haul her into his arms and kiss her. Her breathing hitched, and she realized she wanted exactly that.

Instead, he reached for the handle of her wheeled carry-on bag, and relief hit her. Or maybe it was disappointment.

"I'm glad you're here," Dylan said. "The construction crew is hard at work, but I need to get things rolling on the interior."

"Yes, of course."

His lips curved in a smile, but his expression was as guarded as she recalled. *A man with secrets*—it was a thought she'd had before. Perhaps uncovering those secrets was part of the reason she had decided to come.

Perhaps it was simply that she hadn't been able to think of anything but Dylan Brodie since he had left L.A.

"We need to get your luggage. The baggage claim is off to your right."

"We have to get Finn."

His mouth, which was hard and fit his face perfectly, edged up. "I can't wait to meet him."

Finnegan was her dog, a ninety-pound Irish wolfhound—the runt of the litter. Her closest companion since her fiancé, Jason Russell, had died in a motorcycle accident three years ago. Bringing Finn along was the only way she would agree to come.

They collected her bags, then went in search of her dog.

One of the airport staff released him from his giant cage, and he raced to her side as if she had saved his life. Which she'd actually done when she'd rescued him from the pound just hours before he had been scheduled to be put down.

"You might have mentioned you were bringing your horse," Dylan said drily.

Lane just smiled. "This is Finn." She knelt and put her arms around his neck, gave him a hug. "Good boy," she said. Tall and rangy, he had a coarse gray coat and dark brown eyes that seemed able to look into her soul.

"Were you a good boy on the plane?" Rising, Lane rubbed between his ears the way he liked, calming him a little. "I bet you were."

Finn panted and gave her one of his goofy wolfhound grins. Lane scratched and petted until the stiffness went out of his body and he began to relax. "Finn, meet Dylan. He's a friend."

Dylan closed the distance between them, eased a hand out for Finn to sniff. The dog got a whiff of his scent and relaxed even more.

"He knows the word friend," she said. "He's very intelligent. He's a great watchdog, but he's amazingly gentle."

"You said he was okay with kids."

"Finn loves children."

Dylan just nodded. From the terminal, he led her outside, carrying her heavy suitcase as if it were full of feathers instead of a month's worth of clothes and wheeling her carry-on, too.

"I hope you had a decent flight," he said as they walked along, Finn trotting quietly at the end of his leash.

"As far as I'm concerned, any flight I can walk away from is a good one."

His smile came easy this time, genuine and warm. It made her stomach lift alarmingly. This was the reason she had come, this amazing attraction. And yet it scared her to death.

"Up here, flying's mostly the way we get around," he said. "Maybe I can teach you to like it."

She knew he was a pilot. She had also known he would be flying her into his recently purchased fishing lodge. Instead of heading for the parking lot, he turned and started walking toward the water. Since the Ketchikan Airport was built on an island with only ferry access to the mainland, there were docking facilities for the floatplanes that carried passengers to inland destinations.

"I have a feeling you're a very good pilot," she said. "I'm actually looking forward to the trip." Though she didn't know that much about him, there was an air of confidence in the way he moved, the way he handled himself that made her think he was good at anything he attempted.

Dylan seemed pleased by the comment. "I think you'll find the scenery pretty amazing." But he was looking at her and not the incredible view of the ocean, and Lane was having a hard time catching her breath.

Too late to back out now, she reminded herself. Followed by, *Just remember to keep your head.*

A ramp appeared in front of them, bobbing in the water. It swayed a little beneath their feet as Dylan led her toward a white floatplane with blue striped sides, rocking at the end of its tether.

"Beautiful airplane. What is it?"

"De Havilland Magnum Turbo Beaver," he said proudly. "Some Microsoft exec from Seattle was the original owner.

Sold her to a guy in Newport Beach, but it didn't work out. Now she's mine."

"This is the plane you bought in L.A.?" That was what had led to their meeting. Dylan had stopped to visit his cousin, Tyler, who lived in the city. At the time, Ty, a private investigator, had been working with Lane's best friend, Haley Warren.

"I found her on the Internet. She was in fantastic condition, and the price was right. It was worth the trip down to pick her up."

Since then, Haley had married Ty and become a partner in Modern Design, giving Lane the freedom to make the trip. Her gaze went over Dylan Brodie, looking like every woman's macho fantasy in his worn jeans and plaid flannel shirt. After the shooting at the wedding, while the EMTs had been cleaning the wound in his side, she had seen him shirtless, seen a portion of his incredible body.

Now, just thinking about all that hard male flesh had her nerves kicking up again.

Lane shifted a little closer to Finn as Dylan loaded her bags into the cargo compartment. He urged the dog up into the seven-seat passenger section of the plane and helped her into the copilot's chair. After a final check of the exterior, he climbed aboard, settled himself in the pilot's seat, and began flipping switches.

Her nervousness built. She still couldn't believe he had talked her into leaving her business and flying up for the weeks it would take to complete the remodel job. She couldn't believe she had given in to her wild attraction to him and accepted the job.

But as she looked over at Dylan Brodie, saw the confident way he went through the flight check, the ease with which his hard hands moved over the controls, she understood exactly why she had come.

Not since Jason had died had a man attracted her the way Dylan did. She had dated a couple of other good-looking men, but those few dates had ended in disaster. Maybe it would happen again, but there was something about Dylan Brodie that had convinced her to take the risk.

Aside from his irresistibly challenging project, she was determined to explore the attraction between them. She would take things slowly, keep her emotions in check and make sure she was doing the right thing, but if the feeling was mutual and as strong as it had been before, she would act on it.

She was a woman, after all. She had needs, desires, just like any other woman. After three long years of grieving, she deserved a little physical contact with an amazingly attractive man.

Or at least that was what she had told herself.

Unfortunately, as the plane began to rush through the water, throwing up a frothy wake, traveling faster and farther toward some unknown destination, all her earlier doubts rose into her head.

She didn't have to be psychic to know she was completely out of her league with a man like Brodie. Good Lord, she didn't even know him!

She hadn't been sure what Dylan expected of her when she'd agreed to take the job, but she wasn't going to let him push her into making a mistake. She hadn't had sex in three years. She simply wasn't ready to rush into a relationship, she told herself, as brief as this one would be.

Dear God, she thought in near panic as the engine roared and the plane began to lift out of the sea, *what on earth have I done?*

Chapter Two

Dylan eased the plane into a slow climb, then flattened out and settled at a comfortable altitude above the ocean and deep green forests below.

He flicked a glance at the woman beside him, sitting rigidly in the copilot's seat. She was wearing beige slacks, a peach-colored sweater, and low-heeled shoes. Gold earrings sparkled in her ears, and pale orange fingernail polish gleamed on her slender hands. Not exactly outdoor wear, but he liked it.

He wondered if the tension she was feeling came from the plane ride or just sitting next to him.

He was pretty sure it was the latter.

She'd been wary of him since the moment he had introduced himself one sunny afternoon in California. Over the next few days, she had dodged every effort he had made to get her to go out with him, told him in no uncertain terms she just wasn't interested.

Not in him, or the job he offered.

She owned an interior design firm in Beverly Hills, she'd told him, adding when he'd baited her that she was a damn good designer. Having checked her résumé and the references he found on the Internet, having done all the necessary homework, he knew she hadn't been unjustly boasting. The woman knew interior design, and her credentials said she could handle the job.

Still, she'd said no when he'd tried to get her to come north and take on the project. She'd said no half a dozen times, and it should have been enough.

For reasons he had yet to fathom, he had called her again when he got back home and asked her one last time, offered her way more money than the job was worth.

He'd called himself an idiot a hundred times, been thinking it right up to the moment he'd seen her standing in the terminal and felt that same punch in the gut he'd felt in L.A.

Taller than average, about five-eight, she was twenty-seven years old, slender yet curvy in all the right places. She had wavy, just-below-the-shoulder red hair and eyes greener than a high meadow pine. She had bold yet feminine features, and her skin had a golden cast he didn't think came from the sun. Just looking at her made him hard. God, she was a beauty.

He reminded himself he had fallen for a beautiful woman before and it had ended in disaster. Marrying Mariah Douglas was the worst mistake he'd ever made. But he wasn't interested in marrying Lane. And she sure as hell wasn't interested in tying up with him.

Not for any length of time, at least.

Lane was a sensible woman, a businesswoman sophisticated enough to enjoy a brief, intense relationship and walk away unfazed when it was over.

From the moment he had seen her, he had wanted her. More than wanted her. And though she was skittish and unsure of her feelings, he knew damn well she wanted *him*.

He wouldn't rush her. It wasn't his way. If it worked, it worked. If it didn't, it didn't. But he was a man who went after what he wanted, and he wanted Lane Bishop in his bed.

He thought of his daughter and wondered what Emily would think when he brought another woman into the house. He hadn't told Lane about her. But then what was there to tell? Em lived in a world of her own. She never bothered anyone. And Lane was there to do a job. The two would rarely see each other.

"You were right," Lane said, flashing him a grin, apparently forgetting her nervousness, at least for the moment. "It's spectacular." She went back to looking at the view of deep pine forests stretching endlessly beneath the plane, the landscape interspersed with blue ocean, quiet lakes, and rocky peaks. "It's better than any picture I've ever seen."

He relaxed a little. "I hoped you'd like it." But he hadn't been completely sure. These days, a lot of people were more interested in texting or playing a game on their iPhones than looking at the scenery.

Though his ex-wife had been raised in Wyoming and should have been used to the climate and surroundings, she had hated Alaska the minute she'd set foot on the loamy soil.

Next to him, Lane was still smiling. "I love the mountains," she said. "I grew up in Illinois farm country, but my mother came from Vermont. She always missed it. The snow on the mountains at Christmas, the scent of pine trees. I guess I must have inherited a little of that love."

Of course it was easy to love Alaska in the late spring and summer. The tourist season. It was the rest of the year most people couldn't handle.

"Your folks still around?" he asked.

He caught a flash of sadness in her face. "Dad took a job in L.A. and died of a heart attack right after the move. Mom got breast cancer a few months later. I was in college in Chicago. I quit school and moved out to California to take care of her."

"That had to be rough."

"It was worth it. Over those last few months, Mom and I really got to know each other. I wouldn't trade the time we spent together for anything."

Interesting. He had her pegged as a cooler, less emotional kind of woman. He wondered if that would pose a problem later on. Then again, why should it? Lane was from L.A. No-strings sex was perfectly acceptable there.

She turned back to the window. "Oh, look at those snow-covered peaks! They seem tall enough to touch the sky." She grabbed her handbag and started digging frantically around in the bottom. Behind them, Finn moved a little in his seat, then put his head back down and went back to sleep.

Lane retrieved her digital camera and started snapping away. For the next few minutes she took photo after photo of the incredible view outside the window.

"How far away is the lodge?"

"It's about a hundred miles from Ketchikan to Eagle Bay."

She started snapping pictures again as if she wouldn't have time to get enough. He didn't tell her the view she was looking at went on for thousands of miles.

There was only so much a city girl could take.

Lane enjoyed the flight to Eagle Bay far more than she had expected. She'd been completely caught up in the incredible scenery, the snow-capped ranges that stretched as far as the eye could see, the islands, one after another in the Inland Passage below the plane. She had even spotted a whale, and Dylan had dipped down so she could get a closer look.

For a while she'd even been able to forget the unsettling man beside her. Now they were descending, losing altitude, preparing for a water landing in the bay.

"I'll make a pass over the lodge so you can get a look at what you'll be dealing with."

"That'd be great."

The plane dipped, continued its descent, then began to circle over a structure sitting along the shoreline of the bay. The lodge was larger than she had imagined, big and sprawling, a U-shaped building two stories high, one side a little longer than the other.

"There are two separate wings," Dylan said. "The smaller one's for family, the bigger one's for guests."

"How many rooms?"

"Four bedrooms and a master suite on the residential side, ten rooms in the guest wing. We're knocking out some walls so we'll end up with two suites and six bedrooms with baths in that wing. There's a garage underneath. The center of the lodge is the great hall and dining room, a few miscellaneous spaces."

"It looks a lot bigger than I imagined when I saw the photos." She looked down. "Are those cabins?"

"That's right. Four outside cabins plus the main lodge, and a few outbuildings: sheds, covered wood bins, that kind of thing." One of his dark eyebrows went up. "You can handle it, right?"

A shot of irritation trickled through her. "Of course." She was damn good at what she did. And she had done far bigger projects. She wouldn't have taken the job if she couldn't do it right. She flicked him a sideways glance. "I can handle it. That's why you're paying me the big bucks."

Dylan laughed, a husky, masculine sound that sent a ripple of heat sliding through her, reminding her of the underlying reason she had come.

Dylan circled the plane one more time and some of her unease returned as she realized that as far as she could see there was nothing but forest, miles and miles of deep green woods broken only by blue mountain lakes and long stretches of ocean.

"I thought there'd be a town," she said.

"Not to worry." The engine buzzed as he swung the plane a little to the right and she spotted what looked like structures in the distance, a few scattered homes and businesses. "That's a settlement called Yeil. It means 'raven' in Tlingit."

"Klink-it?"

"That's the way you pronounce it. It's the name of the Indians in this area. There's a small school, a grocery store with a one-pump gas station, and a community center. It's where we get our power, and the cell tower is there. Some of the people who live there work for me."

"I see."

"Waterside is fifteen minutes further north by air. The ferry docks there. That's where we get supplies, pick up guests. There are businesses there, even a movie theater."

"So you can drive there?"

"You can. Or you can go by boat."

"You have a boat?"

"Twenty-five-foot Grady-White. Great for fishing."

"How long does it take to drive?"

"The town's only twenty-five miles away, but the roads are gravel. They aren't too bad this time of year, but if the snow gets too deep, you have to fly or go by snowmobile."

Her stomach knotted. Unless Dylan flew her, or took her in his boat, she was stranded miles from the nearest real town. Why hadn't he mentioned how secluded they would be? Why hadn't she asked more questions? She'd been so damned busy she hadn't had time to do her research.

Or maybe she was afraid if she knew too much, she wouldn't come.

When she turned, she saw him watching her.

"You know you read like an open book. We won't be alone out here, if that's what you're worried about. Other people live in Eagle Bay. They aren't that close to the lodge, but they have homes not too far away. With the remodel, I've got contractors working at the lodge all day. I've got a housekeeper. You don't have to be afraid, Lane."

Her hackles went up, though she had definitely been feeling uneasy. "I'm not afraid. I was just . . . I should have done a little more research."

"I'll tell you anything you want to know."

She sat back in her seat. It would have to be enough. She was here now and she had to admit she was captivated by what she had seen so far. Whatever happened, she would remember this wild place. She figured very few people who saw it ever forgot it.

Dylan made a nice, easy, smooth-water landing, then taxied close to the dock and let the wake nudge him up to the tie-downs. Paddy O'Ryan, the brawny, redheaded

Irishman who worked for him, began securing the lines, attaching the plane so it wouldn't float away.

Dylan climbed out, stepping down on one of the pontoons that replaced the wheels, then reached up for Lane and helped her climb out. She caught Finn's leash and tugged, and the dog jumped out of the plane, nearly knocking her into the water as he shot past her and landed on the dock.

Grinning, Dylan caught her waist to steady her and felt her firm, lean muscles. A jolt of heat shot through him. Lane must have felt it, too. She turned, eyes wide, and quickly stepped onto the dock. Collecting Finn's leash, she led the dog up on the shore while Dylan unloaded her bags and followed.

His best friend, a well-built, dark-skinned man, walked up and grabbed the bigger bag. He was half Alaska Native with a mix of something else that refined his features and made him obnoxiously handsome. "I see you found her," Caleb said.

"Yup, right there at the airport where she was supposed to be." Dylan turned. "Lane, this is Caleb Wolfe. He helps me run the place."

Her green eyes ran along the black hair Caleb wore in two long braids, then traveled six feet down to the soles of his heavy leather work boots. At thirty-one, Caleb was two years younger than Dylan, though his occasional spouting of Indian mythology had a tendency to make him seem older and wiser.

Having seen him as drunk as ten Tlingit braves on homemade beer and barely able to talk at all, Dylan knew better.

Lane extended a hand. "It's nice to meet you, Caleb."

His friend's calloused palm engulfed her slender fingers.

"Dylan's said a lot of nice things about you. I can see they were true."

Dylan inwardly scoffed. He hadn't said squat. Which just went to show that just because a guy wore beads and wove feathers into his hair didn't mean he wasn't full of bullshit.

"This is Finn," Lane said, rubbing the dog's shaggy head. "He's very gentle."

Caleb extended his hand, Finn sniffed, and the two got acquainted. "Nice dog," he said.

"Thanks."

Caleb gave Finn a little scratch beneath the chin and the dog gave him what looked strangely like a smile. "I'll take the bags in," Caleb said. "Mrs. Henry's been cooking all day. I can smell the venison roast from here. She baked an apple pie, too."

"Sounds good."

"I'll see you at supper."

"Mrs. Henry?" Lane repeated as Caleb walked away and they headed up the stone path toward the front door of the lodge.

The lodge regally overlooked the bay, with a covered porch in front, two long balconies that wrapped around the upstairs, and amazing views of the ocean. The sight reminded him why he had purchased the place.

"Winifred Henry," he explained. "The housekeeper I mentioned. She takes care of Emily."

Lane stopped dead in her tracks, Finn right beside her. "Emily? Who exactly is Emily? And you had better not tell me she's your wife."

He chuckled. "No wife. Not anymore. Emily's my daughter."

She didn't move. He could see the temper building,

rippling off her in waves. "You didn't bother to mention the lodge was miles away from a real town, down a nearly impassable road and—"

"Fifteen minutes by plane."

"And you also just happened to forget to mention you had a daughter?"

His amusement slipped away. "Emily won't bother you. You won't even know she's here."

"How old is she?"

"She's eight."

Lane started walking rapidly up the path, and Dylan fell in behind her. As she reached the front door, he caught her shoulder and turned her around. "I didn't tell you about Emily because it was just too complicated."

Those green eyes were spitting. "Since when is talking about an eight-year-old girl too complicated?"

"Emily isn't like other kids. She's . . ." He swallowed. "The problem is, Emily doesn't talk. Not a word. Hasn't said a damned thing since her mother left us three years ago."

Silence fell, then Lane revved up again. "Have you taken her to a doctor, a specialist, someone who might be able to help her?"

He was starting to get mad himself. "What do you think I did? Just pretended she was okay? I took her to every specialist I could find. Seattle. San Francisco. Even Chicago. The doctors ran tests, prodded and poked her till it drove me half crazy. When the tests all came up negative, I took her to a string of psychiatrists."

"And?"

"And in the end they all agreed. Emily was in her quiet world because that was where she felt safe. There was nothing physically wrong with her. Nothing anyone could do."

"So you're saying the reason she doesn't speak is because she doesn't want to."

"Basically, that's right. No one but Emily can break the spell she's put herself under. So far it hasn't happened." Maybe it never would. He didn't want to think about that.

Long moments passed. They were staring at each other, both of them still angry. He should have expected the blow-back. Maybe he had. Maybe he hadn't mentioned Emily because he was afraid Lane wouldn't come.

"Where were you living when this happened?" she asked.

He sighed, suddenly weary. He hated talking about Emily, hated feeling so helpless. It was the reason he mostly stayed away from her.

"We lived in Juneau at the time. I've got two brothers, Nick and Rafe. All three of us live in Alaska. We're spread out pretty good, but we were raised in Anchorage, and Alaska's our home."

"What does Emily do about school?"

"Mrs. Henry homeschools her. She doesn't have a learning disorder—she just doesn't speak."

Her gaze softened and she reached toward him. Before she made contact, she let her hand fall away.

"So you're staying?" he asked when she didn't say more.

One of her burnished eyebrows went up. "As you said, I'm sure your daughter won't bother me. I'll hardly even know she's there."

He just nodded and started walking, feeling a sweep of relief. She was here, and at least for the moment, she was going to stay.

He led her up onto the porch. Outside the ornately carved front door, he gripped the big iron handle, turned, and stepped back out of the way, allowing Lane and the dog to walk past him into the entry beneath a heavy wrought-iron chandelier.

"Oh, my God, Dylan! It's . . . it's spectacular."

He released the breath he hadn't realized he had been holding. "You'll make it even better."

She looked up at him, green eyes sparkling. "You bet I will." Then she smiled. "Thank you for bringing me here. Oh, I can't wait to see the plans for the remodel. I can hardly wait to get started."

Her excitement was contagious, vibrating through her and into him. His pulse began to pound and desire curled through him. He'd wanted Lane Bishop since the first time he'd seen her, all that fiery hair, sweet curves, and a face that could grace the cover of *Vogue*. Now that she was here, he wanted her even more.

Instead, he took a step back, giving them both a little space.

"Welcome to Eagle Bay," he said and led her farther into the house.

Chapter Three

Lane was exhausted. She was always tired after traveling and plane changes, and then that amazing plane ride to the lodge. And there was Dylan himself. The man was even more imposing than she remembered. Imposing, impressive, commanding. Also daunting and slightly over-whelming.

She hadn't missed the scorching looks he'd cast in her direction, the way those incredible blue eyes slid over her, taking her measure.

In L.A., during the few brief times she had seen him, he hadn't made the slightest effort to hide the desire he felt for her. She had tried to hide her attraction to him, but clearly it hadn't worked. She had finally agreed to come, accepted the job in Alaska with her eyes wide open.

And yet she hadn't been quite prepared for the heat that sparked between them the minute she had seen him walking toward her at the airport.

She needed time. She wasn't the sort of woman who could jump into bed with a man she barely knew. She needed to get to know him, feel safe with him, trust him. If she decided to act on the attraction she felt for him, their affair would be brief, just the few weeks she would be in Alaska—she was prepared for that.

But she wanted the time she spent with him to be more than just sex. She wanted them to wind up at least as friends.

They walked through the great hall toward the family wing of the house, stopped in the hallway outside the kitchen.

"Lane, this is Winifred Henry. She's the lady who takes care of us." He smiled down at the woman, who stood several inches shorter than Lane. "Believe me, we couldn't get along without her."

A wide, welcoming smile bloomed on Winifred Henry's round face. "Welcome to Eagle Bay," she said, repeating Dylan's earlier greeting.

"Thank you. I'm excited to be here. It's a wonderful project."

One of the woman's gray eyebrows went up. "Yes, but it's also our home."

Lane didn't miss the note of warning. Whatever she did, she needed to make sure it was a comfortable place for a family to live. "I promise I won't forget that."

Mrs. Henry seemed to relax. She was in her early sixties and twenty pounds overweight, with thick gray hair pulled into a knot at the back of her head and plenty of wrinkles. She looked as if she had lived her entire life in the wilderness and it was exactly where she belonged.

The older woman's gaze ran over her, seemed to take in her fatigue. "I know you're anxious to see the lodge, but I wonder if you'd like to get settled, rest a little first? Dylan can show you around when you wake up."

Gratitude swept through her. "That would be great."

She looked up at Dylan. "If you don't mind, I'd like to be fresh, maybe take some notes as we go through the lodge."

He smiled. "Take all the time you need."

Lane followed the stout, gray-haired woman to an up-stairs bedroom in the family wing next to what appeared to be the master suite. She wasn't sure if that was an accident or part of a plan. Her suitcases were already in the room, she saw when Mrs. Henry opened the door. She hadn't met Emily. Perhaps at supper.

Closing the door behind her, she crossed the room to the window, looked down to see Finn outside in a big, fenced-in side yard he seemed to have fallen instantly in love with. In the corner of her room, she spotted an old blanket put there for him to sleep on when he was in the bedroom.

With a yawn, she unpacked and put away her clothes, then slipped out of her travel-stained slacks and sweater and pulled on a pink fleece robe. The June days were sunny, with daytime temperatures in the low sixties, but the nights would be chilly.

Padding across the room, she climbed up on the high, queen-size bed made of the same golden pine used to build the lodge. The dresser and bedside tables were pine. A hooked rug warmed the wide-plank floors, and the mattress was covered with a handmade quilt patterned in dark red and forest green. Lane found the room charming.

The residential wing of the house had been remodeled a few years back, Dylan had told her. Which accounted for the en suite bath. Nothing fancy, but according to Dylan eventually this wing would also be redone.

Making herself comfortable on top of the covers, she fluffed the pillow and closed her eyes. *Just a few minutes*, she told herself.

Lane didn't remember sleeping for more than an hour, but when she jolted awake, she remembered that she had been dreaming.

Something strange, she recalled with a frown, something about a raven and a cemetery.

Shaking her head at the oddity, she climbed down from the bed. She didn't dream often, but as she hurriedly dressed in jeans and a long-sleeved light blue T-shirt, it remained strangely clear in her head.

A glance at the digital clock on the bedside table said it was 8:00 PM. Hurrying down the stairs, she spotted Dylan as she reached the bottom, his amazing blue eyes swinging in her direction as if he had some secret radar where she was concerned. Her stomach contracted at the smile on his handsome face.

"Feeling better?" he asked, walking toward her.

"I didn't mean to sleep so long. I hope you didn't wait to eat supper."

"This time of year we usually eat a little later in the evening. I'll let Winnie know you're here and probably starving."

She *was* hungry, she realized. Ravenous, in fact.

"Well, you're looking rested," Mrs. Henry said, smiling as Lane walked toward her.

"I hope I didn't keep everyone waiting."

"Not at all. We all work late this time of year."

"In the winter we've only got a little over seven hours of daylight," Dylan explained. "This time of year, it doesn't even start getting dark until after ten. Shall I show you the house while Winnie gets supper on the table?"

She glanced toward the older woman. "Is there anything I can do to help?"

"Heavens, no. You just go along with Dylan, let him give you a tour."

"Maybe I should get my notepad."

"Not tonight," he said, reaching for her hand. "Tomorrow, you can take your time, look the place over top to bottom."

Lane smiled, liking the idea. "All right."

As Dylan started leading her away, she got a whiff of his cologne, something woodsy that made her think of a forest and clean sheets. Her heart was beating a little too fast, she realized and eased her hand away.

She walked beside him up one of the staircases at each end of the great hall. Then he turned and they crossed an open balcony above the room and made their way to the guest wing.

"There's an extra room up here that won't work as a bedroom. I was thinking maybe a study for the guests."

She glanced at the construction in progress around her. "Or maybe a library."

"That might be a good idea. Or a combination of the two."

They continued on into the upstairs portion of the guest wing, where most of the remodeling was being done. The crew had been hard at work, tearing out walls in some areas, rebuilding them in others.

"The rooms were good-sized to begin with," Dylan said, "but some of them didn't have a bathroom originally so we're adding those, and all the heating and plumbing is being redone. We need a couple of suites, and I want some of the bedrooms to have adjoining doors for families who bring their kids."

She started to ask him about his daughter, but decided to wait, see if Emily came down to supper.

The lodge was big and it was old and it was beautiful. Everything about the place charmed her: the hand-hewn logs perfectly notched together, the three-foot irons in the huge rock fireplace, the wide-planked floors.

"You've taken on an amazingly expensive project," she said as they walked along.

"Don't I know it. My dad was kind of an adventurer. He moved our family here from Texas when we were just kids. But he retained his interest in the family ranch. Dad passed away a few years back, then his brother, Jim. When Ty's dad, my uncle Seth, the last of the brothers, died, we sold the ranch—at least most of it—and the proceeds were split among the heirs. Along with the money I've saved over the years, it's more than enough to remodel the lodge and do pretty much anything I want."

"Lucky you," she teased.

Dylan glanced away. "Yeah . . ."

Lane realized he was thinking of his little girl, mute since her mother had left, and wished she could call back the words. She reached out and touched his arm, felt a quick charge of awareness. When Dylan swung his scorching gaze in her direction, whatever she'd been going to say died on her lips.

"Supper's on!" Mrs. Henry called out, ending the moment, thank God.

"We'd better go eat before the food gets cold," Lane said, forcing herself to smile.

"Yeah." But his gaze held hers for several more seconds before he took her hand and they started back downstairs. The kitchen and breakfast nook were behind a wall that separated them from the dining area, which sat at one end of the great hall.

"We usually eat in here," Dylan said, leading her into

the kitchen and over to the long pine table that dominated one side. The scent of roasted meat, vegetables, and freshly baked biscuits filled the air.

At the far end of the table, a little girl with big blue eyes, and chin-length dark brown hair cut in a bob sat staring out the window into the side yard. Her attention was riveted on Finn, who was sniffing around, getting to know his territory.

Lane noticed the deep breath Dylan took before he led her to the end of the table. "Emily, honey, I'd like you to meet a friend of mine. Her name is Lane Bishop. She came up from California to help us remodel the lodge."

The child turned to look at her but didn't say a word.

"Hello, Emily," Lane said gently. "It's very nice to meet you."

Nothing.

Dylan's shoulders looked tense. Lane's heart went out to him. "That's Finn outside," she said. "He's my dog. You'll have to meet him, too."

The little girl's features brightened. She didn't speak, but she was definitely curious about Finn.

Mrs. Henry began setting platters of food on the table as Caleb Wolfe walked into the kitchen along with the brawny, red-haired man who had helped Dylan down at the dock. He had a ruddy complexion and a friendly smile. He cast a quick glance at Winifred Henry before he walked up to the table.

"Paddy, this is Lane Bishop," Dylan said. "She's an interior designer. She's here to help us with the lodge."

He reached up to touch an invisible hat that wasn't on his head. "Pleasure, ma'am."

"It's just Lane. It's nice to meet you, Paddy."

They all found places at the table. Taking a seat across

from Emily, Dylan pulled Lane down on the bench beside him. Caleb sat next to Emily on the opposite side, and once everyone, including Mrs. Henry, was seated, heaping platters of steaming meat and vegetables were passed around. Biscuits followed, with slabs of butter and what appeared to be homemade berry jam.

The food was delicious, the conversation easy and relaxed. Still, it was unnerving to feel Dylan's hard body brushing against her, the heat of his thigh against hers. Her hands were a little unsteady as she passed a big bowl of corn, and she saw him watching her, his thoughts only too easy to read.

Or perhaps they weren't. Maybe she was the only one who knew what he was thinking because her thoughts ran close to the same.

Dylan fought to ignore the press of Lane's thigh against his. He shifted away from her a little, hoping to control the arousal it wasn't the right time to feel.

"How was your nap?" Winnie asked Lane about halfway through the meal. "I hope your room is all right."

"It's a lovely room," Lane said. "And so quiet. I slept longer than I meant to and more deeply than I have in a while. I remember having this dream. I don't usually recall them, but this one was odd and particularly vivid."

"I remember mine sometimes," Winnie said, "not very often."

"As we were flying up here," Lane said, "we talked about Yeil. The Alaska Native village? In the dream, I was watching some kind of ceremony. That's probably why I had the dream."

"Probably," Dylan said.

Lane flicked a glance at Caleb, who was digging into a slice of roasted meat as if he hadn't had a meal in weeks. "Klink-its? That's how you say it, right?"

Caleb nodded, finished the bite he had taken. "But it's spelled T-L-I-N-G-I-T-S. Indians are really into dreams, you know? They think they hold special meaning. So what was it about?"

"You know how weird dreams can be. This one had something to do with a festival of some kind."

"What makes you think they were Tlingits?" Caleb asked.

"I'm just guessing. They were wearing these funny blankets and odd-looking hats. I saw a picture like that on the wall at the airport. I'm sure that's part of the reason I dreamed about them."

"I'm sure it is," Dylan said, hoping to change the subject. Up here, there was always some Indian myth or legend to deal with. He didn't need to hear it from Lane, too.

"Those are Chilkat blankets," Caleb explained. "And the hats are made of roots."

"That's interesting. I've never seen a totem pole, but there was one in the dream. It had a raven on top."

Caleb's fork paused halfway to his lips.

"When I told you about Yeil," Dylan said, "I mentioned the word meant raven."

"Yes, I'm sure that's it."

"What color was the raven?" Caleb asked.

"Red and black. There were animals and different images underneath. They were very stylized. I don't really know what they were supposed to be."

Caleb's black eyes zeroed in on Dylan. "Did you show her the cemetery?" he asked, and Dylan wanted to kick him.

"No."

"What cemetery?" Lane asked.

"The old Indian cemetery up on the hill," Caleb said. "Maybe you saw it when the plane circled over the lodge."

"I don't think so, but I might have. Why? Is that the place I dreamed about?"

"No," Dylan said.

"Could be," said Caleb. "There's a totem pole up there. The colors are pretty much washed away after so many years, but there's a raven on the top and I think it was originally painted red and black."

Dylan set his fork down beside his plate. "You probably saw it from the plane and didn't realize you had. It's just a coincidence."

"Yes, I'm sure you're right. It's kind of odd, though."

The subject changed, shifted toward the remodel of the lodge, and Dylan finally relaxed. They finished the meal in easy conversation, and everyone stood up from the table.

"Are you sure I can't help?" Lane asked.

Winnie just smiled. "I have a job to do and so do you. I'm sure you'll have plenty to keep you busy without volunteering for extra work."

Lane smiled and nodded. It was a little after nine, but the sun still hadn't set. "Did you get that box of samples I shipped?" she asked as he guided her out of the kitchen.

"They're in my office. It's down the hall from Winnie's quarters. There's a computer in there. Satellite feed to the Internet. You won't be out of touch."

"That's great. I brought my laptop. I use it for my design work, but I wasn't expecting to be able to connect."

"I want this place to feel like a home away from home."

Lane smiled. "Way away, from what I can see."

"That's why people come to Alaska. They want a wilderness experience. Here at the Eagle Bay Lodge, they'll get one."

She looked up at him with those big green eyes, and Dylan felt the kick. When they paused in front of the door to the office, he reached up and touched her cheek. "I'd really like to kiss you, but I know it's too soon."

Lane backed away. "We don't . . . don't even know each other."

"Not yet. In time, we will."

She didn't respond, but he could see her mind spinning, trying to work things out.

"I-I'm still kind of tired. If you don't mind, I think I'll bring Finn in and go up to bed."

Just the word *bed* made him start to get hard. "All right." She was still a little afraid of him, he could see, maybe a little afraid of herself. He needed to give her time. He had known that from the start.

"The power can be kind of sporadic," he said. "There's a reading light in your room, and a flashlight if you need it."

"I suppose you have to be prepared up here. I hadn't thought much about how hard it could be to live in a place like this. I guess I really am a city girl."

He chuckled. "Doesn't make you a bad person."

She smiled.

"Good night, Lane. I'll see you in the morning." He started to turn away, stopped at the sound of her voice.

"You're daughter's beautiful, Dylan."

His insides tightened. He just nodded and started walking.

Chapter Four

In the morning, when Lane went downstairs, Dylan's plane was gone and so was he.

"He went to Waterside for supplies," Caleb said as he approached. He had the softest way of walking, so quiet she looked down to see if he was wearing moccasins, then inwardly laughed at herself when she saw his heavy leather boots.

"The boxes of samples you shipped are in the office," he said. "Dylan figured you could set up your stuff and work till he gets back."

"Great. Thanks."

Caleb turned to leave.

"I was wondering . . . if you aren't too busy, could you walk me up to the cemetery? I want to see if the totem pole looks like the one in my dream."

"All right, but Dylan won't like it."

"Why not?"

"Because when he bought this place there were all kinds of rumors about it, stuff to do with Indian legends and . . . things."

"What things?"

"I don't know exactly. Some people died. No one talks much about it. Up here, no one asks. Everyone pretty much minds his own business."

"But people died on the property?"

"The place has been here more than eighty years, Lane. People live hard lives up here. Everyone dies sooner or later."

"True enough."

"You still want to see it?"

"If you wouldn't mind."

He shrugged his thick shoulders and started walking. He was a few inches shorter than Dylan and more muscular than lean. With his shiny black hair and black eyes, he was handsome. She liked that he seemed to respect whatever claim Dylan had on her and didn't come onto her the way a lot of men would.

They went out through the mudroom into the side yard. The fence looked remarkably new, and she wondered if Dylan had enclosed it specifically for the dog he'd known she was bringing. She smiled to think of the surprise he had gotten when he had first seen Finn.

The dog ran up to her, head cocked, panting a little, excitement clear in his doggy eyes. Finn loved the place already. Her yard in Beverly Hills wasn't large. Finn had a sort of freedom here he had never experienced before.

He gave a single low woof as he trotted along beside them. "Yes, you get to go." She rubbed his ears. "Caleb is taking us for a walk."

Caleb chuckled. "That's some dog."

Lane grinned. "He is, isn't he?"

"It's good he's big. He'll be able to take care of himself if he runs into trouble."

She stopped. "What kind of trouble?"

"Bears. Wolves. Moose. This is Alaska, you know."

She tugged on the retractable leash, pulling him in a little closer. Caleb just smiled. They walked in silence for a while, through the forest toward a sloping hill. Behind it, the mountains grew steeper, became a snow-capped range.

"It's over there," Caleb said, pointing in that direction.

Lane spotted a small area on the hillside enclosed by a weathered picket fence with several sections falling down. Inside were remnants of wooden grave markers, and in a front corner, a totem pole that listed slightly to one side and stood maybe fifteen feet high.

All of the wood was weather-beaten. If the fence or markers had once been painted, none of it remained. She wandered toward the markers. Only a few had dates she could read. The oldest was 1896. The most recent, 1934.

"There was a Native village on a plateau about a quarter of a mile from here," Caleb said. "It was abandoned shortly after the lodge was built, and the people moved to Yeil. At least that's what I heard."

She walked over to the totem pole. "That's a raven at the top, isn't it?"

"That's the symbol for it, yes."

There was still a little faded color on the pole. "It was red and black."

"Looks like it."

She felt a little chill. "Does it mean anything special?"

"According to Tlingit legend, the raven was the creator. There are dozens of stories about him—some are serious, some humorous. This pole was a memorial to the dead. It's probably carved out of red cedar. That's all I know."

"It looks like the one in my dream."

"Does it? Maybe you'll have another dream and you can figure out the message."

Lane shook her head. "I hope not."

"Yeah, I don't like that stuff much, either."

They walked back toward the house. By the time they got there, Dylan had returned.

"I was beginning to worry," he said, casting a dark look at Caleb.

"I took Finn for a walk," Lane told him. "Caleb went along to look out for us."

Dylan's mouth edged into a reluctant smile. "You're a terrible liar. You conned him into taking you up to the cemetery, right?"

She grinned. "It was interesting."

"Was it the totem pole in your dream?"

"Maybe, but I'm sure I saw it from the plane."

"Must have." Setting a hand at her waist, he started guiding her back to the house. They left Finn in his new favorite place, the fenced-in side yard. Caleb and Dylan went up to check on the work being done in the guest wing while Lane spent the rest of the afternoon unpacking her samples and taking measurements, doing her best not to think of Dylan.

She wondered again about the raven on the totem pole she had seen and the cemetery and the legends surrounding the lodge. Wondered who might have died there.

Dylan worked with his crew until supper. The replacement of the upstairs plumbing in the guest wing had nearly been completed. It was up to Lane to choose the bathroom fixtures—within a budget they were still discussing.

With that thought in mind, he headed downstairs in search of her.

He figured she was probably in the office, where she had disappeared after the meal. He'd set aside half the room for her use, and she seemed to be making the most of it, spreading the samples she'd had shipped over every available surface.

He found her bent over the desk, examining fabric swatches. Her jeans weren't that snug, but they nicely outlined her curves and made him think of sex. Which, with Lane around, wasn't that tough to do.

She glanced up as he walked through the door and their eyes met. He could almost feel the heat arcing between them.

Lane looked away first. "You're still working?" she asked.

"The last of the crew took off. We're finished for the day. How about you?"

"I was just fooling around with some colors. I had a couple of ideas in mind for the project before I left L.A., but now that I'm here, I've started thinking in a new direction."

"Such as?"

"Log homes, places like this up in the Northwest, most of them are full of animal heads and bearskin rugs, that kind of thing. In fact there are some of those here now."

"And you'd want to get rid of them?"

"Not all of them. It's a lodge. It needs to feel like one. You want your guests to experience Alaska, but it should also feel unique and a little sophisticated."

"Go on."

"It was built in the thirties, right?"

"Around that time. Started a little earlier but finished in the early thirties, or so I'm told."

"That was the Art Deco period. It was an elegant time. I was thinking maybe we could use some of that elegance here, yet keep the rustic lodge feel."

Uncertainty rolled through him. "I don't know. . . . That sounds a little too Hollywood for me."

"Don't jump to conclusions. Have you ever been to the Ahwahnee Hotel in Yosemite?"

He shook his head. "'Fraid not."

Lane walked over to the laptop she had brought with her, which was open and sitting on her worktable. He'd shown her how to access the Internet through his satellite link, password EagleBay123.

"Let me show you what it looks like." Seating herself, she tapped the keyboard and pulled up photos, and his interest sharpened.

High ceilings and heavy wooden crossbeams. Lots of stone and plenty of windows. It was rustic, but there were touches of Art Deco here and there that added a certain elegance. He had to admit it was impressive.

"It's a beautiful place," he said.

"It was built around the same time as the lodge. Eagle Bay won't look the same because it has a character all its own. I just wanted you to see how it could work when you put the different pieces together."

"How'd you come up with the concept?"

"I noticed the wall sconces along the upstairs hallway. They're from the thirties, and I liked how well they seemed to fit. And I love the chandelier in the entry. It's big and heavy. We need a couple more like it, one for the great hall and one for the dining area. I have a contact in Mexico who does wrought-iron work for me. If I send him photos and measurements, he can match it exactly."

Dylan frowned. "That sounds expensive. I wasn't figuring on having things custom-made."

"It's Mexico, remember? Work is done fairly cheaply down there. It's more about the time it'll take to get it finished. And shipping it up here could be a problem, but I don't think it'll cost all that much."

"We're going to need a budget. That's one of the reasons I came looking for you."

"I've been working on it. I know you want the lodge to be first-rate, but I don't imagine you want to run up some ungodly bill, either."

"You got that right." He was glad to know they were on the same page.

"You have some lovely old furniture around. I'm planning to use as much of it as I can. We might need to refinish some of it. We'll need new sofas and chairs, lamps, carpets, draperies. I want to keep the look and feel of the place mostly the way it is, just add some interest and make it all seem new again."

He liked what she was saying. It matched the thoughts he'd had about the lodge. He could feel her excitement, the energy that seemed so much a part of her. He wanted to reach out and touch her, let some of that energy flow into him.

Taking her hand, he pulled her up out of her chair and into his arms, bent his head to kiss her. At the last second, Lane turned away.

"I need time, Dylan." Her hands trembled where they rested against his chest. She eased out of his arms, but her gaze remained on his face. "I won't deny I'm . . . I'm attracted to you. But I'm not ready to jump in bed with you."

"You can have all the time you want. I won't push you. But when I see the same heat in your eyes I know you see in mine, don't expect me not to act on it."

Color crept into her face, which only confirmed he'd been right. She wanted him, too.

"I came here to do a job," she said. "Beyond that, I'm not sure what's going to happen."

"I think you know what's going to happen. I think we both do." Lane had traveled two thousand miles to come to Alaska, and he didn't believe for a minute it was only for the job. "But I won't rush you. Not if you aren't ready." He gently touched her cheek. "You don't have to be afraid of me, Lane. I'd never do anything you didn't want me to do."

Lane nodded, seemed relieved. "It's been a long day. I think I'll bring Finn in and head upstairs."

"I've got to go to Waterside tomorrow. A delivery I've been waiting for came in. Would you like to go along?"

Her features brightened. "I'd love to. What time?"

"After breakfast." A faint smile tugged at his lips. "Did I mention town's only fifteen minutes away?"

Lane laughed. "I believe you did. I'll see you in the morning."

Dylan watched her walk away. He was giving her time, but time wasn't something they had a lot of, and he didn't want to waste it. But, aside from their attraction, she was there to do a job and he intended to let her do it.

Still, he couldn't help wishing she'd be spending the night in his bed—instead of alone in the room next door.

* * *

Lane left Dylan in his office and headed down the hall to get Finn. Her insides were still trembling. He'd almost kissed her. And God, she'd wanted him to. But part of her wasn't ready to move in that direction. She hadn't been with a man since Jason. She needed time to sort things out, prepare herself.

It was dark as she shoved through the door, just a sliver of moon drifting across the sky. Tall pine trees cast shadows across the ground. A faint breeze rustled the needles on the branches.

"Finn! Come on, boy!" She clapped her hands. "Finn, where are you?"

She clapped her hands again, but there was still no sign of him. "Finn! Finn, come here, boy!" Her pulse kicked up as fear snaked through her. *Bears, wolves, moose.* Dear God, had some wild animal gotten through the fence, or had he dug out somehow? It wasn't like him to run away.

Turning, she raced back into the house for a flashlight, saw Dylan striding down the hall.

"Finn's missing! It's too dark to see, but I don't think he's in the yard. I've got to find him!"

He caught her shoulders as she reached him. "Take it easy. He's upstairs with Emily."

She relaxed against him. "Thank God."

"I went upstairs to check on her and there was Finn, sleeping on her bed."

"I'd better go get him. I didn't mean for him to cause any trouble."

Dylan just smiled. "He's fine. Emily must have brought him in."

They went up the back stairs together. When Dylan opened the bedroom door, Emily was fast asleep, Finn sprawled across the mattress at her feet. Spotting Lane, the dog raised his head, jumped down, and trotted over to where she stood in the doorway.

"You aren't supposed to be any trouble," she scolded, but she was glad to see him, which he seemed to know.

"Maybe I should get her a dog," Dylan said. "Maybe it would help."

Lane smiled. "Well, she's got Finn now. I'm happy to share him."

Dylan caught her hand and brought it to his lips, and a delicious little tremor went through her.

"Thanks," he said, letting her go. But his eyes remained on her face. Lane thought how handsome he was and how strongly she was attracted to him. Dylan walked her to her room, and she considered kissing him good night. But she was afraid if she started kissing him, she wouldn't want to stop.

"I'll see you at breakfast," he said a little gruffly.

Lane nodded and ducked into the bedroom. God, she wanted that man. She couldn't remember ever feeling such lust for a man before. Not even Jason. Still, she needed to be sure. Sure of Dylan. Certain of her own emotions. And that took time. Waiting was better for both of them.

Lane brushed her teeth and climbed into bed, read for a while, a book of literary fiction she had been trying to finish for months but which usually put her to sleep. Groggy, she finally set the book aside and turned off the light. It didn't take long to fall asleep.

For the first few hours, she slept soundly. The chill in the room and the thick down comforter she nestled beneath made for perfect sleeping. It was the loud clanging of metal against metal that jolted Lane awake in the middle of the night.

The red letters on the digital clock read 3:10 AM. Heart pounding, ears ringing, she swung her legs to the side of the bed, grabbed her fleece robe, pulled it on, and shoved her feet into a pair of slippers. Grabbing the flashlight off the floor, she hurried to the door.

The clanging continued, loud and grating on her nerves. Dylan was coming out of his room at the same time she was leaving hers. He was wearing a flannel robe, but it gapped open in front, showing a little of his hard-muscled chest.

"What is that?" she asked, trying not to stare.

"Sounds like something's wrong with the pipes. The crew was working on them today. They must have caused some kind of problem." Striding off down the hall, he stopped to make a quick check on his daughter.

"She's always been a sound sleeper," he said and closed the door.

Lane fell in behind him as he turned and headed for the back stairs, and both of them hurried down. Mrs. Henry, a single thick gray braid nestled against her shoulder, stuck her head out the door of her room off the kitchen as they passed.

"What is that awful racket?"

"Problem with the plumbing. Go back to bed."

Lane kept pace with Dylan, wide awake now and curious. Dylan flipped a switch at the head of the stairs, illuminating the basement, which was huge and dark, a big, seemingly bottomless black cavern.

"Stay here." Taking the flashlight from her hand, he pounded down the stairs.

Lane followed him partway down, watched him cross

the room toward the two big propane water heaters that had just been installed. The floor and walls of the basement were made of stone, the ceiling low overhead. The cavernous room was damp, and icy cold seeped beneath her fuzzy pink robe.

The clanging grew louder, sending chills down her spine. As Dylan moved around, shining the flashlight beam into cracks and crevices not illuminated by the overhead lights, the equipment in the room cast eerie shadows against the walls. Lane pressed her hands over her ears to shut out the grating noise, but just then the awful clanging ceased.

Dead silence fell.

Dylan had disappeared, but she could hear his footsteps as he prowled the basement that encompassed the entire footprint of the lodge.

"I didn't find anything," he said as he returned and both of them climbed back upstairs. "I'll have my crew chief take a look in the morning."

"Has that ever happened before?"

"No." He made a last survey of the basement, then stepped into the hall and turned off the lights. By the time they were back upstairs, Lane was yawning.

Dylan opened her door. "Get some sleep. I'll see you in the morning."

"Dylan?"

He turned back, those blue eyes suddenly intense.

What could she say? I've changed my mind? I want you to kiss me? She'd only be sorry in the morning. "Nothing. I'll see you tomorrow."

Dylan disappeared into his room and closed the door. Lane figured if she dreamed tonight, it wouldn't be about ravens—it would be about Dylan Brodie.

Chapter Five

Holding on to Lane's hand, Dylan headed for his plane the following morning. He should have known she would dress up for a trip to town, today in dark brown slacks, a soft yellow sweater, and gold hoop earrings. Since it took awhile for the temperature to warm into the sixties, she was wearing a brown tweed blazer for warmth.

Everyone up here wore jeans, but he liked the classy way she dressed and wasn't about to discourage her.

"I usually don't like flying," Lane said. As the engine roared the plane lifted out of the water and began to climb into the air. "But this is wonderful. On those commercial flights, you're packed in like sardines. You've been searched, poked, and prodded, and once you're in the air, you have no idea who's at the controls."

He followed her gaze out the window, toward the sea stretching ahead of them and the glacial peaks in the distance.

"This is different," she said. "It makes you feel so free."

"My dad was a pilot. He started me flying when I was a teen. I knew right away it was something I wanted to do."

"You were a bush pilot, right?"

"That's right. Still am. Difference is, now I'll be flying my own clients instead of working for someone else."

"As soon as you get the lodge finished," she said.

"That's right. I'll be flying them into some of the nearby lakes. The fishing's fantastic."

"Where will you live in the winter?"

He flicked her a sideways glance. "We'll be right here. We'll close down the guest wing, but the lodge is where we live. Right now Emily's being homeschooled, but I'm hoping eventually she'll be able to go to school in Yeil."

Lane settled back in her seat. "So . . . did your crew chief figure out what was wrong with the plumbing?"

Dylan blew out a frustrated breath. "He checked everything. Swears it's all working perfectly."

"I'm afraid I'd have to differ."

"That's what I said. I've got him making another check. Could be it's something else."

"I hope he finds it. That wasn't the most pleasant way to wake up in the middle of the night."

Dylan shot her a look. He imagined sliding his hands into all that glorious red hair and his groin tightened. "I can think of a far more pleasant way to wake you up in the middle of the night."

Color washed into her cheeks. He wondered how long they could last without giving in to the heat, finding out where it would take them.

"There's the town," she said as he started his descent. Homes sparsely dotted the hillside above the water, and Main Street wound along parallel to the sea.

The ocean was smooth as glass and so was his landing. Creating a sizable wake, he taxied up to the floatplane dock and got the plane secured. A few minutes later they were walking toward Waterside, population a little over three thousand.

His supplies came in at C.J.'s Mercantile, which sat at the near end of the town. The bell above the door rang as he shoved it open and spotted the owner, Charlie Jensen, a squat, heavyset man with thinning gray hair, standing behind the counter.

"Hey, Dylan," Charlie called out.

"Hey, Charlie. You got that package that came in for me?"

"Sure do. It's in the back room. When you're ready to head back home, I'll have Teddy haul it down to the plane and load it for you." Teddy was Charlie's grandson. He worked at the mercantile in the summer when he was home from college.

"That'd be great. Charlie Jensen, this is Lane Bishop. She's an interior designer. She's here to help me with the lodge."

"Nice to meet you, Charlie," Lane said.

"You, too. So what do you think of the place?"

"The lodge is beautiful. I can see why Dylan fell in love with it."

"I was out there once. Took my grandson for a drive. It was empty at the time, some of the windows boarded up, some of them broken. We walked around and peeked inside. I gotta say, the place gave me the creeps."

Dylan felt a shot of irritation. "Empty old buildings will do that."

"I guess so. How are things going out there?"

"We're only a little behind schedule. That's better than I expected."

"That's good to hear. The last couple of owners had, you know . . . some problems."

Unease rolled through him. Charlie was the town gossip. You never knew what he was going to say. "We've been lucky, I guess. Just some plumbing problems, stuff like that."

"There's been a lot of talk about the old place. But I guess you heard the stories before you bought it."

"What stories?" Lane asked.

"'Bout the . . . umm . . . murders."

"I'm not interested in gossip," Dylan said, trying to shut Charlie up. "It's all bullshit as far as I'm concerned."

"What murders?" Lane asked.

"Oh, it goes way back," Charlie said. "No one knows for sure what happened. People say they've seen ghosts up there. Say that's the reason the owners keep selling."

"Well, I'm not selling," Dylan said flatly. "And I'd appreciate if you didn't start those kinds of rumors. It isn't good for business."

Charlie looked down at his feet. "Sorry, Dylan."

Hoping to end the conversation, he began pushing Lane toward the door. "You want to take a walk around, get a look at the town?"

"I'd love to." She flicked a glance over her shoulder at Charlie, obviously wanting to know more, but Dylan nudged her out the door.

"Are you going to tell me what that was all about?"

He sighed, wishing he didn't have to answer, but figuring she'd whittle away at him till he did. "Like I said, it's all just bullshit. The truth is the owner sold the place because living out here isn't for everyone—not because some ghost scared him away."

Lane fell silent as they walked down a sidewalk that was partly wood, partly cement. It wasn't much of a town by most standards, but it was a stop on the Alaska Ferry system so there were lots of tourists this time of year through the end of summer. One of the big white boats was sitting at the main dock. People streamed down the gangway toward town and began to meander in and out of the shops along Main Street.

Dylan took Lane's arm and slipped it through his. Wandering along toward the central part of town, they passed a couple of gas stations and the Sea View Motel. There was a grocery store and an auto repair shop, though there wasn't much traffic since there weren't that many roads.

The town itself had a western flavor, with false-fronted wooden buildings and shutters on the windows. Closer to downtown, they passed the old Hotel Waterside, built just after the turn of the nineteenth century, which was empty now, with a FOR SALE sign in the window.

"Look, there's an art gallery!" Lane said excitedly. "Let's go in." The old hotel sat next to the Whale's Tail, one of three galleries and a couple of gift shops in a town that made most of its money from passengers off the ferry.

Dylan indulged her, shoving open the door and leading her inside. Paintings and Alaska Native artwork, sculpture, and hand-beaded jewelry filled the shop.

Lane started prowling. "When I was in high school, I wanted to be a famous artist. I even majored in art in college."

"What happened?"

"Mom got sick. I needed to earn a living to help with the bills. I learned fairly quickly the term 'starving artist' meant exactly that."

"So you gave up your dream and started doing design work."

She shrugged. "You do what you have to."

"Were you any good?"

She smiled. "Actually, I was."

They strolled through the shop, looking at the different paintings, everything from landscapes to portraits, all with an Alaska Native flare. "Some of these are pretty good," she said.

"You think so? I bet yours were better."

She didn't disagree. And since he knew she wasn't the type to make false claims, she undoubtedly was. He made a mental note to order some art supplies. Maybe she'd have a chance to do a little painting while she was up there.

"You hungry?" he asked.

"After the breakfast Mrs. Henry cooked, I shouldn't be. But I am."

"We've got a couple of places to eat in town. The Grizzly Café is probably best for lunch. Come on." Lane smiled, and he guided her in that direction.

The Grizzly Café was noisy and more than half full, Lane saw as they pushed through the door, ringing the bell overhead. It was a typical small-town coffee shop, with a row of pink vinyl booths and a long Formica-topped counter with matching pink bar stools. Windows beside each booth looked down at the harbor.

A big, chesty blonde in her thirties, with long hair and blue eyes appeared to be the owner, a good-looking woman even in the simple black slacks and white blouse she wore.

She smiled when she spotted Dylan and started in their direction. The smile slipped a little when she realized Lane was with him.

"Dylan," she said. "Always good to see you."

Dylan bent and kissed her cheek. He surveyed the

patrons filling most of the tables. "Looks like you're plenty busy."

"Business always picks up this time of year."

He turned in Lane's direction. "Lane, this is Maggie Ridell. She owns the place."

"Nice to meet you."

"Maggie, this is Lane Bishop. She's here to help me remodel the lodge."

A predatory gleam appeared in the woman's blue eyes. "So you're a decorator?"

"Interior designer," Lane automatically corrected.

"You must be from California." It sounded like an insult.

"Beverly Hills," Lane couldn't resist saying, though she could have lessened the sneer if she had just said L.A.

"We met through my cousin, Ty," Dylan explained. "Lane's done projects like the lodge before."

"I see." That cool gaze zeroed back on Lane. "So I guess you're staying out there."

"That's right. There's a lot of work to do."

One of her blond eyebrows winged up. "I'll just bet there is."

Dylan must have finally felt the tension simmering between them. "I told Lane the food here was good. How about some menus, Maggie?"

"Sure. Coming right up."

Dylan led Lane over to one of the few empty booths and they slid in on opposite sides. Maggie brought menus. Lane took a quick look and ordered a hamburger and fries. Dylan ordered the same. Maggie's swivel-hipped walk carried her back to the kitchen.

"So . . . I guess you have an admirer," Lane said, her gaze still following the buxom blonde.

"Maggie and I are just friends."

"Friends with benefits? Or just regular friends?"

Dylan's mouth edged up. "Regular friends. And I hope what I'm hearing in your voice is a touch of jealousy."

Lane shook her head. "Sorry. I'm not the jealous type." A complete, bald-faced lie. She might not have realized she was the jealous type before, but seeing the looks Maggie Ridell was tossing at Dylan, she was definitely feeling a touch of the green-eyed monster now.

The waitress, a black-haired girl in her twenties, pretty with her high cheekbones and ripe figure, brought their orders and set them down on the Formica-topped table in front of them.

"Hey, Dylan."

"Hey, Holly. Holly, this is Lane."

"Nice to meet you," Holly said.

"You, too." Lane was beginning to wonder how many women in Waterside had a crush on Dylan. But looking at the girl, she didn't catch any of the covetous glances Maggie Ridell had cast his way.

"So . . . umm . . . how's everything up at the lodge?" Holly asked, lingering, it seemed to Lane.

"Work's coming right along." He handed the ketchup bottle to Lane, who squirted some on her burger and handed it back. Dylan buried his fries in crimson, then started on his burger.

"Well . . . umm . . . tell Caleb I said hello."

Dylan smiled. "I sure will."

Holly turned and hurried back to the kitchen, making up the lost time, Lane figured.

"I have a hunch Caleb has an admirer, as well," she said.

"Holly's just moved back to Waterside from Seattle. She was away at nursing school."

"How'd she wind up waiting tables?"

"She's working here part-time till she goes full-time at the hospital."

"I guess you know just about everyone in town."

He picked up a fry and munched it down. "That's the way it is in a place this size. I've only been here a couple of months, and I'm already part of the community. Here, people care what happens to you. It's kind of nice."

"I've never really had that. Aside from everyone knowing everyone's business, I think in most ways it *would* be nice." They chatted through lunch, running over some ideas for the window treatments in the great hall. Dylan paid the bill and left a tip, and they headed back to the mercantile to pick up the load of drywall tape and heavy-duty staples Dylan had come to get.

From there, they returned to the plane for the quick flight home. She'd had fun, she realized as she strapped herself into the seat. Dylan was a very good host and he seemed resigned to giving her a little breathing room and a chance to get better acquainted.

Of course, he had Maggie Ridell to fall back on if things didn't work out. Lane didn't like the idea.

As the plane made the short trip south from Waterside back to Eagle Bay, her thoughts returned to Charlie Jensen and the ghosts he had mentioned.

She really couldn't say she believed in ghosts or spirits, and clanging pipes in the middle of the night certainly weren't enough to convince her. Clearly, Dylan didn't believe the stories either or he wouldn't have purchased the lodge.

Of course there was that crazy dream. . . . Lane shoved the thought away and settled back to enjoy the ride.

* * *

Lane spent the afternoon working, laying out color boards, looking at fabric samples, and going over measurements. They broke for supper at eight, then went back to work for a while.

It was after ten when Dylan walked her upstairs to her room.

"I really enjoyed the day," she said, turning to look up at him in front of her door. "And even with the trip to town, I got a ton of work done."

"I don't expect you to work this late every day."

"I don't mind. I get pretty wound up when I'm on a new project. I prefer to be tired enough to sleep."

He caught her chin, tilted it up so she was staring into his face. "Come to bed with me and I promise you'll sleep like a baby."

Her pulse shot up a notch. She told herself to back away, but when he bent his head and very gently kissed her, she couldn't resist. Those hard male lips were softer than she had imagined, and they fit perfectly with hers. He smelled like the forest, and hard work, and man.

A soft sigh escaped. She didn't remember sliding her arms up around his neck or opening to take the kiss from a slow, leisurely exploration to deep, hot, and wet. She only knew she didn't want to stop. Ever.

Dylan groaned. His hands slid into her hair, fisted, holding her immobile as he deepened the kiss. Lane's insides were quaking, her knees weak. It took all her will to end the kiss and back away.

She looked up at him, tried to even her breathing. *Just a little more time*, she told herself. *Just a few more days.*

Why she needed them, she was no longer sure. "I'd better go in. I've got a lot of work to do tomorrow."

"Are you sure that's the way you want it?"

She wanted to drag him into her room, wanted to tear off his clothes and ravish him. "For now," she said.

He kissed her softly one last time, waited for her to disappear inside her bedroom and close the door. She could hear his heavy footsteps as he padded down the hall and went into his own room.

Lane released an unsteady breath. Every part of her body tingled. She could still taste him on her lips. Her skin felt hot and tight and her breasts ached.

But she was two thousand miles from home, in the middle of a job she was committed to finishing. If the sex was disappointing, if for some reason it didn't work out between them, it would be a disaster.

She thought of Maggie Ridell. Dylan had said they were only friends. But she wasn't completely sure she could trust him. He had lied about Emily—or at least lied by omission. And the Ridell woman definitely had more than a casual interest in him.

She had to be certain she was making the right decision, but she had wanted Dylan since the moment she had met him. She had to wait, but God, it seemed like she had been waiting forever.

Determined to think of something else, she stripped off her clothes and slid naked between the covers. Even though the sheets were cold, she enjoyed the freedom.

Finn was already in the room, asleep on his bed in the corner. Lane turned off the lamp on the nightstand, exhaled an exhausted breath, lay back, and closed her eyes.

She wasn't sure how long she slept before the faint

sound slowly reached her. It stirred images in the back of her mind that eventually nudged her awake, and for several seconds she stared up at the ceiling trying to figure out what it was.

Then she knew. *Crying.* It sounded like a child. *Emily.* Grabbing her robe off the foot of the bed, Lane tugged it on, grabbed the flashlight off the nightstand, and hurried out the door.

There was no one in the hallway, but the crying grew louder as she moved along the corridor and opened the door to Emily's bedroom. Careful not to frighten her, Lane shined the flashlight into the room, spotted Emily lying on the bed, and stepped quietly inside.

The crying stopped as Lane approached. She saw that the little girl's eyes were open and staring up at her, and it didn't appear she had been crying at all.

"Are you all right, sweetheart?" Lane perched on the chair next to the nightstand. Emily surprised her by nodding.

"Were you crying?"

She shook her head.

"Did you hear it?"

Emily nodded.

"Do you know who it was?"

Emily shook her head, closed her eyes, and snuggled back down in the bed.

Lane listened, but heard only silence. Surely it had been Emily. There was no doubt it had been a child and she was the only child in the house. Or was she?

Lane gazed back down at the little girl, who was already fast asleep.

A chill slipped through her. Charlie Jensen had said there were ghosts in the house. He had implied they had driven past owners away. It was ridiculous. It must have been Emily. Probably she just didn't want Lane to know.

Still, Lane intended to talk to Caleb, see if he knew more than he had told her.

Making her way back to her room, Lane went in and closed the door. But she wasn't able to fall asleep.

Chapter Six

Dylan checked his watch: 8:00 AM. In the mornings, they started at six, worked for a couple of hours, then took a break for breakfast. Winnie was setting food on the table, but Lane still hadn't appeared. She was usually downstairs by seven. Dylan was beginning to worry when he looked up and saw her walking into the kitchen.

"Sorry I'm late," she said, taking her usual seat beside him at the table. He wished it didn't feel so good to have her there. "I woke up in the middle of the night and didn't get back to sleep until almost dawn. I should have set the alarm."

"It's all right, we just sat down." Dylan did his best to ignore the jean-clad thigh brushing his, tried not to think of the scorching kiss they'd shared in the hallway last night.

Lane spread her paper napkin over her lap and glanced over at Emily, who was sitting across the table next to Caleb. Emily's eyes swung to Lane's, and for a moment neither of them looked away. Dylan wondered what his little girl was thinking, wished she were able to tell him.

Knew that she could if she wanted. The thought made his chest feel tight.

"I saw an old friend of yours yesterday," he said to Caleb as he passed the bacon and scrambled eggs, then filled his plate as the pancakes went by.

Caleb slid a load of bacon onto his plate. "Oh, yeah? Who was it?"

"Holly Kaplan."

Caleb grunted. "I heard she'd moved to town. Got her nursing degree."

"She's working part-time at the Grizzly. Said to tell you hello."

"Like she thinks I care?"

"So you don't?"

"Not anymore. Not since she decided she'd rather be with Eddie McGuiness than me."

"That was awhile back, if I recall. When we were still living in Juneau." Where he and Caleb had first met and become good friends.

"What difference does it make where we lived? Doesn't change what happened."

Lane set her coffee mug down on the table. "She seemed like a nice girl. Maybe you should give her another chance."

"I will. When hell freezes over." Caleb turned to Winnie, who sat at the end of the table. "Would you pass me some more of those blueberry pancakes, Mrs. Henry? They're really delicious."

Winnie passed the platter, always pleased when the guys cleaned up all of her cooking. "I'm glad you like them."

They finished the meal in easy conversation and everyone headed off in different directions. "I'll see you later," Dylan said to Lane, who'd been unusually quiet through the meal.

He hoped she wasn't regretting that kiss.

He sure as hell wasn't.

Lane caught up with Caleb in the hall outside the kitchen. "Could I talk to you a minute?"

"Sure." He wore his usual long black braids, as glossy as the feathers of the raven they had talked about. "What's up?"

"Yesterday when we were in town, Charlie Jensen at the mercantile said this place was haunted. He said that was the reason people kept selling and moving away."

Caleb just smiled. "Charlie's a busybody. Worse than a woman." He grinned. "No offense."

She smiled back. "None taken. I was just wondering . . . he said something about a murder. You mentioned people had died here. Do you know what happened?"

"Not really. I heard some of the guys from the village talking. One of them said the last owner sold the place because he kept hearing footsteps in the hall and no one was there. Stuff like that."

"By 'the village' you mean Yeil?"

"Yeah. About a hundred people live there. Lots of them are Tlingits, probably more than half."

"Have you ever heard them?"

"What?"

"The footsteps."

Caleb shook his head. "But I live in one of the cabins. Far as I know, nothing like that has happened since we've been here."

Lane hesitated. No way could she mention the crying she had heard to Dylan. He'd be sure it was Emily, and Lane didn't want to lose the little girl's trust. Still, she needed to know if something odd was going on.

"Last night I heard a child crying. When I went into Emily's room, she was awake, but she said it wasn't her."

His obsidian eyes widened. "She talked to you?"

"No, but when I asked her about it, she shook her head. I asked her if she heard the crying and she nodded."

He shrugged. "Probably just the wind. It makes some pretty weird noises."

"I suppose. But it might be interesting to know the history of the lodge. Got any idea how we might find out?"

"It was built in the early thirties, or somewhere thereabouts. There are some elders in the village who might know something about it."

"Maybe you could take me to see them."

Caleb shook his head. "No way. Not without Dylan. He's my friend, and I'm not about to go behind his back. If he wants to go, I'll take you."

"He won't want to go. He's convinced there's nothing to the rumors."

"He's probably right."

"Probably."

Caleb sauntered off down the hall, headed for the guest wing, where the crew was hard at work. Lane went to work in the office, trying to decide on the bathroom fixtures, which would have to be ordered and shipped to Waterside. She wanted something with a hint of Art Deco but not too expensive.

Most people thought of that period as Erté-style sculptures and drawings of sleekly beautiful women, but there had also been great usage of geometric lines and angles, giving the style what looked like an Indian flare. That was the look she wanted.

Sitting down, she started sifting through catalogs.

* * *

Dylan walked into the office before supper to find Lane on the Internet. He came up behind her, looked over her shoulder.

"You're on Facebook?"

She nodded. "I don't go on that often. But being so far from home, it helps me feel connected."

He studied the monitor. "You posted the photos you took from the plane."

"Some of them. And some pictures of the lodge. It's just so beautiful."

He read the posts, which said how amazing the scenery was, how much she was enjoying working on the project, and how glad she was she had come.

Dylan pulled her up from the chair and into his arms. "I'm glad you came, too." He kissed her briefly, lightly, felt her tense, and backed away. "You ready for supper?"

"I'm going to check on Finn first, then I'll be in."

"I'll go with you."

She didn't protest when he walked her down the hall, through the mudroom, and out into the side yard. Finn was in the far corner, sniffing something beneath a bush next to the fence.

"Oh, crap." Dylan started running, but it was too late. Finn made a shrieking sound and leaped straight up in the air.

"Finn!" Lane started running. Dylan caught her before she got too close. "What happened? What's the matter with him?"

"Porcupine. Finn!" Dylan called. "Come here, boy."

"Finn, come here, baby." The big dog slowly crossed the

yard, head down, tail tucked between his legs. Porcupine quills stuck out of his muzzle and all around his face.

"Oh, my God, my poor baby."

"I'll get the pliers. You keep him calm."

"Oh, Finn, it's okay, boy. We're going to fix you."

When Dylan returned, he was surprised to see Emily sitting on the ground next to Lane and Finn. The little girl was petting poor Finn, who was trembling all over, while Lane talked to him softly.

For the next half hour, he worked over the dog, pulling the quills out one at a time, a painful procedure since they were barbed at one end. All the while, Emily and Lane kept the dog quiet.

"Could have been worse," he said as he finished.

"Worse? Finn was really hurting."

"I know. But sometimes the quills get inside the animal's mouth. It's really hard to get them out." He went back inside the house and brought out some spray antiseptic, and gave the dog a good dose.

"He'll be okay. Hopefully, he's smart enough not to go near one of those things again."

"I don't think he will."

"Good." He smiled. "At least we don't have to worry about skunks."

"Skunks? Oh, my God."

Dylan laughed at the look of horror on Lane's pretty face. "Take it easy. There aren't any up here. They're all farther south. No snakes, either. Frogs are about it."

"Except for bears, wolves, and moose."

"Well, yeah."

Lane smiled and shook her head. "I think Mrs. Henry is calling us to supper." She extended a hand to Emily. "Come on, sweetheart. Let's go in and eat."

Dylan watched the emotion playing across his daughter's face. Uncertainty. Anxiety. Longing. For several seconds, she just stared up at Lane. Dylan's chest squeezed when Emily took hold of the hand Lane offered, and Lane led her into the house.

It had been another long day and yet Lane felt exhilarated in a way she hadn't in a very long time. Maybe never. As a child in rural Illinois, she had loved the open spaces, the clear skies, the green fields stretching along the highway. She'd been living in L.A. so long, fighting the traffic and smog, she had forgotten how good it felt to breathe fresh, clean air.

At night she was exhausted, but also excited to be working on such an amazing project. And there was Dylan.

Her attraction to him seemed to grow every day, more so perhaps, now that he was giving her the time she needed to know him. He had walked her to her room and given her one of those mind-blowing, world-rocking kisses, but he hadn't pressed for more.

Lane almost wished he would.

Almost.

At the tap of doggie nails on the floor, she glanced over at Finn. Amazingly resilient, he trotted up to her as she got ready for bed. Careful not to brush his injured muzzle, she gave him a few quick back scratches and he headed for his place in the corner.

Tired to the bone, Lane climbed into bed and turned off the lamp, closed her eyes, and slid into a deep, mindless sleep. It wasn't until sometime after midnight she began to toss and turn, her mind flashing with erotic images, her body growing hot and damp.

She was no longer alone in the bed. Dylan was there, kissing her, pressing her down in the mattress, his strong hand fisting in her hair. The muscles in his long, hard body tightened as he moved, as his powerful erection thrust deep inside her. She was on fire for him, moaning, straining toward release.

She was almost there, teetering on the edge of climax, whimpering softly. "Dylan . . ." she whispered. "Dylan, please . . ."

Footsteps sounded in the hall, jerking her from sleep to wide awake in an instant. Eyes wide open, she listened for Dylan's knock at the door.

Embarrassment washed over her. Dear God, had Dylan heard her moaning? Calling his name? Heaven only knew what else she might have said. She waited, wondering if she should invite him in, let him make love to her, give her what her hot, erotic dream had promised.

She heard the heavy thump as the footsteps moved closer to her door, then they stopped, as if the person stood in the corridor just outside. But no knock came at the door.

Surely it was Dylan. But when he didn't knock or didn't move away, a shiver ran through her. Caleb had said the former owner had heard footsteps in the hall but no one had been there. Heart pounding, she grabbed her robe off the foot of the bed, tiptoed to the door, and cautiously pulled it open. No sign of Dylan or anyone else.

Just then, his door swung open and he stepped into the hall. He was barefoot, wearing only his jeans. His magnificent chest was bare, and he held a flashlight in one hand.

"Was that you I heard in the hallway?" he asked.

"I thought it was you."

He shook his head. "Stay here." Striding off down the hall, he went into Emily's room, apparently found her asleep, then checked the other bedrooms in the wing, which were empty.

A memory of her erotic dream surfaced as she watched him walking back toward her, and color washed into her cheeks. She hoped it was too dark for him to see.

She still couldn't believe she had almost climaxed in her sleep. It had certainly never happened before. Dylan headed downstairs and Lane waited in the corridor. The only footsteps she heard were Dylan's bare feet on the stairs as he climbed back up to the second floor.

"Must have been the wind," he said.

"It sounded like footsteps."

"Weather's coming in. Supposed to rain tomorrow. It was just the wind."

"I guess." But Lane was no longer certain the happenings in the house could be explained so easily.

"Will you be able to get back to sleep?" Dylan asked, and even in the dim light in the hall, she could feel those hot blue eyes on her.

Desire slipped through her and she fought not to tremble. "I'll be all right. Good night."

"Good night, love." He waited till she was safely inside, the door closed behind her, before he returned to his room.

Chapter Seven

After breakfast, Dylan went over Lane's choices for the plumbing fixtures, impressed by the interesting geometric designs that gave them an Indian flavor. The fixtures were perfect for the concept Lane had presented, yet the price was well within the budget he had mentally calculated as he'd laid out his plans for the lodge.

"I'll put the order in today," she said.

"Sounds good."

Lane went over to the computer and pulled up the product distributor on the Net. Dylan walked up behind her, set his hands lightly on her shoulders. He thought it was a good sign that she didn't pull away.

"I was thinking . . . you know, we work hard around here, but once in awhile we deserve a little time off. I thought maybe you'd like to take a boat ride, do a little camping."

She swiveled around to face him. "Camping?"

"Sure. I know a good place. We can take Emily and Finn. We'll pitch a tent big enough for all of us, just take enough supplies for one night."

"I don't know. I've never been camping."

"You're kidding, right?"

She shrugged. "My dad was more into sports. It just never happened."

"Then we'll make it happen. Soon as the weather clears, we'll go."

She smiled up at him. "Okay, it sounds like fun."

He liked that she seemed to have an adventurous spirit. Completely unlike Mariah. But then, everything about Lane was different from his ex-wife.

He let her go back to work and went upstairs to check on the crew. The drywall was up in the bathroom additions. In an area downstairs, some of the walls between the bedrooms had been removed, making the rooms large enough to create two suites. Those would have gas fireplaces that looked liked old iron stoves.

It was lunchtime before he saw Lane again. When Dylan walked in, she was sitting at the kitchen table next to Caleb, getting ready for the chicken salad sandwiches Winnie was serving for lunch. Lane was so engrossed in her conversation, she didn't see him.

"I heard them last night," she was saying. "When I went out in the hall, there was no one there. But Dylan heard them, too."

Irritation slid through him. "I told you last night it was only the wind."

Lane turned as he walked toward the table. "I know that's what you said. I'm not sure I believe it."

"Why not?"

"Because Caleb said the last owner heard footsteps, too. And there were other things. It was the reason he sold the lodge."

"Jeff Fenton sold the lodge because his wife didn't like living in Alaska." Just like Mariah. He understood that only too well. He turned a hard look on his friend. "I'd appreciate it if you didn't encourage her. We've got enough problems already."

"Sorry."

"I heard crying the other night," Lane said. "It sounded like a child, but it wasn't Emily. I checked."

Worry trickled through him. "You're sure it wasn't her?" But she rarely cried and not at all in the last few years.

"It wasn't her, but she heard it, too."

He didn't ask how Lane knew. She seemed to understand his daughter in a way he was no longer able. "Until we get the place sealed up, the wind is going to make strange noises. That's all it is."

"I want to find out what happened here. People gossip about it. Once we know, we can deal with it."

"If something happened, it was a long time ago and it doesn't mean the lodge is haunted."

Silence fell over the table. None of them had ever said the word out loud.

"Fine," he grumbled. "How do you suggest we find out what happened—assuming something actually did?"

Lane gazed up at him excitedly. "We could start by looking at county records. We find out the names of the owners through the years, then look at newspaper accounts, see if there's anything there."

"It's a borough," he said darkly. "The borough of Waterside."

"When are you going there next?"

"I don't know for sure."

"How about today?" She grinned. "It's only fifteen minutes away."

He couldn't stay mad at her. Not when she looked so damned cute. "Fine. If it isn't raining, we'll go this afternoon."

Just then, Emily walked into the kitchen and conversation came to a halt. Since Dylan was sick of hearing about ghosts and sounds in the night, he was damned glad for the moments of silence.

It rained all day. A downpour that hammered against the windows and beat down on the heavy slate roof. Transfixed, Lane watched the deluge that churned the smooth water in the bay into whitecaps and left the sky a leaden gray.

In L.A., the weather was always the same. Sunny, sunny, sunny. It was wonderful, but occasionally boring. For a while, she stood in the great hall staring out the windows, watching the shifting clouds, the heavy mist hanging over the ocean, the endless buckets of rain.

Emily came in and stood beside her for a while, neither of them speaking, just watching the storm.

"It's beautiful, isn't it?" Lane finally said, not expecting an answer. She was surprised when Emily reached over and took hold of her hand.

They stood like that for another few minutes before, by unspoken agreement, they wandered back to what they'd been doing, Emily returning to her studies with Mrs. Henry while Lane went back to the office to check on her e-mail.

Being able to connect on the Internet had made working at the lodge far easier than she had expected. She was able to stay in touch with her friend and partner, Haley Brodie, and keep an eye on Modern Design.

Having been best friends in college at the University of Illinois, the two of them had reconnected when Haley had come to L.A. to investigate the death of her father. There, she'd met Dylan's cousin, Tyler, a private investigator. The two had fallen in love and married.

Haley was now in charge of art acquisitions and placement, her area of expertise. As an added benefit, she seemed to have a knack for knowing how to handle the three temperamental designers who also worked at the studio.

Lane checked her messages, saw a couple from Haley that had just come in, updates on current projects. Though Lane was enjoying her stay in Alaska, she felt a pang that everything seemed to be running so smoothly without her.

She e-mailed Haley back.

Glad to hear all is well. Things are interesting here. We may have a ghost in the lodge.

Haley answered right away, clearly sitting in front of her computer. Wow, that's cool. Have you seen it?

No, and I hope I don't. We're investigating. I'll let you know what we find out.

What about Dylan? How are you two getting along?

We're taking things slowly, getting to know each other.

That's a good idea—considering what happened with the last guy you dated.

Lane laughed. She had only gone out with Kyle Whitaker a couple of times before she'd realized that as good-looking as he was, the man just wasn't her type. *Only guy I ever dated who wound up in jail,* she thought. She didn't think she had to worry about that with Dylan.

But then, she'd had rotten luck with every man she'd dated after Jason. She had loved him so much. No other man could compare.

She finished her e-mail and signed off, thinking of Dylan. He was completely different from the fiancé she had loved and lost, less self-absorbed, less demanding. Lane realized that aside from the incredible attraction she felt for him, she was actually coming to like him very much.

The question remained, was she ready to sleep with him? Her brain said no, but her body whispered a determined *yes.*

The rain didn't let up. It was just part of living in such a scenic place. It rained a lot in the panhandle, but it also kept the landscape green and lush, kept the glaciers on the distant mountain peaks gleaming with snow year-round, and the water in the bay mirror-clean.

And when it stopped two days later, everything sparkled as if it were newly created, reborn in some way.

Dylan looked up as Lane bounced into the kitchen, a big smile on her face. Damn, she was pretty. He wanted to haul her back upstairs and into his bed. He wanted to keep her there for the rest of the day. Hell, the rest of the week.

"The sun's out," she said. "I'm ready to go to Waterside whenever you are."

Inwardly, he groaned. He'd been hoping she'd forget about the lodge's past, and ghosts, and instead focus on work and maybe a little on him. "You're sure you want to do this?"

"Are you kidding? You never know what we might find out."

True enough. Which was a good reason to stay home. But he loved to fly and with all the work on the lodge, he hadn't been doing a whole lot of that lately.

"All right, we'll head to town as soon as we're finished with breakfast."

They ate French toast drenched in butter and Winnie's homemade maple syrup, thick slices of bacon, and gallons of hot black coffee. The crew was hard at work by the time Dylan was ready to leave. He was waiting for Lane when she stepped out of the office into the hall, looking a lot less buoyant.

"What is it?"

She ran a hand through her heavy red hair and Dylan felt a deep jolt of lust. He wanted to see that glorious hair spread out on his pillow. He just flat wanted her. *Damn.*

"I did some checking. The ownership records for the area are kept in Ketchikan. We'd have to go all the way down there to get a look."

A smile broke over his face. "Helluva lot more fun than a fifteen-minute flight to Waterside. Grab your bag and let's go."

"Really? You'll take me?"

"It's only a hundred miles. We'll be there in time for lunch."

She rushed upstairs and grabbed her jacket and her purse and came back down, her hair pulled into a ponytail. "I can't believe I'm actually looking forward to the flight."

"It grows on you. I've always loved to fly. Up here, it's like being close to heaven."

They headed for the float dock and a few minutes later were up in the air. The trip went smoothly, Lane snapping more pictures with her small digital camera. As he began his descent, she started pointing wildly toward the ground.

"Oh, my God! There's a bear right there on the beach! I can see it from here, Dylan!"

He chuckled, swooped a little lower, circled around so she could get a shot before the big bear lumbered back into the woods.

Lane leaned back in the seat. "That was amazing."

He was glad she was enjoying herself. They didn't have that much time before she'd be heading back to L.A. The thought had the smile sliding off his face.

The recorder's office was on Main Street in Ketchikan, a town of around eight thousand whose economy was based on tourism and salmon fishing.

As they approached the counter, a plump, gray-haired woman wearing jeans and a white knit sweater walked up. "May I help you?"

"My name's Dylan Brodie and this is Lane Bishop. I own a piece of property near Waterside. We'd like to do an ownership search, find out who built the place originally, get the names of the people who've owned it since."

"We're in the process of putting everything on the computer," the woman said, "but I'm afraid we aren't quite there yet. A lot of it's still on microfilm. I'm Mrs. O'Neal. Maybe I can help you find what you need."

"That would be great."

"First we'll need to locate your property on the map," she said, "find out the tax parcel number. Then we can go back through the records. Or we can start with your name and the date of your purchase and go back that way."

"Sounds good."

They ended up using a combination of both his name and the date he'd bought the place, then going backward on the computer as far as the sixties. When the records got older and harder to sort out, they went to the map, located the acreage on Eagle Bay, and searched for the original owner.

The microfilm machine whirred. "Here we go." Mrs. O'Neal hit the button, printing a copy of the earliest documented land ownership record. "On May 2, 1928, the property was deeded to a man named Artemus Carmack."

"That would fit with what little I know," Dylan said. "I was told the lodge was built in the late twenties, early thirties."

Even though they were getting copies, Lane took notes for quick reference, carefully checking the spelling and transaction dates of each sale.

"It looks like Carmack owned the property till September of 1939," Mrs. O'Neal said. "It was sold to a man named Roland Murray." She went back to the parcel map records. "After that I don't see anything till the end of the war."

Lane stacked another document copy on top of her pile.

"I see a couple of transfers in the fifties," Mrs. O'Neal said. "Looks like it was tied up in an estate for more than fifty years before it sold again in 2008."

"Jeff Fenton bought it then," Dylan said. "He did some major repairs and remodeled the family wing. I bought it from him this spring."

"I think we've got what we need," Lane said, smiling.

"Thank you, Mrs. O'Neal," Dylan added. "We appreciate your help."

Lane gathered up the printed pages, paid a small fee for the copies, and they left the records office.

"I'm starving," Dylan said. "How about you?"

"Definitely. I seem to have a lot bigger appetite up here."

"It's the fresh air. Seems to have that effect on people." They went to lunch at a place on Front Street called Annabelle's Keg and Chowder House, then wandered back along the harbor to the plane.

"So what's your next move, Sherlock?" Dylan teased.

"The newspaper office in Waterside," Lane said. "The *Sentinel*'s been in business since 1902." She grinned. "I looked it up on the Internet. We need to run down these names, see what turns up."

"We can stop on the way home if you want."

"Are you sure? It's getting kind of late."

"Doesn't get dark for hours." He grinned. "And it's only fifteen minutes from home."

Lane laughed. Dylan reached down and caught her hand. She didn't resist when he brought her fingers to his lips. "Time's running out, Lane. I want to take you to bed."

She moistened her lips. "I want that, too. I just . . ." She glanced away.

"Is it him? Jason? I know you took his death really hard."

Her eyes clouded. "I loved him. I was going to marry him. But Jason's been gone three years. It's time to move on, take the next step forward."

"Take that step with me, Lane."

She stopped on the sidewalk, turned to look up at him. Sliding her arms around his neck, she went up on her toes and very softly kissed him.

Dylan's whole body clenched. Wishing they were somewhere besides the middle of the sidewalk, he kissed her back. "Jesus, I want you."

When she made no comment, he took her hand. "Let's go find a ghost."

Chapter Eight

It was late afternoon when they made an ocean landing and taxied up to the floatplane dock in Waterside. The city was so small everything was in walking distance, and fortunately, the *Sentinel* office was still open when they got there. The smell of newsprint and ink tinged the air as Lane walked ahead of Dylan through the front door.

So far, the day had been lovely. She enjoyed Dylan's company, and just being with him had kept her heart racing with excitement. Every time those amazing blue eyes swung in her direction, her breath hitched. When her nipples tightened, she pretended it was the cold mountain air.

The truth was, the man just stirred her up. She wished she had the nerve to do something about it. *Soon*, she told herself. It had to be soon or she was going to go crazy.

A big, dark-complexioned man with short, straight black hair walked up on the opposite side of the counter. With his strong nose and blunt features, she thought he was at least half Alaska Native.

"Hey, Dylan, nice to see you."

"Been awhile." Dylan stuck out his hand. "John Ivanov, this is Lane Bishop. She's here—"

"—to help you decorate the lodge," the man finished.

"Maggie mentioned it the last time I was over at the Grizzly." He stuck a big meaty hand out to Lane. "Nice to meet you."

"You, too, John. Ivanov? Is that Russian?"

He nodded. "My father's side. Russian fur traders were the first white people up here. On my mother's side I'm Tlingit."

He turned his attention to Dylan. "So what brings you here? You aren't thinking of putting something in the classifieds? I didn't think the lodge was ready for guests."

"We're not there yet. Lane was just curious about the history of the place. We dug up a list of owners. We thought we'd run down the names, see what might have been written about the lodge over the years."

John's black eyes fixed on Lane's face. "There're lots of stories about the place. I don't know how much is true or if any of it found its way into the paper."

"Maybe we should have come here first," she said. "What stories have you heard?"

John looked at Dylan, who gave a resigned shrug. "You might as well tell her. She's determined to dig around, see what she can come up with."

"I guess if I don't tell you, sooner or later, someone else will. Word around town is the old place is haunted. People have been saying it for years. The owners never stayed long after they bought it, and they always had some tale to tell about ghosts."

"Fenton didn't say anything," Dylan said. Lane could hear the annoyance in his voice.

"Not to you," John said. "He was looking for a buyer. But rumor was, he heard strange noises in the middle of the night. It scared the hell out of his wife. That's the reason he put the lodge on the market."

Dylan shook his head. "It's all a crock of bull. The house is old and it isn't sealed up as tight as it should be. The wind blows through cracks and crannies and makes spooky sounds. Most of it'll stop once we get the remodel done."

"Probably. But you know how people are."

"Yeah, unfortunately, I do."

"So where do you want to start?" John asked.

Lane moved forward, pulling out the copies of the ownership records she had gotten at the recorder's office. "We might as well start at the beginning."

"Fenton told me it was built in the late twenties, early thirties," Dylan said. "According to what we found in Ketchikan, the owner at that time was a guy named Artemus Carmack."

"What's the date of the purchase?" John asked.

Lane shuffled through the papers. "May 2, 1928," Lane said.

John led them back behind the counter, into the bowels of the newspaper office. The printing press wasn't twenty-first century, but it wasn't ancient, either. With so many newspapers going out of business these days, it was nice to see the *Sentinel* still selling. But then everything moved at a slower pace up here.

"The newer editions are on the computer," John said, "but all the old papers are on microfiche. You know how to use the machine?"

"I do," Lane said. "I dug around in the microfiche doing research for an art history project in college. I'm hoping you have some kind of an index."

"We do. Eagle Bay is what you need to look under. Or Yeil. That's the closest village to the lodge. Once you know the dates of the articles, you can locate the film in the file drawers."

"I'll get the index cards," Dylan said to Lane. "Make a list of the dates, and pull the sheets. You can do the digging."

"Perfect."

"All right, then," John said, "I'll leave you to it. Let me know if you've got any questions."

He left them in the back room and Dylan went to work on the index cards. As he located the articles that had referenced Eagle Bay over the years, he wrote down the dates and where to find them. The first posting of interest was the sale of the property in 1928. Dylan pulled the sheet of microfiche from the file and handed it to Lane.

She shoved it under the viewer. "Here it is." She read it on the screen. "The article describes Artemus Carmack as a wealthy entrepreneur from San Francisco. It mentions his plan to build a fishing lodge for the use of his family and friends in the summers."

Dylan handed her the next sheet of microfiche. "Look for an article on June 4, 1929. That would have been a little over a year later."

She found it easily, skimmed the information on the screen. "This one talks again about the plans Carmack had for the property. Oh, look! There's a photo of the lodge under construction."

"That would have been a very big deal up here, especially back then." Coming to stand behind her, he leaned over her shoulder to look at the photo projected on the viewing screen. Lane had to force herself to concentrate.

"Looks like a beehive of activity going on," she said, examining the old black-and-white photo. Mule teams pulled wagons loaded with lumber, boats sat in the bay loaded with building supplies, construction workers were everywhere.

"I wonder how long it took them to finish," Dylan said.

"From the amount of work being done, I'd say it had to be quite awhile."

"And most of it stopped in the winter."

"So what's the next date?"

He handed her another sheet of microfiche. "This is two and a half years later. October 21, 1931."

Lane pulled it up on the screen. "It talks about how the project was encountering problems, taking far longer than anticipated."

"Figures. Just getting the equipment they needed up here had to have been a helluva job. There were logs to mill, then set in place, stone to haul for the fireplaces, all the finish work. Then they had to bring up the furniture once the lodge was finished. They probably used a lot of Indian labor from the village."

The next date was May 31, 1933. "The headline reads, 'Carmack Celebrates Completion of Long-Awaited Eagle Bay Lodge.'"

There was no photo, but the article talked about Carmack bringing his family—his wife, Olivia, and his daughter, Mary—up to enjoy the lodge for the first time. Another article mentioned the names of several San Francisco politicians who had come for a visit that summer. Even one of Roosevelt's vice presidents had spent a week at the lodge.

"Aside from the historical interest," Lane said, "so far I don't see anything that would account for the ghost stories."

Dylan pulled another section of microfiche. "Check this one out. It's a year later, July 1934."

She took the slide, slid it under the viewer. The headline jumped out at her. "Oh, God, Dylan."

"What is it?"

"'Massacre at Eagle Bay.'" A chill ran up her arms.

"Massacre? What the hell?" He moved closer to study the screen.

Lane read the article out loud. "'Olivia Carmack and her eight-year-old daughter, Mary, were killed on Monday in a violent attack at the Eagle Bay Lodge. San Francisco entrepreneur, Artemus Carmack, is said to have barely escaped with his life.'"

"So that's what happened."

Lane turned to look at him over her shoulder. "Caleb said people had died. That's who it was. Olivia Carmack and her daughter, Mary."

"Keep reading."

She skimmed the printed page. "It says they were killed with a shotgun when intruders entered the home in the middle of the night. 'So far no arrests have been made.'" A lump swelled in her throat. "Mary was the same age as Emily. God, Dylan, who would murder an innocent woman and child?"

He handed her the next slice of microfiche, his mouth thin, his jaw set in a grim line. Lane's hand shook as she slid it under the viewer, forced herself to read.

"'Two men, members of the Bitter Water Tribe from nearby Yeil, were arrested for the murders committed at the Eagle Bay Lodge.'"

Standing behind her, Dylan took up the reading when her throat felt too tight to go on. "It says Will Seeks and Thomas Shaekley were taken into custody by the foreman of the lodge, Tully Winston, and several men from Carmack's personal staff. Justice was dispensed at the site."

She looked up at Dylan, a knot forming in the pit of her stomach. "Justice was dispensed? What . . . what does that mean?"

He just shook his head and handed her another piece

of microfiche, which she forced herself to slide into the machine.

"It's a follow-up article," Dylan said, reading over her shoulder. "Printed in the *Sentinel* a week later. 'Before their deaths, the two men arrested admitted their guilt in committing the murders. Unverified reports say that harsh working conditions and too little pay may have been the motive for the shooting. Justice was swift and severe. The assailants were hanged, then buried in the nearby cemetery.'"

Lane trembled. "That's . . . that's the one up on the hill behind the lodge."

Dylan made no reply, just flipped to the next date on the index, slid another section of microfiche into the viewer. "'Lodge abandoned,'" he read. "'Harsh memories of the painful murders of his family make it impossible for owner Artemus Carmack to revisit his beloved Eagle Bay Lodge.'"

Feeling sick, Lane looked down at the ownership notes she had made. "Carmack sold it to a man named Roland Murray five years later, in 1939."

Dylan found an article printed a few weeks after the sale. "It just says the lodge has a new owner who plans to make repairs on the structure and use it for family vacations."

He went back to the index. "There's nothing here until Murray sells the place after the war. That's the end of the microfiche. From then on, everything's on the computer."

Lane looked down at the transfer documents. "There were two sales in the 1950s, then nothing for almost sixty years, not until Jeff Fenton bought it in an estate sale in 2008."

"We know how that went," Dylan grumbled. "Fenton heard noises, his wife got scared, and he sold the place to me."

Lane leaned back in her seat, exhausted.

"Well, now you know," Dylan said darkly.

"Yes."

"Doesn't mean the place is haunted. Hell, I don't even believe in ghosts."

"I don't, either. Didn't, at any rate."

Dylan paced away, stopped, and turned, paced back to where she still sat in front of the viewer. "So what do you want me to do? There are enough rumors about the place already. You tell people what happened out there, my fishing business will never get off the ground. The Eagle Bay Lodge will fail before it ever gets started. Is that what you want?"

Lane came up out of her chair. "No, of course not."

"What then?"

Her heart went out to him. Dylan loved the lodge. It was his dream to make it into a successful business. Aside from that, he wanted to make a home for himself and his daughter.

She reached up and touched his cheek, felt the roughness of his afternoon beard. "We won't say anything, okay? So far all that's happened is we've heard some odd noises in the night. The clanking might actually have been the pipes. It hasn't happened again."

"And the crying? The footsteps?"

"If it keeps happening after you have guests, you'll just explain that the lodge has a resident ghost. You'll tell them he's harmless. People love that kind of thing."

Some of the tension went out of his shoulders. Dylan rubbed a hand over his face. "All right, that's it then. We keep quiet and hope for the best."

Lane just nodded. She could handle noises in the night.

She just prayed she didn't see an actual ghost in her bedroom.

Chapter Nine

Dylan and Lane hadn't yet returned from their trip to Ketchikan, and though Caleb had the job running fairly smoothly, the plumber had run short of the PVC pipe he needed to finish one of the upstairs bathrooms.

With a cell tower in Yeil, he was able to phone Mack's, the plumbing, heating, and electrical supply store in Waterside, and get what he needed. Then he headed out to his pickup for the long drive down the muddy gravel road into town.

He'd bring back the pipe, but the trip was mostly an excuse to see his ex-girlfriend, Holly Kaplan. He'd been thinking about her since Dylan had mentioned her the other day, hadn't been able to get her out of his head.

He had met Holly in Juneau six years ago, when he was twenty-five and she had just turned twenty-one. He'd fallen hard for Holly and planned to ask her to marry him. Instead, she'd taken off with another man.

Caleb hadn't seen her since the breakup, but he knew she had gotten her nursing degree and recently taken a job in Waterside. Several of his friends had hinted that he was the reason she was there.

Caleb paid for the pipe, and while it was being loaded into the bed of his pickup, walked over to the Grizzly Café.

The lunch hour was over. As he shoved through the door, ringing the bell, he saw that only a couple of tables had customers.

He also saw that Holly was busy working, refilling coffee cups, clearing away empty dishes.

She looked good. Beautiful, in fact, with her smooth olive skin and her sleek black hair loose around her shoulders. Though she was petite, she had plenty of curves, and watching her stirred memories he thought he'd forgotten.

Like the exact shape and heavy weight of her breasts, the dark areolas at the crest. He remembered how much he loved the feel of them in his hands, the taste of them in his mouth.

He remembered a lot of things about Holly. Most of all, he remembered that she had told him she loved him, then run off with Eddie McGuiness, the hotshot son of a local car dealer. He remembered that Holly Kaplan had broken his heart.

He sat down in a booth in front of the window, smelled coffee and clam chowder as he waited for her to notice him, saw the color rise in her face when she did.

Coffeepot in hand, she took a deep breath and started toward him, stopped in front of the booth where he sat.

"Caleb. It's good to see you." She smiled. "The years have certainly been good to you. You're even more handsome than you were before."

"You look great, Holly. I heard you were in town."

"I'm a nurse now. I've got a part-time job at the hospital. I start full-time in the fall."

"Good for you."

"I hear you're working for the guy who bought the lodge in Eagle Bay. Maggie says you're his foreman."

"That's right. Dylan Brodie. We met when he was flying out of Juneau. Got to be friends. He needed someone to help him run the place, offered me the job and I took it."

"I bet you're good at it. You always were good with people."

"Except for you."

She glanced away, looked down at the mug still turned upside down in front of him. "You . . . umm . . . want some coffee?"

"I've got to be getting back. I just stopped in to say hello." He rose from the table.

"I was hoping we might, you know, get together sometime, do a little catching up."

"What about Eddie?"

She shrugged. "That didn't work out. We broke up a couple of years ago."

"So now you're looking for a replacement and you're thinking it might be me."

Holly didn't back off. "I never got over you, Caleb. I was hoping you might still have some . . . you know, feelings for me."

He used to wonder what it would be like if they had stayed together. But deep down he knew.

"I'm seeing someone, Holly." He had only been out with Jenny Larsen a couple of times, but they had clicked really well and he wanted to see her again. "She's a first-grade teacher here in Waterside."

"Is it . . . is it serious?"

Was it? Maybe it could be. "Listen, I've got to go. It was good seeing you, Holly."

"You too, Caleb."

Turning, he strode across the café and pulled open the door, stepped out into the cool, fresh air. He'd been crazy about Holly, but seeing her again had cleared his head. Revisiting their disastrous relationship, going down that painful road again, wouldn't be good for either one of them.

Caleb headed for his truck.

Dylan was in a foul mood. It was after midnight. The house was closed up, everyone sound asleep.

Everyone but him. Feeling restless and moody, he pulled on his jeans and wandered barefoot through the house. He went into the kitchen and opened the fridge, but nothing looked appealing. Deciding against a glass of milk, he wandered out into the great hall, stood there staring out the window.

A quarter moon sent a slice of silver across the open water. Towering pines cast long shadows onto the shore. It was beautiful here. Beautiful and peaceful. He'd loved the lodge the moment he had seen it. During the weeks he had investigated the purchase, he'd heard rumors about the old place being haunted, but he had ignored them.

For chrissake, he didn't believe in friggin' ghosts.

He'd figured it was just that the lodge had sat empty for so many years, with just a smattering of owners coming and going through the decades.

Jeff Fenton had owned it since 2008, but had never gotten around to the main remodel and only stayed at Eagle Bay a few months in the summer.

Now that Dylan knew about the murders, he wasn't sure how he felt about the place anymore. Wasn't sure he could go on with the plans he had made.

A faint sound reached him, soft feminine footfalls

padding across the wide-plank floor. He turned to see Lane approaching in her fluffy pink fleece robe.

"I couldn't sleep. I heard you leave your room. I thought I'd see if I could find you."

"I'm surprised you didn't think it was a ghost," he said darkly.

She just smiled. "I heard you close your door." She stuck her hands into the front pockets of her robe, stared out over the water. "You're thinking about what happened here. You're thinking about the lodge and the murders."

He followed her gaze through the massive front windows, out to the silvery sea. "I'm trying to figure out how I feel."

Lane turned to look at the great hall, tilting her head to survey the huge pine logs above their heads, taking in the massive stone fireplace, the wood plank floors, then turned back to the windows and the spectacular view of the bay in the moonlight.

"It's a beautiful place," she said, "the mountains and the forest. The lodge itself is beautiful. It took a tremendous amount of hard work to build it. It deserves a second chance to be what it was meant to be."

"What do you think that was?"

"A place for people like me to come and experience the uniqueness of a wild place like this."

It was the reason he had bought the lodge. He'd wanted to share the beauty of the wilderness. And he'd wanted to make a home for himself and Emily here.

He looked into Lane's green eyes, saw that she understood, and something tightened in his chest. Framing her face in his hands, he bent his head and kissed her. It was meant to be tender, just a thank-you for her thoughtful words. But the moment their mouths met, the instant her pretty lips softened under his, heat arced between them. His body tightened and desire exploded in his blood.

"Lane . . ."

Her arms went around his neck and she leaned into him, parted her lips, inviting him to take more. Dylan didn't hesitate, swept his tongue in to taste her, breathed in the soft feminine scent of her that wrapped around him.

He parted the robe and slid his hands inside to cup her breasts, tested the size, the way they tipped faintly upward, felt her nipples harden beneath his palms.

Lane whimpered, and the kiss went deeper, hotter. He kissed the side of her neck, trailed kisses over her shoulders, claimed her mouth again. His blood was pounding, his groin pulsing, the blood flowing thick and hot through his veins. He slid his hands from her breasts to the curve of her waist, moved lower, reached around to cup her sweet little ass.

Lifting her into the V between his legs, he let her feel the heavy erection throbbing beneath the fly of his jeans. Jesus, he was on fire for her.

Lane moaned.

Dylan slid the robe off her shoulders, let it fall to the floor. Bending his head, he tasted those pretty breasts, first one and then the other, rolled his tongue over the pebbled tip, felt her trembling. He palmed her sex, stroked her, felt how wet she was, and knew she wanted him as much as he wanted her.

Lifting her into his arms, he carried her to the worn sofa in front of the empty fireplace. He wished he had a big fire roaring, wished he could make love to her on a thick bearskin rug in front of the flames.

"We've waited long enough, Lane," he said, as he rested her on the sofa.

"Yes . . . I think we have."

He kissed her again, left her only long enough to strip off his jeans. Careful to keep his weight off her, he settled himself between her legs and kissed her, long and deep. He loved the taste of her, the softness of her lips, the way they melded with his. He loved her feminine, floral scent.

He felt her fingers sliding into his hair, the press of her breasts against his chest. Moving restlessly beneath him, she arched upward against his arousal, encouraging him to give her what she needed. What both of them needed.

He parted her legs with his knee and eased his erection into the slick, hot, softness of her passage, clamped down hard to stay in control.

She was tight and wet, and as her body grew accustomed to his size and length, gloved him perfectly. He tried to go slowly, meant to, but Lane would have none of it. She arched upward, driving him deeper, and her breath slid out on a sigh.

"Lane . . ." She felt so good and he had waited so long. Hanging on to his control by a thread, he started to move, clenched his jaw against the powerful sensations and his overwhelming desire for her.

Out and then in, out and then in, the rhythm increasing, Lane moving with him, their bodies in perfect unison. She came swiftly, unexpectedly, and the hot spasms pouring through her body drove him over the edge.

He pounded into her, driving hard, taking, taking, and Lane came again, her whole body shaking with the force of her release. Dylan's muscles contracted, clenched so hard they vibrated as he followed her over the edge.

Long seconds passed and neither of them moved. He could hear the creak of the aging timbers, the lap of the water against the shore.

Keeping his weight on his elbows, he bent and kissed her softly one last time, then lifted away and settled himself beside her. For several moments, neither of them spoke.

Lane traced a finger over his chest. "That was . . . amazing."

"We were good together. I had a feeling we would be."

"It's been three years. There's been no one since Jason."

Dylan leaned over and kissed her. "I'm glad it was me."

She nestled against him. "We . . . umm . . . didn't use protection," she said into the darkness.

He should have. He had a box of condoms in his bedroom, but his seduction hadn't been planned. "I didn't mean for this to happen, not tonight. If there are consequences—"

"I started on the pill before I came up here. I wanted this to happen. I wanted you, Dylan."

He'd wanted her, too. Since the moment he had first seen her. There was something about her, something that called to him as no woman had for as long as he could remember.

He traced a finger along her cheek. "I didn't plan this, but I'm glad it happened. It's been awhile for me, too. I've been tested. We're safe."

She nodded, snuggled against his bare chest, yawned. "I could sleep right here."

Dylan chuckled. "Mrs. Henry might be in for a shock when she walked in on us in the morning."

She sighed, yawned again. "I guess we ought to go upstairs."

"Yeah." But neither of them moved. Not until the pipes started their violent clanking, jolting both of them up off the sofa. "Son of a bitch!"

"There's our ghost. The pipe ghost, at least."

Dylan grabbed his jeans. Lane hurried over and grabbed

her robe as Dylan headed for the stairs in the hallway leading down to the basement. He flipped on the light at the top of the stairs but only made it as far as the bottom tread when the obnoxious clatter ceased.

He gritted his teeth. At least his ears had stopped ringing. Heading down the stairs, he took a walk around the cold stone floor, checking for anything that might have caused the commotion. The old basement was huge and the lighting wasn't good, leaving much of it in shadows. It smelled of mold and dampness.

Seeing nothing that would account for the racket, he returned upstairs to find Winnie standing in the hallway next to Lane.

"That is the most annoying sound," his housekeeper said.

"We'll figure it out. If we're lucky, it won't start up again tonight. Go back to bed. I'll check on Emily when we go upstairs."

Winnie glanced between them, taking in their bare feet and disheveled appearances, but made no comment, just shuffled back down the hall and disappeared into her room.

Dylan sighed. He had hoped to spend the rest of the night making love to Lane, but one glance at her cool expression and he knew that wasn't going to happen. She was already having regrets, worrying whether or not she had done the right thing. But Dylan had no regrets. He only wanted more of her.

They climbed the stairs together, and both went down to Emily's room. When he opened her door, he saw she was still fast asleep.

"I think she could sleep through an earthquake," he said.

Lane looked up at him. "I . . . umm . . . think I'll be able to sleep now, too."

He reached out and cupped her cheek, read her uncertainty, didn't say what he could see she didn't want to hear. "Good night, love."

"Good night, Dylan." He kissed her at the door to her bedroom and saw Finn standing guard just inside the door, tail wagging as he waited for his mistress to come back inside.

Running a hand through his hair, Dylan returned to his room, doing his best not to think of Lane, trying not to want her again so soon.

He almost smiled. Clanging pipes aside, he had a feeling tonight they would both be able to sleep.

She shouldn't have done it. At the time, it had just seemed so right, so perfect. Now she worried that she should have waited, been more sure of him, been more sure of herself.

But when she had heard him leave his room, Lane had known the reason, known it wasn't ghosts but the murders in the lodge that haunted him. When she had found him standing in front of the window in the great hall, long legs splayed, the muscles in his broad back tense as he stared out at the sea, her heart reached out to him.

She shouldn't have made love with him. Not yet.

But she had, and the truth was, it had been amazing. She had climaxed twice, which had never happened to her before.

Guilt swept through her. She thought of Jason and how much she had loved him. They'd had sex often and it had always been good between them. But there was none of the hunger, the deep restless need she felt for Dylan, none of the hungry need he seemed to feel for her.

She wasn't sure what to do next. She still wanted him, ached for more of the bone-deep satisfaction he had given her. But she was thousands of miles from home, and though she was enthralled with the beauty up here, she couldn't stay.

She owned a business. She had clients, responsibilities. She had mortgage payments, rent on her studio, people who worked for her. The hard truth was, she had a life and it would never include Dylan Brodie.

As she tossed off her robe and climbed into bed, she thought about the reasons she had come to Alaska. She had wanted an adventure. Wanted to visit a beautiful place she had only seen in pictures. She'd wanted to tackle an intriguing, challenging project that paid extremely well.

And she had wanted to sleep with the ruggedly handsome man she'd been attracted to since the moment she had set eyes on him.

Lane relaxed against the pillow. Everything would be all right, she told herself. All she had to do was remember the reasons she had come. She was here, enjoying the adventure, enjoying the work she was doing on the project.

And after three long years of mourning for Jason, she deserved to enjoy a satisfying physical relationship.

For as long as it lasted, Lane intended to do just that.

Chapter Ten

Two days passed. Dylan was giving Lane time to deal with her past, but he wasn't going to wait much longer. Sex with Lane had been even better than his fantasies about her. Physically, they clicked in a way he never had with another woman. And he could tell by her body's response that she had felt it, too.

Tonight, after Emily was asleep and Caleb had gone out to his cabin, Dylan intended to pay a visit to Lane's room. After the heated glances they had shared through supper, he didn't think she would turn him away.

In the sitting room of the master suite, he set aside the book he'd been trying to read and checked the time. Midnight. Barefoot and wearing just his jeans, he started for the door to the hallway, hoping he had read the signals right and Lane would welcome him into her bed or join him in his.

He had almost reached the door when a woman's high-pitched scream sliced through the silence. Jolted into action, Dylan jerked open the door and spotted Lane standing in the hallway, her eyes huge and her body trembling.

"I-I saw it, Dylan! The ghost! I-I saw it!"

After a scream that would awaken the dead, even Emily

had been roused. She stuck her head into the hallway and Finn trotted out of the room beside her. Dylan strode toward her, leaned down, and gave her a hug.

"It's okay, honey. Lane saw a vole and it scared her." A vole was the Alaskan version of a mouse, which so far he hadn't seen inside the lodge. "Everything's okay. Go back to sleep."

"Everything all right up there?" Winnie called out.

"Everybody's fine."

Emily looked up at him, then reached down and stroked Finn's furry head. She patted her leg, silently calling the dog back into her room, went inside, and quietly closed the door.

Dylan checked the empty bedrooms and found nothing. He headed downstairs and made a quick search of the house, then came back up to where Lane still stood in the hall. Leading her into his sitting room, he eased her down on the sofa in front of the fireplace and went into the bathroom to get her a glass of water. When he returned, he pressed the glass into her hand.

"Here, drink this."

She accepted the glass, but her hand was shaking so badly she spilled some of the liquid over the rim. Dylan steadied her hand, held the glass to her lips.

"All right," he said. "Everything's okay. Now tell me what happened."

She swallowed, looked up at him. "I was . . . I was coming to your room. I thought it was what you wanted. It was what I wanted, too."

"It's exactly what I wanted. I was coming to you, Lane."

She nodded, swallowed a little more water, set the glass down on the coffee table. "It was just like before. I heard footsteps in the hall, but I thought it was you. I went to the door and pulled it open, but you weren't . . . you weren't there. Instead I saw this . . . this thing, this man standing in the hallway. An Indian in full warrior dress—like those pictures I saw at the airport. He was covered in blood and he had a kn-knife in his hand."

Dylan tried to be sympathetic, but part of him was getting annoyed. "There was no one out there, Lane."

She looked up at him. "I know, but I saw him."

"You saw a blood-covered warrior in the hallway."

"Not exactly." She took a deep breath, released it slowly. "The thing is, he was a man, but . . . Dylan, he was kind of this weird blue color and I could . . . I could see right through him."

Dylan slammed a hand down on the arm of the sofa. "Goddammit." He got up and paced over to the window, stared unseeing out into the darkness. Turning, he paced back to where she sat. "Do you know how crazy that sounds?"

Lane moistened her lips. "I know. I wouldn't believe it either, if I hadn't seen it myself."

"There was no one in the hall, and I don't believe in ghosts. You read what happened in the newspaper, how the Natives murdered Carmack's wife and daughter. Now you're imagining things."

She shook her head. "No. I was wide awake. I saw it clearly. It was a ghost."

He was angry now. Everything he had worked for was in danger. He towered over her. "There are no such things as fucking ghosts."

Lane pushed him back, came up off the sofa. "Yesterday I would have agreed with you. Not now. Not after what I saw tonight." She was angry, too. "I'm going to bed. I'll see you in the morning." Turning, she stormed away from him out into the hall. He didn't relax till he heard her door close a little too firmly behind her.

Dylan raked a hand through his hair. He didn't believe in ghosts. But he had seen Lane's face and he didn't believe she was simply making things up. Whatever had happened, she believed she had seen something out of the ordinary.

An idea began to form in the back of his mind. He had a friend, a psychiatrist he had met after Mariah had left, when he had been flying out of Juneau.

Amelia Boyle had been in a group he had taken on a sightseeing excursion. She was pretty and smart and easy to talk to, and they had wound up in bed. At the end of the week, Amelia had gone back to Seattle, but they had stayed in touch over the years, seen each other a couple of times when he had been in Seattle. Though he hadn't heard from her in at least two years, tomorrow he was going to call her.

Maybe Amelia could help him figure out what the hell was going on.

Dylan made the call to Amelia Boyle, PhD, as soon as her Seventeenth Avenue office in Seattle opened the following morning.

"I'd like to speak to Amelia," he said to the receptionist who answered. "This is a friend of hers, Dylan Brodie."

"I'm sorry, the doctor is in with a patient. If you'll leave your number, I'll have her return your call."

Dylan left his cell number, then paced back and forth in the great hall, waiting for the phone to ring. Never a patient man, he went upstairs to check on the crew. Caleb was working, helping them put up some wallboard. Spotting Dylan, he motioned him down the hall, out of earshot of the men.

"What's up with you and Lane? You two have been looking daggers at each other all morning."

Dylan sighed. He hadn't mentioned the murders they had uncovered or what had happened last night, but he trusted Caleb and he could use the input. He started to fill him in when his cell phone began to ring.

Dylan dug the phone out of his pocket and pressed it against his ear. "Brodie."

Caleb waved as he walked back to join the crew, and Dylan headed for the stairs, moving away from the clatter of hammers and the buzz of saws where he could have some privacy.

"Hello, Dylan, it's Amelia," a familiar voice said. "My secretary gave me your message. Are you in Seattle?"

He kept walking, heading back to the windows in the great hall, where he could talk without being disturbed.

"'Fraid not. This is kind of a professional call, Amelia. I'm hoping you can help me."

A faint pause. "All right. Tell me what's going on."

"The thing is, this problem isn't the kind you usually deal with and it isn't me, it's a friend of mine." Briefly, he told her about the lodge he had purchased, told her that in the mid-thirties, a woman and child had been brutally murdered, and ever since, people had been claiming the lodge was haunted.

"Lane and I researched the archives in Ketchikan and Waterside. That's how we found out about the murders. It's been on both of our minds ever since. Last night, Lane freaked out. She believes she saw the ghost of a warrior covered in blood. It really shook her up." Hadn't done him a whole lot of good, either, but he didn't say that.

"Lane? That's your friend?"

"That's right. She's an interior designer. She's up here helping me remodel the lodge."

"I see."

He wondered how much she really did see and if it bothered her to think of him with another woman. They hadn't been together in years. But still . . .

"Isn't there something called hysterical hallucination?" he asked. "Where a lot of different people claim to see the same thing at different times?"

"There is. You're talking about something like when people say they've been abducted by aliens and all report the same experiences."

"Yeah, I guess."

"In this case, people hear the house is haunted and convince themselves they've seen a ghost. But hallucinations can also be a sign of alcoholism, a lot of different things."

He shook his head. "A lot of people besides Lane say they've seen things, heard things. And Lane isn't much of a drinker."

"You say this happened in the middle of the night?"

"Yes. Lane walked out of her bedroom into the hall. That's where she claims she saw it."

"There's a mental pathology called hypnopompic hallucination. Hang on a minute. I've got a text right here. Let me refresh my memory on this."

She came back on the line a few minutes later. "Here it is. Hypnopompic hallucination is a state of consciousness leading out of sleep. It's something certain people experience in the first few moments after they wake up. The hallucinations may vary. People can experience an actual physical sensation, a smell, a sound, even an image that isn't really there."

"You're saying the person is still partly asleep."

"Yes. It's emotional and credulous dreaming."

He thought of the dream Lane had had of the raven and the cemetery. "So she might have been having the remnants of a dream though she was mostly awake."

"It isn't really that uncommon. And if the two of you had just been discussing the murders, that might have led her to dream something about them."

"Sounds plausible. Thanks, Amelia. I think maybe that's what happened. I really appreciate your help."

"Call me if you come to town."

"Sure." But he wasn't planning a trip to Seattle anytime soon, and he had no real desire to see Amelia again. At the moment, the only woman he was interested in was barely speaking to him.

Dylan ended the call and inwardly groaned when he turned to see her standing right behind him, her arms crossed over her chest.

"Hallucinating? That's what you think. You think I'm crazy?"

"I don't think you're crazy. Other people claim to have seen ghosts here, too."

"Who the hell was that?"

"A friend of mine in Seattle. A psychiatrist."

"Amelia? Someone you used to date, right?"

"It was years ago, and that isn't the point. Dr. Boyle thinks maybe what happened is that you weren't completely awake when you walked out into the hall. You saw something that was an extension of a dream you were having. It's not uncommon. It's called a hypnopompic hallucination."

"That is so much bullshit. I was wide awake when I stepped into that hallway. Do you know how long I lay in bed trying to work up the courage to knock on your door before I left my room?"

He hadn't considered that, but he could imagine how hard it would have been for her. "Maybe you fell back asleep for a few minutes, then woke up again."

"That's not what happened. And the next time you decide to have one of your ex-girlfriends psychoanalyze me—don't."

When Lane turned and marched out of the great hall, Dylan didn't try to stop her. Lane wasn't crazy, and eventually she would at least entertain the possibility that what she had seen was something other than a visitor from the other side.

At least Dylan hoped so. In the meantime, all he could do was leave her alone and hope in time they could get past this. He still wanted her. Badly.

That she claimed to have seen a ghost didn't change that. *Damn.*

"So what's going on?"

Dylan, who'd been tackling a pile of logs he had cut and brought down from the forest but hadn't yet split and stacked, looked up to see Caleb walking toward him. They hadn't had a chance to talk since his blowup with Lane.

Dylan set a log on the stump, swung his ax, and split the wood into pieces that flew into the air.

"Lane saw a ghost," he said.

"Shit."

"Exactly." Dylan stripped off his plaid flannel shirt and the T-shirt he was wearing underneath and tossed them over a bush.

"Man, that sucks," Caleb said as Dylan picked up his

ax again. "The last thing we need is for our guests to freak out in the middle of the night or not come out here at all."

"It gets worse." Dylan swung the ax, splitting another log in two. "During our little research expedition the other day, we found out the original owner's wife and daughter were murdered in the lodge. The killings were headlines in old *Sentinel* newspaper accounts."

He went on to tell Caleb about the brutal murders and the two villagers who had been hanged for the crime and buried in the cemetery.

"Jeez. I heard something had happened. Never knew exactly what it was. Lane's pretty rock solid. Even if she thought she saw a ghost, I'm surprised she said anything."

"Are you kidding? She screamed the house down."

Caleb grinned. "What'd she say it looked like?"

Dylan felt a trickle of irritation as he remembered her description. "I'm supposed to believe he was an Indian warrior covered in blood, except he was blue, and she could see right through him."

"Whoa."

"Any idea what could have set her off?" Dylan asked.

"She must have seen something. She doesn't strike me as the type to make up something like that."

"She knew about the Carmack family murders. We'd talked a lot about it. Amelia Boyle thinks it was kind of a half-awake dream."

"Amelia? The shrink? The one you used to sleep with? You called her?"

He nodded.

"Tell me Lane didn't find out."

"Walked up behind me when I was on the phone."

Caleb whistled. "No wonder she's pissed."

Dylan whacked a couple more logs, splitting them.

Then he picked up the pieces and tossed them into the pile. He was glad for the exercise. He needed to get his head on straight. He needed to find a way to mend things with Lane.

"She's convinced she's right," he said.

"What if she is?" Caleb asked.

Dylan looked up. "You think that's possible?"

"I'm half Tlingit. To us, ghosts are no big deal."

Dylan set the ax aside. He was beginning to perspire and it felt good. "I don't believe it. In a way, I wish I did. Might make things easier."

"I guess you could pretend."

He chuckled. "I'm not a good liar."

"So what are you going to do?"

"Talk to Lane. Maybe we can agree to disagree. We still have to work together."

"And there's the matter of how hot she is and how bad you want her."

"That, too." The sound of an engine on the road had Dylan glancing in that direction. A battered old white pickup rolled toward them down the gravel road. "Looks like we've got company."

He wasn't sure who it was, but as the truck got closer, he could see a petite woman with long, coal-black hair behind the wheel. Holly Kaplan. "I've got a hunch she's here to see you."

Caleb swore softly and began walking toward the truck.

Dylan put another log on the stump, picked up the ax, and started swinging.

Chapter Eleven

Caleb watched the old truck pull up under a pine tree. As the engine went still, he walked up to the driver's side window.

Holly rolled it down. "Hey, Caleb."

"Hey, Holly." She looked as pretty as ever, her long hair gleaming like black silk around her shoulders, the swell of her breasts faintly visible at the top of her scoop-necked sweater, her lips full and pink. "Didn't expect to see you out here."

She smiled and he felt a little jolt of the old desire. But he knew where sex with Holly would lead, and he wasn't going down that road again.

"We didn't really get a chance to talk the other day. Today's my day off." She glanced toward the lodge. "I've never been out here, but I've heard about it. I thought maybe you could show me around."

Considering how long it had taken her to get there, it didn't look like he had much choice. "I'm . . . uhh . . . pretty busy, but I guess I can spare a few minutes."

Holly frowned.

Caleb opened her door and stepped back as she climbed

down from the truck. "Mrs. Henry keeps a pot of coffee brewing in the kitchen. Let's grab a cup and I'll give you a quick tour."

"Sounds good."

The kitchen was empty, though there were books and papers spread out on the long pine breakfast table. Through the window, Caleb saw Emily out in the side yard throwing a stick for Finn.

He grabbed a couple of heavy china mugs out of the cupboard and filled them from the pot Mrs. Henry kept on the counter. "There's cream and sugar next to the pot if you need it."

Holly took the cup from his hand. "I'm good."

Caleb led her out of the kitchen, through the formal dining area with its view of the bay on into the great hall.

"The lodge was built over eighty years ago," he said. "Must have been a helluva job."

"It's beautiful." She looked up at the heavy iron chandelier above the entry, down at the wide-plank floors. "You can see the care that went into it, even if it does need work."

"We're getting it back in shape, little by little. It's going to be spectacular when we're finished."

Holly continued across the room to the big plate-glass windows, but she didn't seem interested in the view. Instead, she turned and looked up at him.

"I came out here, Caleb, because I wanted to talk to you. I've been thinking about us ever since you came into the café. I think we should spend some time together, see where it leads."

"I told you I'm seeing someone. And even if I weren't, there's too much water under the bridge."

Holly moved closer, set her palms on his chest. She was

almost a foot shorter than he was. "We're older now, completely different people. Everyone deserves a second chance."

Caleb looked down at her and thought how much he had loved her. Maybe it would be different this time. Maybe she had changed as much as he had. He thought of Jenny Larsen, the cute little blond schoolteacher he had only taken out a couple of times. He really liked Jenny.

"I don't know, Holly."

"When are you coming to town again?"

"I'm not sure. I may bring the boat up sometime over the weekend, or maybe I'll make the drive."

"Call me. We'll just go out for something to eat, no expectations, no big deal. Just a little time to talk."

A noise caught his attention. He glanced up as one of the workmen came thumping down the stairs for another load of material. "I need to get back to work," he said.

"At least think about it."

He'd think about it, but his instincts were screaming for him to stay the hell away. "Come on. I'll walk you out."

Caleb took her hand and led her out of the great hall, dropped their coffee mugs off in the kitchen, then led her outside to her truck. He opened the door and helped her climb up in the cab. "Be careful driving back. The roads are still slick."

"I'll be careful." She dug into her purse and pulled out a piece of paper, pressed it into his hand. He looked down to see her address and phone number scrolled in familiar letters. Holly leaned out the window, pressed a soft kiss on his mouth. "Call me."

She tasted like strawberries, got his heart beating a little too fast. She was a beautiful woman and he knew what she was offering, remembered how good it had been.

But Holly was right about one thing. He was a different man now. Smarter. Less naïve. Happier.

He stuffed the paper into the pocket of his jeans. Caleb wanted to stay that way.

Unable to concentrate on the fabric she was trying to choose for the sofas in the great hall, Lane finally gave up and left the office.

She and Dylan were barely speaking. He didn't believe she had seen a ghost and he had gone as far as to call some woman psychiatrist, clearly a female he knew extremely well. He had even admitted to a former relationship. Or maybe not so former.

A fresh rush of anger moved through her. Dammit, she shouldn't have slept with him. She didn't know enough about him. She blew out a frustrated breath. At the very least, she deserved to know the truth about him and *Amelia*.

Or maybe she just wanted to see him.

Lane searched the house. Earlier, Emily had been outside playing, but now she was back in the kitchen with Mrs. Henry, working on addition and subtraction.

"How's she doing?" Lane asked the gray-haired woman as she walked over to where Emily sat at the breakfast table.

"She's gotten every problem right so far," Mrs. Henry said proudly. "I told her if she got the next ten examples correct, she could go back out and play with Finn."

Lane squeezed the little girl's shoulder. "I bet you'll get them all." Emily looked up at her and grinned. Bending her dark head over the numbers, she started adding the columns again.

"She loves that dog," Mrs. Henry said.

"I think he loves her, too." Lane felt a pang at the thought of taking Finn away from the little girl when they went back to L.A.

Still looking for Dylan, she wandered outside, spotted him working on a pile of logs next to the wood bin. He was shirtless, all those glorious muscles gleaming in the sun, bunching as he swung his heavy ax in an arc above his head.

Her stomach contracted just watching him. Lane found herself walking toward him as if drawn by some invisible cord. Dylan spotted her and set the ax aside. He grabbed his T-shirt, used it to wipe the sweat off his face and chest, and tossed it on the stump.

"Looks like hard work," she said.

"I brought this load down from the mountain last week, haven't had time to split it. The smaller pieces are easier to handle and they burn a lot better." He leaned the ax against a stump and walked toward her, stopped in front of where she stood. "Lane, I'm sorry about what happened."

"You mean about calling Amelia?"

He nodded. "I just . . . I thought maybe she could help me find some rational answer for what you thought you saw."

"I can't believe you called your ex-girlfriend and talked to her about me."

Dylan shrugged his wide shoulders, drawing her attention to all that bare skin. "We're friends. I haven't slept with her in years. Like I said, I was hoping she could give me some answers."

"The answer is the house is haunted."

Intense blue eyes bored into her. "Are you really that sure?"

Was she? "I saw him. As clearly as I'm seeing you now. What other explanation is there?"

"You saw a person—except he was blue."

She glanced down, embarrassed though she shouldn't have been. "Yes. Kind of blue, anyway."

Dylan just shook his head. "I'm sorry, but I can't buy any of it. Is there any chance we could give it a little more time, see what happens next?"

Her anger was fading. He didn't believe she'd seen a ghost, but was it really fair to ask him to?

"All right, I guess I can agree to that." A faint smile touched her lips. "But I hope to God the next time some blue Indian is loitering in the hall, he scares the hell out of you and not me."

Dylan laughed, easing the last of the tension. Leaning over, he kissed her softly on the mouth. "If I wasn't so sweaty, I'd drag you off somewhere and ravish your beautiful body."

Lane smiled and moved closer. All that sweat-slick muscle was calling and her body was only too ready to respond. She slid her arms up around his neck and leaned into him, the dampness of his skin soaking through her pink T-shirt. He smelled like hard work and man, and desire curled through her.

"Dylan . . ." she breathed into his mouth, opening to invite his tongue in to tangle with hers.

Dylan pulled her hard against him, kissed her long and deep. Scooping her up in his arms, he started striding off into the woods. Long, jean-clad legs ate up the distance along the forest path, setting giant ferns in motion as he passed, his heavy work boots thudding softly on the damp, loamy soil.

He didn't go far, just out of sight of the lodge and the men who were hard at work inside, stopping in a clearing surrounded by massive, towering trees whose branches cast the area in dappled shadows. There was a fire pit lined with stones in the middle, a picnic table, and benches next to the stones.

Dylan set her down on the end of the table. Beads of dew soaked through the seat of her jeans, but Lane didn't care. Dylan pulled her T-shirt off over her head, unfastened her bra and slipped it off, bent and took a nipple into his mouth. Need and fierce, burning desire washed through her.

He untied the laces on her sneakers and pulled them off, popped the snap on her jeans and lifted her enough to slide them over her hips and down her legs.

In an instant, her panties were gone. Dylan kissed her again, deep and thoroughly, making her insides go hot and damp. She heard the jangle of his belt buckle being unfastened, then the buzz of his zipper sliding down. Dylan lifted her off the table, wrapped her legs around his waist, slid a hand into her heavy red hair. With a single deep thrust, he was inside her.

Both of them stilled. He was thick and hard, and she loved the way he filled her. Dylan kissed her again, slowly, erotically. She loved the way he kissed, loved the control he used to keep them both on the edge. Trailing hot, wet kisses along the side of her neck.

"I can't get enough of you, Lane," he said, kissing her deeply once more. "All I can think of is having you again. Anyplace, anytime, anywhere."

Gripping her bottom to hold her in place, Dylan started to move, driving deep, taking what he wanted. Giving her what she wanted, too. Her eyes closed and her head fell back as the pressure built inside her. She came with a shuddering moan that trembled through her body, but Dylan didn't stop, just pounded into her until she came again.

A low groan slipped from his throat. His jaw tightened and his muscles clenched as he reached his own release.

Moments passed, their hearts pounding, the sounds of the forest beginning to reach them.

"You okay?" he asked.

Lane just nodded. With her head against his shoulder and her arms around his neck, she leaned into him as he set her back down on the table, kissed her softly one last time.

Dylan's jeans were unzipped and hanging low on his hips. Lane was completely naked. The chill in the air finally reached her and goose bumps dimpled her skin. Dylan picked up her T-shirt and handed it over, along with a handkerchief out of his back pocket that she used to freshen herself.

He lifted her down from the table, and she went in search of her panties, dragged them on, and located her bra, jeans, and sneakers. With much of the sunlight obscured by the branches, and missing the warmth of Dylan's hard body, she shivered.

"I better get you back," he said. "You need to get into dry clothes and get warm."

She nodded. She didn't say anything more about Amelia. They needed to trust each other. And there was something sincere about Dylan Brodie she had noticed from the moment she had met him.

He took her hand as they started back down the path to the lodge. He didn't mention the ghost and neither did she.

* * *

Lane finished choosing the sofas and chairs for the living room. One grouping would be tufted leather, the other overstuffed and trimmed with old-fashioned brass tacks. She had yet to pick the fabric, but her workday was over and she needed a break. Wandering into the kitchen, she found Mrs. Henry hard at work on supper.

"What can I do to help?" Lane asked. "And don't say it isn't my job. I'm done for the day and I could use a little female companionship."

Mrs. Henry smiled. "In that case, why don't you peel the potatoes? We're having meat loaf, mashed potatoes, and gravy."

"That sounds great."

She handed Lane an apron, which she tied around her waist. Lane set to work at the sink, digging into what looked like enough potatoes to feed an army. Mrs. Henry worked efficiently a few feet away, putting the meat loaf together in a big stainless-steel mixing bowl.

Lane picked up another potato and started peeling. "So how did you happen to take a job way out here? Did you know Dylan before he bought the lodge?"

"Lord, I've known the Brodie family for years. I kept house for Dylan's father in Anchorage. He was raising Rafe, Dylan, and Nick all by himself. It wasn't easy."

"He was divorced?"

She shook her head. "His wife, Caroline, died of breast cancer. The boys were in their teens by then, but it was still hard on them."

"My mother died the same way. I helped nurse her through those last awful months. It was a very special experience. We became more than just mother and daughter. We became best friends."

Mrs. Henry cast her a look that seemed to hold a hint of approval. "After Clay died—that's Dylan's father—the brothers drifted apart. Dylan got married, and Emily was born. One day I got a phone call from Dylan, asking me to move to Juneau and work for him."

As she stirred the hamburger in the bowl, she flicked a glance toward the door to be sure no one was listening. "Mariah wasn't much of a mother." Another quick glance. "Or wife, for that matter."

The words stirred Lane's interest. "Why did Dylan marry her?"

"I think she just swept him off his feet. He was younger, wilder. And Mariah was beautiful. One of the most beautiful women I've ever seen. Blond and fair and way too pampered. They met in college in Seattle. Dated for less than a year, then got married. I think Mariah thought she could convince Dylan to stay in Seattle, but Alaska is his home."

"Yes, I can see that."

"Dylan took a flying job in Juneau and loved it, but Mariah never got used to Alaska. The remoteness, the weather. She always hated it up here."

"I think it's beautiful."

"Yes, but it's hard living. If you aren't born to it, it takes a special kind of person." Mrs. Henry's direct look was assessing and tinged with warning.

"If you're wondering what my intentions are toward Dylan, you don't have to worry. We're attracted to each other, and I like to think we're friends. But neither of us is interested in a long-term relationship. I have a business in Los Angeles, a company to run. My home is there."

"I didn't mean to pry," Mrs. Henry said, though Lane felt sure she was completely unrepentant.

"Dylan and Emily are your family. You have a right to protect them."

The older woman relaxed. "I can see why Dylan and Emily like you so much."

Lane smiled, pleased by the notion. "You're wonderful with Emily."

Mrs. Henry sighed. "I keep hoping she'll get past whatever keeps her from speaking, but the doctors all warned us not to push her too hard."

"Dylan said something about her mother leaving. I gather that was the cause."

The older woman broke a couple of eggs into the bowl with the meat. She grunted. "Damned woman just up and left one night. Didn't even say good-bye to her daughter. Ran off with some salesman headed back to Seattle."

"Seattle isn't that far. Doesn't she see her daughter at all?"

Mrs. Henry's eyes sharpened on Lane's face. "Why, no. I thought you knew. Mariah was killed in a car accident six months after she left. Her drunken boyfriend got both of them killed."

The potato peeler paused in Lane's hand. How sad for a child to lose her mother at so young an age. It had been nearly unbearable for her, and she'd been twenty years old.

"So Emily's mother's death compounded the problem," she said. "It made Mariah's leaving final."

"That's what the doctors say. It's hard to know the mind of a child."

"Especially one who won't tell you what she's thinking."

The older woman sighed. "It's been very hard on Dylan."

"Yes, it has. I can see the hurt in his face every time he looks at her."

Mrs. Henry went back to her meat loaf and Lane didn't say more. She wished there was a way to help Emily, but she wouldn't be staying in Alaska. Encouraging the little girl to form an attachment would only end up hurting her.

Lane finished the potatoes in silence and set the peeler on the counter. "Is there anything else I can do, Mrs. Henry?"

"I appreciate the offer, dear, but I'm kind of set in the way I do things." She smiled. "And I think it's time you called me Winnie, don't you?"

Lane felt a soft pang in her chest. "I'd love that, Winnie." Lane untied the apron and handed it back, then turned and left the kitchen, glad Dylan and Emily had someone like Winifred Henry to look after them.

She recalled the subtle warning she had received. Winnie was afraid Dylan would get involved with another woman who would abandon him and his daughter. It wasn't going to happen. She and Dylan were friends. They lived two different lives in two different worlds.

There was nothing either of them could do to change that. Lane ignored a little pinch in her heart.

Chapter Twelve

Flames licked over the grate in the small rock fireplace in Dylan's sitting room, lighting the area with a warm red-and-orange glow. Lying spoon-fashion on the sofa, Dylan drew Lane a little closer against him. He loved the way her slender curves fit so perfectly with his, loved the feel of her silky red hair against his cheek. They had made love once already. It was ridiculous to want her again.

He smiled. Lane's eyes were drifting closed, and he had to admit, it had been a long day for him, too.

"It's getting late," he whispered, gently kissing the nape of her neck. "Why don't we go to bed? We'll sleep a lot better in there than on the couch."

She murmured something and slowly opened her eyes, sat up on the sofa, and yawned. She was wearing one of his T-shirts and nothing else, and as far as he was concerned, even that was too much.

His groin tightened. He couldn't remember a woman who turned him on the way she did.

She glanced toward the door. "I don't think that's a good idea, Dylan. What about Emily and Winnie?"

At supper, he'd noticed the change in Lane and his

housekeepers' relationship. Winnie clearly approved of Lane, and yet he knew with certainty the older woman wouldn't encourage any sort of relationship that went beyond friendship, even if they were just sleeping together, which she could pretend to ignore.

Winnie hadn't liked Mariah. She wouldn't want him to risk falling for an outsider again.

Dylan caught Lane's chin, leaned down, and very softly kissed her. "I get up early. I can wake you when I leave and you can go back to your own room."

She glanced back at the door. "I don't know. . . ."

Before she had time to argue, he lifted her into his arms and started striding toward his bedroom. He would let her get some sleep, though he'd rather make love to her again.

He had almost reached the bedroom door when he heard it. Soft and unidentifiable at first, then growing louder, becoming crystal clear. It sounded like a child crying.

"There! Do you hear that?"

Unease trickled through him. "Stay here." Setting Lane on her feet, he grabbed his jeans off the floor and pulled them on, then walked over and opened the door.

The crying continued, a sort of sniffling and then more tears. At least there was no ghost in sight.

Dylan strode down the hall and quietly opened Emily's door, but she was sound asleep, Finn draped over the foot of her bed. He closed the door and turned, caught a glimpse of something in the hallway, something hazy and without much form; then it was gone.

"Did you see that?" Lane was dressed in her jeans and T-shirt and standing in the doorway of the suite.

"I'm not sure what I saw."

"I think . . . I think it was the ghost."

"Bullshit. There's no such thing."

Her chin hiked up. "Then who was crying?"

Dylan gritted his teeth. "I don't know. Maybe the wind has found a spot to seep through that makes a sound like that."

"You saw something. Admit it."

"I didn't see a blue Indian."

"No, but—"

"Look, Lane. I'll admit something unusual is going on. Tomorrow I'll do whatever it takes to figure out what it is. In the meantime, why don't we try to get some sleep?"

Lane shook her head. "I'm awake now and it's getting late. I think I'll stay in my own room."

He could see by the stubborn tilt of her chin it wouldn't do any good to argue. "All right. If you're sure that's what you want."

She bit her lip. He could read the indecision in her pretty green eyes. It relieved him a little to know she didn't want to sleep alone, either.

"I think it's for the best."

He just nodded. "I'll see you in the morning." Holding open her door, he waited till she disappeared inside, then closed the door and walked back into his sitting room.

Dragging a chair over to the doorway, he sat down facing the hall. Lane was right about one thing. Something was definitely going on.

Three hours later, he woke up still sitting in the chair, irritated at himself for falling asleep. The only thing he had to show for his efforts was a stiff neck and a bad disposition. Whatever was happening in the house, clearly he wasn't going to figure it out tonight.

Dylan yawned. Setting the chair back in place, he closed the door and padded off to bed. He hoped like hell he'd be able to sleep.

* * *

Breakfast was a quiet affair the next morning. Emily finished early and went outside to play with Finn. Neither Caleb nor Paddy O'Ryan had shown up. Lane and Winnie weren't doing much talking, either.

"Sleep okay?" Dylan finally asked Lane, just to stir her up a little and see what she'd say.

Faint color rose beneath the bones in her cheeks. "Actually, I did. After the excitement was over, I slept very well."

Winnie looked up from her place at the end of the table. "What excitement?"

"Last night, we heard something that sounded like a child crying," Lane said. "I've heard the same sound before."

Winnie wiped her mouth with a paper napkin. "It wasn't Emily, was it?"

"No," Dylan said.

"I've heard it a couple of times," Winnie said, suddenly unable to meet his eyes as she toyed with the food on her plate. "I checked on Emily, but she was asleep."

The bite of eggs Dylan had taken seemed to stick in his throat. "Why didn't you mention it before?"

"I knew you'd heard the rumors. You had enough on your mind trying to get this place in order, and I didn't want to upset you. But now that we're talking about it, I might as well tell you the rest."

Dylan set his fork down next to his plate. "Crap, what else?"

"At night, before I go to bed, I always check the windows, make sure they're locked. But every once in a while when I get up in the morning they're unlocked."

His stomach was churning. "Anything else?"

"The pictures on the walls . . . sometimes I find them hanging upside down."

"Jesus."

"I saw a ghost, Winnie," Lane said. "It was an Indian warrior, but it was kind of blue and I could see right through it. I saw it upstairs in the hall outside my bedroom. I think it was there again last night."

"Oh, dear."

Stifling a curse, Dylan looked up to see Paddy O'Ryan walking into the kitchen with Caleb right on his heels.

"We got a problem, boss," Paddy said, his red hair sticking up, windblown, and in need of a comb.

"Some of the crew heard about the murders that happened out here," Caleb said. "One of the guys claims he was driving home after dark a couple of days ago and saw blue lights in the attic window. This morning, there was writing on the wall in one of the bathrooms we've been working on in the guest wing."

"Writing," Dylan said darkly.

"That's right," Paddy said. "And it looks like it was painted in blood."

Dylan came up off the bench, slammed his napkin down on the table. "Son of a bitch!"

"Most of the crew took off—all the guys from Yeil. The plumber headed back to Waterside. They say they aren't making enough to work in a haunted house."

Dylan's jaw felt tight. "I've got to see this. Upstairs or down?"

"Downstairs," Caleb said.

Heading out the kitchen door, he strode through the formal dining room, across the great hall, and into the guest wing. Just as Caleb had said, a wall in one of the bathrooms had been painted with streaky red letters. Crimson dripped eerily all the way to the floor.

"Tlingit?" he said to Caleb.

"Looks like it."

"What's it say?"

Caleb's mouth edged up. "I don't have a clue. But one of the guys from Yeil is a full-blood. He claims it says, 'Leave. Now.'"

Dylan walked over and ran a finger through one of the red streaks on the wall.

"Is it blood?" Lane asked, appearing in the doorway, her face a little pale. Dylan hadn't realized she'd followed them.

He sniffed the red on his finger, recognized the coppery scent. "Yeah, it's blood."

"Oh, my God."

"Take it easy—all of you. Okay, I won't argue anymore. I'm convinced something strange is going on. As of right now, I'm not stopping until I figure out what it is."

Lane and Caleb exchanged a glance. Neither of them believed he would find anything normal that could explain the odd happenings.

"Caleb, as soon as you and Paddy finish breakfast, we're going to do a room-by-room search of this place. The crew won't work. Guests won't come if they think the place is haunted. I still don't believe in ghosts, but I'm beginning to believe someone wants us out of here. We're going to find out who the hell it is—and why."

While the men finished eating, Dylan went back to the guest wing bathroom. Using a clean square of white cloth, he took a sample of the blood on the wall. Back in the office, he phoned a friend who worked at the DNA Diagnostic Center in Juneau. The lab was mostly used for paternal DNA testing, but Rex Doheny, an avid outdoorsman and fishing buddy, would be able to tell him whether or not the blood was human.

"You got a sample?" Rex asked, after Dylan explained the situation, calling the incident vandalism—which he actually believed it was.

"I've got one. I'll bag it and fly it up to you this afternoon." The fastest he could get a letter or package to Juneau from Waterside was seventy-two hours. Taking his own plane, at a hundred and fifty miles an hour, it was less than a two-hour flight from Eagle Bay. He could be up and back before nightfall.

"Give me a call when you get to the airport," Rex said. "I'll come pick you up. Give us a chance to catch up and save you a trip into town."

Relief trickled through him. "That'd be great. I appreciate the help. I owe you and Sarah a weekend at the lodge once we get it finished."

"Sounds like a deal to me. I'll see you late afternoon."

Dylan ended the call. He needed to get the sample to Rex as quickly as possible and get back home. Things were happening he didn't understand, things that could wind up putting people in danger. Until he knew exactly what was going on, he needed to be here making sure everyone was safe.

"You're flying up to Juneau?" Lane stood a few feet away. He hadn't heard her walk into the office.

"That's right. I need to know if this is human blood. I don't think it is, but I need to be sure."

"If you think it was vandalism, why don't you call the police?"

"Because I'm trying to keep a lid on things. And I want to take a look at the house, see what I can find out."

Caleb walked in just then, his jaw set, a long black braid resting on each shoulder. As part of the deal they had made, Caleb owned a percentage of the lodge. He wanted it to be successful as badly as Dylan did.

"Where do you want to start?" his friend asked.

Dylan raked a hand through his hair. "Upstairs in the family wing, I guess. That's where most of the activity has been. We'll search every inch of it, see if we can't find something out of place."

"We're gonna need a ladder and some flashlights," Caleb said. "I'll go get them."

The men walked out into the hall to find Paddy O'Ryan waiting, looking as grim-faced as he and Caleb. While Caleb took off in search of a ladder and flashlights, Dylan and Paddy headed upstairs.

He didn't expect Lane to fall in behind them, but it was all right with him. Lane was smart and she had seen the "ghost." Maybe she could be of some help.

"What're we looking for?" Caleb asked when he arrived on the second floor, setting the ladder down in the hall and spreading it open.

"Could be anything. We heard crying. If it wasn't real, it had to have been recorded and delivered through some kind of speaker."

Caleb nodded, beginning to get on board with the idea. "Okay, so we look for a speaker that's small and unobtrusive, probably wireless."

"Sounds right."

"What else?" Paddy asked.

"If the windows were opened at night, it had to have been done from inside. Same with the pictures being turned upside down, and the writing on the wall. We've got hand-locking dead bolts on all the doors, so a key isn't going to work. Look for some sort of secret panel, some kind of entrance that would let someone into the house."

"That's a scary thought," Lane said.

"Makes sense," said Caleb.

"Paddy, you take the two empty bedrooms up here. Caleb, you and I'll work the hall."

"Emily's outside with Finn," Lane said. "I'll look around in her room."

He smiled, appreciating the fact she was willing to keep an open mind and not just dig in her heels about what she had seen. "Thanks."

He watched her disappear into Emily's bedroom. As far as they knew, nothing had happened in there, but Em wouldn't have said anything if it had.

Paddy headed for one of the empty bedrooms while Caleb went up on the ladder and began searching the seam between the wall and the ceiling. Dylan got down on his hands and knees and ran the light along the baseboard.

For the next half hour, he and Caleb quietly searched the hall, floor to ceiling, even pulled up the rug in a couple of places. Nothing.

Finally, Paddy came out of an empty bedroom, shaking his head.

"Nothing?" Dylan asked.

"'Fraid not, boss. Maybe there really is a ghost. You ever seen that movie, *Amityville Horror*?"

"No, and I don't want to. Why don't you take a look in the attic above this wing? There's an access panel in the ceiling at the far end of the hall."

"Will do." Paddy borrowed the ladder to climb up in the attic; then Caleb carried it back to where he had left off his search. Minutes dragged as the search quietly continued. Dylan was beginning to wonder if his idea was as crazy as it sounded.

"Hot damn!" Caleb called out. "I found something."

Dylan stood up, his adrenaline kicking in. He shined his light toward the ceiling, where Caleb used his pocket-knife to pry out a tiny plastic circle. "What is it?"

Caleb tossed the object down to Dylan.

"Son of a bitch. I knew it. It's a miniature speaker."

Caleb moved the ladder, climbed back up. "There's another one in the same place on the opposite side of the hall."

Dylan shined the flashlight on the second speaker, then scanned the ceiling farther along the corridor. "Here's another one. There's another one across from it." They were the same off-white color as the walls and wedged in out of sight.

"I bet they bought them on the Internet," Caleb said. "All kinds of sites sell stuff like this: miniature speakers, recorders, cameras—you name it."

"We need to find the device they were using to play the recordings."

"The speakers are wireless. Could be anywhere in the house."

Down the hallway, Emily's bedroom door burst open and Lane hurried into the hall. "I found something."

"So did we." Dylan held up one of the speakers. "Speakers. We've got four of them so far."

"Wow. That's how they faked the crying child."

"Looks like. And don't forget the clanging pipes."

Lane turned and started back the way she had come. "Wait till you see this."

Dylan almost smiled at her enthusiasm. Clearly she'd changed her mind about the haunting. One less obstacle to overcome.

Lane knelt next to the little rocking chair in Emily's bedroom. "Down here," she said. Dylan knelt beside her on the carpet, close enough to make her skin tingle. She shoved aside thoughts of the fantastic sex they'd had last night and pointed to a tiny piece of clear nylon string attached to the leg of the rocker.

"Fishing line," Dylan said.

"See where it goes?" She followed the fine piece of nylon to where it disappeared into a section of the baseboard. Removing the cut-out piece, she pointed to a homemade device with an arm that swung back and forth like a metronome. When she tugged on the fishing line, the rocker moved back and forth as if it were occupied by some invisible force.

"The arm that moves is attached to parts from a wind-up alarm clock," she said. "That's what makes it work."

"Damn. I've seen the chair moving. I thought it was just the wind."

"Pretty clever, don't you think?"

Dylan's features tightened. "Clever, yes. But someone has to be coming into Emily's room to wind it up and that scares the hell out of me."

Caleb frowned as he looked at the rocker. "Probably used some version of the trick on Jeff Fenton's family to drive them out of here."

Lane thought of the eerie sounds she had heard and a

chill went through her. "What about the ghost? I definitely saw a blue Indian warrior in the hall. How did they do that?"

Since no one seemed to have the foggiest idea, they all filed back into the corridor. Lane looked up at the sound of Paddy's voice.

"Hey, boss, there's something up here." The ruddy-faced man leaned down through the opening into the attic. "I got no idea what it is."

Lane exchanged a glance with Dylan. Caleb grabbed the ladder and put it in position beneath the opening. They each grabbed a flashlight and climbed up into the attic.

There wasn't much up there, just a wooden floor and a small window letting in light from the far end of the room. It was the odd-looking apparatus on the floor that snagged their attention.

"What do you think it is?" Paddy asked.

Dylan crouched down to examine the equipment, which involved mirrors, something that looked like a laser projector, and a photographic plate. "Whatever it is, it wasn't here when I bought the lodge."

"There! That's him!" Lane pointed to a photo of a Tlingit warrior in full battle dress. "That's the ghost I saw at the end of the hallway—except he was blue and kind of wavy."

Dylan looked back down at the equipment. "I don't know much about this kind of thing, but I think what you saw was a hologram." He skimmed his flashlight over the floor of the attic, looking for the opening where the image had been projected onto the floor below. "Here it is."

There was a well-disguised hole they would have eventually discovered if they had examined more of the second-floor ceiling.

Paddy looked over at the holographic apparatus. "Should we take the damned thing down, or leave it here?"

"Leave it," Dylan said. "If we have to call in the police, maybe they can get some fingerprints or something."

"I usually hate admitting I'm wrong," Lane said, "but not this time."

"At least we found our ghost," Caleb said with obvious relief.

Dylan flicked a dark glance his way. "Great. Now all we have to do is figure out who the fuck is trying to scare us the hell into leaving—and why."

Lane thought of the house, of the murders all those years ago, tried to imagine who might be prowling the corridors while they were asleep, and felt an ominous shiver.

Chapter Thirteen

It was overcast, but only slightly windy. Dylan made the trip to Juneau, left the blood sample with Rex, and was on his way back to the lodge by early evening.

Now that he knew the haunting was a hoax, he needed to know how far the perpetrators were willing to go to get him to follow in his predecessor's shoes and abandon the lodge. He needed to make sure the blood on the wall wasn't human.

With everything that had happened, he hadn't wanted to leave his family alone, but he needed the information. Flying up with the sample was the fastest way to get it. While he was gone, Paddy and Caleb planned to search the outside of the house to try to find out how the intruders were getting inside. He hoped they'd been successful.

Across the water, the sun was just setting, turning the sky a pinkish orange that tinted the snow-topped peaks in the distance, a sight that packed a punch he never got tired of. Dylan started his descent, skimming the surface of the ocean, setting the pontoons gently on the top of the sea.

As he reached the dock and turned off the engine,

Paddy began the task of securing the plane, and Dylan climbed down from the cockpit.

"Find anything?" he asked the brawny Irishman.

Paddy shook his head. "We didn't find squat, boss. No door, no secret entrance. Nothing."

"Could be a tunnel comes up somewhere under the floor."

"Could be. We'll start looking again at first light."

"Until we find it, we need to make sure everyone is safe."

They'd discussed security before he left. Tonight, Caleb would be sleeping in one of the upstairs bedrooms. Paddy, who lived in a small log home off the road between the lodge and Yeil, had volunteered to spend the night in Caleb's cabin, keep an eye out for anyone who might be prowling the grounds. Dylan and Caleb planned to take two-hour watches, hoping to catch whoever was sneaking inside.

"Welcome home." Lane smiled as she walked toward the float dock, and a warm feeling expanded in his chest.

"I heard the plane landing," she explained. "I've been worried. I'm glad you're back safe and sound."

Dylan reached out and touched her cheek. He'd been worried about her too, worried about all of them since he'd left that afternoon. Lane must have read his thoughts. She moved closer, leaned into him, and Dylan folded her into his arms. For long seconds, he just held her.

"We're going to figure this out," she said softly.

We. The word tightened something in his chest. He was used to fighting his battles alone. He didn't want to think how good it felt to know Lane was willing to help.

"Rex is testing the sample," he said. "He'll let us know sometime tomorrow."

"Rex. That's your friend at the lab?"

He nodded. "Old fishing buddy."

"Whatever he finds, at least now we know the lodge isn't haunted."

Dylan bent his head and very softly kissed her, felt the immediate kick of sexual awareness, forced himself to pull away. "That's something, I guess."

"Yes, it is. It's easier to fight a flesh-and-blood enemy than one you can see through."

He found himself smiling, and some of the tension he was feeling slipped away. "Good point."

Draping an arm around her shoulders, he walked her back toward the lodge. Caleb was coming from the opposite direction, a serious expression on his face.

"What is it?" Dylan asked. "Not more trouble, I hope."

"Nothing new. Just that I've been thinking about that message on the wall."

"And?"

"It was written in Tlingit, right? Two braves from the village killed Carmack's wife and daughter. That's the reason the ghost Lane saw was dressed as a warrior."

"That's got to be right," she said. "Anyone who's heard the story would understand the threat. Those braves were hanged. If you stay here, they'll come back and take revenge on you."

"Stay and you could be murdered too," Dylan added.

"The braves that were hanged came from the village," Caleb repeated. "Whoever did this—there's a good chance someone from Yeil is involved."

Dylan had already come to that conclusion.

"Couldn't it just be kids?" Lane asked. "Maybe a group of teens? Lots of people seem to think the lodge is haunted. Maybe whoever it is just thought scaring us would be funny."

"Pretty sophisticated equipment for kids," Dylan said.

Lane arched a burnished eyebrow. "Are you serious? The average twelve-year-old today knows more about computers than most adults."

"Good point. Whoever it is, before we make accusations, we need some kind of proof."

"I think we should talk to the village elders," Caleb suggested. "We tell them what's been going on, see if they'd be willing to help."

"All right. And we need to get the word out, let the construction guys know it's all a hoax and nothing to be afraid of. Maybe the elders can help with that, too. Can you set up a meeting?"

"I know some people in Yeil. I'll head over there first thing in the morning."

Dylan looked up to see Winnie walking toward them across the grass, a scowl on her wrinkled face. Clearly, she had overheard their conversation. "All right, you three, that's enough talk about ghosts and murder. Supper's ready. It's time to eat."

Lane looked up at him. "Emily's with Finn. I'll go get her."

Dylan watched her leave, his gaze going from the dark red hair around her shoulders, past her small waist, down to her sexy behind. He clenched his jaw as he started getting hard.

Damn. He had wanted Lane Bishop from the moment he had seen her in L.A. Stupidly, he'd hoped that once he'd had her, his hunger would lessen. Instead, he lusted after her worse than ever. He hoped to hell he could end his obsession by the end of summer.

But as he watched her striding away, remembered the way those long legs felt wrapped around his waist as he moved inside her, Dylan was beginning to doubt it.

* * *

As Emily tossed a stick for Finn, Lane crossed the side yard in the child's direction. Finn dropped the stick, woofed, and trotted toward her, all long legs and shaggy gray head. Emily stayed where she was.

Lane kept walking, Finn falling in beside her. She rubbed his ears as they reached the little girl, and Lane knelt at her side.

"Did you and Finn have fun playing?" she asked.

Emily nodded. She was a pretty little thing with her big blue eyes and glossy dark hair. With a father as good-looking as Dylan, it wasn't surprising.

"Finn never gets tired of playing. But it's time for us to go in. Mrs. Henry has supper ready. I bet you're hungry after being out here so long with Finn." Lane rose and reached out a hand. Emily hesitated only a second before she placed her smaller hand in Lane's and the two of them started back to the house.

Every time she was with the child, it took all of her self-control not to encourage Emily to speak. But Dylan had tried for years and so had Winnie. Nothing they had done so far had worked.

They went inside and headed for the kitchen. Still holding Emily's hand, Lane inhaled the succulent smell of roast chicken. "Smells good, doesn't it?" She smiled down at the child. "I love chicken, how about you?"

Emily nodded vigorously. What kept her from speaking? What would unlock the words she kept inside? Lane wished she knew how to help, but winning the child's trust would take time, and time wasn't something she had.

She kissed the top of the little girl's head. "You better go wash up. Finn is a sweetheart, but he loves to get dirty."

Emily giggled and raced away. Lane watched her go, aching for the child and the father who loved her. Lane turned to find Dylan watching them, saw something in his face she could only call regret.

Regret that his little girl refused to speak? Or that she would be leaving? Either way, Lane felt a touch of that same regret.

Lane extended her hand to Dylan, who caught it, pressed his mouth against her fingers, and let her lead him into the kitchen.

The men were taking two-hour shifts, making rounds through the house, then taking a position in the shadows, hoping to spot whoever was sneaking into the lodge.

With Caleb and Dylan prowling the darkness, Lane slept fitfully, waking every couple of hours to the sound of muffled voice, straining at every creak and groan that might be a possible intruder.

A little before dawn, she fell asleep, then overslept and missed breakfast. Wearily she headed for the shower. She had just turned off the water, stepped out, and wrapped herself in a towel, when a knock sounded at the door.

Red hair pinned up, damp tendrils stuck to the back of her neck, she hurried to open it and found Dylan standing in the hallway, looking tired and frustrated and sexier than any man had a right to.

"I just came by to tell you . . ." His words trailed off as his eyes ran over her half-naked body. "Jesus, you look good enough to eat." Dylan backed her into the room and closed the door, hauled her into his arms and kissed her, a fiery kiss that deepened into something erotic and had her moaning into his mouth.

Dylan Brodie was her weakness, like eating chocolate bonbons, or curling up in the sun with a really good book. From the moment she had seen him crossing the deck with his cousin Ty in L.A., striding toward her as if he already knew what was going to happen between them, she had wanted him.

She wanted him now.

Lane slid her arms around his neck and kissed him back, her towel falling to the floor. Dylan filled his hands with her breasts. She could feel the calluses of a hardworking man abrading her nipples, inhaled his clean woodsy scent, and heat poured through her.

"I missed you last night," he said, kissing the side of her neck as he kneaded her breasts, then moved down to cup her bottom and pull her against him. She could feel the thick, hard ridge inside his jeans, and a sharp stab of need cut through her. Her body burned for him the way it always did, and her heart beat so hard she could hear it.

"I missed you, too," she whispered, nipping his earlobe, then kissing him hotly again. When he lifted her, she wrapped her legs around his waist, felt the washboard muscles beneath his flannel shirt as he carried her across the room and set her down on the edge of the bed.

Lane gasped as he eased her back on the mattress, parted her legs and knelt between them, kissed and nipped his way from her breasts to her belly, then lower, tasting her and making every nerve ending in her body jump.

She was shaking, hot and wet and needy. Lane cried out at the feel of his mouth and tongue, teasing and tantalizing, driving her to the brink of climax. Trembling all over, she laced her fingers in his thick dark hair and a wave of need washed through her.

Her climax hit hard, pleasure spreading through her

body, sliding out through her limbs. Before she had time to spiral down, Dylan came up over her, pinned her wrists above her head to hold her in place, and drove himself deep.

Lane moaned. In seconds, she was tipping into another powerful climax, the sensations so hot and sweet she could taste them on her tongue. Dylan followed her to release, his body going rigid, a low growl locked in his throat.

For several long moments, neither of them moved.

Dylan kissed her softly one last time, then lifted himself away and began to straighten his clothes. He bent and retrieved her towel, tossed it in her direction.

"I can't believe that happened." He raked a hand through his hair. "I've got a thousand things on my mind and none of them include having sex with a beautiful woman. One look at you in that towel . . ." He shook his head. "Jesus, Lane."

Ridiculously pleased she could affect him that way, Lane sat up on the bed and wrapped the towel around her, tucking the end between her breasts to hold it in place.

"If you have so much to do, why are you here? Did something happen last night?"

He sighed. "Not a damn thing happened last night. Probably because of the wireless mini-cam we found this morning in the stairwell, aimed down the hall. They could have watched us taking down the speakers or heard us talking. Odds are they know we're onto them."

"With a camera focused on the hall, they could play one of their recordings—footsteps or crying—then watch to see what happened when we heard it."

"That's right. And they'd also know when to make the ghost appear. I'm pretty sure that's how they scared the Fentons into selling."

"And maybe other people over the years."

"That's the way it looks."

"Everything's wireless. All they need is a laptop somewhere within range to make their equipment work."

"Except for the rocker." His jaw tightened. "Someone had to come upstairs for that."

"I'm surprised no one saw them."

"Maybe we did and didn't realize they were part of this."

Her eyes widened. "You aren't thinking it's someone who works for you?"

"It's a possibility I'm not willing to overlook."

"Oh, Dylan."

"We're going to search outside this morning, see if we can find a tunnel that leads into the house."

"I think you should go to the police. We know the house isn't haunted. We know someone is playing a very serious hoax. The police can help us find out who it is."

"I'd like to meet with the elders first. Everyone in Yeil probably knows the story of the murders. Maybe someone there will know who's behind this. If there's any way to handle the problem ourselves, I'd rather keep the police out of it."

She wasn't sure that was a good idea. But Dylan had a business to run. And she was beginning to realize how independent and self-sufficient the people who lived in the Alaskan wilderness were.

Dylan bent his head and softly kissed her. "You'd better get dressed. If you don't, you won't be getting out of here for at least another half hour."

Lane grinned. "You're insatiable, you know that?"

He cocked an eyebrow meaningfully in her direction.

"Okay, I see your point, but I didn't plan for that to happen, either."

Dylan chuckled and headed for the door. It closed softly behind him as he returned to work.

As soon as he was gone, Lane headed back to the bathroom, her body pulsing softly, reminding her of their unplanned encounter. Dylan Brodie was the sexiest man she had ever met. Even Jason hadn't been able to stir her body the way Dylan could.

Guilt slipped through her. Comparing the two men was wrong and completely unfair. She had loved Jason. She only lusted after Dylan.

Or was it more than that?

A sliver of unease went through her. The consequences of falling in love with Dylan would be dire for both of them. She couldn't stay here. He couldn't leave. And there was Emily to think of. Lane refused to do anything that would hurt Dylan's little girl.

She could handle it, she told herself. She just had to be careful.

Dressed at last, her hair pulled into a ponytail, she headed downstairs, her body still humming with remnants of sexual pleasure. She hoped it didn't show on her face.

Her stomach rumbled. She'd missed breakfast, but there was always something to eat in the kitchen. She grabbed a leftover biscuit and went into the office, sat down, and booted up her laptop.

She needed a little girl talk. Lane opened her e-mail and started typing a message to her partner and friend, Haley Brodie. She wanted to update her friend on the nonexistent ghost, check on her business, and see how the newlyweds were getting along.

One thing she knew for sure. If Ty Brodie was as hot in bed as his ruggedly handsome cousin, Haley was doing just fine.

Chapter Fourteen

Dylan grabbed his cell phone, punched in his brother's number, and headed outside to get some fresh air.

Nick answered on the second ring. "Hey, 'bout time you called. It's been so long I was about to break down and call *you*."

His brother, one year younger, was an ex-Army Ranger, a homicide detective in Anchorage. Or he had been, until he'd helped apprehend a killer who was torturing and murdering young women. The job, combined with his years of fighting in Iraq and Afghanistan, had begun to weigh on his mind. A few months back, Nick had taken a hiatus, bought a place a few miles north of Anchorage, and was doing his best to recover from a heavy dose of burnout.

"Been meaning to phone," Dylan said. "Kind of got sidetracked."

"With the pretty lady from L.A.?"

Dylan chuckled. The last time they'd talked he had mentioned Lane Bishop, the interior designer from Beverly Hills he had hired. His brother, knowing him a little too well and being a former detective, had apparently checked out Lane's website. One look at her picture and he had assumed Dylan's interest went beyond remodeling the lodge.

"She's an interesting woman," Dylan said, "and good at her job."

"And . . . ?"

"And that's all you need to know. How are things up there?"

"Quiet. It's a nice change after being a cop for so long." Not to mention Nick's years in Special Forces.

"I'm surprised you aren't getting bored."

The silence on the other end of the line told Dylan he probably wasn't too far off the mark. Sitting around the house wasn't his brother's style, even if he had convinced himself it was.

"Listen, I've got a problem," Dylan said. "I thought you might be up for giving me a little advice."

"Fire away," Nick said.

For the next few minutes, Dylan filled his brother in on the hoax, and the vandalism that had caused his crew to walk off the job.

He could almost hear Nick's mind spinning on the other end of the line.

"If this has been happening for as many years as you think it has, it isn't personal," Nick said. "There's got to be something else going on. You need to find out what it is."

"Yeah, and who the hell is behind it," Dylan added.

"That's right. So far no one's been hurt, but I can tell you from experience that can change in a heartbeat. This sounds like a pretty elaborate hoax. There's a reason for it. Until you find out what it is, stay alert."

It was good advice. But then that was the reason he had called. "We're being careful," Dylan said. "I'm hoping to talk to someone in authority in Yeil, see if they can help us find out what's going on."

"You want me to come down there? You know I will."

"I know that. I'll let you know if I need you."

"Okay, but don't wait too long." Nick signed off and Dylan ended the call. He hadn't missed the worry in his brother's voice. They needed answers. They needed this to end—before someone got hurt.

Caleb returned from the five-mile trip to Yeil just before noon. Dylan and Paddy had been going through the house, looking for other surveillance equipment and thankfully finding none.

"I talked to Andy Payuk," Caleb said to Dylan, referring to a framer on the construction crew. "I told him it was all a hoax, told him we had proof, and asked him if he could set up a meeting with his grandfather."

Dylan nodded. "Jacob Payuk's a powerful man in Yeil."

"I've met him once or twice. Andy's supposed to call me this afternoon with a time for us to meet."

"Sounds good."

With the meeting coming together, Dylan, Caleb, and Paddy went outside to search for a tunnel or some other way of getting inside the house. Each armed with a flashlight, they split up, Caleb checking the grounds, Dylan searching the two-car garage under the house. Paddy searched the empty cabins.

The garage, a big empty space beneath one end of the lodge, had yielded nothing. He was just walking back outside when his friend appeared.

"I think I've found it," Caleb said. "I don't know how we missed it yesterday, but we did."

Dylan followed him around to the north side of the lodge, where he stopped in front of a pair of bushy shrubs against the outside wall. Leaning forward, his black braids sliding around his shoulders, he shoved the bushes aside, and a small wooden door appeared.

"It's well hidden," Dylan said. "Only four feet high, same cedar as the lodge. It blends right in. Unless we'd pulled up the shrubs, we never would have noticed it. You know where it leads?"

"Not yet. Figured you'd want to be here when I went in."

There was no lock on the door. Dylan lifted the wrought-iron latch and pushed, and the door swung open, the rusty hinges recently oiled and making not a sound. There were stairs leading down into a remote section of the basement. He and Caleb followed them down.

Dylan shined his flashlight around the rock walls, spotted a set of wooden shelves at the opposite end. "The damned basement's so big I never paid any attention to this area."

"Plus, if I remember right, the boiler's on the other side of those shelves. This old storeroom is tucked away and probably hasn't been used in years." Caleb shined his light around the musty room that was no more than eight by eight feet square. Inside the room, hidden behind the battered wooden shelves, sat two folding chairs, a card table, and a desk lamp.

Dylan reached down and clicked on the lamp, lighting the small, dusty chamber. "Two chairs, probably two people," he said. He shined his light on the table. A thin layer of dust formed a square where a laptop had been sitting.

"This is it. My guess, they had a computer right here. That's what they used to run their equipment."

"Probably took it and cleared out when they figured out we were onto them."

"Which means," Lane said, having followed them into the low-ceilinged room, "they won't be back."

Caleb sighed. "I guess that's something."

But Dylan felt a trickle of unease. He had hoped to catch the bastards sneaking back into the house. Until they caught whoever was behind the hoax, there was no telling what they might do.

He walked over to the wooden shelves and shoved. They moved a couple of feet, creating enough of an opening that anyone in the room could walk into the basement on the other side.

"Through the outside door into the basement," he said, calculating the route, "then up the back stairs to the ground-floor entrance in the guest wing. They could unlock windows, turn pictures upside down. Once they had the holographic apparatus installed in the attic, they could turn it off and on wirelessly with the laptop."

"And view the mini-cam," Lane added.

"And play their recordings," Caleb finished.

"We need to lock this place down good and tight. I don't want them getting back in."

"I can handle that," Caleb said. "Then we'll be able to sleep tonight."

Dylan's mind shot forward to the evening and having Lane back in his bed. At least there was some good news.

"Let's get the hell out of here," he said, urging her back the way they had come, and they all headed out through the little door.

* * *

Rex called from the lab in Juneau that afternoon. "It's blood, all right," he said, "but not of the human variety. It's pig's blood."

Sitting in the office, Dylan felt a wave of relief. "That's good news."

"Yeah, at least you know these guys aren't out there hacking people up."

Dylan smiled. "Not so far. I really appreciate this, buddy. I won't forget that weekend I owe you."

Rex chuckled. "Sarah would love it, and maybe you and I could get in a little fishing."

"Count on it. I'll keep you posted." Dylan ended the call and shoved his cell phone back into the pocket of his jeans just as Caleb and Lane walked into the office.

"Your friend at the lab?" Lane asked.

Dylan nodded. "Rex says the writing on the wall was pig's blood."

Lane plopped down in the chair in front of her laptop. "That's a relief."

"Yeah," Caleb agreed. "And guess where they raise pigs?"

"I'm betting on Yeil," Dylan said.

"Yup. It's kind of a local endeavor. Homegrown pork is popular. Winnie buys it at the market once in a while. Wouldn't be hard to get your hands on enough blood to write that message."

"Any word from Payuk?" Dylan asked.

"Andy called this morning. His granddad's out of town, but he'll be back late tomorrow night. Andy talked to him on the phone. He can see us Monday morning."

"I guess we can hold on till then."

"I got the entrance to the basement locked down. No way those bastards are getting in here again."

"Well, that's one problem solved."

"I was kind of wondering . . ." Caleb said. "It's Saturday. I was planning to make the drive into Waterside, come back in the morning. I'll cancel my date if you think you might need me."

Dylan's mouth edged up. "Which one is it? Jenny or Holly?"

"It's Jenny, smart-ass. If you think it's safe for me to leave, I'm taking her to the show."

"Whoever is behind all this, they've never used violence. We'll be fine."

"You sure?"

"I've got my Browning twelve-gauge in the gun safe along with the .44 Mag I carry for bear protection in the woods. I'll take them upstairs before I go to bed."

"So you're okay with me leaving?"

Dylan cocked an eyebrow and Caleb smiled. "You're right. I wouldn't want to be on the other end of your .44 or your shotgun." He tipped his head toward Lane. "Dylan's lived in Alaska all his life. He's a crack shot with just about anything, even a bow and arrow."

Lane smiled. "I had a feeling I'd be safe."

"Safe from intruders, at least." Caleb winked, and Lane blushed. Dylan cast a warning glance at his friend.

"I'd better get going," Caleb said unrepentantly. "I'll see you in the morning." He headed for the office door.

"I like him," Lane said as Caleb's retreating figure disappeared. "He seems like a really good guy."

"Caleb's the best. He's smart and loyal. I'd trust him with my life." Dylan smiled. "He's a little too good-looking, but the ladies don't seem to mind."

Lane cocked an eyebrow. "So he has two girlfriends?"

"Not exactly. He's been seeing a little blond school-teacher in town. Holly's his ex. I have a hunch she isn't happy he's seeing someone else. Jenny's great, but Holly's bad news."

"If Caleb's as smart as you think, he'll figure that out."

Dylan grunted. "Long as he keeps thinking with his big head instead of his little one, he'll be fine."

Lane laughed. It was Saturday, but both of them were working. They got back to it. There was plenty to do.

It was after 10 PM. The show at the Waterside Theatre, *Pirates of the Caribbean*, was over. It was an older release, but the theater often ran old movies, and even the new films were at least six months old. No one seemed to mind.

Caleb sat across from Jenny Larsen at the Silver Salmon Bar and Grill, the place locals gathered for conversation, a hamburger or pizza, and a pitcher of beer. The decor wasn't much, just a bar with a row of stools, a wood stove against the wall, and a room full of tables and chairs. But a digital jukebox sat in the corner and someone was always feeding it money.

Caleb looked over at Jenny. She was fair and slender, with a pretty face and big blue eyes that tilted upward at the corners. She was smiling at him softly, still a little shy around him.

"So what'd you think of the movie?" he asked as they waited for their pizza to arrive.

"That's the second time I've seen it. I love Johnny Depp."

He chuckled, took a sip of his beer, Alaskan Amber, a local favorite. "He makes a great pirate."

She looked up at him with those big pixie eyes and he felt a little kick.

"You'd make a great pirate," she said. "Let's see. . . . You're tall, dark, and handsome, and you have a ton of sex appeal."

He grinned. "You think so?"

"Long black hair, sexy dark eyes. Put an earring in your ear, you'd steal the heart of every woman in the theater."

His gaze sharpened on her face. "Then maybe I should carry you off someplace and have my way with you."

Jenny blushed. She was a really sweet girl. He'd been taking it slow with Jenny. She deserved more than a one-night stand. But tonight, he found himself wanting to take the next step, explore the attraction he felt for her that grew every time they were together.

"I don't know if I'm ready for that," she said, reading his mind and glancing away.

Caleb reached across the table and took her hand. "I want you, Jenny. I'm not going to lie about it. But I'm not going to rush you. When you're ready, we'll see if this thing between us is real."

She looked up at him earnestly. "It's real for me, Caleb. It didn't take me long to figure out what kind of man you are. A man I can trust and respect. I just need to be sure it's right."

He nodded, squeezed her hand. He liked that she wanted something more than just sex. He liked that she valued herself highly enough to believe she deserved more than that.

They started talking about what was happening in their lives, Jenny telling him about the antics of a cute little first-grade boy in her class, Caleb telling her about the fake ghost and haunting at the lodge.

"We're going to find out who's involved," he said. "Once we do, they'll be lucky if Dylan doesn't press charges." He started to say something more, glanced up as a shadow fell across the table.

"Hello, Caleb." Holly Kaplan stood next to him, her pretty face a stiff, unpleasant mask. She turned to Jenny.

"I'm Holly Kaplan. Caleb's girlfriend. I'm sure he's told you about me."

Jenny's face went pale.

"That isn't true, Jenny," he said, pushing up from the table. "What the hell do you think you're doing, Holly?"

"You said you were going to call me."

"That's bullshit. I didn't promise you anything." In fact, Holly had called him a couple of times after she'd come to the lodge, but after the first call, he had let the rest go to voice mail.

Jenny slid out of the booth. "I'm going home. Don't worry, I'll find my own way."

Caleb stepped in front of her, blocking her path to the door. "You came here with me. If you want to go home, I'll take you." He tossed some money on the table, enough to cover the bill, and cast Holly a look of disgust. Taking Jenny's arm, he started guiding her toward the door. He could feel Holly's dark eyes burning into his back all the way.

Out in the parking lot, Caleb opened the door to his pickup and helped Jenny into the passenger seat. Her face was pale and she was shaking as she pulled her seat belt across her lap and clicked it into place.

Caleb slammed the truck door, rounded the vehicle to the driver's side, and slid behind the wheel.

He turned to Jenny. "What Holly said in there . . . it isn't true. We dated once, but it was a long time ago. It's been over for years. She just moved to Waterside a few weeks back. She wants to take up where we left off, but I'm not interested."

Jenny's eyes zeroed in on his face. "She said you promised to call her."

Caleb sighed, resigned to telling her the rest. "She came

out to the lodge. I didn't invite her, she just showed up. She asked me to call if I got to town. I never said I would."

"It's getting late. I need to go home."

"Dammit, Jenny. I'm not seeing Holly. You're the only woman I'm interested in, the only woman I want to see."

He caught the sheen of tears an instant before Jenny brushed them off her cheeks.

"I'm telling you the truth, honey. I wouldn't lie to you about something like this. Holly's bad news. It's been over between us for years. I'm asking you to believe me."

She gazed up at him, studied his face in search of the truth. A soft breath whispered out. "I believe you."

Caleb leaned across the seat and very gently kissed her. He could feel her lips trembling under his, feel her mouth begin to soften, her response begin to build. For an instant, he deepened the kiss, letting her know that she was the woman he wanted, not Holly Kaplan or anyone else.

He forced himself to end the kiss, though he wanted to kiss her until she begged him not to stop.

"Now, I'll drive you home."

If he'd been the least bit tempted to see Holly again, that temptation was gone. She was trouble. Always had been. He wanted no part of it, or her.

Caleb looked over at Jenny, thought of those soft lips and trusting blue eyes, then reached down and started the engine. There was something good between them. Caleb wasn't about to mess it up.

Chapter Fifteen

It was after 1:00 AM, the night sounds intruding into the bedroom. The wind in the trees, the hoot of an owl on a limb somewhere nearby. Curled into Dylan's hard body, Lane stirred and slowly opened her eyes. A faint trace of moonlight slanted down through the window. Tall pines cast dark shadows across the deck outside the bedroom.

Lane drowsed, her body warm and languid. She thought of Dylan's amazing lovemaking, and a faint smile curved her lips. The man was a very demanding lover and yet he never took without giving back. Her body was beginning to crave him like a drug.

Her smile slipped away. She had to remember this was only a summer affair, a sinfully delicious episode, a respite from the real world that she had allowed herself. Both of them knew it couldn't last; both had accepted that before the affair ever started. Maybe they would see each other once in a while, when they could fit it into their busy schedules, but it was hardly a secret that long-distance affairs never worked.

Lane didn't want to think about that. Not now. Not when he slept so peacefully beside her.

She listened to his even breathing against the side of her neck, turned onto her back so she could study his face, the carved cheekbones, the curve of that hard mouth. When he shifted onto his back, intriguing bands of muscle tightened across his powerful chest.

She loved his body. Long, lean, and hard, every ridge and sinew honed for stamina and strength. She loved the way he knew exactly how to use it to bring them both pleasure.

She loved his protective nature, his commanding presence, his work ethic, the way he took control. She loved—

Lane broke off. She loved too many things about Dylan Brodie. She had to be careful, had to protect herself. She couldn't allow herself to get in too deep.

Instead of touching him, rousing him from slumber and making love with him again as she wanted, she turned back onto her side and stared out the window. The curtains were open, giving her a clear view of the black night sky and jewel-bright stars, nothing like the view through the haze in L.A.

She was staring at a cluster of sparkling white dots, trying to recall the name of the constellation, when she saw him. A man, tall, his shadow moving stealthily, soundlessly across the deck. A cry locked in her throat, and she started to tremble. Moving toward Dylan, she barely touched his arm before he came awake.

"What is it?"

"There's a man . . ." She pointed toward the window. "Outside on the deck."

"Stay here," he commanded as he climbed out of bed. Jerking on the jeans he had slung over a chair, he grabbed his pistol off the nightstand and shoved it into his waistband. "The shotgun's under the bed. There's a safety on top. Don't shoot me."

Lane swallowed and nodded as she watched him stride toward the bedroom door that led out onto the deck. He didn't ask if she knew how to use the weapon. He just assumed she could handle the job if it needed to be done. No man had ever treated her so much as an equal.

Her heart raced as she watched him quietly disappear out the door. Hurrying to the window, she surveyed the wooden deck that wrapped around the bedrooms on this side of the lodge, but the man was already gone.

She thought of the moment he had realized she had seen him, the faint hesitation in his step. He was wearing a sweat-shirt with a hoodie that shadowed his face, and though she couldn't really see him, she could feel the power of his gaze, burning into her.

Lane shivered. *No one can get inside*, she reminded herself. Caleb had personally seen to that. She was safe. They all were. Still, she didn't relax until Dylan returned to the suite.

She met him at the door. "Did you see him?"

He shook his head. "Nobody there." There was something in his manner, something he wasn't saying.

"What is it? Tell me."

He sighed, raked a hand through his sleep-mussed hair. "There was nothing. Not a trace. Not a footprint. Nothing."

Her chin inched up. "I saw him, Dylan. You doubted me about the ghost, but I was right. It might not have been real, but it was there. And I saw someone out there tonight."

His mouth edged up. "All right, you saw someone. I believe you. Let's just hope whoever it was got the message that he's no longer welcome. Maybe now he'll leave us alone."

Lane relaxed.

Dylan draped an arm around her shoulders. "Come on, baby. Let's go to bed. We'll take another look around in the morning. Caleb'll be back by then. I'm a good tracker, but Caleb's better. If the guy left any sign, we'll find it."

Maybe they would. Lane hoped so. Anything that would bring all this to an end.

"In the meantime," Dylan said, "maybe we can find a way to get back to sleep."

Lane's insides warmed at the thought of that incredible male body pressing her into the mattress, moving deep inside her. Amazing how the man always seemed able to read her mind.

But as they passed the window, she thought of the shadowy figure on the deck, remembered the stealthy way he'd moved, then just seemed to disappear, and a chill slipped down her spine.

Who was he? What did he want? She couldn't help wondering if any of them would truly be safe until they found out what was going on.

Dylan took another look around Sunday morning, but it had rained in the hours just before dawn. He'd found no footprints last night, and with the ground so wet, the chances of finding anything now were slim to none.

Instead of continuing to search, he went back to the lodge and phoned Jeff Fenton. He needed to know for sure if Fenton had been a victim of the hoax, and if so, what exactly he and his wife had experienced. He needed as much information as he could get before he talked to Jacob Payuk in Yeil Monday morning.

Cell phone in hand, Dylan walked outside where the reception was better and sucked in a lungful of crisp mountain air. He couldn't stand to be cooped up for long, not even in the lodge. He liked the pine scent of the forest, the rich, musky smell of the soil beneath his feet, liked to look up at the clear blue sky above his head.

He found Fenton on his contacts list and punched in the number. It took the man a few rings to answer. "Fenton."

"Hey, Jeff, it's Dylan Brodie. You got a minute?"

"Yeah, I guess." Dylan didn't miss the slight hesitation that had crept into Fenton's voice.

"We've had a little trouble up here. I'm wondering if you might have had some of the same stuff happening to you while you were here."

A long silence ensued. "I don't know what you mean."

"I think maybe you do. I want to know what went on in the lodge, what you heard, if you saw something out of the ordinary."

"Look, Brodie. A deal's a deal. The lodge is your problem."

"I'm not trying to back out of the deal or hold you responsible for anything. If it'll make you feel any better, it was all a hoax. I found wireless speakers and a mini-cam in the hall. Someone was using an old supply room off the basement, running the equipment with a laptop. I'm trying to find out who it was and why."

A sigh whispered out on the other end of the line. "So the footsteps and the crying were nothing but a prank. I tried to tell my wife it was all a crock of bull, but she was convinced. I should have told you, I guess, but no one told me, so I figured tit for tat."

"So you heard footsteps and crying? A kid, right?"

"That's right. Sounded like a little girl. We'd heard stories . . . something about some Indians that murdered a woman and her child."

"Anything else happen?"

"Stuff misplaced then showing up the next day, windows opening and closing. Dark shapes outside at night."

"Ever see a ghost?"

"No ghost, but it was damned unnerving, that's for sure. After the first year, Millie wouldn't go to the lodge anymore. I'd come for a few weeks of fishing in the summer, but I usually stayed in one of the cabins."

"So you finally had enough and sold the place to me. The question is, do you have any idea what the motive for all this could be? They forced you out and they're doing their damnedest to get me out, too."

"I wish I knew. I'm still trying to wrap my head around the fact it was all just a con." He chuckled into the phone. "I guess in a way it helped you. You got one helluva good price for the lodge."

Dylan smiled. "That's something, I guess. Listen, Jeff, thanks for being straight with me."

"Past time, I guess."

"Maybe so. Take care and if you think of anything that might help, give me a call."

"Will do. You calling the police?"

"I'm not sure yet. I may have to."

"At least I'll have the pleasure of telling Millie it was all a load of crap."

Dylan chuckled and hung up the phone. He glanced up to see Lane walking toward him across the grass, thought how pretty she looked with the sun shining down on her burnished hair, tried not to think how good it was to have her sleeping in his bed.

"I saw you on the phone," she said.

He nodded. "I called Jeff Fenton. He didn't see the ghost,

but the rest of it was about the same. He wasn't much help."

"Maybe the hologram was the latest addition."

He cocked an eyebrow. "You think they've been getting more sophisticated over the years?"

"It's only logical. In the old days, they could scare people off just by making a few weird noises and moving some candles around upstairs. Once the ghost stories got started, the lodge sat empty. It would have taken a little more effort in modern times."

"Good point. You coming with us to Yeil tomorrow?"

"I'd really like to. I wasn't sure you'd take me."

Dylan shrugged. "Alaska Natives live in a matriarchal society. They respect women so that isn't a problem. You're helping me rebuild this place. You deserve to be kept in the loop."

Lane's smile was wide and warm. Damn, she had the prettiest smile. "I appreciate that," she said.

"Hey, Dylan!" Caleb walked toward them, a cardboard box in his hands. "Your package came in. I stopped at the mercantile to see if there was anything to pick up, and Charlie asked me to bring it out to you."

"That's great." Dylan took the box, turned, and handed it to Lane.

"What's this?"

"Just something I thought you might like." They headed back toward the house, stopped at the picnic table next to the built-in barbecue on the sloping front lawn. It was warming up nicely. He made a mental note to have supper outside one evening. Emily always loved it when he barbecued. Or at least she used to.

He looked back at Lane, who was carefully examining the package.

"It's sealed up pretty tight," she said.

Dylan pulled his big folding knife out of his pocket. It was a notch up from his old Swiss Army knife, a SOG military issue that Nick had given him a few years back for Christmas. He also carried a Tool Logic Survival Card with a fire starter and a mini-light, an amazing little piece of gear the size of a credit card that fit neatly into his wallet. The stuff had come in handy out in the woods more than once.

Dylan took the knife and popped it open, used it to slice through the packing tape. Lane opened the box and looked up at him, her green eyes wide with surprise.

"Art supplies?"

"That's right. You told me you used to love to paint. Scenery doesn't get much better than this. I thought you might like to try your hand again."

Lane sorted excitedly through the box that contained an artist palette, brushes of every size and shape, and tubes of acrylic paint in more than a dozen different colors.

"I got home pretty late last night," Caleb said. "The canvases are in my cabin. I'll go get them, take them into the office."

Her eyes were shining. "Thank you, Caleb."

"Don't thank me—thank him. I just picked them up." Turning, he strode off across the yard.

Lane studied the items in the box. "This is a wonderful present."

"I didn't know exactly what you'd need. I asked Penny Hawks over at the Whale's Tail Gallery. She gave me a list of the basics and I ordered them off the Web. I figured we could get whatever else you need."

She hugged the box against her chest. "I can hardly wait to get started. Thank you, Dylan." She went up on her toes and kissed him softly on the mouth. When she tried to back away, he took the box out of her hands and set it down, dragged her into his arms, and kissed her the way he'd been wanting to all morning.

A faint sigh slipped out when the hot kiss ended.

"That's more like it," he said as he reluctantly stepped away.

Lane just grinned, turned, and went back to digging through the box. Clearly, he'd hit a home run. He was surprised how much it pleased him to give her this one small gift.

Chapter Sixteen

It was Monday morning, the weather cool, but the sky had mostly cleared, just a few fluffy white clouds in a crystal-blue dome. Lane was still thinking about Dylan's present as she sat next to him in his big, dark brown extended-cab pickup, rolling along the gravel road toward Yeil.

Art supplies. It was as if he knew she had looked at those gorgeous mountains a hundred times since her arrival and imagined putting them on canvas. She had wanted to be a painter since she was a little girl. In college she had taken every art and design class she could find.

At the University of Illinois, she had met her best friend and now business partner, Haley Warren Brodie, in an art history class. Haley had graduated and gone to work in a prestigious gallery in downtown Chicago, but Lane had been forced to give up her dream in order to nurse her mother.

She had never regretted the decision, though it had ultimately changed her life. Instead of becoming an artist, she'd wound up in the interior design business, a far better-paying endeavor. She was good at it, she'd discovered. Exceptional, in fact.

But deep in the marrow of her bones, she still carried a secret yearning to paint. And somehow Dylan had known.

Last night she'd held a paintbrush in her hand for the first time in years. Since it was Sunday, Winnie had cooked an early supper, giving everyone a little time afterward to enjoy themselves before the new workweek began.

After they'd eaten, Lane had pulled on a sweatshirt and set up a makeshift easel on the porch in front of the lodge.

Her excitement grew as she mixed brilliant blues and greens, tans and browns, and several shades of white. Her fingers felt clumsy as she held the palette. Her brush-strokes were jerky, the thickness of the paint uneven, but eventually the picture in her mind began to show up on the canvas.

What little she had painted—a view out toward the snowy peaks across the bay—wasn't very good, but it was a start. And the joy she felt as she warmed to the task still amazed her. She hadn't really known how badly she had missed this lost part of herself.

The pickup bumped into a hole, jerking her thoughts back to the present. Wedged between Dylan and Caleb, she tugged her seat belt a little tighter, got a smile from Dylan that made her heart beat a little faster.

"You okay?" he asked.

"Are you kidding? This is more fun than a roller coaster."

He chuckled and returned his gaze to the muddy gravel road. In completely different ways, he and Caleb were two of the best-looking men she had ever seen—though as far as she was concerned, Caleb's exotic dark features, high cheekbones, straight nose, and sleek black brows couldn't compare to Dylan's deliciously masculine, amaz-ingly sexy, rugged good looks.

And those eyes. The most stunning shade of blue

she'd ever seen. She felt them slice in her direction, and her stomach floated up beneath her ribs. She told herself the pickup had only hit a low spot in the road.

"You're smiling. You're supposed to be thinking about fake ghosts and finding out who the hell has been trespassing in my lodge."

Her smile widened at the teasing note in his voice. "I was thinking about how good it felt to paint again." Well, partly. Mostly, she was trying to ignore the heat curling low in her belly whenever Dylan glanced her way. "The painting I started isn't very good, but it feels great to have a brush in my hand again."

Dylan chuckled. "You'll get the hang of it."

They rode the last few miles in silence, passing a couple of small houses set back in the trees, Lane taking in the extraordinary scenery that appeared at every turn. Bright pink wildflowers along the road gave depth to awe-inspiring vistas of sea and mountains and moss-draped woods.

The road curved and Dylan slowed. "Moose," he said, pointing to the massive four-legged creature grazing peacefully in a meadow just a few feet off to the side near the trees.

Lane's breath caught. "Oh, he's beautiful."

"It's a she. Cow and calf." He pointed again. "See the little guy in the bushes?"

"I see him! Oh, he's so cute. I can't believe the way they blend right into the landscape."

"They may be cute," Caleb said, "but a moose is the most dangerous animal in the forest. More people are killed by moose than grizzlies."

"You come up on one when you're hiking," Dylan warned, "steer clear."

But she was too busy working on the remodel to be

doing much hiking, and she didn't know enough about surviving in the forest to go by herself.

And she wouldn't be staying long enough to learn.

The thought put a damper on her musings. She was here to do a job and then she'd be heading home. Dylan and Caleb were focused on the meeting ahead, and Lane forced her mind in that direction.

The road they were on went all the way to Waterside, but Yeil was only five miles from Eagle Bay so they were almost there.

Dylan glanced over at Caleb. "You think Payuk will be any help?"

"Maybe. Depends on what he knows. In a place as small as Yeil, people stick together. His first loyalty will be to his family and friends."

Dylan turned off the main road, traveled another half mile, and the village came into view—what little there was of it. The largest building in town, the Yeil Market, was a one-story wooden structure with an overhanging porch and a pair of outdated gas pumps in front.

A sign above a brick building a little farther on read YEIL COMMUNITY CENTER. The roads were unpaved, the town close to the water, with a floating dock where a few small boats bobbed peacefully in the sea. A scattering of wood-framed houses dotted the surrounding landscape.

"The market's pretty much all there is," Dylan said. "It's got the bare necessities, and there's a food counter inside. They make sandwiches, serve frozen pizza they nuke in a microwave. You can get coffee, an egg wrap in the mornings, some packaged bakery goods."

"Not exactly Beverly Hills," Caleb joked.

Lane grinned. "Not exactly."

"Payuk's house is the one down the road on the right."

Caleb pointed toward a wood-frame structure with a porch in front, pretty much what all of the houses looked like.

Dylan pulled up in front and turned off the engine. Cracking open his door, he stepped down, then reached up to help Lane down from the truck. The minute his big hands wrapped around her waist, she felt the sizzle. It zipped through her body all the way to her toes and every womanly place in between.

When she looked at Dylan, she saw the heat, the hunger that said he'd felt it too. She took a deep breath as he swung her to the ground, and Dylan let her go.

Thinking how much the lodge meant to him, she hoped the trip would be successful, that Jacob Payuk could help him put an end to the problems he had been having. Whatever happened, she needed to be sure he was okay when she returned to L.A.

Dylan guided Lane up on the porch and rapped on the door. He could hear footsteps on the other side as Caleb and Lane joined him. An instant later, a heavyset, dark-skinned man with thick gray hair pulled back in a ponytail opened the door.

"Dylan Brodie?"

"That's right."

"I am Jacob Payuk."

Dylan gave a nod of respect. "Elder Payuk. Thank you for seeing me. You know Caleb Wolfe, and this is Lane Bishop. She's a friend."

Payuk's keen black eyes moved over the three of them. "My grandson, Andy, has told me what has been happening at the lodge. He told me you wished to see me. Come inside."

They walked into the house, which had a living room with a hall leading to the bedrooms and a kitchen off to one side.

Payuk led them into the living room, furnished simply with a brown vinyl sofa and chairs, end tables, a couple of nondescript lamps, and an older-model TV. But the walls were filled with colorful Tlingit objects: woven rugs in red and black, carved wooden masks of animal totems colored in turquoise and red, intricately woven baskets. A carved wooden whale painted red and green sat on the coffee table.

He noticed Lane eyeing the pieces with interest. "Your artwork is beautiful," she said with obvious appreciation. "We're planning to use pieces of Native artwork throughout the lodge."

Dylan assumed that would make Payuk happy, but instead he just frowned. "The others will be here soon," he said.

They didn't have to wait long before a knock came at the door. Payuk walked over and pulled it open, inviting two more men into his small house. They were clearly Indian, black-eyed, sharp-featured, their skin a burnished brown. Both were dressed in jeans, T-shirts, and a light jacket of some kind.

"This is my brother, Reggie, and this is George Tuck."

Dylan made a polite inclination of his head. "Elders." He introduced Caleb and Lane to the new additions.

"Please sit down," Jacob said, and Dylan, Lane, and Caleb lined up on the sofa like recalcitrant kids. Dylan figured with the age difference that was about the way the elders saw them.

The brothers took seats in overstuffed chairs, and

George Tuck brought a wooden chair in from the kitchen and settled himself between them.

"You have asked to see us. We are here. Tell us why you have come."

Dylan looked at each of the men, giving them equal respect. "As you all must know, I'm the most recent owner of the Eagle Bay Lodge. I'm here because of the problems I've been having since my daughter and I moved in, problems that have continued to worsen over the past few weeks."

He went on to tell them about the crying in the night and the footsteps, the ghost of a warrior that had appeared in the hallway.

"Perhaps you have angered the spirits," George Tuck said.

"I've angered someone. It definitely isn't a spirit." He went on to tell them about the hoax, about the fake ghost, the camera he had found, and the speakers someone had been using to make the eerie noises.

"The last owner believed the lodge was haunted," he said. "Some of these same things happened to him and his wife. His wife was afraid to stay there. Finally, he was forced to sell the lodge, and I was the man who bought it. Fortunately, I discovered what was really going on. What I want to know is who's responsible. I came to you hoping you could tell me why this has been happening over the years."

The older men spoke between themselves. Heads were shaking, the conversation low and much of it in Tlingit.

Jacob Payuk, who appeared to be the oldest and the leader, finally answered. "We do not know who has done these things."

There was something in the careful way he said the words, something he wasn't saying. "All right—you don't know who's involved. But I have a very strong suspicion you know the reason this has been going on. You may not know who's responsible, but you know why they want the lodge to fail."

A long silence ensued. The men exchanged a few more glances. Jacob Payuk spoke again. "Do you know about the murders?"

"I do. Ms. Bishop and I researched the history of the lodge, starting with the man who built it, Artemus Carmack. We went to the newspaper office in Waterside, read old *Sentinel* accounts of the murders of Carmack's wife and eight-year-old daughter. Two Tlingit villagers were responsible."

"That is not true!" George Tuck was on his feet, his dark skin flushed beneath his high cheekbones.

"The paper said something about bad working conditions," Dylan pressed. "Something happened to set the men off. That night they broke into the lodge and killed Olivia Carmack and the little girl, Mary. Will Seeks and Thomas Shaekley were found guilty of the crime, hanged, and buried in the cemetery at Eagle Bay."

"All lies! All of it!" Tuck was shaking.

"Sit down, George," Jacob said firmly.

Tuck's jaw looked tight as he sat back down in his chair. Dylan remained silent.

"There are few in Yeil who do not know the story of the murders," Jacob said. "Though they happened over seventy years ago. Most of those who live here know the truth."

Dylan straightened. "Exactly what truth is that?"

"That the men who were hanged that day were innocent. They were good men, family men. Not the sort to murder a woman and child."

"Artemus Carmack was a cruel, violent man," George Tuck said harshly. "He had been drinking that night. He and his wife fought bitterly. In a fit of rage, Carmack killed her and his small daughter."

Reggie Payuk's hand tightened into a fist on the arm of his chair. "It was easy for him, a man of great wealth and power, to blame the men who worked for him. The villagers spoke no more than a few words of English. They could not defend themselves."

Lane's face looked pale as she leaned forward on the sofa. "If Artemus Carmack killed his family, he got away with murder. Do you have any proof?"

Reggie Payuk merely shook his head, as did the other two men.

Dylan finally understood. "That's it, then. Someone wants the lodge to fail as payback—revenge for the two innocent men who were hanged."

"The men were from Yeil," Jacob said. "They have clansmen here and in other villages. Tales of injustice do not end with a single generation. They are handed down from family to family, father to son. Perhaps destroying the lodge is someone's way of finding justice for the innocent men who were hanged."

But the hangings had happened decades ago and he hadn't had a damned thing to do with them.

"It can't continue," Dylan warned. "You realize that. If you decline to help me, I'll be forced to bring the police in from Waterside. Is that what you want?"

Reggie Payuk looked unmoved. "We do not know who is responsible for these acts."

"And if you did?"

He shrugged his thick shoulders. "A wrong must be righted. Perhaps this is the way."

All three men stood up from their chairs. "We cannot help you," Jacob Payuk said flatly.

Dylan rose as well, anger and frustration humming through him. He had uncovered the hoax, but there was no way to know what else the perpetrators might do. Lane and Caleb joined him as he made his way to the door.

He paused when he reached it. "You're leaving me no choice. If we have more problems, I'll have to go to the authorities. If you don't want to see someone end up in jail, at least put the word out. I don't want anyone getting hurt, and I think we all know that could happen."

Jacob hesitated, flicked a glance at his brother, then looked back at Dylan and nodded. "We will tell our people what you have said. We do not wish to bring trouble to our homes."

He felt a trickle of relief. "Thank you." The elders wouldn't intervene on their behalf, but at least they would put out a warning.

With any luck, the guilty parties would accept the fact their hoax had been discovered and get on with their lives. Dylan damned well hoped so.

He just wished he could make himself believe it.

Chapter Seventeen

The crew was back on the job, had been for the past few days. Lane hadn't seen anyone on the deck or prowling the grounds at night. By Thursday, she was beginning to relax, and some of the tension seemed to have faded from Dylan's shoulders. Maybe Jacob Payuk's warning had been enough to end the troubles at the lodge.

Trying to get as much done as possible before the long Fourth of July weekend, she and Dylan were both hard at work late that afternoon. The weeks had flown by so quickly Lane couldn't believe she had been in Alaska for almost a month. She couldn't afford more than a two-month hiatus from her business in L.A., but she'd figured it would be enough to finish the project and enjoy the much-needed break she had earned.

And in the early evenings, she had been able to paint. Lane smiled to think how quickly her skills were improving. Like riding a bicycle, she thought. Painting had become part of her DNA.

She looked down at the thick sample books on top of a two-foot stack. She had found the right fabric and ordered the sofa and chairs for the great hall. A brocade pattern in green velvet for the grouping in front of the fireplace, a style that looked old and interesting but was comfortable and long-wearing.

Rich dark leather would cover the sofa and chairs in a second conversation area. Bright throw pillows made of a heavy woven fabric in Art Deco geometric patterns and colors that would complement the Alaska Native artifacts would finish the look.

Seeing the wonderful pieces of artwork at Jacob Payuk's house had given her some fresh ideas about the accent pieces she would be putting on walls and setting in bookshelves, but today she was choosing the material required for the ten-foot draperies that would hang at the windows.

She was busily going through catalogs, trying to decide between a contrasting color or a matching shade of dark green when Caleb walked into the office.

"You seen Dylan?" he asked, a worried look on his face.

"He's upstairs checking with the guy who's installing the baseboard. I think he's trying to get a completion date. What's up?"

Caleb hesitated only a moment. They were becoming close friends. In a place as rural as Eagle Bay, everyone looked out for each other, and it didn't take long to form strong bonds.

"I've got to go to town. I got a call from Jenny. We were supposed to go out this weekend, but she phoned and canceled. When I asked her why, she started crying. Holly Kaplan called her. Fed Jenny a bunch of crap about the two of us being together. Now Jenny won't see me. I've got to talk to her."

Dylan stood in the doorway, eavesdropping without a hint of guilt. "The person you need to talk to is Holly. If it's really over between you two, you need to tell her that in no uncertain terms."

Caleb grunted. "It's over, all right. I might have been a little curious about her, but not anymore. The last thing I want in my life is a woman like Holly Kaplan."

"We've got everything covered here. No new problems with the ghost or anyone else. Take whatever time you need to get this handled."

"Thanks, Dylan."

"No worries. I'll see you when you get back."

"It might be tomorrow. I've got a couple of other things I need to do." And no one liked to drive the narrow gravel road late at night. Better to grab a room at the Sea View Motel, or in Caleb's case, stay with a friend.

Lane almost smiled. If things worked out, maybe he'd be staying with Jenny.

Caleb waved over his shoulder as he walked out the door. Dylan headed back upstairs and Lane returned to her fabric samples. She'd been working about an hour when Emily walked into the office. She held up Finn's leash.

Lane smiled as she rose from her chair. "You want to take Finn for a walk?" She and Emily had a silent way of communicating that neither of them quite understood but somehow seemed to work. The little girl came over and took hold of Lane's hand. "Oh, I see. You want both of us to take him out."

Emily shyly nodded.

A noise caught their attention. For the second time that afternoon, Lane looked up to see Dylan standing in the doorway. "It's a beautiful day," he said, the look in his gorgeous blue eyes softening as they studied his daughter. "I think getting out a little is a great idea."

Emily seemed uncertain, but Lane was sure spending time with her father was exactly what the little girl needed.

"I've got an idea," Lane said brightly. "Why don't I grab some crackers and cheese, maybe a couple of apples, and some Cokes. We'll have a little picnic." They'd had lunch earlier, but an afternoon snack wouldn't hurt anyone.

Dylan smiled. "Good idea. I'll find a blanket for us to sit on."

Emily's uncertainty turned to excitement that had her hopping up and down. Lane grabbed the child's hand and led her to the door. "You go get Finn ready. I'll let Mrs. Henry know where we're going and get the food."

Emily nodded vigorously and raced out into the hall, Finn's leash rattling as she rushed toward the side yard.

"There's a place I've been wanting to show you," Dylan said. "It's not that far away. I think it would be great for a picnic."

"I'd love to see it."

They completed their tasks and met up in the side yard, Finn dancing around Emily, eager to get on the trail, a silly dog grin on his face.

Along with a blanket, the snacks Lane had collected were in the backpack Dylan wore slung over his impressive shoulders. Each of them carried a lightweight jacket.

"Let's get this show on the road," Dylan said, smiling. Finn gave a joyous woof, and they were on their way.

Leaving the lodge behind, they walked single file along a narrow trail winding through the marsh grass and trees at the edge of the bay. They climbed over boulders and a few downed trees fallen across the path, but it was an easy hike. When Lane followed Dylan and Emily up the last rise, she could see for miles out over the ocean.

"So what do you guys think? You like this place?"

Lane's chest squeezed at the beauty. "It's perfect, Dylan."

Emily's head went up and down, moving the dark, blunt-cut hair along her jaw. Dylan slung the backpack on the ground, took out the blanket, and spread it open on a flat, dry spot in the sun beside a big granite boulder.

Emily took Finn off his leash, and they raced toward the trees, Emily searching the ground for exactly the right throwing stick for the big dog to fetch.

"Don't go too far," Dylan called after her. "Stay where I can see you."

Emily gave him a quick wave and went back to her search. Dylan watched her a moment before joining Lane on the blanket. It was warm there, the rock blocking all but a slight ocean breeze. They busied themselves setting out the snacks, then Lane leaned back against the sun-warmed boulder.

"I think this must be what heaven is like," she said, surveying the magnificent vistas around them.

Dylan's gaze followed hers, and for a moment he seemed lost in the beauty here, which was so all-consuming. He looked back at her and began to frown.

"Unfortunately, days like this are few and far between. Rain and cold are part of the price of living up here. Most people can't handle it."

"I guess I'm lucky I live in sunny California."

"In some ways, I guess."

But she knew how much he loved Alaska. She also knew he was thinking about Mariah and Emily, and the disaster his marriage had been.

Lane glanced over to where the child played with Finn, patiently tossing the stick again and again, laughing at some of the big dog's antics as he tirelessly returned it and readied himself to play the game again.

Lane fixed her attention on the man sitting on the blanket across from her. "When you said that, you were talking about Mariah. You think her leaving is the reason Emily doesn't speak."

"I'm sure it is." He ran a hand over his face. "The whole thing is my fault. I never should have married her."

"If you hadn't, you wouldn't have your daughter."

His gaze found hers. "That's the only thing good that came out of it. The truth is, I drove my wife away. I should have moved back to Seattle the way she wanted. If I had, Mariah would still be alive, and Em wouldn't hate me."

Shock rolled through her. "You think Emily hates you?"

His glance swung to where she played with the dog. "She blames me for her mother leaving. Now Mariah's dead and Emily won't talk to me. What other reason could there be?"

"I don't know. But I don't think she hates you. I see the way she looks at you when you aren't watching. There's this longing in her face. She doesn't hate you, Dylan. She loves you."

He shook his head. "I don't know. Maybe. Whatever it is, I wish I could change it. I wish she'd talk to me."

Lane reached for his hand, gave it a reassuring squeeze. "Just make time for her. Like you are today. For now, that's all you can do."

He nodded, came up with the trace of a smile.

Lane began setting out the snacks, including three big chocolate chip cookies that Winnie had sent for dessert. They called Emily over, and she plopped down next to them on the blanket. Finn dropped his stick beside her, looking hopeful.

"That's enough," Lane said. "Go lie down." The big dog

cocked an ear, turned, trotted a few feet away, then dropped down on the warm, grassy earth. "That's a good boy."

The food was delicious, not enough to stuff them too full for supper, but enough for an afternoon treat. As the wind came up and the temperature began to drop, they refilled the backpack and started back toward the lodge.

The path home seemed a little farther or maybe it was the extra food in their stomachs. Even Finn seemed ready to get home.

The lodge appeared ahead, but instead of walking faster, Dylan began to slow his steps. He walked off the trail to examine something Lane couldn't see.

"Go on," he said. "I'll be there in a minute."

Wondering what had snagged his attention, Lane watched his long strides carry him into the woods. "Come on, sweetie." She took hold of Emily's hand. "We're almost home."

As the lodge drew near, Lane could see the bedrooms on this side of the building, the deck sweeping around them, the stairs leading up from the ground below. She paused, her hand tightening around Emily's. She could see into the bedroom she and Dylan had been sharing, into the guest room next to it that she had been using since her arrival.

She let go of Emily's hand. "Go ahead, honey. Get Finn settled in his yard. Your dad and I will be there in a minute."

The little girl dashed away, but Lane stayed on the trail waiting for Dylan. Her palms had begun to sweat and her heart was pumping too fast when he appeared a few minutes later, striding up the path with a fierce scowl on his face.

Lane hurried toward him. "He was here—wasn't he? The man on the deck. He's been watching us from some-where nearby."

He held up a few strands of greenish-brown thread. "I noticed this as we passed. It was caught on a bush." It was nothing she would have noticed, but she didn't live in Alaska, didn't know how to track an animal, didn't hunt food for the table.

"There's a spot near the bottom of a pine tree. The grass is a little mashed down. Looks like an animal's been bedding down there, but it wasn't an animal."

"Are you . . . are you sure?"

He glanced back the way he had come. "He was lying on his stomach, using binoculars. You can tell by the elbow marks."

"Oh, my God."

He caught her shoulders. "Look, it just means whoever has been bothering us still may want to cause trouble. It doesn't mean we're in any sort of danger."

"I don't like it. We don't know who he is or what he's thinking—or even if there's more than one person."

"You're right, and I don't like it, either. I'll call the police, tell them what's going on, but I'd rather do it in person. Saturday's the Fourth of July. That's only a day away. I was thinking maybe I'd fly us all over to Waterside. We could watch the parade, maybe even stay for the fireworks. I'll talk to the police while we're there."

She nodded, trying to bring her worry under control. "All right, that sounds good. I'm sure Winnie would like to see the show, and I think Emily would love it."

"She used to love the fireworks show they had in Juneau,"

Dylan said with a note of regret. "We haven't watched them together since her mother took off."

Lane managed to smile. "Then this is definitely a good idea. And maybe the police will have some idea who's behind all the trouble."

Dylan's jaw hardened. "If they don't figure it out, I'll find out myself. I'm through waiting for something to happen. One way or another, this is all going to be over very soon."

Lane took one look at the grim set of his features and knew he meant every word.

It was cloudy, looked as if a storm was moving in, by the time Caleb pulled his truck up in front of Jenny Larsen's small house a few blocks from the elementary school where she worked. The house, wood-frame with a covered porch, wasn't much, probably built in the forties.

But it sat on a knoll that looked out over the ocean and the views were spectacular. A white picket fence enclosed the front yard, where Jenny had planted yellow marigolds and purple iris and some pretty pink flowers he didn't know by name.

Caleb thought the place fit her perfectly.

He steeled himself for the less-than-friendly greeting he expected, opened the little white gate, and strode up onto the porch.

He rapped lightly and the ruffled curtains moved at the windows. She'd seen him, but he wasn't sure she would let him in. He breathed a sigh of relief when the door swung open.

"Hello, Caleb."

"Hi, Jenny. Can I . . . uhh . . . come in? We need to talk."

She moistened her lips, the same pink as her flowers. "I'm sorry, Caleb. I don't need trouble and apparently that's what you are." She tried to close the door in his face, but he blocked it with his work boot.

"Just give me a minute to explain." He saw fear leap into her face and silently cursed. "Dammit, Jenny. I'd never hurt you. Surely you know that."

Her pale blue cat eyes filled.

"Don't cry, honey. I'll move my boot. I won't try to come in. I'll let you close the door in my face if you'll just give me a couple of minutes to explain."

Jenny swallowed, dashed away tears. Finally, she nodded.

"Okay. You said when you phoned me that Holly called you. She told you I loved her. She said for you to stay away from me. Is that about it?"

"She . . . she was angry. She said I was the reason the two of you were having problems. She warned me to stay away."

Caleb clamped down on his temper. He didn't need to upset Jenny any more than she was already. "I don't love her, Jenny. I thought I did when I was younger, but that was years ago. There's nothing between us. Nothing at all. I'm going to talk to her, make her understand it's over."

"I . . . I'm a teacher, Caleb. I love my job. I can't be involved in something like this."

"You're right. I know that and I understand. Let me take care of it. I won't bother you again until I've got everything straightened out. But don't give up on me. Not yet. Okay?"

She bit her lip. Finally nodded. "Okay."

"I was . . . you know . . . looking forward to taking you

to the fireworks show on the Fourth, but I guess that's off for now."

Jenny didn't answer.

"I'll call you, I promise. I'll let you know when I've got this handled."

"Bye, Caleb."

"I'll see you soon, honey."

Jenny closed the door, and for long moments he just stood there. With a calming breath, Caleb descended the porch stairs, pulling his cell phone out of his pocket as he headed for the gate. He found Holly's number on the calls received list and pressed the SEND button. Her phone rang, but Holly didn't pick up.

Maybe she was at work, either at the hospital or the café. She probably worked odd hours so he drove to the home address she had given him that day at the lodge, an apartment on Third Street. Maybe she was asleep or something.

Caleb knocked on the door, knocked again, but nobody was home. From there he drove to the hospital, but the receptionist told him Holly wasn't on call until tomorrow.

He headed for the Grizzly Café. The bell rang above the door as he pushed it open. It was after 8:00 PM, the supper crowd mostly served. Maggie looked up from where she stood behind the counter and smiled as he walked inside.

"Hey, handsome."

"Hey, Maggie." She was a good-looking woman, big, blond, and buxom. She had the hots for Dylan, but he never seemed to notice. "I'm looking for Holly. I thought maybe she was working."

She cast him a knowing glance, as if she knew what he was thinking. He didn't bother to tell her that she was dead wrong.

"She worked the early shift today. Did you try her apartment?"

"She wasn't there. I went by the hospital. No luck there, either. Any idea where I can find her?"

Maggie cut a wedge of cherry pie and slid it onto a plate. "Can't say for sure, but sometimes she goes over to the Pelican Pub. Or she might be at Mad Jack's."

The Pelican Pub was a beer bar, not so much a family place as the Silver Salmon, but a good place to let off steam. Mad Jack's Saloon was a little rougher, a bar with a couple of pool tables and a band on Thursday, Friday, and Saturday nights. Lots of sportsmen went there, hunters and fishermen, guys off the ferry.

"I'll check it out. Thanks, Maggie." Caleb headed for the door as Maggie whisked the pie off to a waiting customer. Caleb hoped to hell Holly was at the Pelican or Mad Jack's. He needed to find her, make it crystal clear—once and for all—that their relationship was over.

He thought of the tears in Jenny's pretty blue eyes and warned himself not to lose his temper.

Chapter Eighteen

Dylan left Lane in the middle of his big king-size bed. They had made love earlier—on the rug in front of the fireplace in the sitting room. He didn't want to close the bedroom curtains. He didn't want to do anything that would give away the fact he had discovered the watcher's location on the hill.

Dressed in jeans, a sweatshirt, and a green and dark-brown camouflage jacket, he glanced at the clock on the bedside table: 11:00 PM. It had been late the night Lane had spotted the man on the deck, but there was a chance he was already out there. If not, Dylan wanted to be in position, be ready when he arrived.

He picked up his .44 Colt Anaconda off the nightstand, shoved it into the holster on his belt, flipped his jacket over it.

"Be careful," Lane whispered from her side of the bed. He wanted her there as a lure for the watcher—and in her skimpy little pink teddy, she was one helluva lure.

His jaw tightened. How often had the son of a bitch watched them? How much could he see?

He smiled grimly. The shotgun was still under the bed.

After the last incident, he'd shown her how to take off the safety, point, and shoot. If she had to, he didn't doubt she'd pull the trigger.

He almost wished the bastard would try to break in.

Dylan headed downstairs, slipped quietly out a door on the north side of the lodge, and began circling slowly around through the woods toward the spot in the grass on the south side he had found that afternoon.

With a thick layer of clouds rolling in, the moon wasn't giving off much light. As he moved silently through the trees, his camouflage jacket helped him blend into the landscape. Dylan found the game trail he had scouted that afternoon and followed it toward the depression in the grass the watcher had left on a small rise off the path.

His adrenaline was pumping. There was a chance the guy was already there. He slid the gun from its holster. He didn't know his opponent, only knew how determined he was. The last thing he wanted was to underestimate his enemy.

The depression in the grass was up ahead. Earlier, he had left a tiny mark on a nearby tree so he wouldn't miss the spot as he moved through the darkness.

His pulse kicked up as he approached, setting one boot quietly in front of the other. He could see the spot now, see the grass that was already beginning to spring back into its normal position.

He clenched his jaw.

No one there.

Disappointment filtered through him. He wanted this to end. Dylan moved deeper into the shadows and settled in to wait.

* * *

Caleb shoved through the swinging doors of Mad Jack's Saloon. He had phoned Holly a couple of times, but never reached her. He'd been to the Pelican Pub, hung around a while, stayed long enough to eat a hamburger and fries, but she'd never shown up.

Thursday through the weekend, Mad Jack's didn't really get going till after ten, when the band started playing. If Holly was headed there, it wouldn't be till late. The band was just ending an old Brad Paisley country song when he walked in. They finished the tune and the musicians set their guitars aside, taking a break as Caleb crossed the wooden floor to the bar.

In a heartbeat he spotted Holly, gleaming black hair, curves that made a man's mouth water. A skirt so short it barely covered her very nice ass. She was talking to the guy next to her, Jimmy Brock. Jimmy managed a local gas station. Nice guy, but he was married.

As Caleb walked up to them, Holly spotted him and grinned. She whirled on the bar stool and threw her arms around his neck.

"Caleb! Hey, baby." She tried to kiss him, but he turned his head away, removed her arms from around his neck. Jimmy took the opportunity to slide off the stool and slip away.

"I need to talk to you," Caleb said. "I called, but you didn't pick up."

She dug her phone out of her purse, shrugged. "Dead battery."

Typical Holly. She never bothered to think very far ahead.

"I'm glad you're here," she said. "The band's great. You used to be a really fun dancer."

"Yeah, well, that was a long time ago." He took her arm, urged her down off the stool, over to a table in the corner.

Holly grinned. "Cool. It's nice and dark over here. Remember how we used to make out? Anytime, anyplace. Boy, you could really kiss." She leaned toward him for a sample. Caleb backed away, sat her down in one of the battered wooden captain's chairs, and took the chair next to her.

"You're drunk, Holly."

"So what? You used to like it when I got drunk. You used to like the things I did to you." She started to rise. "Come on, let's go outside and I'll—"

"No, goddamn it!" He shoved her back into her chair, looked up to see a couple of people staring at them, lowered his voice. "Look, Holly, I came here to tell you I'm just not interested in picking up where we left off. It didn't work then. It wouldn't work now. I want you to leave me alone. I want you to leave Jenny alone. You understand?"

She leaned toward him, slung her arms around his neck, and tried to kiss him.

"Stop it! I'm telling you to leave us alone. If you don't, you're going to be sorry. I don't want to be with you—I want to be with Jenny. You got that?"

She stiffened, shot up out of her chair, propped her hands on her hips. "You bastard! You're just mad because I told your mousy, skinny little blond girlfriend about us."

"There is no us! I'm warning you, Holly. I'm not putting up with this any longer."

He tried to clamp down on the fury pumping through him. Turning away from her, he stormed toward the door. It occurred to him the place had gone quiet, that half the bar was watching.

Dammit, the last thing Jenny needed was gossip. With any luck, the jokers in the bar would get good and drunk and forget all about the scene he'd just made.

Caleb jerked open the door and stepped outside. At least he'd made sure Holly finally got the message.

He just hoped Jenny would want to see him again.

Dirty bastard. Who the hell did he think he was? Holly still couldn't believe Caleb was treating her this way. He'd always been so easy to manage. Back when they'd been together, he would have crawled over broken glass for her.

She walked back to the bar and climbed up on the stool she had vacated, took a long drink from the bottle of beer she'd left behind.

Holly grimaced, set the bottle back down. It was warm now, and she was out of the mood to party anyway. When the band started playing and one of the locals asked her to dance, she just shook her head. Slinging the strap of her purse over her shoulder, she slid off the stool and headed for the door.

At least that bozo Jimmy Brock had paid for her beer. She pushed through the swinging doors and stepped out on the boardwalk in front of the bar. A guy sat on one of the benches along the wall smoking a cigarette, the tip glowing in the darkness.

She recognized him from a night a few days back, remembered how good-looking he was, remembered he was really built.

"Hey, darlin'," he said from his place in the shadows. "You're leavin' early."

She thought he might have a slight Southern drawl. Southern men were so sexy. "It's boring in there."

"You think so? You wanna have some fun?"

She hitched her purse up on her shoulder. "I might."

He rose from the bench, even taller than she remembered, ground his cigarette out on the bottom of his boot, stuck the stub into his shirt pocket. His eyes were gleaming as he walked toward her, lean and lanky, sexy as hell.

He didn't ask permission, just hauled her into his arms and kissed her, long and deep. She was breathless when he stopped. His eyes held hers, dark brown and hungry. He didn't ask, just took her arm and started walking, hauling her off into the woods.

She liked a man who knew what he wanted. Her heart was beating really fast. One kiss and she was hot and wet between her legs. He knew where he was going, she could tell, letting him tug her along the path in his wake. By the time he reached the edge of the meadow beneath a pine tree, spread his jacket on the grass, and pulled her down beside him, the music sounded far away.

He didn't bother with the niceties, just started kissing her, and he was good at it. She gasped as his big hands slid beneath her short skirt, grabbed the silky thong panties that were all she wore under her clothes and ripped them away. Then his fingers were inside her and she was so hot.

"I don't . . . don't even know your name," she panted.

For a minute she didn't think he was going to answer. "My friends call me Dusty," he said, the words muffled by the sound of his zipper sliding down. She caught the flash of silver as he tore open a condom and sheathed himself, spread her legs with his knee, and plunged inside her.

He was big and he was hard. In an instant, Holly started coming. Wow, this guy was good. She bucked against him as he moved, heard his hiss of pleasure, smirked as she thought of Caleb. Caleb didn't know what he was missing. Well, he did, but he'd forgotten.

"You like this, don't you? I bet you like it a little kinky."

Holly moaned as he plunged into her again and again. God, it felt good, and yet there was something. . . .

His hands moved to her neck, circled her throat. "This'll make you even hotter, I promise." He pretended to choke her, just a little, as he withdrew and drove into her again. It was a game some men liked to play. Women, too. She went along with it for a while, pretended he was taking her against her will, let the excitement build.

She started coming a second time, and she could tell he was close. The hands around her throat went tighter. Tighter. Some of her enthusiasm faded even as her orgasm hit and pleasure rushed through her. Dammit, she could barely breathe.

"Stop . . . it . . . Dusty." She tried to force out the words, but they were locked inside by his relentless grip on her neck. She tried to suck in a breath, but her chest wouldn't move. She squirmed frantically beneath him, her air supply almost gone, her vision beginning to blur.

"Stop!" She wasn't sure if she actually said the word or if she just screamed it inside her head. Her limbs felt weak, her strength nearly gone. She used the last of her energy trying to pry his hands off her neck, but he was oblivious to her struggles. He just kept pounding away, driving toward the climax he was determined to reach.

Her mind was spinning. Spots appeared in front of her eyes. She felt his hard body stiffen the instant before her vision faded to black. He was finished, she thought vaguely, her limbs suddenly weightless. Surely, she'd be okay. It was only a game, after all.

Holly had always been good at games.

* * *

Friday morning, the crew was hammering away up in the guest wing. Winnie was working upstairs with the girl who came in once a week to help her clean, but downstairs everyone was walking on tiptoes, including Lane.

It was raining outside, a real gully washer that had started in the early hours of the morning. After the night he had spent outdoors, Dylan had eaten breakfast, then gone into the great hall to check on a measurement, sat down on the old sofa, and fallen dead asleep. The poor man had spent half the night in the forest, hoping to catch the person who had been watching them.

Terrified something might happen to him, Lane had barely slept herself. She had finally fallen asleep for a couple of hours just before dawn, after Dylan had returned soaking wet. She'd kissed him, then gone back to her own room before the household awakened and found them together.

He was sound asleep now. Even the hammering, the buzzing of a saw chewing through a stack of two-by-fours hadn't disturbed him.

Lane checked her watch. He'd been in there at least three hours. She was sitting at her desk in the office going through her e-mails when Caleb walked through the door.

"You seen Dylan?"

"He fell asleep on the sofa," she said as she answered an e-mail from one of the designers who worked at Modern Design. "Yesterday, he found a spot where a guy had been watching the lodge. He was out all night trying to catch him."

"Damn. I should have been here."

"Wouldn't have mattered," Dylan said as he walked in yawning, carrying a mug of coffee and rubbing his eyes. "The guy didn't show."

"You think he spotted you?"

"I doubt it. Might have been watching from a different location, but I did a surveillance round every hour. Didn't pick up any sign."

"We can try again tonight. I'll be here to help. We'll take shifts."

Dylan nodded, yawned again. "How'd it go with Jenny?"

Lane could tell by the look on Caleb's face it hadn't gone well.

"I talked to her. Jenny's afraid of a scandal. She's worried it could affect her job."

"She's a first-grade teacher, right?" Lane said. "There's probably a chance it could."

"I promised I wouldn't call her again until I had the problem solved with Holly."

"And?" Dylan asked, taking a sip of coffee.

"And it took me all day and half the night to find her. We had a scene at Mad Jack's. It wasn't pretty."

"I presume Mad Jack's is a bar," Lane said.

Caleb nodded. "She was there, already half drunk. It got loud. I warned her in no uncertain terms to stay away from me and Jenny."

"Do you think she will?" Lane asked.

"Yeah, I think so. I think she was testing the waters. She's the kind of person who knows how to get what she wants, and wants whatever it is she can't have. I made it clear it wasn't going to happen this time."

"That's good," Dylan said. "Maybe that'll be the end of it."

"I'm hoping."

Footsteps hurried toward them down the hall. Winnie came bustling in, a worried look on her face.

"What is it?" Dylan asked.

"The state police are here. They want to talk to you and Caleb."

Dylan drained the last of the coffee in his mug. "Jesus, what now?"

Lane felt a tug at her heart as she noticed the weary lines in his face. Dylan walked out of the office and Caleb fell in behind him. Lane and Winnie followed the men down the hall.

Lane hoped it was good news for once instead of bad. Maybe it was something to do with the incidents that had been happening at the lodge. Maybe the police had stumbled across information about the man or men who'd been watching the house.

Trying to stay optimistic, Lane followed the men out of the lodge. Winnie, who usually stayed out of these kinds of things, marched out right beside her. One glance at the worried look on her face, and Lane's optimism went right out the window.

Chapter Nineteen

As Dylan walked through the door to the side yard, an Alaska State Trooper's white-and-gold SUV sat in the parking area at the end of the gravel road.

"You don't think Holly did something stupid?" Caleb said, spotting the two men in blue uniforms and flat-brimmed hats. "Oh, shit, Jenny!" He started forward, but Dylan caught his arm.

"Take it easy. Before you panic, we need to find out what's going on."

Caleb took a deep breath, nodded. "Sorry."

But as the troopers approached, not a hint of friendliness in their expressions, Dylan felt a shot of worry himself.

He stopped in front of the men. "I'm Dylan Brodie. My housekeeper says you're looking for me. What can I do for you?"

"I'm Trooper Drake. This is Trooper Everett." Drake was tall, athletically built, and sandy-haired, his partner dark-haired, young, and stout as a bull.

Trooper Drake's attention shifted to the man with the long black braids. "Are you Caleb Wolfe?"

"That's right."

"I'm afraid you're going to have to come with us."

Caleb blanched.

"Wait a minute," Dylan said. "What's this about?"

"Last night a woman named Holly Kaplan was murdered." Drake's gaze sliced back to Caleb. "You were seen talking to her at Mad Jack's Saloon last night. According to witnesses, the two of you got into a heated argument. Now the Kaplan girl is dead. We'll need you to come with us, answer some questions."

Caleb's dark face looked pale. "It's true we argued. But then I left. Holly was still in the bar. You should be able to verify that."

"Where did you go after you left the bar?"

"A friend of mine has a cabin at the edge of town. He lets me stay there when I'm in Waterside."

"So you didn't come back to the lodge."

"I don't like to make that drive at night. Not unless I have to."

"What time did you get to your friend's cabin?"

"I wasn't paying attention to the time. I'd say around eleven, maybe eleven fifteen."

"What's the name of the man who owns the place?"

"Wally Sturgeon."

"So your friend, Wally, can verify you were there from eleven o'clock till morning?"

"Wally's visiting some friends in Anchorage. I stayed at the cabin by myself."

"The medical examiner places Holly Kaplan's death sometime between eleven and two PM last night," the younger trooper said. "Very shortly after the two of you had a bitter fight. This morning, a hiker found her body floating in Bristol Cove. Looks like she was dumped in the river and floated downstream to the ocean."

Caleb's breathing went shallow. "For chrissake, I didn't kill her. She was perfectly fine when I left her. Ask anyone who was there."

"The problem is, Holly walked out of the bar by herself, but her car was still in the parking lot this morning. There were half a dozen phone calls from you on her cell. You threatened her in the bar. Now Holly is dead and you don't have an alibi for your whereabouts at the time of the murder."

"I told you I went to Wally's cabin."

Dylan interrupted the trooper's reply. "How was Holly killed?"

"She was strangled."

Caleb's eyes slid closed.

"Raped?" Dylan asked.

"We're waiting for the coroner's report." He returned his attention to Caleb. "Do you have any problem with us taking a look at your truck?"

"No. Why?"

"We believe she was killed somewhere else and transported to the river."

"You won't find anything in my truck. Go ahead and look."

But it had been raining like hell since well before dawn. If there had been anything in the bed of the truck, odds were it would have been washed away on Caleb's trip from Waterside to Eagle Bay. Or at least the police would see it that way.

The troopers made a cursory examination of Caleb's

white Chevy pickup, careful not to touch anything in the cab or the bed of the vehicle, then returned.

"We appreciate your cooperation, but we need to question you further. I'm afraid you'll have to come with us."

Caleb's eyes swung frantically to Dylan. "I didn't kill Holly. I was mad at her, but I wouldn't kill her."

Dylan set a hand on his friend's thick shoulder, felt the tension running through him. "I know that. I've got a friend in Anchorage. Peter Keller's a top-notch criminal attorney. I'll call him, make arrangements for him to represent you."

"Fuck, Dylan, I didn't do it."

"I know you didn't do it, all right? We'll figure this out. Till we do, don't say anything more until you talk to Keller."

Caleb nodded. "So I'm under arrest?" he said to Drake.

"We're bringing you in on suspicion of murder. We can hold you up to forty-eight hours before we have to arraign you. You cooperate, it might not be necessary."

But Dylan could tell by the hard set of the men's faces they were ninety percent convinced Caleb had committed the crime.

The troopers turned him around and locked a pair of handcuffs on his wrists. Caleb made no protest as the troopers led him over to their big SUV and settled him in the backseat. A woman had been killed. Caleb was a powerful man. The troopers were only doing their job.

Dylan stood rigidly as the engine started and the SUV pulled off down the gravel road leading back to Waterside. He felt Lane come up behind him, her fingers reaching out to clasp his hand.

"He didn't do it," she said. "They'll figure that out."

Dylan's jaw hardened. "Let's make sure they do." He

headed into the house to make the phone call to Keller. But he didn't let go of Lane's hand.

Lane waited in the kitchen with Winnie while Dylan went into his office to call his attorney friend in Anchorage.

"I'm so worried, I can't think straight," Winnie said, wiping her hands on her apron for the third time in the last five minutes. "The first person they suspect is the husband or the boyfriend."

"Caleb and Holly broke up years ago. It shouldn't be too hard to prove Caleb was no longer involved with her."

"He was mad at her for upsetting Jenny. He fought with her in a public place. There were any number of witnesses."

"She was alive when he left her in the bar."

"He doesn't have an alibi for the time she was murdered. They'll say he could have waited for her outside. They could have started fighting again and he could have killed her, loaded her into the back of his pickup, driven her to the river and dumped her body. We need to find a way to prove he didn't do it."

Lane's stomach knotted. Winnie was right. Caleb was the obvious suspect. The only suspect so far.

"I read a lot of mysteries," Winnie continued. "Caleb had motive—he was mad at Holly for causing trouble with Jenny. He had means—the man is strong as a horse, powerful enough to strangle a woman. He had opportunity—he could have been waiting for her outside the bar."

Lane turned as Dylan walked into the kitchen. "We have to find out who killed Holly," she said. "The evidence points to Caleb. It won't take much more to convince them he's guilty."

A muscle tightened in Dylan's cheek. "Keller's agreed to represent him. He'll fly directly from Anchorage to Waterside and do what needs to be done to get him released."

"We have to do something, too," Lane said. "We need to go to Waterside, find out who else could have killed Holly."

"I'll fly over in the morning. Start digging, see what I can come up with."

"I'll come with you."

He didn't agree, but he didn't say no, either. And she was going—one way or another.

"Looks like the fireworks show is out," he said. "We need to be home before dark."

She wasn't in the mood to celebrate anyway. Not with Caleb in jail. Another thought occurred. "You want to get back before dark because of the man who's been watching the lodge."

"That's right. This isn't a game anymore. A woman's been murdered. Since Caleb didn't do it, the guy's still out there. I'm on my way to Yeil. I need to talk to Jacob Payuk, tell him what's happened, try again to get his cooperation."

Lane's worry increased. "You don't really think the murderer could be the man in the woods?"

"I doubt it. At the moment, I don't see any connection. On the other hand, we can't be sure what the hell is going on, and until we are, I'm not taking any chances."

"Are you going to tell the police?"

"When I get to Waterside on Saturday, I'll talk to Frank Wills. He's the chief of police. I'll bring him up to speed on what's been going on—the hoax, the break-ins, the man or men who've been watching us."

"You want me to come with you to Yeil?"

His gaze swung to hers. "That might be a good idea."

"Let me grab my jacket." Turning, she started for the door.

"And put on your hiking boots. It's muddy as hell out there."

It was quiet in the forest. He could hear a woodpecker battering the trunk of a tree, hear the sound of the water in the creek splashing over the rocks, the soft drip of the rain that had fallen in the night.

He liked the quiet, liked that it gave him a moment's respite from the voice inside his head.

Hell, he hadn't meant to do it. He'd just gotten carried away. He wasn't a fucking murderer.

You killed her, said the voice. *You're worse than an animal.*

"That's not true. It was an accident. We were just play-ing a game." But the words rang hollow as he sat in a spot above the cemetery, a secluded place on the hill behind the lodge.

The voice spoke to him again. *They'll hunt you down. They'll put you in prison. Is that what you want?*

"I told you it was an accident. It was just sex. I didn't mean to kill her."

You've got to run. Get away before they find you.

He clenched his jaw. "They won't find me. Not if I don't want to be found. I'm not leaving until I finish what I came for."

He waited for a reply, but this time the voice didn't answer. Sometimes it happened that way. He'd speak, but there would only be silence. Other times, the voice would be crystal clear.

He'd been hearing it for years, off and on since he was

twenty-five, a soldier in the Army. Delta Force. He was good. The best.

Except when he heard the voice. Then he couldn't concentrate, couldn't focus. The doctors had put him on Prozac, tried a couple of other meds. He could lead a normal life, they'd said. But it didn't matter. The Army didn't want him anymore.

He was thirty now, on his own, but trouble always seemed to follow wherever he went. He hadn't meant to kill the girl, but he wasn't about to change his plans.

He settled his back against a boulder, reached into his pocket, and pulled out the little wooden totem he had found on an antique table in the great hall, rubbed his fingers back and forth across it. He could just make out the roof of the lodge through the trees.

Did they really think boarding up the place was going to keep him out if he wanted to get in?

He chuckled, stuffed the totem back in his pocket, and started moving silently off into the forest. It was only a few miles' walk to the place he had found deep in the woods, an old hunting cabin. Its owners were long gone, making it the perfect place to take shelter from the wind and rain.

Tomorrow he'd drive the Jeep he'd rented into town and pick up supplies, enough to last at least a couple of weeks. Plenty of time to complete his plan.

After that, after things were settled, he would leave.

"I'm glad you came," Dylan said to Lane, keeping the wheel steady as the big, extended-cab pickup slopped through the mud holes on the road to Yeil. "We need to talk."

Lane felt a trickle of unease. "What about?"

"When we made the deal for you to come up here, neither of us expected any of this trouble. The hoax was bad enough. Now it looks like they haven't given up, that at least one of them is out there watching the house. Worse yet, there's been a murder and Caleb's the number-one suspect. I think it would be best if you went back to L.A."

Something pinched hard in her chest. Yes, Dylan was having problems, but she'd thought they were friends. Friends didn't leave when the going got tough.

Another thought struck, and the tightness returned to her chest. "Are you . . . are you tired of me? Is this just an excuse to get rid of me?"

Dylan slammed on the brakes so hard the truck fishtailed in the mud and Lane jerked against her seat belt. He jammed the gearshift into park.

"Getting rid of you is the last thing I want! I just want you safe, dammit! If you stay, I can't guarantee you will be. You'll be out of danger if you're back in L.A."

Her heart was beating hard, drumming against the wall of her chest. The fierce look on his face said it was the truth, and the frantic beating began to slow. He was worried about her. He was trying to protect her. The tight feeling eased.

"Caleb didn't kill Holly," she said. "And you said yourself you don't have any reason to believe whoever's been watching us is the murderer."

"It doesn't seem likely, no. But there's no way to know for sure. Like I said, I want you safe. If that means leaving, then that's what I want you to do."

But she wanted to be there for Dylan when he needed her. And there was the job she had undertaken. She wanted to see all of it put together, wanted to see the finished design. And she wasn't ready to give Dylan up.

"I'm not afraid, Dylan. Whoever is behind the hoax, the fact is no one has ever been hurt, not during all those years. There's no reason to think that's going to change. The interior isn't finished. I'm waiting for the furniture to arrive. I just got the draperies ordered. I'm waiting for the wrought-iron chandeliers to get finished, shipped up here, and hung. I want to see what the Eagle Bay Lodge looks like when it's ready for its first guests."

"You'd be safer in L.A."

She hadn't been safe since the day she had met him. He was like a dangerous drug she couldn't get enough of.

"You hired me to do a job. I want to finish the project."

Those intense blue eyes remained on her face. "Is that the only reason you want to stay?"

Her heart squeezed. Lane reached up and touched his cheek, felt the roughness of his afternoon beard. "You know it isn't. We both work hard. We deserve this time together. I'd like to stay, but only if you want me here."

Dylan popped his seat belt, leaned across the seat, slid a hand behind her neck, and dragged her mouth up to his for a deep, very thorough kiss. Lane felt the heat all the way to the bottom of her hiking boots.

"I should make you go back," he said, kissing the side of her neck. "It'd be the safest move. But dammit, I don't want you to leave."

Lane popped her seat belt, leaned in for another scorching kiss. "I'm staying," she whispered when the hot kiss ended. She took a steadying breath. "With both of us working together, we can solve whatever problems come up."

Dylan shoved wavy red hair back from her face, bent, and kissed her one last time. "Maybe we can."

"I know we can."

He smiled but didn't look away. "We need to go."

She nodded. Easing back into her seat, she clicked her seat belt back in place. "Then let's get rolling."

Dylan cranked the ignition.

Dylan walked Lane up on the porch and knocked on Jacob Payuk's door. A few seconds later, it swung open and the older man with the long gray ponytail stood in the opening.

"I'm sorry I didn't call," Dylan said, "but there really wasn't time." And he hadn't been sure Payuk would agree to see him. "Things have happened since we last spoke. Someone has been hiding in the woods behind the lodge, spying on the people inside, and last night in Waterside, a woman was murdered."

The old man's wrinkled features tightened. "I had not heard this news."

"The state troopers are involved. I don't know if the murder and the incidents at the lodge are related, but I'm not willing to take the risk. I'm responsible for everyone at Eagle Bay. My daughter is there. My foreman is a suspect and sitting in jail for something he didn't do. I need to know the names of the people behind the hoax. I want to know who's been watching the lodge."

Payuk stood rigidly near the door. "I have told you from the start, I do not know who is behind the hoax. That has not changed."

"Maybe not. But I believe a man of your great influence could persuade the guilty party to come forward. Now that the troopers are involved, I'll have to tell them what's been happening. It would be better for all of us if whoever is behind the hoax came forward."

A long pause ensued. Payuk finally nodded. "What you

say makes sense. I have responsibilities, also. To the people in Yeil, my family and clansmen. I will do everything in my power to convince the parties involved to come forward."

Dylan nodded. "That's all I can ask. Tell them if they agree to a meeting and are willing to stop what they've been doing, I won't press charges."

"Do you believe the police will come to Yeil?"

"I think, until the murder is solved, they'll look at every possibility."

They spoke a few more moments; then Payuk walked them out onto the porch.

"Thank you, elder," Dylan said.

Payuk just nodded and closed the door.

As the truck slid through the ruts in the muddy road on the way back to the lodge, Dylan's iPhone started to ring.

He pulled over to the side, dug it out of his jeans. Recognizing the caller ID, he pressed the phone against his ear. "Hey, Rafe."

"Hey, brother, how's it going?"

It felt good to hear his older brother's voice. "We're making progress. Running a few days behind schedule, but that's pretty much what I expected."

"I hear you got some trouble down there with ghosts," Rafe said, a hint of amusement in his voice. "Among other things."

Dylan should have known this was more than a social call. After his conversation with Nick, his younger brother would have phoned Rafe, given him a heads-up on the problems he'd been having at the lodge. Now they were worse.

"Ghosts aren't a problem anymore, and the crew is

back to work." He didn't mention the watcher. He was hoping Payuk would help him solve that particular problem. "The bad news is, Caleb's in trouble. His ex-girlfriend was murdered and the state police like Caleb for the crime."

"Son of a bitch. He in jail?"

"For now. They picked him up this morning. Peter Keller's flying in tomorrow to get him out. I'm flying into Waterside to meet him. I'll do some digging, ask some questions, see what the police might have missed. We need to find this guy."

"You want some help?"

"Not from you. This time of year, you're busier than a one-armed stripper." His brother owned a fleet of charter fishing boats in Valdez. With the silver salmon about to run, all of Rafe's boats would be completely booked.

"Caleb's a friend. I'll help any way I can."

"I know that. I might call Nick, but I'm hoping I don't have to. He's doing his best to get out of the murder business."

"He'll be there if you need him."

"I know that and so does Caleb."

"All right—for now. So how's your lady?"

Dylan flicked Lane a sideways glance, felt a little punch just seeing her there beside him. "I can tell Nick doesn't have enough to do if he's got time to gossip. She's fine. I tried to convince her to go back where it's safe. Says she's going to stick it out here."

Rafe's tone changed. "Safe from what? You don't think Caleb's guilty?"

"Hell, no."

"You got a reason to think the killer might be somewhere around the lodge?"

Dylan sighed, unwilling to lie by omission. "We've had someone watching the place. No reason to think it's the guy who murdered Holly Kaplan. More likely, it's one of the people who set up the phony haunting."

"But there's no way to know for sure."

"No. Like I said, I tried to get Lane to go home. She's staying."

Rafe made a sound of approval. "I think I'm going to like her." But his brother wouldn't get the chance to meet her. Lane would be gone by the time Rafe was finished with the tourist season and able to come down for a visit. Dylan forced the thought away.

"I've got to get going," Rafe said. "I got a couple of boats about to head out."

"I'm under the gun, myself. Thanks for calling." Dylan hit the END button and stuffed the phone back into his jeans.

"I take it that was your brother."

He reached down and started the engine. "My older brother, Rafe. The three of us are each a year apart."

"Your daddy was a busy man."

He chuckled. "We were lucky to have each other. We lost my mom when we were in our teens, but we had a really great dad."

"It broke my heart when I lost my father, but my mom was terrific. We had some great years together before she died. I guess we're both orphans now."

Dylan cast her a glance. "Good thing we've got each other." But they both knew it wouldn't be that way much longer. Dylan forced himself to concentrate on the road.

Chapter Twenty

It was the Fourth of July, an exciting day in a place as small as Waterside. Dylan knew Winnie had been looking forward to the trip, knew Emily probably was, too. He looked over at Lane, who sat in the copilot's seat. At the last minute, he had decided to bring Emily and Winnie along for the day after all.

He wanted to keep a sense of normalcy, stay positive, focus on something good. Whatever was going on, it wasn't fair for his daughter and Winnie to miss out on such an important day.

Lane gave him a smile as he made a smooth water landing, idled the plane up to the float dock, and shut down the engine.

The town was bustling as they walked up the hill from the dock, everyone excited about the annual parade that was scheduled for 11:00 AM. Dylan intended to leave Emily with Winnie in front of the Grizzly Café. They could watch the parade while he and Lane met with Peter Keller.

The attorney had decided to fly in last night instead of this morning. He'd called Dylan to let him know he was scheduled to meet with Caleb at 8:00 AM. It was ten thirty now. Dylan was set to meet with Keller in his room at the Sea View Motel.

As he reached the boardwalk at the edge of town, Dylan crouched in front of Emily. "You ready to watch the parade?"

Emily vigorously nodded. "Then we'd better get going. It's almost time for it to start." He flicked a glance at Lane as he took hold of Emily's hand and saw her smiling softly down at the little girl.

"I just love holidays," Winnie said as they walked along the crowded street. "The Fourth is one of my favorites. It always makes me feel so patriotic."

Especially when the whole town was decorated in red, white, and blue. Flags flew everywhere. Bunting was draped across second-story railings all over town. Emily pointed and laughed as they passed a little boy whose face was painted in red, white, and blue stripes. The boy grinned and waved, and Emily waved back.

It was the warmest day of the year so far, and everyone was in T-shirts and short-sleeved shirts. Dylan wore a black tee with an eagle on the front. Lane had a little rhinestone flag pin on the collar of her white cotton blouse. Emily wore a bill cap in red, white, and blue that Dylan had bought her in Juneau. And Winnie wore a bright red T-shirt with U.S.A. proudly stamped on the front.

He could see the Grizzly Café up ahead. There was an American flag in the window, and Maggie had piped John Philip Sousa marching band music out onto the sidewalk in front.

"Okay, you two," Dylan said to Winnie and Emily. "Have a good time and enjoy the parade. We won't be gone long. If the parade's over before we get back, we'll meet you at the café. All right?"

Emily nodded.

"We'll be there," Winnie said. Her smile slid away. "Go take care of our boy."

Dylan reached over and squeezed her hand. "I will. Don't worry." But he knew she wouldn't stop fretting until Caleb was in the clear.

Dylan took Lane's arm and wove it through his as they headed back up the street to the motel. All the rooms in the two-story building faced the harbor. Peter had taken rooms 212 and 213 on the second floor.

They climbed the outside stairs and crossed the balcony, which was draped with red-white-and-blue bunting. Dylan took a deep breath and knocked on the door of 213, where the meeting was to be held.

The Sea View was one step up from a Motel 6. Nothing fancy, but great scenery outside the windows and easy access to town. Keller had set up one of the rooms as an office. Dylan raised a hand to knock when Keller opened the door.

"You're right on time. Come on in."

As he stepped into the motel room, Dylan felt a shock of relief to see Caleb standing next to the round Formica-topped table in the corner. He caught the quick flash of tears in Lane's eyes when she saw him.

"Thanks, Peter," Dylan said as they walked in and the men shook hands.

Keller smiled. "Just doing my job." Although he was only thirty-three, the same age as Dylan, Keller's hair was prematurely silver. He was six feet tall, lean, and always perfectly groomed. Today he wore a white Izod pullover and navy-blue slacks, his feet shoved into an expensive pair of navy-and-yellow Nike sneakers.

Caleb walked over and clasped Dylan's shoulder. "Thanks, buddy."

"You okay?"

Caleb still looked a little pale and slightly shell-shocked. Dylan didn't blame him. "Better now that I'm out of jail. Thanks to you and Peter."

Lane leaned over and gave Caleb a hug he briefly returned. "I'm really glad you're here."

He smiled. "Thanks."

"Lane, this is a longtime friend of mine, Peter Keller. We went to school together in Anchorage when we were kids. Peter went on to law school at Berkley, graduated at the top of his class. At the moment, I'm damned glad he did."

Dylan turned his attention to the attorney. "Peter, this is Lane Bishop. She's helping me remodel the lodge." Even as he said the words, they didn't sound right, didn't sound like enough. Lane meant more to him than just a woman he had hired to do a job.

"Nice to meet you, Lane." Keller shook hands with her, then tipped his head toward the table in the corner. Four black vinyl chairs surrounded it. "Why don't we all sit down?"

Dylan seated Lane, then took a seat himself. Caleb and Peter also sat down.

"So how did you get him out?" Dylan asked.

"Caleb hadn't been arraigned yet, so there was no way to post bail. The thing is all the evidence against him is circumstantial. I told them they would be looking at a lawsuit for false arrest if they kept him locked up. I also said if they'd release him, you'd personally guarantee he didn't leave the area. I hope that was okay."

"No problem."

"The bad news is, their case is beginning to look pretty good."

Dylan's stomach tightened. "So they've come up with new evidence?"

"Yesterday afternoon, they found the primary crime scene. It was fifty yards from Mad Jack's Saloon. One of the high heels Holly was seen wearing in the bar was found in the bushes, along with a thin silver chain she was known to wear. That was confirmed by a woman named Maggie Ridell, the owner of the Grizzly Café where Holly worked part-time."

"Evidence of rape?" Dylan asked.

"Medical examiner says the vagina showed no signs of tearing, no bruising, nothing like that. There was evidence she'd had sex, but it looks like it was consensual, and the guy was wearing a condom."

Caleb looked sick.

"So no DNA," Dylan said.

"The river isn't far from Mad Jack's," Peter continued. "Her body was waterlogged and battered pretty badly by the rocks as it floated to the sea. But those injuries were postmortem. She wasn't beaten, died before she had a chance to put up much of a struggle. The supposition is, whoever killed Holly carried her to the river after she was dead and dumped her body to make sure they didn't find any DNA."

"And it worked."

"Apparently it did. The police believe Caleb waited for Holly outside Mad Jack's. They had sex in the woods, started arguing again, and he killed her. Maybe it was an accident. Maybe he did it on purpose."

"I didn't kill Holly," Caleb said darkly.

"No one here believes you did," Dylan said.

"Did they find her purse?" Lane asked, drawing Dylan's attention and a hint of respect, since it was a damned good question.

"It wasn't in her car or at the crime scene. They figure he took it with him, probably tossed it into the river along with the body."

"Who reported her missing?" Lane asked.

"Her car was still in the lot, registration in the glove box. One of the local cops saw it and put two and two together."

Lane reached for Caleb, gently touched his arm. "Dylan and I are going to find out the truth. We're going to dig around, ask questions, see if we can find the person who killed her. There were people in the bar that night. Someone has to have seen something that can help us."

Caleb sat back in his chair. "In the meantime, what am I supposed to do? I can't just sit around and wait for them to put a noose around my neck."

Keller leaned toward him. "That is exactly what you're going to do. You're going to put yourself under house arrest. You're going to go back to Eagle Bay and stay there. You're going to make sure someone knows where you are every minute of the day and night. You got it?"

Caleb's black eyes studied Keller. "You aren't worried there might be another murder and I'd get the blame?"

"It's happened before," Keller said.

Caleb rubbed a hand over his face.

"You listen to your attorney," Dylan warned. "You sit back and let us do the work."

Caleb sighed. "Okay, okay. I'll do whatever you say. I didn't kill anyone and I don't want to go to jail."

"Anything else we need to know?" Dylan asked.

"Not at the moment. I'll be heading back tomorrow.

The police aren't ready to press formal charges. They want to be sure they have all their ducks in a row."

Peter stood up from his chair and the others got up, too. "I'll be in touch," Keller said. "Keep me posted on whatever information you come up with."

"Will do."

"It might be a good idea to hire a private investigator. But sometimes you can make more headway going in low-key. You know these people, Dylan. I'm guessing they like and trust you. Give it a go, see if you can make any progress."

He nodded. "If I hit a brick wall, I'll call Nick. Till then, we'll do what we can on our own." Dylan shook Peter's hand, then settled a hand at Lane's waist and urged her toward the door.

"Winnie and Emily are with us," he said to Caleb. "I'll be flying all of us back home this afternoon. In the meantime, it's the Fourth of July. Let's go watch the parade."

Caleb actually managed to smile.

The Waterside High School band was bringing up the rear of the parade, marching down the street playing "The Stars and Stripes Forever." The Wolverines cheerleading squad darted along beside the band, shaking blue-and-gold pompoms in their hands.

As the crowd began to disperse, Lane spotted Winnie and Emily up ahead. Emily ran to Caleb, and he caught her in his arms and swung her up on his shoulders. Lane could see the disappointment on Dylan's face that his little girl hadn't dashed over to him.

"How's my favorite kid?" Caleb asked, but of course Emily didn't answer.

"I'm starved," Dylan said. "Anybody else hungry?"

"I could eat a bear," Winnie said, clearly relieved to see Caleb. "Tail end first."

Emily laughed. Caleb set her on her feet as they reached the door to the café, and Dylan pulled it open, ringing the little bell above. There weren't too many customers inside. A lot of people were heading for the picnic in Waterside Park that Winnie had told Lane about.

Dylan spotted a booth that had just emptied out and started guiding them in that direction. He had almost reached it when Maggie came out from behind the counter and stormed toward them, wedging herself between Caleb and the rest of their party.

"You aren't welcome in here," she said, clamping her hands on her curvy hips. "Not anymore."

Caleb's dark features went pale. "You think I killed her? You think I killed Holly?"

The customers all turned in their seats, their attention locking on the scene playing out in the middle of the café.

"The two of you were involved. You'd been sleeping together. She told me so herself."

"Well, she was lying. I've only talked to her a couple of times and I haven't slept with her since we broke up six years ago."

"I want you to leave. Holly's dead. She was only a kid. If it turns out I'm wrong about you, I'll apologize."

"That's enough," Dylan warned. "Let's go." He urged them firmly toward the door. "We don't need the hassle." As they walked outside, he stopped and turned back. "I'm going to hold you to that apology, Maggie." And then they were outside and back on the boardwalk.

Winnie was utterly horrified. "Well, I never. I always liked that woman. Not anymore."

"Holly was Maggie's friend," Caleb said, defending her even after what she had said.

"Well, she's no friend of yours."

Caleb made no reply.

"I'd rather have pizza anyway," Lane said brightly, reaching down to take Emily's hand. "How about you, Em?"

Emily looked at Caleb as if she wanted to say something but couldn't force out the words. In the end, she just nodded.

Dylan led the small group down the walk and turned onto a side street. The Pelican Pub was a wooden building with neon Bud Light beer signs in the window.

"Best pizza in Waterside," Dylan said.

"That's right," Winnie agreed. "And the service is as good as the food."

And with any luck, Lane thought, the owner wouldn't accuse Caleb of murder.

After the scene at the Grizzly Café, Dylan changed his plans. He'd intended to go to the police, tell them about the man who had been watching the lodge. Trouble was there was a good chance the police would think Caleb was that man.

Since Caleb lived in one of the cabins by himself and hadn't been there the night Lane had seen a man on the deck, there was no way to prove it wasn't him.

Deciding, at least for the moment, to try handling the problem himself, after they finished their pizza, Dylan rounded up his small group of travelers and headed back to the plane.

He wanted to be sure the lodge was locked up tight before dark, and he planned another night of lying in wait for the watcher. With Caleb and Paddy's help, maybe they'd get lucky and catch the son of a bitch. If not, he'd talk to Payuk again, see if he had made any progress.

Tomorrow, he'd return to Waterside and start digging. He wanted to talk to the employees at Mad Jack's Saloon, speak to some of Holly's friends, and take a look at the crime scene.

There had to be something, some piece of evidence that would send them in the right direction—and clear Caleb's name. Dylan was determined to find it.

Chapter Twenty-One

It was a long night, but with Dylan, Paddy, and Caleb all taking shifts, the men got at least a few hours of sleep. The bad news was—or maybe it was good news—the watcher never appeared.

Or at least they never spotted him.

It took less effort than she had imagined for Lane to convince Dylan to take her with him to Waterside the next morning. She figured he could use all the help he could get. They left right after breakfast, making the short flight north along the coast to the small Alaskan town. Dylan had called ahead and had a rental car waiting in the parking lot near the float dock—though the faded, powder-blue Toyota with the dented front fender hardly looked like it was part of the Avis fleet.

"Runs better than it looks," Dylan said. "And it's got front-wheel drive so you can get around town in the winter. You can find a decent rental at the airport, but it's a little tough to get out there. Johnnie Mellon, the mechanic down at Pete's Garage, keeps this one for the guys who fly into the float dock."

"At least it's clean."

"There should be a key hidden under the bumper."
Dylan groped beneath the front, found the key, and opened
the door for her. The interior of the little car was clean and
smelled like the pine-scented deodorizer Johnnie must
have used.

"So where are we headed first?" Lane asked as she
buckled the seat belt across her lap.

"Let's take a look at the crime scene, see what the cops
might have missed. Let's hope the yellow tape is gone.
We don't need any more trouble."

"If the tape's gone, how will we find the spot?"

"It happened fifty yards from the bar. The cops will
have tromped all over the area around it. I'll find it."

Lane didn't doubt that. The man seemed able to do
anything he set his mind to. She hoped he could find
something that would clear Caleb of murder.

She wondered why she was so certain he was innocent. Maybe it was Dylan's unshakable belief in him. But
Lane thought it was something else, a gentleness of spirit,
a kindness she had sensed in Caleb the moment she had
met him.

Dylan started the engine and headed out of the parking
lot, pulling onto one of the few paved roads in the area. The
little blue banger carried them out to Mad Jack's Saloon
at the edge of town, a distance they could have walked if
they'd had time. But they had other stops to make, and
every minute counted.

He parked the car in the gravel lot across from the bar
and they both got out. The wooden building was rustic, the
kind of place where you'd expect to see Harley motorcycles
sitting out front. A gleaming black one with a lot of chrome,
and a metallic blue with flames on the side rested there
now, though it was only ten in the morning.

"This way." Dylan took her hand and led her toward the forest east of the parking lot.

He was right. The trail into the forest was obvious. State troopers, EMTs, the medical examiner, and God knew how many other people had been tramping back and forth to the murder scene. Lane shivered as she thought of Holly's body lying lifeless in the woods.

"You cold?"

"No. I just . . . I feel sorry for her. She was too young to die, and in such a brutal manner."

He stopped on the trail and turned back to her. "You can wait here if you'd rather. This isn't your problem. You don't have to put yourself through this."

She felt an unexpected pang. Caleb was Dylan's best friend, but he was her friend, too. On top of that, she wanted to help Dylan. She'd thought he understood that. Thought he knew that at some point during her time in Alaska, his problems had become her problems, too.

"I might see something you miss. I don't believe Caleb killed her. I want to help any way I can."

Dylan bent his head and very softly kissed her. "You're a good friend, Lane. Caleb's lucky to have you on his side."

She hoped she was Dylan's friend, too. But deep down she knew friendship wasn't what she felt for him. It was crazy, but she wanted more from him than that.

"It's not far now," he said, taking her hand. Dylan continued toward the crime scene and she realized he was pacing off the fifty-yard distance. The closer they got, the tighter her stomach went. She was glad for the warmth of the strong fingers wrapped around her hand.

He came to a halt beneath the branches of a thick-trunked pine tree that sat at the edge of a meadow.

"This is it. About fifty yards out and you can tell the

ground has been disturbed by any number of people. This is where he killed her."

Her stomach knotted. The yellow tape was gone, but there was no doubt this was the place it had happened. "It looks like the area has been thoroughly searched. I can't believe there's anything left for us to find."

Dylan made no reply, just started walking, stopping every few feet, crouching, examining the spot, crouching again, studying every blade of grass, every pinecone.

"See this?" He pointed to another trail that ran into the tall meadow grass from the murder scene. It was almost nonexistent except for a patch of green that was flattened, followed by another a few feet away. "This is the path he made as he carried her body to the river."

Dylan started down the trail, moving from one footstep to the next, Lane following behind him. Her heart was pounding. It was all too easy to imagine the young woman's lifeless body slung over the killer's shoulder as he walked to the river rumbling in the distance.

"Do you think the police got any boot prints or anything?"

Dylan shook his head. "Rained too hard that night." He took her hand, moving carefully along the trail, looking for something—anything—the police might have missed.

"He's tall," Dylan said. "Strides as long as mine, and purposeful. No hesitation. Always moving forward. He knew what to do with the body, figured if he put her in the river, any DNA would be washed away."

"Not everyone would know something like that."

He looked off toward the sound of the rushing stream. "The guy knew what to do. My guess, he's seen death before."

"How can you tell?"

"It's like hunting. First-timers get nervous. They get buck fever, sometimes can't even pull the trigger. Afterward, they're unsteady. Sometimes they even get sick. A seasoned hunter lays out a plan, locates the game he's after, takes the kill shot, then does what's necessary to bring back food for his family. I don't know if this guy killed Holly on purpose, but dealing with her body didn't shake him up."

"That isn't Caleb."

"No, it isn't. Caleb gets upset when a bird flies into a window. Once Holly was dead, the killer did what had to be done to keep from getting caught."

Dylan started walking again, leading Lane along the faint trail through the deep grass onto the bank overlooking the water.

"This is the north fork of Copper Creek," he said. "Lot of guys fish it."

The river wasn't that wide, but it was frothy and churning as it poured itself toward the sea. Dylan followed the muddy bank, carefully examining the ground, the twigs and leaves along the route. Lane mimicked his search, being careful not to fall in. They looked the area over for half an hour before Dylan gave up and grimly shook his head.

"Nothing. Whoever did this took his time, cleaned up after himself." He urged her back down the trail. "Let's head over to Mad Jack's. See what else we can find out."

With her hand in his, Dylan led the way. They walked in silence, taking a shorter route back that avoided the spot where the murder had taken place. At the edge of the parking lot, he paused.

"Before we go in, I need to make a phone call." With a glance back toward the crime scene, he dug into the pocket of his jeans and pulled out his cell phone. "Three bars. Service isn't a problem."

"Who are you calling?"

He raised a finger, silencing her question, as the phone was quickly answered. But Lane had a pretty good idea who was on the other end of the line.

Dylan waited only a single ring before Nick picked up.

"Hey, bro," Nick said. "I'm glad you called. I've been worried. Rafe phoned this morning, brought me up to speed. How's Caleb?"

"Hanging in there. Keller got him released so he's home. Listen, Lane and I just left the crime scene. I was hoping you could give me a little input."

A heartbeat passed. "I'll do what I can."

Dylan knew his brother was trying to take a break from the murder and mayhem he had dealt with in his job. Still, this was Caleb. Dylan knew he could count on Nick's help.

Over the next few minutes, he laid it all out: what the cops had found—or hadn't; what the scene looked like; the conclusions he had drawn.

For several moments, Nick was silent on his end of the phone. "From what you've said, this guy sounds like a pretty cool customer. Nothing at the scene that could incriminate him. They found a shoe? A chain? So what? Purse is gone, so no ID. No blood. No DNA. This may not be his first rodeo."

"I was afraid you'd say that."

"He might have hoped the body wouldn't show up for a while, but he was ready if it did. On the other hand, could be this was a sex game gone wrong. She wasn't beaten. She wasn't raped. His stride matches yours so we know he's tall. Powerful enough to strangle her. Could have been he just got carried away. Whatever happened, if you're reading this right, he knew what to do once she was dead. The guy was no stranger to death. I have a hunch this joker's a professional."

"You mean like a hit man?"

"More like a cop or soldier. Didn't seem intimidated by being in the woods. Found a place to take her for sex, someplace close enough to the bar so she wouldn't be scared but far enough away they wouldn't be heard."

"Maybe he's a local."

Nick picked up on the tone of his voice. "But you don't think so."

He didn't. He couldn't say why, just one of those hunches he had listened to over the years. "We've never had any problems before. Nothing like this. Ferry comes in and out. Could be some drifter who got off for a visit."

"Could be."

"Anything else?" he asked.

"Not without coming down there."

"Let me do some legwork first. See if we can get this done ourselves."

"You're using the plural, brother. If you mean you and Lane, you better take care or you'll be in deeper shit than you were the last time."

The words were sobering. Lane would be leaving. He couldn't afford to get in too deep.

"I'll keep that in mind. In the meantime, I'll keep you posted. Thanks for the help." Dylan hung up the phone.

"That was your brother, Nick, the policeman?"

"Homicide detective. Or was. He says the guy sounds like a professional, a cop or ex-military."

"Because he didn't get rattled after he killed her."

"That's right. Think how you would feel. The average guy would go ballistic. Unless he had it planned, which considering the timing—she could have walked outside any time that night—I don't think it was."

"But you think it's a stranger, not someone local, maybe someone who came in on the ferry."

He nodded. "Holly hadn't been in town that long. And she was concentrating on Caleb. As far as we know, she wasn't involved with anyone in town—the cops would have checked that angle."

Lane looked up at him. "If he came in on the ferry, he might need transportation."

Dylan's interest sharpened. "You're right. He could have walked from town to the bar, but if he's staying somewhere out of town, he'd need a way to get there." He smiled. "I knew you were more than a pretty face." Reaching for her hand, he started across the parking lot.

Lane stopped him at the door. "Okay. Before we go inside, let me put this together. We're looking for someone as tall as you and probably as strong. He's purposeful. Not a wimpy kind of guy. Probably attractive or Holly wouldn't have had sex with him."

He nodded. "Sounds right."

"Maybe someone who's been a cop, or in the military, or someone who spends a lot of time outdoors." She glanced up at him. "That leaves a lot of possibilities."

"Not so much in a place the size of Waterside." Dylan led her up on the porch and pushed through the swinging doors. He'd been in a few times. Caleb liked to go there once in a while to listen to the band. Occasionally, he'd talked Dylan into going with him.

The wooden floor creaked beneath his feet as he walked to the long oak bar. A row of stools ran the length of it and there was an old-fashioned back bar behind it. Dylan recognized the guy using a rag to wipe off the counter.

"Hey, Brian, how's it going?" He waited for Lane to sit down on one of the stools, then sat down beside her.

The bartender slowed the spin of the rag to a stop. "Dylan, right?" He was thin to the point of skinny, dark-haired, with lip whiskers and a pointy little goatee. He looked like a dumbshit, but he seemed like a pretty decent guy.

"That's right," Dylan said. "I was in here a couple of times with Caleb."

"I . . . uhh . . . heard about the murder. I guess he's under arrest."

"Released him yesterday. The evidence is all circumstantial."

"Doesn't mean he didn't do it."

Dylan's jaw clenched. He forced himself to relax. "Were you working the night of the murder?"

"I was here for a while."

"When Caleb and Holly were in here?"

"Look, Dylan, they had a fight, okay? Caleb left. Holly left maybe fifteen minutes later. That's what I told the troopers and that's all I know."

"Fair enough. You ever see Holly in here with another guy?"

"You mean like a date? No. She was a real cock tease, though. She was always coming on to some guy. Got them to buy her drinks, but she usually didn't leave with them."

"I'm thinking of someone in particular," Dylan said. "About my height. Athletic. Confident. Maybe even arrogant."

"Good-looking," Lane added.

Brian's dark eyebrows drew slightly together. "I don't know. . . . Doesn't sound like any of the regulars."

"Could be an ex-cop," Dylan added, "or maybe ex-military."

Brian's head came up. "Now that I think about it, there was a guy . . . been in a few times over the last couple weeks. Mentioned being in Iraq." Dylan and Lane exchanged glances. "But he wasn't with Holly. At least not on my shift."

"But he may have been in here that night."

"I don't know. Might have been in the night before. Good-looking S.O.B."

"What color hair?"

"Brown, I think."

"Eyes?"

He shook his head. "Don't recall. A couple of girls came onto him, but he didn't seem that interested."

"Did he come off the ferry?" Dylan asked.

"I don't know. I don't think he's from around here, though. I'd never seen him in here until lately."

"You catch a name?"

Brian just shook his head. "Sorry. He kind of kept to himself. He'd just leave money on the bar when he left and slip out real quiet like." He swirled the rag on the bar top. "He was just a guy, you know? This time of year, we get lots of people in here."

Dylan pulled out his wallet, took out an Eagle Bay Lodge card. He tossed the card down with a pair of twenties.

"We appreciate your help, Brian. If you think of anything else, give me a call."

Brian nodded. "If it's worth anything, I don't think Caleb did it."

Lane flashed the bartender a smile. "Neither do we. Thank you, Brian."

Dylan rested a hand on her waist and led her outside. He tried not to think how well she fit with him, how she steadied him somehow. Considering how fast the summer was passing, it was an unsettling thought.

Even more unsettling was his brother's warning. He told himself to be careful, keep his distance. He tried to remember what had happened with Mariah.

But when he looked at Lane, his mind refused to go there.

Chapter Twenty-Two

Convenient Rental Car at the Waterside Airport was closed on Sundays. Prearranged car pickup and returns only.

"We'll have to come back tomorrow," Dylan grumbled as they walked back across the parking lot to the beat-up blue Toyota.

But Lane's hopes had been lifted. "We got a lead, Dylan. Brian told us about a guy in the bar who fit our description. It could be him."

Dylan scoffed. "We have no idea if our theoretical killer is the man at Mad Jack's. The killer could have been some guy she was conning out of money."

"Look, I watch those detective shows on TV. Stuff like *Blue Bloods*, reruns of *NYPD Blue*. The cops come up with a theory, then try to prove it. We've got a theory. Until we prove ourselves wrong, we push forward."

A slow grin spread across Dylan's face. He pulled her into his arms. "Damn, I'm crazy about you." A little thrill slid through her as he bent his head and kissed her.

It was followed by a jolt of alarm. "Please, Dylan, don't

say that. We . . . we have to be careful. We can't let this whole thing get out of hand."

A muscle ticked in his cheek, and he glanced away. "I know."

Steeling herself against the sudden tightness in her throat, Lane went up on her toes and kissed him. As always, the heat was there, the hunger. She eased away though she didn't really want to.

She pasted on a smile. "Where should we go next?"

Dylan gave her a last slow glance, then looked back toward the rental car agency. "We can't talk to these guys till tomorrow. But if our suspect came in on the ferry, he had to have transportation to get out here. There's a couple of drivers who meet the boat when it docks, hoping to get a fare. One of them works with Johnnie at Pete's Garage, but they're closed on Sundays, too."

A small plane, the commuter from Ketchikan that Dylan had talked her out of taking so that he could pick her up and fly her back himself, buzzed overhead.

"You know, he didn't have to come in on the ferry. He could have flown into the airport."

"I thought of it. That would mean Waterside was his final destination. He'd have to have a reason for coming. Working on our theory, according to Brian, the guy in the bar has only been in town a couple of weeks. I haven't heard of any new jobs opening up, something big enough to attract someone from someplace else."

"That makes sense. It looks like most of the businesses are owned and run by locals."

"If he's a loner, he probably didn't come up with friends to go fishing. More likely, he's a drifter, some guy just following the ferry route north, taking a look at Alaska."

"All right, then what about talking to some of Holly's friends?"

"I guess we could try Maggie, but she seems pretty convinced Caleb did it. I doubt she'll be much help."

"How about some of the people she works with?"

He nodded. "We need to do that. At least the hospital's open."

But none of the nurses or any of the staff at the Waterside Medical Center had been particularly close to Holly. None of them knew anything about her private life or the men she was involved with. Dylan did get her home address, an apartment in a four-plex walking distance from the hospital, which meant it was also close to town.

"You think we can get inside?" Lane asked as they climbed back into the Toyota and started in that direction.

"We'll drive by, see if there's a manager. Maybe he'll let us in."

The two-story building on Monrovia Road sat on a hillside overlooking the sea. It was painted brown and yellow, and like most of the buildings in Waterside, had a really great view.

As they crossed the grassy knoll in front, Lane spotted a sign on one of the apartments downstairs. MANAGER. Lane flashed Dylan an excited glance as he knocked on the door.

There was a shuffle of feet, and then a short, bald-headed man in faded jeans and a long-sleeved T-shirt opened the door and looked up at them. "What can I do for you?"

Dylan smiled. "I heard you had a vacancy coming up. That right?"

"Looks that way. Word sure travels fast. Young woman who lived here just died a couple of days ago."

Dylan flicked Lane a glance and settled into his role. "Not inside, I hope."

"No, nothing like that. Police came by yesterday, spent a couple of hours going through her things. They said she was murdered."

"That's terrible. Maybe renting the place would be bad luck."

The little man shook his head. "No reason to think that way. 'Course, the apartment won't be available till the end of the month. That's when Holly's rent was due."

"Any chance we could see it?" Dylan asked.

"Couldn't have yesterday, but it looks like the police are finished in there now. Trouble is they dusted for fingerprints so it looks pretty bad in there. Kind of small for the two of you, anyway."

"I was looking at it for a bachelor friend of mine," Dylan said. "He doesn't need all that much."

"I guess I could show it to you."

They climbed the outside stairs and the little man shoved a key into the lock. He turned the key, then the knob, and the door swung silently open. As Lane walked inside, her throat closed up. A young woman was dead, her life over. What kind of man would commit such a horrible crime?

"Terrible thing," the manager said, echoing her thoughts. "Too bad they can't give the bastard the needle."

Maybe so, Lane thought but first they needed to find the right man.

"Did you know her well?" Dylan asked. As the manager had said, the apartment had been thoroughly searched, stuff moved on top of the coffee table, the lampshades slightly askew. Black fingerprint powder coated every surface.

"She kept pretty busy. She worked two jobs, you know? And she liked to go out."

Lane glanced around. Holly might have been busy, but

she'd kept the apartment clean. No dishes in the sink, her clothes hanging neatly in the closet.

Lane swallowed past the lump in her throat. "Did she have any family here?"

"Told me once her folks live in Juneau. I don't think they were close. She had some guy she was sweet on, but I don't think he ever spent the night. Holly was always by herself."

"You know his name?" Dylan asked.

"I think she said Carlos or Carter or something. Said they'd dated once before."

Not Carter. Caleb. Lane was beginning to realize how determined Holly had been to rebuild her relationship with the man who'd once loved her.

"The apartment's nice," Dylan said. "I'll mention it to my friend, but I don't think you'll have any trouble renting it."

"Nah, stuff goes quick up here. Not much around."

That was for sure. Not many people. No need for more than a handful of apartments. They headed back downstairs, paused in front of the manager's place.

"Thanks, Mr. . . . ?"

"Granger. Harlan Granger. Let me know if your friend wants the place."

"I will."

Thinking of the woman whose life had so senselessly ended, Lane reached for Dylan's hand as they crossed the lawn. When she climbed into the car, she slumped against the seat.

"I'm beginning to feel like I know her. It's really sad, Dylan."

"Yes, it is. But it'll be a lot worse if they convict an innocent man."

"Oh, God, Dylan." She thought of Caleb and how scared he must be. "We can't let that happen."

Dylan sighed, rubbed a hand over his jaw. "The day's pretty well shot. We need to get back. We'll fly in again tomorrow, talk to the rental car people."

A worrisome thought occurred. "When's the ferry due back?"

Dylan's blue eyes swung to her face. "I think it's in next week. You're thinking our guy might get on the boat and leave?"

"If he hasn't already gotten on a plane."

Dylan shook his head. "I don't think so. This guy is careful. He'll be worried about the police. My hunch is he hasn't left yet. Probably lie low for a couple of days, let things settle down, get back to normal."

But there was no way to be sure. She read the same worry she was feeling in Dylan's face.

"We'll start again tomorrow," he said. "We need to catch this guy—and we need to do it soon."

Lane couldn't agree with him more.

By the time Dylan got back to the lodge, he was worried and angry. Worried that Holly's killer would find a way to leave before they could catch him. Angry at himself for relaxing his guard, letting himself get in so deep with Lane.

I'm crazy about you. What the hell was he thinking? Sure, they were good together. And he was damned glad to have that sharp brain of hers as they tried to track a killer. But it couldn't be more than that.

There was no way in hell Lane Bishop would stay in Alaska. She had a home, a business, friends in L.A. She was a city girl, for chrissake. She lived in fucking Beverly Hills. No way was she cut out for hard winters and loneliness, for raising a child with emotional problems, for living in the wilderness. It took a special breed of person, and Lane Bishop, interior designer, wouldn't last a year.

His jaw felt tight by the time he walked her into the lodge, left her in the office, and headed back outside. It was getting on toward supper. He needed to work off some of the restless energy that still raced through him. Heading out to the woodpile, he picked up the ax, cut half a cord of wood, and began stacking logs next to each of the four outside cabins.

The crew had worked them over a little, gotten them ready to rent. They were the most recent additions to the lodge, built by Jeff Fenton, so they didn't need to be completely remodeled. Since the old furniture still looked pretty good, Lane had just ordered a few new pieces to bring them up to date. She'd done some stuff with the curtains, added throw pillows to the small living rooms to brighten them up and make the rustic cabins look cozy.

Lane. Just thinking about her made him mad all over again. He dumped a last load of wood next to the cabin on the end, stacked it neatly, carried a smaller stack inside, and set it on the hearth next to the fireplace. His brother was right. He had to get his head on straight, put his summer affair with Lane into perspective.

He wanted her, yes. He considered her a friend—more than a friend—but that was all she ever could be. He knew it. She knew it. All he had to do was keep his feelings in check.

He looked up just then, spotted her standing in the open doorway as if his thoughts had brought her there, felt the swift, hard punch in the gut, the sweep of hunger he felt every time he saw her. His jaw tightened. One of his hands clenched into a fist.

She strode toward him, stopped right in front of him.

"All right, what's going on? You brought me back and dumped me off like a sack of dirty laundry. If you're worried about Caleb, that's one thing. If it's me—"

"Goddamned right, it's you." He hadn't meant to say it out loud, but now that he'd started he couldn't seem to stop. "I can't get you out of my head. I think of you night and day. I have you, and it isn't enough. Just looking at you standing there in a pair of goddamn jeans makes me want to fuck you."

Her eyes widened. He didn't talk that way. Not to Lane. Not to anyone. But he meant every word. She was a fire in his blood, a soul-deep need he couldn't seem to quench.

He raked a hand through his hair. "Look, I'm sorry, okay? I just need to work a few things out. Go on back to the house. I'll be there as soon as I'm finished."

Lane just closed the door.

"What are you doing?"

She unbuttoned her white cotton shirt as she walked toward him, slid it off her shoulders, tossed it onto the sofa. His mouth went dry when she unhooked her bra and tossed it on top of the shirt, revealing her pretty breasts.

"You want me?" she said. "Here I am."

He started shaking his head. "I'm not in the mood for slow and easy."

She just kept coming. "Neither am I." She framed his face between her hands, pulled his mouth down to hers for a kiss that was long, wet, and deep. If he'd wanted her before, he was on fire for her now. He filled his hands with those lovely, rose-tipped breasts, felt her tremble.

He was rock-hard and aching, no longer thinking of consequences or unwanted emotions, filled with nothing but raw aching need. The kiss went deeper, hotter. He reached for the snap on her jeans, popped it. She gasped as he turned her around, slid her pants down her long legs, and bent her over the back of the sofa.

She was wearing a tiny pair of blue bikini panties. Fuck it, he'd buy her a new pair. She made a little sound in her throat as he ripped them away, spread her legs, and filled her.

Lane moaned.

God, he didn't want to hurt her. But when he started to pull away, she arched her back, taking him deeper, making him even harder than he was before. The hunger burned through him. Heat and need and a desire for her he had never felt for a woman before. He drove into her, gripped her hips, and took her. Took her until all he could think of was Lane and how right it felt to be inside her.

She cried his name as she reached release, but Dylan didn't stop, just pounded into her until she came again. Reaching the limit of his control, he allowed himself to follow, jaw clenched hard against the rush of pleasure.

Quiet settled over him. The self-directed anger was gone. He'd needed her and she'd needed him. Whatever he felt for Lane, he would deal with it when the time came for her to go.

He pulled her back against him, kissed the side of her neck, pulled her jeans back up around her waist. He wanted to say he was sorry, but it would be a lie.

Lane turned in his arms. "Everything'll be okay," she said, resting her palm against his cheek. "We'll make it be okay."

Dylan just nodded. He wanted to believe it. Maybe by summer's end he would. Dylan didn't think so.

Chapter Twenty-Three

Winnie met them at the mudroom door as Lane walked next to Dylan back to the lodge. Her face was still flushed, her body still humming. God, the man was amazing. She forced herself to focus on the robust woman in the doorway, hoped she couldn't guess what they had been doing.

Winnie's shrewd gaze ran over them and her mouth tightened. Clearly she hadn't been fooled. She was protective of Emily and Dylan. She loved them. She had a right to be. But she and Dylan were both adults. Both knew this would be over at the end of summer. Lane ignored a sharp pinch in her heart.

"Jacob Payuk just called," Winnie said to Dylan, holding open the back door so they could walk in. "I told him you'd call him right back."

"Did he say what he wanted?"

"Something about a meeting. I told him you'd phone as soon as you got back to the house."

Dylan didn't waste time. Lane watched as he pulled out his cell and found Payuk's number. He pressed the iPhone against his ear. "Jacob, this is Dylan Brodie."

The village elder said something, and Dylan started

nodding. "An hour?" He flicked a glance at Lane. "That'll work. We'll see you then." He ended the call, shoved the phone back into his jeans. "Payuk's set up a meeting. He's convinced the people responsible for the haunting scam to come forward. I guess this murder thing has got them scared. They don't want to turn up on the suspect list."

She thought of Caleb. "I don't blame them."

"Payuk wants me to bring you with me. I think he figures having a woman along will soften the situation, keep things from getting too heated."

"I'd like to come."

He turned to Winnie. "Where's Caleb?"

"He and Emily went fishing. They're on the dock out in front."

He nodded. She could tell it bothered him that his daughter was so much more at ease with his friend than she was with him. Lane wondered how the two had grown so far apart—and what it would take to bring them back together.

"We'll probably be late for supper," he told Winnie.

"I've got a nice baked ham, mashed potatoes, red-eye gravy, and some biscuits. You just deal with those fools in Yeil, and I'll keep it warm."

"Thanks, Winnie."

Dylan set a firm hand at Lane's waist, reminding her of their encounter in the cabin. Just thinking about it made her feel like blushing.

"We need to talk to Caleb," Dylan said. "Let's go this way."

Lane walked beside him through the lodge into the great hall. Moving beneath the wrought-iron chandelier, they made their way out the door. Eagle Bay stretched in front of them, the inlet calm, the blue sea barely lapping against the sandy shore in front of the lodge.

Lane spotted Finn, prancing along next to Emily. The little girl walked beside Caleb, who had a pair of fishing poles riding on one powerful shoulder.

"Catch anything?" Dylan asked as the two of them approached.

Caleb patted the canvas creel on his hip. "Couple of pinks, a little over three pounds, maybe. Be good to go with supper." Caleb's smile faded. "How about you? Your fishing trip do any good?"

Dylan glanced back toward the house. "Come on in. We'll fill you in on what we got."

Caleb nodded. "Let me get these cleaned and I'll be right with you."

Emily clapped her hands for Finn to follow her, smiled at Lane, and rushed off to play in the side yard.

She and Dylan headed back into the great hall, walked over and sat down on the old sofa and chairs in front of the empty hearth. It was quiet in the cavernous room without the crew at work upstairs. The chaos would start all over again tomorrow, but even without much furniture, it was a good place to sit.

It was only a few minutes before Caleb walked into the lodge minus his fishing creel and came over to join them.

"We may have found something in town," Dylan said, stretching his long legs out in front of him. "Or more specifically *someone.* At the moment it's all just conjecture, but if the pieces keep coming together, we may have a suspect."

Caleb sat forward in the overstuffed chair. "Who is he?"

"We don't have a name. Maybe by tomorrow we will." Dylan went on to tell Caleb about visiting the murder scene, tracking the killer to the river. He explained their theory about the man's size and capabilities.

"I pretty much fit that description, too," Caleb said darkly.

"Yeah, but you didn't kill anyone."

"No."

Dylan explained Nick's take on the crime, and the bartender's confirmation that a stranger fitting that description had been in Mad Jack's at least a couple of times in the last two weeks.

"Have you seen anyone around who fits our profile?" Lane asked.

"Besides yourself," Dylan said with the hint of a smile.

Caleb just shook his head. "Doesn't ring any bells with me, but I haven't been spending much time lately in Waterside."

Sensing the worry he was feeling, Lane reached over and touched his arm. "We've got a lead, Caleb. There's a chance he's the man who did it."

"It's pretty slim."

"It's more than we had before," Dylan said. He looked down at his watch, told Caleb about the call he'd gotten from Payuk. "We've got to get going. We need to be in Yeil when these guys show up."

"You want me to come along?" Caleb asked.

"I think it'd be best if you stay out of this. You've already got more on your plate than you can handle. We'll bring you up to speed when we get back."

Caleb ground his jaw, finally nodded.

Lane reached over and squeezed his hand. "We're going to find him, Caleb. You didn't do it. Proof of that has to be out there. Sooner or later, we'll find it."

Caleb didn't look all that convinced, but Lane gave him a smile she hoped would reassure him. She and Dylan left the great hall and headed out to the garage where his truck was parked.

A few minutes later, they were heading down the gravel road. Lane's adrenaline was pumping, her hopes once again high. She prayed at least one of Dylan's problems was about to be solved.

It was definitely Sunday in the tiny town of Yeil. Though the afternoon was waning, the sun was still bright, and people were fishing out on the dock or just sitting in folding chairs beside the water. A couple of aluminum boats floated in the sea, poles sticking over the sides.

The kids were riding their bikes up and down the streets. A boom box roared next to a man who worked under the hood of his car.

There was a church in town, such as it was, white clapboard with a bell on top and a wooden cross out in front. People were heading inside for the Sunday evening meeting. Aside from the glaciers in the distance and the forested hillsides, Lane thought the town looked much the same as a lot of rural mountain communities in America.

Payuk must have seen them drive in. He waited on the porch, a stern look on his dark, weathered face. As they climbed the steps, he wordlessly turned and pushed open the door, beckoning them inside.

Three people stood in the living room. Two young men and a young woman. The boys' appearance hinted at their Alaska Native heritage, black hair and dark skin, but their features were more refined, clearly several generations removed from full-blood Tlingit. The girl had light brown hair, blue eyes, and a pixie nose.

They were dressed more like college kids than locals, the boys in Nikes and Reeboks, Izod pullovers, and chinos. The girl wore a short white skirt, a red-and-white-striped top, and sandals.

Either boy was tall enough to have been the figure she had seen outside the window. It didn't really matter which one it was as long as the boys stopped terrorizing the people in the lodge.

With a shock, Lane realized she had seen the girl before. Her name was Heather and she came to the lodge once a week to help Winnie with the heavy cleaning.

Jacob Payuk spoke to the three young people standing rigidly in his living room. "You will say your names and what you have done."

The tallest boy straightened. "My name is Alex Kramer. This is Jared Deacon, and that's Heather Nolan."

"I've seen Heather at the lodge," Dylan said. "My housekeeper told me she was a student at the community college in Ketchikan. What about you two?"

"We were born in Yeil," Alex said. "We go to school with Heather, but we're home for the summer."

"We didn't hurt anyone," Jared said, a note of belligerence in his voice. "We were only defending our ancestors' honor."

"We weren't the first to do it," added Alex. "There were others before us. After the murders, everyone thought the lodge was haunted anyway. All we did was give them a few more reasons to believe it was true."

"We couldn't let the crimes go unpunished," Jared said darkly.

"I just made the rocking chair move," Heather said, her blue eyes darting worriedly between Lane and Dylan.

"The hologram was a nice touch," Dylan said. "Impressive. I guess you learned that at school."

Alex shifted from one foot to another.

"I understand why you did it," Dylan pressed on. "Jacob has told me the truth about Artemus Carmack and what happened at the lodge all those years ago. But that was then and this is now. I had nothing to do with the murders or the hanging of innocent men."

The boys didn't reply.

"This ends now," Dylan said, his blue eyes cold and unrelenting. "No more sneaking into the lodge. No more prowling around outside at night. If anything else happens—anything at all—I go to the police. Since they're currently looking for the man who murdered a young woman in Waterside, now would not be a good time for your names to come up."

Payuk spoke directly to the boys. "Many years have passed since our great-grandfathers were wrongly accused and punished for a crime they did not commit. It is time to put the past aside and move on with our lives."

Alex and Heather were nodding. Lane figured they wanted no part of Dylan Brodie. Clearly, Heather wasn't Tlingit. Likely, she was Alex's girlfriend, just helping her boyfriend out.

Jared still looked unconvinced, his jaw set, tight lines around his mouth.

Lane focused her attention on him. "Have any of you ever tried to prove Will Seeks and Thomas Shaekley were innocent of the crime?"

Jared scoffed. "It happened a long time ago. Tales handed down by our forefathers are all the proof we have."

"Dylan and I were able to dig up the story of the

murders—or at least one version of it. Maybe you could go online, do some research on Artemus Carmack. Find out what happened to him after he left Eagle Bay. Maybe he killed someone else. Maybe there's something out there that will help you prove your version of what happened is the truth."

Jared was shaking his head. "I don't think it would work."

But Alex had brightened. "It might be worth a try." He turned in Lane's direction. "If you would be willing to help."

Lane inwardly groaned. She should have known she was shooting herself in the foot with this idea. "I can tell you what I did. Give you some ideas where to look. Maybe you can find someone still living who was there that night or perhaps the child of someone who was there. Even if you can't completely prove Carmack's guilt, you could write about it, present the facts you *can* prove, or at least the facts as you know them. You could post the article online, at least stir up some doubt."

"It would be a great service to our people," Jacob Payuk said.

The three of them put their heads together and started whispering. When Lane glanced over at Dylan, those cold blue eyes had warmed, and approval faintly curved the edge of his mouth.

"We'll try it," Alex finally agreed.

"I want your word," Dylan said, putting himself directly in front of the boy. "I want to know that my family and friends, the guests who come and stay at the lodge, can feel safe."

Alex shuffled his feet. "All right. We won't bother you anymore."

Dylan drilled him with a look. "Your word this is finished."

Alex straightened, took a deep breath. "You have my word."

"On the blood of our ancestors, you have my word," Jared added.

Dylan cocked an eyebrow. "Heather?"

"All I did was make the rocking chair move."

"If you want to keep your job, you won't do it again."

Her eyes widened. "You aren't going to fire me?"

"Not if you give me your word."

"Okay, sure. I promise."

"Good. Then we're finished here." Dylan turned to the elder. "I appreciate your help in this matter, Jacob. I believe it serves all of us well."

"I also believe that is true."

Dylan set a hand at Lane's waist and started toward the door. She stopped long enough to scribble a note and hand it to Jared. "Here's my e-mail address. Drop me a note, tell how your research is coming. If I can help, let me know."

For the first time, the boy relaxed enough to smile. It made him look younger, like the college kid he was. "Thanks."

Dylan led her out of the house, and both of them took a deep breath of the crisp, clean air.

"That ham and biscuits is beginning to sound really good," Dylan said.

"And Winnie made apricot cobbler for dessert. I saw it on the kitchen counter."

Dylan smiled. "Let's go home."

Lane smiled back as they headed for the truck. The ghosts were gone. Things could get back to normal.

Except they still had a murderer to find before Caleb wound up in prison.

The wind whispered softly through the pine boughs. The moon was rising, traveling between the clouds moving in from the sea. He hadn't been back inside the house in days, not that he couldn't get in anytime he wanted.

For a while, the stupid kids had made it easy. He'd watched them going in and out, scaring the crap out of people in the middle of the night. He'd used their secret entrance, prowled the whole house, walked the same halls the others walked.

But after what he'd done to the girl, his thoughts had been weighed down with regret. He'd just wanted sex. So had she. He figured he'd make it good for both of them. It was only a game he played with women sometimes. No one had ever gotten hurt.

But sometimes accidents happened. He'd seen it a dozen times in the Army. Guys getting killed during training exercises. Parachutes that didn't open. Hell, sometimes they just weren't paying attention and stepped in front of an armored vehicle. In an instant, deader than dirt. It was sad, but it was just the way life was.

At least the voice had been silent, giving him a chance to think, a chance to plan. A chance to finish what he'd come here to do.

He continued moving quietly through the forest. He wore camo head to foot, and a black wool cap. Had wrapped his boots in long strands of grass, muffling the sound of his footsteps and making him harder to track. His favorite spot wasn't much farther up the game trail.

He frowned when he reached it. He hadn't been there in days, had mostly stayed up on the hill above the cemetery, but he knew exactly where it was. Knew that someone else had been there. Dylan Brodie, the owner of the lodge, had been raised in Alaska. He'd read that on the Eagle Bay website.

Brodie would know the woods, know that someone had been out there watching them. Brodie would be able to track him.

He didn't like the idea. He prided himself on being as invisible as air. But even if Brodie had found the spot, the man had no idea who he was or why he was out there.

He was the only one who knew the answer to that.

Still, he changed his location, moving a little farther away from the lodge. It took awhile to find the spot he wanted, flat and grassy, slightly elevated yet hidden beneath the trees.

He settled into position, took a look through the binoculars around his neck. He could see into the bedrooms on this side of the house, though tonight the curtains were closed in the larger room, the one Brodie occupied. He liked the times he could look at them but they couldn't see him.

Soon, he would move forward with his plan, but not yet.

For now, he would just watch and wait.

Chapter Twenty-Four

The sun was up, the day slipping past. Dylan and Lane were gone, on their way back to Waterside. Frustrated that he had to remain behind while they tried to prove his innocence, Caleb worked with the construction crew. He'd heard them mumbling, talking among themselves. Though no one had made any accusations, he wondered if they thought he was guilty.

Winnie was in the kitchen with Emily, going over some math problems. Just because the rest of the kids her age were out for the summer didn't mean there were no lessons for someone being homeschooled. But Emily loved learning new things so she didn't seem to mind.

Caleb poured himself a cup of coffee from the pot on the counter, walked over to gaze through the window looking into the side yard. He was surprised to see a woman near the gate, bending to let Finn sniff her hand. When the big dog began wagging his tail, she lifted the latch and started walking toward the back door.

Caleb's heart jerked as he recognized the slender blonde. *Jenny.* Setting his mug down on the counter, spilling a little over the rim as he rushed out of the kitchen, he ran down the hall into the mudroom and opened the door.

Standing on the outside step, Jenny smiled up at him. "Hi . . ."

He didn't hesitate, just pulled her into his arms. "God, Jenny. Honey, I'm so glad to see you." Bending his head, he kissed her and prayed she wouldn't pull away. Instead, she kissed him back, then leaned into his chest.

"I heard what happened," she said. "I heard you were arrested."

"I didn't do it, honey. I swear I didn't kill her."

"I don't believe you'd ever kill anyone."

He led her over to a bench beneath a big red cedar and sat down beside her. "After I talked to you that night, I went looking for Holly. I found her in Mad Jack's. I told her to leave us alone and we fought about it." He sighed, rubbed his face. "A lot of people saw us arguing. I didn't stay, and when I left for Wally's, she was fine. I didn't know anything about the murder until the troopers came out to the lodge the next day."

"What are you going to do?"

"Dylan hired an attorney. He got me released from jail, but I'm not supposed to leave Eagle Bay. Dylan and Lane have been digging around, asking questions. They're back in Waterside now."

"Dylan's a good friend. I really like him."

Caleb's mouth edged up. "Just don't like him too much."

Jenny smiled and slid her arms around his neck. "I like you, Caleb. A lot."

Caleb kissed her, soft and slow. He wanted her to know how much she meant to him. When the kiss was over, he ignored the heat in his groin that it was the wrong time to feel.

"Dylan and Lane are working this lead they came up with. Dylan's brother, Nick, helped. They think they may have found someone who could have killed Holly. Unfortunately, they don't have a name."

"Nick's a policeman, right?"

"He was a homicide detective in Anchorage, but he quit. Wants to do something else with his life. Dylan's been trying to keep him out of this as much as he can."

"So they're trying to find this person who might have done it?"

"That's the idea. Even if they do, it's a long shot he's actually the guy who killed her. Hell, it could be anyone."

Jenny reached up and touched his cheek. "Anyone but you."

Caleb caught her hand and kissed the palm. "You shouldn't be out here, Jenny. You're a schoolteacher. You can't be involved with a guy suspected of murder."

"What kind of a person would I be if I didn't stand up for what I believed in? I don't believe you killed that girl. I wanted you to know that, so here I am."

Caleb eased her into his arms and just held her. They sat that way, just listening to the birds, feeling the faint whisper of a breeze. Then he took her hand and they walked for a while, ending up at the old cemetery on the hill. The totem pole watched over it, the faded raven, wings spread, sitting at the top.

Caleb had told Jenny about the fake haunting. As they stood there, he told her about the kids who had done it and why.

"I heard people talking, saying it was all a hoax," she said. "For Dylan's sake and yours, I'm glad it's over."

"We're going to make this place work." His gaze went back to the lodge. He'd grown to love the place as much as Dylan. He wanted to build a house somewhere near, make Eagle Bay his home.

"I know you'll succeed."

He looked down at Jenny, thought of the possibilities of a life that might include her.

Then he thought of Holly Kaplan floating dead in the water and his chest clamped down. "I hope so. All we have to do first is prove I'm not guilty of murder."

Once more behind the wheel of the rented, banged-up Toyota, Dylan drove Lane from the float dock back out to the airport. Finding their theoretical suspect through the rental car agency was a long shot, but a slim chance was better than no chance at all.

If it turned into a dead end, he'd try talking to Maggie. Sooner or later, almost everyone who came to Waterside ended up at the Grizzly Café. Maybe Maggie would remember their suspect. Of course, there was no way to know if the guy the bartender had seen at Mad Jack's had anything to do with the murder.

"Well, this is it." Dylan pulled the car into one of the parking spaces in the airport parking lot and turned off the engine.

"I'm keeping my fingers crossed," Lane said as she climbed out of the car.

Dylan locked the doors and they headed for the metal building that served as the terminal. A couple of Alaska Airlines commuters flew in and out, an express mail plane arrived every three days. The rest were private planes, mostly guys coming in to hunt and fish.

Inside the building, the terminal was empty, the passengers from the last flight having all dispersed. Just the few people who worked there remained, one of whom stood behind the Convenient Rental Car counter.

The little brunette watched as Dylan approached. She was late twenties, pretty, no wedding ring, and she was looking at him the way a woman did who liked what she saw. There was a time not long ago he would have asked her out, might have ended up taking her to bed.

He flicked a glance at Lane. Sunlight slanting through the windows gleamed on her glorious red hair. She smiled and he felt a jolt. He looked at the brunette, thought how little appeal she held for him. How long would it take to forget Lane once she was gone?

"May I help you?" the brunette asked. Her name tag read ELAINE.

"I hope so. My name's Dylan Brodie. This is Lane Bishop. We're looking for someone who might have rented one of your vehicles."

"It would have been a couple of weeks ago," Lane added. "Good-looking guy, brown hair, about Dylan's height."

"What's his name?"

"That's the problem," Dylan said. "The bartender at Mad Jack's mentioned him. Said he was ex-military." There was a flash of recognition in the brunette's dark eyes. "I might want to hire him," Dylan went on. "I've got a security job for a man who knows what he's doing. If I could find him, it might be good for both of us."

The brunette bit her lip. "I don't think I'm supposed to give out customer information."

Lane smiled. "Jobs are hard to find in a place like Waterside. You'd be doing him a favor."

Elaine walked over to her computer, started pulling up rental contracts. "I remember a guy like that." She looked over at Lane. "Tall. Amazing body. Really sexy. I thought he was going to ask me out, but he didn't. He rented the car for two weeks."

"You got a name?" Dylan asked, his adrenaline beginning to pump. But even if they found him, it didn't mean he was a killer.

She spotted the name on the screen, still looked uncertain. "I don't know if I should do this."

Dylan pulled out his wallet, slid a hundred-dollar bill across the counter. "Like I said, this could be good for both of us."

Elaine took the bill, shoved it into the pocket of her slacks, turned back to the computer screen. "Here he is. Dusty Withers. He flew in ten days ago."

"Does it say where he's staying?"

"We don't ask for that information."

"What kind of car did he rent?"

"Jeep Wrangler. Dark green."

"Do you have a home address?" Lane asked.

Elaine looked down at the screen. "1561 Crestline Court, Fort Bragg, North Carolina, 28310. No phone number, though."

"The address makes sense," Dylan said to Lane. "There's a big Army base in Fort Bragg. Maybe he stayed after he left the service."

Lane looked at the girl. "Is there anything else you remember about him?"

"Just that he was hot. I remember he paid cash. We usually insist on credit cards. I had to get an okay from my superior."

"Be hard to steal a car from Waterside," Dylan said. "Roads don't go far in any direction. You can only get a vehicle in and out on the ferry, and it's expensive."

Elaine shrugged. "I guess that's what my boss figured. He didn't want to lose a customer."

"When's Withers due back?" Lane asked.

"Looks like four more days, but he can extend if he sends us more money."

"You got a driver's license number?" Dylan pressed.

Elaine looked back at the screen, wrote the number on a piece of paper, and handed it over. Dylan flashed her a grateful smile. "Thanks, Elaine. You've been a really big help."

"You're welcome." She gave him a friendly smile. "Good luck, Dylan."

They left the terminal and headed back to the Toyota.

"He's still here," Lane said excitedly as she climbed in the car and slammed the door.

"Don't get your hopes too high. There's no reason to believe he's a killer."

"But he could be. He fits our profile. Your brother's a detective and he helped us come up with it. We need to find him."

Dylan slid the key into the ignition but didn't start the car. Pulling his iPhone out of his pocket, he called Nick. A single ring later, his brother answered, a sign he had nothing much going on. Dylan wondered how much longer Nick would last before he went back to doing what he did best.

"Hey, bro, what's up?" Nick said.

"We got a suspect who fits our profile. Haven't located him yet, but we got a name and driver's license number."

"There's that word *we* again."

Dylan ignored the reference to him and Lane. "We need to find this guy, Nick. Can you run a background check?

Maybe he's got a record, something that could help us. Hell, maybe he's got a parking ticket."

"Let me grab a piece of paper."

When Nick came back on the line, Dylan rattled off the name, home address, and license number.

"I've still got friends in the department," Nick said. "I'll give one of them a call. How's Caleb holding up?"

"He's pacing the floor, worried as hell and trying not to show it."

"Then I better get this done. Back to you soon." The line went dead. Dylan pocketed the phone.

"How long do you think it'll take him?" Lane asked.

"Longer than it would have before he left the force. In the meantime, what do you say we make a stop at the Grizzly Café? Everyone in town goes in there. Maybe Maggie can tell us where to find Dusty Withers."

The last place Lane wanted to go was the Grizzly Café. She didn't like Maggie Ridell. The woman had condemned Caleb without a moment's hesitation. And as much as Lane hated to admit it, she was jealous of the buxom, blue-eyed blonde. Maggie Ridell was clearly interested in Dylan. And Maggie would be here after Lane was gone.

Still, Dylan was right. Everyone wound up at the local café. There was a good chance Dusty Withers had been in at one time or another.

The bell rang above the door as they walked inside. Instead of heading for a booth, Dylan led Lane up to the counter. Only a few minutes passed before Maggie sashayed up on the opposite side in front of Dylan.

She cocked a golden eyebrow. "Well, look who's here."

Dylan smiled. "I hope I'm still welcome."

Maggie smiled in return. "Of course you're welcome. You didn't murder anyone."

"Neither did Caleb," Dylan said. "I wish you'd at least give him the benefit of the doubt."

The woman's full lips tightened. "He was sleeping with Holly, then sneaking around with that schoolteacher on the side. They fought about it and he killed her."

"Are you sure about that? You don't think maybe Holly was fantasizing, hoping to get back with Caleb? You don't think it's possible what she said never actually happened?"

Maggie sighed. "I don't know. Someone killed her. Poor little thing was so crazy about him. I felt sorry for her."

Dylan tipped his head toward Lane, sitting on the vinyl-covered stool beside him. "You remember Lane Bishop."

Maggie nodded. "From Beverly Hills. I remember. Nice to see you." But the look in her eyes said she couldn't wait for Lane to leave.

Dylan turned over his white china mug and shoved it toward her. Maggie grabbed the coffeepot off the burner and filled his cup.

"Coffee?" Maggie asked Lane.

"Please." She turned over her mug. "Is there any chance Holly was seeing someone else?"

Maggie poured the dark brew into the cup. "I don't think so. I never saw her with anyone else."

"Did she ever mention a man named Dusty Withers?"

"Not that I recall."

"Maybe you saw him in here," Dylan said. "Flew in from Fort Bragg. Tall, good-looking. Ex-military."

"Sounds like Holly's type, all right, but I don't recall seeing him." She set the coffeepot back down on the burner. "You think he killed her?"

"At this point we just want to talk to him."

"I'll keep an eye out." Maggie shook her head. "What happened to Holly . . . that just wasn't right. This guy comes in, I'll call you."

"That'd be great."

She looked over at Lane. "So when will the lodge be ready to open?" Translation: *So when will your job be finished and you'll be out of Dylan's life for good?*

"We should have the interior finished by the middle of August," Lane said, wishing August weren't so near.

"I'm hoping to have guests in by the end of the month," Dylan added. "Tourist season'll pretty well be over, but we should get some fishermen, maybe a few hunters."

"I'd like to see it after it's finished," Maggie said. She sliced Lane a glance that said, *As soon as you're out of the picture.*

Dylan finished the last of his coffee, set the mug back down on the counter. "Once we're done, I'll be happy to show you around. Maybe you can send me some customers."

Maggie smiled. "You bet I will." With a wave over her shoulder, her hips swaying in the tight jeans stretched over her voluptuous behind, she headed off to take care of another customer.

Lane slid down from the stool as Dylan tossed money on the counter for the bill, and they left the café. Back in the Toyota, she pulled the seat belt across her lap and shoved the buckle into the slot. "So how are we going to find him?"

"I think it's about time we got some help. Let's head over to the police department. I've met the chief a couple of times. We've got a name now. Maybe he'll be willing to help us run this guy down."

It sounded like a good idea. They could certainly use

some help. Proving Caleb's innocence came first, but Lane still had a lot of work to finish if Dylan wanted the lodge to open the end of August. As soon as it was ready, she would be heading back home.

It was a depressing thought.

Chapter Twenty-Five

The police department was on Monrovia Street near the south end of town. Dylan's cell rang as he drove the Toyota into the parking lot and turned off the engine. Pulling the phone out of his pocket, he checked the caller ID, recognized his brother Nick's number.

"I'm here," he said. "What have you got?"

"I haven't got jack shit. The license is a fake. No Dusty Withers. No Fort Bragg address."

"Son of a bitch."

"Calm down, there's some good news in this."

"Yeah, what is it?"

"I think you've got yourself a viable suspect. This guy's off the grid. There has to be a reason. Maybe he's got a record. Maybe he's wanted for something. Whatever it is, he doesn't want his real identity known."

"You're right. Maybe that'll be enough to get the cops to take a look at someone other than Caleb."

"And there's something else. That fake license was good enough to get him on a plane, get him a rental car. Odds are he had it made—which means he had to know who to pay in order to get it done. I'm definitely thinking military, and I'd say Special Ops. Rangers, D-boys, SEALs. Those guys know how to get whatever it is they need."

Dylan thought of the man who had murdered Holly. The way he had handled the body, the way he had managed to just disappear.

"That makes sense. My next stop's the chief of police. We'll see what he has to say."

"Keep me posted."

"Will do." Dylan ended the call and stuck the phone back in his pocket. "The ID was fake. No help there. But Nick thinks this could be our guy. He also thinks he could have been Special Ops."

Lane's eyes widened. "Like a Navy SEAL?"

"Or Delta Force, maybe a Ranger. Unfortunately, if that's the case, it's going to make catching him a whole lot harder."

"God, Dylan."

They got out of the car in front of the police department and headed for the door. There were only sixteen officers on the Waterside force. As they walked inside, a female officer in a dark blue uniform came out from behind her desk and walked up to the counter.

"May I help you?" She was black-haired with Asian features, in her early thirties, and a little overweight.

"I'm Dylan Brodie. This is Lane Bishop. We'd like to see Chief Wills." He'd met Frank Wills a couple of times, once at the Chamber of Commerce when he was working on plans to promote business for the lodge. "It's in regard to the Holly Kaplan murder."

"If you'll wait here, I'll let him know you want to see him."

A few minutes later, they were ushered into his office.

A big man with salt-and-pepper hair, Wills rose from behind his desk.

"Brodie. Good to see you. Been awhile."

"Couple of months. Trying to get the lodge up and running has been taking up most of my time. Frank, this is Lane Bishop. She's helping me get the place ready to open."

"Nice to meet you." He turned back to Dylan. "Officer Holder says you're here in regard to the Kaplan murder."

"That's right."

Wills indicated the pair of chairs in front of his desk. "Why don't you have a seat and tell me what's going on."

Dylan flicked a glance at Lane, received an encouraging smile. "I realize Caleb Wolfe is your primary suspect and I understand your thinking. But ten days ago, a man with a fake driver's license flew into Waterside, a man we believe may have murdered Holly."

"Go on."

"The bartender at Mad Jack's mentioned seeing him there a couple of times before the murder. He's about my size, dark-haired, apparently served in the military. Maybe Special Operations."

"He rented a car at the airport," Lane added. "The young woman who works there said he was extremely good-looking. The kind of man Holly might have left the bar with the night she was killed."

"Were they seen together?"

"Not that we've been able to confirm," Dylan said. "Doesn't mean they didn't know each other."

"What else have you got?"

"That's about it so far. But the fact he's using an alias ought to at least make him a person of interest to the police."

"So you're basing your entire theory on the fact the man

is traveling with a fake ID." He frowned. "By the way, how did you come up with that information?"

Dylan wasn't about to cause his brother any problems. "A friend with connections."

"But you aren't saying who."

Dylan passed over the slip of paper with the name Dusty Withers, his fake address, and the driver's license number written on it. "You can check it out yourself."

"I'm happy to look into this. But I've got to tell you, Dylan, in most of these cases, the killer is someone the victim knows. A husband or boyfriend. In this case, Caleb Wolfe was known to have been seeing the Kaplan girl. He fought with her the night she was murdered."

"He wasn't seeing her. And when he left the bar, Holly was alive."

"That's right. Then he waited for her outside and convinced her to have sex with him before he killed her."

"That isn't what happened."

"You don't think your friend Wolfe has anything to do with this?"

"Not a chance. Caleb Wolfe is no murderer. You need to find this guy, Chief. Before something happens to somebody else."

Frank Wills studied the piece of paper, then rose from behind his desk, an imposing man though clearly he wasn't convinced. "We'll follow up on this. But odds are this guy has a warrant out somewhere he's trying to dodge or, like a thousand other people, just wants to disappear in Alaska for a while. Wolfe and Kaplan have a history. In the end, that's usually what this kind of crime is about."

Dylan didn't say more. He could read a man well enough to know Frank Wills had made up his mind. Dylan also believed the police chief wouldn't ignore the lead he had been given. Maybe they'd get lucky and something would turn up.

In the meantime, he had every intention of finding the man who called himself Dusty Withers. Those hunches he got were warning him loud and clear this guy was a killer.

They stopped in at a couple more places before they were ready to head back to the lodge. The Pelican Pub, the Silver Salmon Bar and Grill, the mercantile, even the Sea View Motel. As they drove toward the float dock, they stopped in at the grocery store. If Withers wasn't staying in town, he'd need supplies. Surely someone in the store had seen him.

But no one recognized the name Dusty Withers, or had seen anyone who looked like him.

It was a solemn trip back to the lodge. Lane could read the tension in Dylan's shoulders, knew his worry had increased. Her own frustration had her nerves strung taut.

It was late afternoon by the time the plane descended and skimmed over the surface of the water. Then Dylan slowed the engines and the floatplane eased up to the Eagle Bay dock. Paddy O'Ryan came out to help Dylan secure the aircraft while Lane headed back to the house.

The day had been long and they still had no idea where to find their suspect. Lane was edgy and restless as she walked through the door. She needed something to do that would occupy her thoughts and ease some of the tension running through her.

Collecting her easel and paints, she started toward the front porch, then changed her mind. She had painted the mountains across the sea a dozen times. Instead, she headed in the opposite direction, carrying her painting gear along the trail to the old cemetery on the hillside.

She wanted to capture the view up the mountain, with the old totem pole and the tombstones as part of the scene.

She set up the easel and went to work mixing paint and applying it to canvas. In minutes, she found herself submerged in a world of vibrant colors, the challenge of capturing the essence of the landscape that went beyond what the eye saw into the realm of what the heart felt.

Her knowledge of the murders, and the innocent men who had been hanged and buried in the graveyard, made the painting take on the subtle blue and gray tones of grief. Time drifted past as each stroke slid onto the surface, the work absorbing her completely, the way it always did.

She had no idea how long she'd sat on the tree stump, her gaze fixed on the old wooden fence around the cemetery and the rugged mountains behind it. She only began to notice that her back was aching and her bottom felt numb.

Getting up from the stump, she stretched her stiff muscles and glanced around. She suddenly had the oddest feeling someone was watching her. She looked up the mountain into the woods, but saw no one there.

Turning, she glanced down the hill toward the lodge, spotted Emily sitting on a log a few feet away, Finn lying quietly at her feet. Lane wondered how long the child had been there watching her. Emily rose as Lane walked toward her.

"I'm not finished with the picture, yet," Lane said with a smile. "It'll take me a while to get it exactly the way I want."

Emily looked up at her, then walked over to the painting. She pointed to the grave markers in the cemetery, then back to the canvas. There was something infinitely sad in the little girl's face.

Lane suddenly knew what it was. "You're thinking of your mother," she said as Emily walked back to her. "You must miss her very much."

The little girl's eyes filled. When the tears spilled onto her cheeks, she quickly dashed them away.

"It's okay to miss her," Lane said, going down on a knee beside her. "My mother died, too, and I miss her very much." She reached out and hugged her. "Your mom's gone, but you've got a father who loves you very much."

Emily's features crumpled. Looking stricken, she turned and raced back down the hill toward the lodge. Trembling, Finn stood watching her, his shaggy head turning from Emily to Lane and back again, uncertain whether to follow the child or stay with his mistress.

"Go ahead," Lane said softly, her heart aching for the little girl. "Emily needs you." She pointed toward the small retreating figure running down the path, and Finn bolted after her.

Not sure what had just happened, Lane sighed and walked back to her easel. But her focus was no longer on the painting but on the little girl. Gathering her easel, palette, and canvas, she followed Emily back to the lodge. Whatever was going on with the child, no one but Emily knew what it was.

If only she would talk. Only then would Emily and the father who loved her be able to work things out.

Lane thought of Dylan. She and Dylan couldn't really talk, either. Not about their emotions, their feelings for each other. She knew he cared for her. She didn't know how much.

And she was completely certain Dylan didn't know that she had fallen in love with him. Lane had only just lately managed to figure that out herself.

* * *

"So how did it go?" Wiping her hands on a dish towel, Winnie walked toward him across the kitchen.

"We made some progress," Dylan said. "The guy we're looking for flew into town a couple of weeks ago. Unfortunately, he's using an alias. We asked around, but we weren't able to find him."

"Did you talk to the police?"

He nodded. "Chief Wills." He walked over and poured a cup of coffee, took a sip. "They still like Caleb for the murder, but I think Frank will follow up, at least try to find the guy we told him about." He glanced around. "Where's Lane?"

Winnie frowned at the inquiry. "She took her easel and paints and went up the hill toward the cemetery. She's been gone a while. Emily took Finn and went to look for her."

Unease trickled through him. He started to leave, go check on them. The cemetery wasn't that far away and men were outside working, but still . . .

Winnie's words stopped him in the doorway. "If you aren't careful, Dylan, that little girl of yours is going to get hurt all over again. She's falling in love with Lane—just like you are."

His chest clamped down. "I'm not falling in love with Lane. We're just friends."

Winnie cocked a silver eyebrow. "That's what you're telling yourself? You're just friends with benefits?"

"Something like that." But deep down he knew it was more. And Emily wasn't the only one who was going to get hurt.

"Lane won't be here much longer," he said. "Another few weeks at the most."

"What about Emily?"

"Dammit, Winnie. What am I supposed to do? I brought Lane up here to do a job. She's planning to see it through. You want me to fire her, send her back to Beverly Hills? I've got money, but not an endless supply. I need to get this place up and running." But the real truth was, he didn't want Lane to leave—at least not until their time together was over.

The older woman sighed. "I know you've got responsibilities, a business to get started. It isn't your fault. It's not Lane's fault, either. I don't suppose either of you planned to get in quite so deep."

Hell no, he hadn't. He had no idea what he'd been planning when he got the idea of hiring her. He'd wanted her. She was good at her job and he needed the help. Bringing her to Alaska had seemed like a good idea at the time.

Unfortunately, the attraction between them was even more powerful than he had suspected. Now he was in over his head and barely treading water. He couldn't afford to let himself get in any deeper. As soon as the lodge was finished, Lane would be leaving, returning to the life she'd had before. A life that suited her as this one never would.

Whatever happened, he couldn't afford to make the same mistake he had made with Mariah.

And Winnie was right. If he wasn't extremely careful, Emily would be the one to suffer. Sweet Jesus, he wished he knew what to do.

At the moment, he just needed to find her, make sure she was safe. Dylan felt a sweep of relief when he saw her walking through the back door.

It changed to uncertainty when he saw Emily holding on to her hand.

* * *

The evening meal was stilted. Caleb was silent and brooding as he passed around the platter of roast beef, taking a smaller portion than usual. Dylan's mood seemed equally bad.

The sun was still bright when supper was over. Deciding to get some fresh air, Lane collected her gear and returned to the cemetery to work on the painting she had started that afternoon. She'd only been working half an hour when Dylan arrived, his mood still not improved.

"I don't want you up here this late in the day. The animals start moving around, foraging for food. I don't want a moose wandering down or maybe a bear."

Her head came up. "A bear? You think a bear might come here?"

For an instant, his mouth edged up. "Lots of bears here. This is Alaska."

"I know, but . . . but the lodge is just over there." She pointed down the hill.

"Now that I think of it, I guess you need to learn the difference between a black bear and a brown bear. That way if you run into one, you'll know what to do."

"I know what to do—run like hell and hope I get away."

Dylan laughed. He went on to explain that a grizzly had a hump and a dish-shaped face. "If it's a griz, you freeze. If he charges, you get down on the trail and curl yourself into a ball, put your hands over the back of your neck."

"And kiss your ass good-bye."

He grinned, shook his head. "With a black bear you make yourself as big as you can. Be aggressive. Try to scare him away. Most of the time, it works."

"Most of the time?"

Dylan's mouth edged up, but he made no more comment. His brilliant blue eyes had moved to the easel. "Wow, that's an amazing piece of work. When you said you could paint, you weren't kidding."

She smiled. "You like it?"

"It's beautiful, Lane. You're a fabulous artist. I saw that talent in some of your other work, but this piece . . . I don't know. In some way it's disturbing."

"It's the cemetery. This place has a soul." She glanced around at the old wooden grave markers. "I can feel it."

Dylan stared at the canvas. "I believe you. It shows in your painting." Over the years, the old grave markers had settled deep into the earth. There was something so forlorn about them, it touched a place deep inside.

His gaze moved toward the horizon. "The light's beginning to fade. You ready to come in?"

She sighed, hating to stop. "I suppose." Dylan helped her carry the easel and paints back to their place in the mudroom. But as the evening progressed and they went upstairs to get ready for bed, his dark mood returned.

They made love, but it was different this time. The hunger was there, sparking into a wildfire between them, but the emotional connection she always felt with him was over-powered by the physical act. Whatever time they had left wasn't enough.

Dylan had begun to distance himself.

Lane told herself she should do the same. But the hard truth was, it was already too late.

Chapter Twenty-Six

It was late in the night when the cry of an animal awakened her, the deep throaty howl of a wolf. She had never seen one except in a zoo, but there was no mistaking the sound that sent a faint tremor down her spine.

Dylan slept peacefully beside her. She knew how worried he was, knew he had been sleeping fitfully all week. He was quiet now and she didn't want to wake him. Slipping silently out of bed, she grabbed her robe off the chair, slid it on, and padded over to the window, pulling the curtains partly open.

She loved looking out at the endless vistas outlined in the moonlight, the peaks of the trees silhouetted in the distance, the amazing wash of stars, sparkling like jewels in the black night sky.

She stood there awhile, soaking up the beauty of a land that was unlike anyplace she had ever been before. The kind of place you never forgot, that stayed forever in some private place in your heart.

The wolf howled again, his call drifting away on the soft night breeze. She could hear the hoot of an owl in a distant pine tree.

Lane yawned, beginning to feel sleepy. She started to turn away from the window and return to bed when a faint movement caught her eye. Shadows were shifting in the distance—a lone figure, standing at the edge of the forest, blending in as if he were part of the night.

Her heartbeat quickened. She told herself it was one of the kids from Yeil. Kids loved to do the exact opposite of whatever they'd been told to do. The shadowy figure stepped away from the trunk of a tree. His form long and lean, he moved fluidly, effortlessly, with an almost ghostly grace.

She watched him fading into the darkness, blinked and he was gone. She could almost convince herself he had never really been there.

She turned toward the bed. Dylan was sleeping so soundly. And whoever had been out there was gone. Not even Dylan would be able to find him, at least not in the dark.

Lane shrugged out of her robe and slipped back into bed, easing closer to Dylan's warmth. She thought of the man at the edge of the forest. Nothing about him reminded her of Alex or Jared, the boys from Yeil.

Still, there was something about the way he moved. Something strangely familiar. She thought of the man they searched for, Dusty Withers. She didn't know anyone by that name.

But there *was* someone, a man named Kyle Whitaker. Dark hair. About Dylan's height, his body equally lean and fit.

She had dated him for a very brief time. A case of bad judgment, she'd told herself when she had ended their involvement at the end of the second week. She hadn't gone to bed with Kyle, though he had been amazingly good-looking.

A memory tugged at the edge of her mind. Had Kyle mentioned a friend named Dusty? She worked to bring the memory into focus, but it remained elusive.

A shiver went through her.

It was ridiculous. Even if there were similarities between Kyle Whitaker and their suspect, Kyle was in jail. A week after she'd last seen him, he'd been arrested for beating a man unconscious after a Lakers basketball game. He was serving a six-month sentence.

It wasn't him.

Couldn't be.

Kyle wouldn't even know she was in Alaska.

But as she tried to fall asleep, her mind kept circling back to the man in the forest. What was it about him that made her think of Kyle?

In the morning, she was going to tell Dylan what she had seen. She would also make a phone call to Haley. Haley was married to Dylan's cousin, Ty, who was a private investigator. He could make certain Kyle was still locked up in jail.

She wasn't about to mention anything about the man to Dylan. Not until she had information that pointed in Kyle's direction. Dylan had more than enough to worry about already.

The plan eased her mind. Still, it was more than an hour before she fell asleep.

Sitting at his desk in the office, Dylan looked up to see Lane walking into the room. Some of the accessories, lamps and shades, a few small tables, even some throw rugs, had arrived yesterday. One of the crew had brought them in from town, and though they wouldn't be placed until the rest of the furniture arrived, Lane had been busy making sure the boxes got into the right rooms.

He'd told himself he was glad she wasn't around.

"There you are," she said as she walked into the office. "You missed breakfast. I've been looking for you all morning."

He'd had some chores to do. But mostly, he'd been avoiding her. He needed to put some distance between them. He should have eased back long before now.

"I had some things to take care of outside. Winnie kept a plate warm for me. What's going on?"

She looked like she didn't want to tell him, like she needed to build up her courage.

"Whoever was watching us before? He was out there again last night."

He came up out of his chair. "You saw him? Why didn't you wake me up?"

She nervously bit her lip. "It happened so fast and you were sleeping so deeply. One minute he was there, the next he was gone. I figured it was the boys from Yeil. Besides, there was no way you could have found him in the dark."

He raked a hand through his hair. "Those f-ing kids again. They gave me their word. I'm not putting up with it. I'm calling Payuk. He'll rattle their chains but good." He reached for the cell phone lying on top of his desk.

"Dylan, wait. Maybe it was someone else."

"It wasn't someone else. Those kids were spying on us for weeks. They have no business being out there at night."

He punched the SEND button, got Jacob Payuk on the line, told him what had happened.

For several seconds, Payuk remained silent. "You are certain it was one of the boys from Yeil?"

"I don't know for sure. But they were here before. I don't want them out there again."

"I will speak to them. But these are good boys. I do not believe they would give you their word and then break it."

A thread of unease slid through him. "I need the truth, Jacob. Someone was out there. I'm just trying to keep my family safe."

"I understand. I will find out." Payuk signed off and Dylan hung up the phone.

"What . . . what did he say?"

"He says the boys wouldn't break their word."

Lane wet her lips. She seemed so uncertain; the shot of lust he felt looking at that pretty mouth gave way to worry. "What is it, Lane? What aren't you telling me?"

"It's nothing. I'm sure when your cousin calls me back—"

"You called Ty? Why the hell would you be calling my cousin?"

"I called Haley. Ty was there when I phoned. I asked him to help me find out if . . . if—"

"If what, Lane?"

She sighed. "I knew someone back in L.A. Seeing that man in the woods last night . . . there was something about him that seemed familiar. The way he moved, maybe. Or the way he just sort of vanished into the night. I don't know why, but it made me think of . . . of . . . this guy named Kyle."

Dylan felt the heat rising at the back of his neck. "Who

the fuck is Kyle? Some old boyfriend?" He hated the rush of jealousy, fought to ignore it. "Spill it, Lane. I'm not playing twenty questions."

She sank down in one of the office chairs. "Kyle Whitaker was never my boyfriend. I went out with him a few times over a couple of weeks."

"You sleep with him?"

"No. After a few dates, I began to sense something about him was a little off. He couldn't stay focused, lost track of the conversation. He kept saying how perfectly we were matched. I didn't think we matched at all, so I broke it off. A week later, Kyle went to jail for assault. As far as I know he's still there."

"But you want Ty to make sure he is."

She nodded, looked miserable. "It can't be him, Dylan. He wouldn't even know I'm up here and even if he found out, he'd have no reason to come after me."

"Except that he thinks you're his perfect match." And for some unfathomable reason that annoyed him. When had he started thinking Lane belonged to him? Christ, she was only going to be there a few more weeks.

"Kyle's in jail," she said firmly. "Ty's going to call and tell us that."

He hoped like hell that was true, but when he looked over at Lane, he could see she wasn't completely sure.

A sudden thought occurred to him. "Wait a minute. You aren't thinking this guy could be our suspect?"

She glanced away. "We don't even know if it's Kyle."

"What else do you know about him? Was he in the military?"

"I don't know."

"What's he look like? Good-looking, I imagine, or you wouldn't have been interested in him in the first place."

She just nodded.

"My height, right? Dark hair?"

She nodded again. "It's just a coincidence. I never even thought of it until last night."

"But now that you have, we need to know."

Her cell rang just then, and she started scrambling to pull it out of her pocket. Dylan resisted the urge to snatch it out of her hand.

"Hi," she said. She flashed Dylan a glance, and as the conversation continued, the color drained from her face. "Thank you, Ty. I appreciate your help."

Before she could disconnect, Dylan grabbed the phone. "He's out of jail, right?"

"Well, nice to talk to you, too, cuz. I'm doing great. Thanks for asking."

"Cut the bullshit. He's out, right?"

"Got out three weeks ago. Good behavior."

"Any prior arrests?"

"Nope. Clean until a fistfight after a basketball game. Fight got out of hand. Whitaker went to jail." He chuckled. "Lane said someone was peeking in your windows. I guess she has an admirer."

"I guess maybe she does. I also guess she didn't tell you that besides being a Peeping Tom, this guy might be a murderer."

Dylan didn't miss the tension that crept into his cousin's voice. "You gonna need some help?"

"Thanks for the offer, but not at the moment. I do need a photo. We need to see if Whitaker is using the alias Dusty Withers."

"I'll send his booking photo to your cell phone."

"Thanks."

"Don't hesitate to call if you need me. I owe you one, remember?"

A couple of months back, Dylan had helped Ty with a

case he and Haley had been trying to solve. Dylan had managed to take a bullet for his efforts. "You're right, you do. I'll let you know if I need you." Dylan hung up the phone.

"He . . . he can't be the man in the forest," Lane said, her voice little more than a whisper.

"But there's a chance he is." His phone chimed as the arrest photo came in. Dylan pulled up a picture of Kyle Whitaker in a prison jumpsuit. "He's got dark hair, but he doesn't look anything like me." He hated the rush of relief he felt knowing Lane wasn't attracted to him because of some joker in L.A.

He held it up for her to see. "Orange just isn't his color."

Her pretty lips faintly curved. Dylan thought of her in his bed the night before, her sweet cries as he'd moved inside her. Jesus, what was wrong with him?

"He's kind of a pretty boy," Lane said. She cast him a teasing glance. "I prefer the ruggedly handsome type."

Dylan leaned down and kissed her. "That's good to hear." He looked at the picture. "How did you meet this guy?"

"He works in construction. He was on the crew doing a remodel down the block from Modern Design. I met him in a bar across the street. Sometimes I meet my girlfriends there for a drink after work." Her smile slowly faded. "We still don't know if Kyle is Dusty Withers."

Dylan's jaw tightened. "Not yet, but we're going to find out."

Lane looked down at the picture and her eyes filled. "If Kyle's out there because of me, I've got to leave. I can't put all of you in danger."

He caught her shoulders. "You aren't going anywhere. Not yet. It's possible this guy killed Holly. I'm not sending you back where he can get to you. We're going to catch him right here."

When she started shaking her head, Dylan's hold tightened. "Listen to me, baby. This isn't your fault. Just because you went out with this lunatic a couple of times doesn't make you responsible for what he may or may not have done."

For several long moments, those green eyes remained on his face. A shuddering breath whispered out. "Even if it's Kyle, he might not have killed Holly."

"That's right. At the moment it's all speculation. We've got his picture now. We'll see if the bartender and the girl at the airport recognize Kyle as Dusty Withers."

"If he's here, how did he find me?"

"Good question. We need to know more about him. Once we put it all together, we'll talk to the police, tell them what's going on."

Just then, Caleb walked into the office. His black eyes zeroed in on Dylan's stony features, then traveled to the tears on Lane's cheeks. "While you're at it, maybe you'd better tell *me* what the hell is going on."

Dylan spent the next few minutes filling Caleb in on the man Lane had seen outside the lodge last night.

"Could be it's one of the kids from Yeil," Dylan said, "but Jacob doesn't think so. There's a chance it's a man named Kyle Whitaker that Lane knew in L.A."

One of Caleb's black eyebrows went up. "That so?"

"Not in the biblical sense," Dylan said darkly, bringing an amused smile to Caleb's lips.

Dylan ignored him. "The problem is Whitaker fits our

suspect's description, so he could have been the guy who killed Holly."

"Was he ever in the service?" Caleb asked.

"I don't remember him talking about it," Lane said, "but I only went out with him a couple of times so I really don't know."

"Any way we can find out?" Caleb asked. "The bartender mentioned it, right? And Withers used Fort Bragg as the address on his fake driver's license. Fort Bragg's an Army base."

"I'm on it." Dylan picked up his cell and punched in his brother's number. "I need another favor," he said when Nick picked up. "We've got a name. Kyle Whitaker. Turns out he may have followed Lane up here. He's got a record for assault in L.A., just got out three weeks ago. Can you see if he's been in the Army? He could have been stationed at Fort Bragg."

"I'll find out. Stay close to a phone, I'll call you back." Nick ended the call.

"You gonna phone the police?" Caleb asked.

"Not yet. We need to get our ducks in a row. Chief Wills is going to need convincing, something more than we've got right now."

"Even if Whitaker is Withers, there's no connection between him and Holly. Nothing but the fact the bartender saw him in Mad Jack's a couple of times."

"First things first," Dylan said. He reached for Lane's hand, tugged her over beside him. "I'm going to Waterside. We need to show this photo around."

"I want to go with you."

His gaze sharpened on her face. "Oh, you're going, all right. Until we know exactly what's going on, I'm not letting you out of my sight."

Chapter Twenty-Seven

It was noon by the time they were ready to make the short flight to Waterside. While they were gone, Caleb was going to look around, see if he could find any sign of the man Lane had seen outside the lodge last night. Paddy O'Ryan had volunteered to help.

"Caleb's a helluva tracker," Dylan said. "He may be able to find something."

"We don't really know who's out there. If he and Paddy go after him, it could be dangerous."

"They'll be armed. They'll be all right."

A chill slid through her. Kyle Whitaker had gone to prison for aggravated assault after beating a man so badly he had wound up in the hospital. She couldn't stand to think of something happening to Caleb or Paddy.

On the other hand, they needed to know what they were facing. Maybe the trip to Waterside would give them the information they needed. In the meantime, she prayed the men would be safe.

"Let's get going," Dylan said, guiding her toward the door.

The sun was overhead by the time they started down

the hill toward the float dock, where the plane sat bobbing in the water. They had almost reached it when Lane spotted Emily running toward them, her cheeks flushed and her eyes wide. She slid to a stop in front of them.

"F-f-f-f." She pointed madly and kept repeating the sound. "F-f-f-f." But the word remained stuck in her throat.

Lane followed the direction of the small shaking finger—the side yard. "Finn! Oh, God, Dylan." She started running. Dylan scooped the little girl up in his arms and ran after her. When they reached the yard, Lane saw that the gate was open and Finn was gone.

Emily pointed wildly.

"Did you see where he went?" Lane asked, worry pouring through her.

Emily shook her head and started pointing at the open gate.

Dylan set her on her feet. "It's all right, honey. He probably just wandered off. We'll find him."

Winnie must have heard the commotion. She opened the mudroom door and walked out on the porch, Caleb and Paddy right behind her. "What's going on?"

"Finn got out," Dylan said. "We need to find him."

But Lane was already running up the hill toward the cemetery. "Finn! Finn! Come on, boy! Finn, Finn!"

Dylan started calling and so did Winnie, Paddy, and Caleb. They branched out in different directions, Winnie circling the house with Emily, while Caleb and Paddy moved off into the woods. Lane headed for the cemetery, hoping the dog had gone back to the place where she had been painting. But when she arrived, there was no sign of Finn.

Her worry mounted. It wasn't like him to take off that way. She thought of the moose and bears Dylan had mentioned. Had Finn run after some wild animal? Had the animal attacked him? Was he lying in the forest some-where, hurt and unable to get home?

"Finn! Finn!" Her throat tightened. Finn hadn't been raised in the wilds of Alaska. The dog was as out of his element up here as she was. What had she been thinking to bring him with her? She should have known something could happen. It wasn't safe for a dog up here.

She stopped when Dylan came up behind her. She hadn't realized she was crying until he turned her into his arms.

"It's all right, baby. We'll find him. He's been here long enough to know where the lodge is. Even if he got lost chasing a deer, he should be able to find his way back."

She looked up at him. "Do you think so?"

He brushed a tear from her cheek. "Yeah, I do."

"He doesn't belong here. It's too dangerous out in the woods. I should have left him in L.A."

Something moved across Dylan's features. "Maybe. But he's here now and we need to find him." Turning, he headed farther up the trail, calling Finn's name.

Lane fell in behind him. What she'd said wasn't true. Finn loved it here. He was the happiest she had ever seen him. She loved it here, too. Maybe she and Finn didn't know their way around, didn't know one animal from the next, didn't know how to survive in the forest. That didn't mean they couldn't learn.

A kernel of something slowly broke open inside her. What if she stayed? Would Dylan want her here? Could she make him happy? Could she be the mother Emily never had? Was she up to the long winters and the remoteness?

She didn't know the answer.

She thought of the dog she loved and the lump returned

to her throat. "Finn! Finn!" She continued up the trail behind Dylan. If Finn was hurt or dead . . .

She shouldn't have brought him, she thought again.

Maybe she shouldn't have come up here in the first place.

Lane just wasn't sure anymore.

He watched from his place in the high branches of a tree. Since he was wearing camo and hidden by the heavy pine boughs, they walked right beneath him, searching, calling the animal's name.

Damn dog. He hadn't wanted to hurt him. He was usually in the yard in the daytime, in the house at night. But today one of the construction workers had left the gate open. The dog had spotted a squirrel on the other side of the fence and taken off after it. The squirrel had escaped, but the dog had picked up Kyle's scent. The stupid beast had tracked him all the way to the cave he had been using as a day camp, that he'd slept in a couple of nights when he hadn't felt like hiking back to the abandoned cabin four miles away.

He'd hated to kill the damn dog.

You shouldn't have done it, the voice said. *He was only a helpless creature.*

"I didn't have any choice. He tracked me to the cave. He could do it again."

So what now? Lane doesn't want you. She's found someone else. You need to leave her alone.

Jealousy burned through him. He couldn't stand to think of Lane with Brodie. Couldn't stand to think of the man touching her, making love to her.

"It's my fault," he said. "If I hadn't gotten into that fight, we'd still be together. I just need to spend some time with her, make her remember how good we were together."

The voice in his head started laughing. *You're a fool, Kyle.*

His features tightened. "I came here to get her. I'm not leaving without her."

It hadn't been hard to find her. He'd hacked into her e-mail before he'd been released from prison, found her on Facebook. He'd started making plans even then. Now he was here, ready to execute those plans. He'd done the necessary recon, knew the area for miles around.

The cabin he had been staying in was only a few miles down the road. It was clean and nicely furnished, a hunting cabin sitting empty, at least for now.

He glanced over at the well-oiled .30-06 he had found in a locked cabinet in the tiny bedroom. When he'd come to Alaska, he hadn't expected to need a weapon. But things had changed. He knew better than most how important it was to be prepared.

Just a few more days, he told himself as the small group passed beneath him on their way back down the hill.

They hadn't found the dog. He didn't think they would, considering he had left its body at the bottom of a ravine.

Now he needed to get rid of Dylan Brodie. As soon as Brodie was out of the way, he would come for Lane.

They searched for Finn until dark. Caleb found some footprints, but they disappeared into the rocks near the top of the hill. By the time they returned to the lodge, all of them were exhausted.

Emily was inconsolable. She had closed herself up in her room and lay in bed weeping. Nothing Lane or Dylan could say could make her feel better. Lane knew exactly how the little girl felt.

She looked up as Dylan walked over to where she sat in the great hall, staring at the hearth. It was as empty and cold as her heart.

"Come on, baby. In the morning, I'll get some of the crew and we'll start looking again." He reached out a hand, and Lane took it, let him help her up from the couch.

"It's a hard life here," he said as he led her toward the hallway. "People freeze to death, get lost in the woods and die of exposure. Animals live by survival of the fittest. None of them die a natural death. I'm sorry this happened. I hope we get lucky and find him. But at least you can see why it would . . ." He broke off, glanced away.

"Why it would never work between us?"

Those incredible blue eyes swung to her face. "Yes."

Lane made no reply. Maybe he was right. Maybe she could never make it in the harsh Alaskan environment.

She swallowed past the lump forming in her throat. "I appreciate all you did today. I know you had more important things to worry about than finding a dog."

He caught her chin, forced her eyes to his face. "Finn's your family. While you're here, he's part of our family, too. We'll try to find him again tomorrow."

She just nodded. Her throat was aching. Finn was lost and soon she was going to lose Dylan. She was in love with him. She hadn't considered even the possibility of that happening when she had taken the job in Alaska.

She had given herself this time with Dylan and this incredible adventure. She had finally put her grief for Jason aside. Now she would grieve just as deeply for Dylan.

Sliding her arms around his neck, she went up on her

toes and kissed him. Dylan drew her against his chest and deepened the kiss. She could feel the hunger, knew he wanted her, and yet it was the most achingly tender kiss she had ever known.

She reached for his hand, started leading him down the hall toward the back stairs. She needed him tonight, needed him to hold her, make love to her. Neither of them spoke as they headed for his rooms upstairs.

If they weren't being so quiet, she might not have heard them: the soft, muffled cries of pain she knew belonged to Finn.

"Finn!" Lane raced into the mudroom, unlocked the door, and jerked it open. They had left the gate open in the hope he might find his way home. Injured and bleeding, he had.

Finn lay on the porch, his chest rising and falling with each labored breath, his shaggy coat matted with blood.

Shaking all over, Lane knelt beside him. "It's all right, boy. I'm here." She stroked his head, felt him tremble. "You're home now. You're going to be okay."

"He needs a doctor," Dylan said. "There's a vet in Waterside. Once I get the plane warmed up, we can be there in fifteen minutes."

"I'll call ahead," Winnie said, hearing the commotion and hurrying up beside them. "I'll let the doctor know you're coming." The heavyset woman raced away, and Lane looked down at her big gangly dog.

Her throat closed up and her eyes stung with tears. "It's all right, boy. We're going to take care of you. We're going to get you well." Her voice broke. Finn tried to raise his head, whined, and lay back down on the porch. At least he was still alive.

"Get some bandages," Dylan said. "We need to stop the bleeding."

Lane took off running, ran into Winnie, who had anticipated her needs and handed over gauze pads and a roll of flexible, self-adhesive tape, then took off to make the call.

Lane raced back to the porch. "Get the plane ready. I'll do this."

Surprise flickered in Dylan's eyes. "You sure?"

She nodded. She could do this. She had tended her dying mother, though it wasn't the same. Still, she didn't have any other choice. "I'll take care of him. Go!"

As Dylan ran for the plane, Caleb appeared in the darkness across the yard, standing in the doorway of his cabin. Seeing them gathered on the porch, he hurried through the gate to join them. "Jesus, what happened to Finn?"

"I don't . . . don't know. He's badly injured. We need to stop the bleeding."

Caleb crouched beside her. "Where's he hurt?"

Everywhere, she wanted to say, since he was scraped raw all over and covered in blood. "I think it's his chest." She searched through his fur, found the gash, pressed a couple of big gauze pads over the wound. "If you lift him, I can wrap the tape around him to hold the gauze in place."

"You got it." As gently as possible, Caleb lifted the big dog off the porch and Lane wrapped the elastic tape around him, pressed it into place.

Winnie appeared in the doorway with a sheet. "The vet is going to meet you at the dock and take him back to the clinic. He and his wife live in the apartment above. I brought this." She held up a sheet. "I thought you could put him on this and use it as a stretcher to carry him out to the plane."

"Good idea." Caleb grabbed the sheet, folded it to a

double thickness and laid it down on the porch next to Finn. Very gently, he lifted the dog onto the sheet.

"I'll get one end, you get the other," Lane said.

Just then Emily appeared in the doorway, squeezed past Winnie, and ran out on the porch. She was making horrifying sounds in her throat, pointing at Finn and crying.

Winnie pulled the child into her arms. "They're taking him to the hospital, sweetheart. Your dad and Lane are going to make sure he gets well."

The little girl's hand shook as she leaned down and carefully stroked Finn's bloody head, then she turned back into Winnie's arms and started sobbing.

"We're going to take care of him, sweetheart," Lane said. "We'll call as soon as we know he's okay." Knowing they didn't dare wait any longer, Lane picked up two corners of the sheet while Caleb picked up the other two.

Moving carefully, they headed for the gate. Once they were out in the open, they made their way down the slope toward the water.

Finn didn't move.

On the floating dock, they laid him down next to the door of the plane.

"Flight check's done and we're ready to go," Dylan said. "We just need to get him aboard."

Lane looked down at Finn, lying limp and unmoving, and her heart squeezed. "Is he . . . is he still breathing?"

Dylan knelt beside him, felt for a pulse, checked for breath. "He's alive. We need to go."

She nodded. Lane climbed in first and helped Dylan and Caleb lift Finn into the plane, settle him next to her behind the pilot's seat. Dylan climbed aboard and strapped himself in while Caleb threw off the lines.

The engine roared to life, and they pulled away from

the dock. Then they were skimming over the water, lifting into the air, swooping upward, flying over the sea that dropped away into the darkness beneath them.

"How's he doing?" Dylan shouted over his shoulder.

"He opened his eyes once. But he's . . . he's unconscious again." Finn had looked straight at her, his dark eyes filled with pain. It was as if he were trying to thank her, as if he were saying good-bye.

Her throat tightened. "Stay with me, boy," she whispered, running a trembling hand over his head. "I love you, Finn. I don't want you to go."

"Just hold on!" Dylan shouted. "We'll be there soon."

Those fifteen minutes in the air seemed like hours. Then the plane was descending, winging over the flickering lights of Waterside. Dylan dropped the plane into the sea. The aircraft slid over the surface and roared up to the float dock, making a bigger wake than it usually did, waves that rocked the plane.

In minutes, the engines were shut down, the plane was tied up, and they were lifting Finn out onto the dock. A young man in jeans and a T-shirt raced toward them. With his blond hair and light blue eyes, he looked more like a student than a vet.

"I'm Dr. Kennedy. The white SUV is mine. Let's get him in the back."

Grabbing two corners of the sheet, Dylan and the doctor carried Finn up to the parking lot and loaded him into the back of the SUV. They all jammed into the vehicle, and Dr. Kennedy drove away.

It didn't take long to reach the clinic, a two-story white stucco building with the doctor's office below and an apartment above. The lights were on in both floors. The doctor moved with efficiency, hurrying them inside, through the waiting room, into a room in the back, where they set Finn down on a surgical table.

"You can wait out in the reception area. I'll let you know what's going on after I take a look at him."

"If you need some help—" Lane offered.

"That's my wife, Sherry." A pretty little blonde hurried down the stairs. "She's also my nurse." A warm look passed between them. Lane felt better knowing Finn was in good hands.

The doctor and his wife disappeared into the surgical room with Finn, while Lane and Dylan found seats in the waiting room.

"He looks competent," Dylan said.

"Yes, he does."

"I think he'll do his best for Finn."

Lane just nodded.

Silently, she prayed that his best would be enough to save Finn.

Kyle peered through his binoculars, scanning the lodge below. It was nearly midnight, but some of the lights in the house were still on. He'd seen the plane take off, seen them load the dog aboard. He figured they'd headed to Waterside to find a vet.

Damn dog. He thought he'd killed it. The good news was even if the animal survived, it was injured too badly to track him. In a way, he hoped the poor beast lived.

Whatever happened, Kyle just hoped Lane never figured out he was the one who had hurt her beloved pet.

He took a last look down on the lodge. As late as it was, Brodie probably wouldn't be back until tomorrow.

Coming up off the ground, Kyle collected the rifle he

had found in a closet in the cabin and started to carry it, then used a couple of branches to erase the place he had been.

Instead of heading up the mountain to the cave, he started north, to the cabin he'd discovered. It didn't look like anyone had been staying there lately and it was well off the beaten path. Lots of places up here were only used part-time.

He moved his Jeep into the lean-to that served as a garage and made a check of his supplies. He was thinking it might be a good place to take Lane for a couple of days, give them time to renew their acquaintance before he used the open-ended tickets he had bought for the ferry that would get them the hell out of town.

In the meantime, he had to get rid of Brodie.

Kyle still hadn't quite worked out how he was going to accomplish that.

Chapter Twenty-Eight

Dylan dozed in the waiting room at the clinic, sleeping off and on with his head against the wall. Lane slept against his shoulder.

It had been nearly three hours and Finn was still in surgery. He'd called Winnie and let her and Emily know the dog was in with the doctor; then they'd settled in to wait.

His muscles were stiff by the time the door to the back room opened and Dr. Kennedy walked out. Lane straightened against him, her nails digging into his arm as they stood up from the blue vinyl couch and looked at the man in the light green scrubs.

"Finn's out of surgery," the doctor said, pulling off the cap he wore. "He isn't completely out of danger, but it looks like he's going to make it."

Lane made a sound in her throat, half sob, half cry of relief.

"Thank you, Doctor," Dylan said. "Finn's a great dog. We really appreciate your helping him that way."

Sherry Kennedy walked up beside her husband. "That's what we do," she said with a smile. "And when things go right, it's a very rewarding job."

"When can he go home?" Lane asked.

"We need to keep him under observation for a while," the doctor said. "He'll need antibiotics to fight off infection. We'll know more in a couple of days."

Lane nodded. "Can I see him?"

"He's still out from the anesthesia. If you're in town in the morning, you can see him then."

Lane looked up at Dylan for confirmation and he nodded. "We'll be here."

He planned to spend the night, show Whitaker's photo around tomorrow. "What happened to him, Doc?" Dylan asked. "He have a run-in with a bear or something?"

Kennedy shook his head. "Finn had a run-in with a knife. A big one. He's lucky to be alive."

Dylan's chest clamped down. Angry heat rose at the back of his neck. Someone was trespassing on his land. Someone dangerous. More and more, he believed his instincts were right. The man who was out there was a killer. And Kyle Whitaker was that man.

He settled a hand at Lane's waist. "We'll be back in the morning to take care of our bill and see Finn. Thanks again—both of you. If you need us, we'll be staying at the Sea View Motel."

"Do you need a ride?" Dr. Kennedy asked.

Lane looked up at Dylan. "If it's okay with you, I'd rather walk. I need to clear my head."

"I'm with you there." He glanced back at the doctor and his pretty blond wife. "Thanks again."

Urging Lane toward the door, Dylan stepped out into the cool night air, started walking the few blocks to the motel.

"Someone stabbed him, Dylan."

A fresh shot of fury boiled through him. "That's right."

"I don't think it was those boys from Yeil or anyone from around there."

"Neither do I." Dylan didn't say the man who had done it was very likely Kyle Whitaker.

And that none of them would be safe until he was caught.

Dylan phoned the lodge as soon as they checked into the motel. He was worried about Emily. He figured the child wouldn't be able to sleep until she knew Finn was okay.

Winnie answered the call. "I'll tell her. She tried to stay awake till you called, but she finally fell asleep in my bed. I don't think she'll sleep long, not until she knows Finn's going to be okay."

Dylan hung up the phone, relieved he'd been able to give his daughter good news. He knew how much she loved that dog. It was going to break her heart when Lane took him home.

Something else he was to blame for.

He glanced over at the bed, where Lane had fallen asleep. She was exhausted. Outside the window, a purple dawn hovered on the horizon. He had so much on his mind, so much to do, but he wouldn't be any good to anyone if he didn't get some rest.

Sliding into bed next to her, he eased her back against his chest, holding her spoon-fashion against him. He bent and kissed the side of her neck, heard her soft purr. His erection stirred. He wanted her as he always did, but she needed to sleep as much as he did.

He settled against the pillow, worried he wouldn't be able to sleep with so much on his mind, but the next time he opened his eyes, it was ten thirty in the morning.

He smiled at the feel of soft lips trailing over his chest. He knew he should get out of bed and head for the shower, but whatever willpower he had evaporated like mist on a breeze.

"Time to get up," Lane teased, nipping him playfully. "Oh, I see you already are."

Dylan laughed and pulled her beneath him, came up over her, and slid himself deep inside.

They made love slowly, enjoying each other until both of them were sated. He would have dozed again if they didn't have so much to do.

"We'd better get dressed," he said against her hair, loving the silky feel of it trailing over his skin.

She looked up at him, looped her arms around his neck. "I'd rather stay here. We could spend the day in bed, pretend none of this is happening."

"I wish we could, love. I truly do." Reluctantly, he eased himself off her, sat up on the edge of the mattress.

Lane sighed as she slid out of bed and padded into the bathroom. While she showered, Dylan phoned Johnnie Mellon down at Pete's Garage and told him he needed to use the Toyota again. Johnnie told him it was still parked in the gravel lot behind the float dock, the key under the bumper.

Dylan showered and dressed, then checked them out of the room, and they walked down to retrieve the car. He dropped Lane off at the clinic so she could spend time with Finn and drove out to Convenient Rental Car. The brunette who'd helped them before was working in the booth.

Dylan got in line behind a customer, waited till she had finished with the rental contract and handed the balding man the keys, then stepped up to the counter.

"Hi, Elaine," he said, flashing her a smile. "I'm Dylan Brodie. You helped me a couple of days ago."

She gave him a friendly smile in return. "I remember." Her smile slipped. "I can't give you any more information, Dylan. I might get into trouble."

He wondered what new information she might have, but let the comment pass. "No problem. I just came to show you a picture." He pulled out his cell and brought up the booking photo of Kyle Whitaker in an orange jumpsuit. "Is this Dusty Withers?"

Her eyes widened. "Is he a convict?"

"No, he's served his time." He held out the photo. "Is this Withers?"

"He's better-looking than his picture, but yeah, that's him."

He took a chance. "His car rental's almost up. Have you heard from him?" She took a step back as if to avoid the question. "Keep in mind the orange jumpsuit."

She sighed. "He left an envelope full of money, enough for another week. He shoved it through the mail slot. We found it on the floor when we opened the day after you were here."

Dylan smiled. "Thanks, Elaine." He'd figured the bastard was about to leave. He just wasn't ready quite yet.

"Are you going to call the police?"

"Like I said, he's served his time." Dylan headed out the door. He needed to pick up Lane, tell her Whitaker and Withers were one and the same. He was crossing the lot when his cell started ringing. "Brodie."

"Hey, bro." Nick's deep voice drifted over the line. "I got that intel you wanted on Whitaker."

"Was he Army?"

"Special Forces. His file says he was given an honorable medical discharge, but it doesn't say what for. Guy was a real hero, though. Silver Star, all kinds of commendations."

"Anything else in the file?"

"Not enough. I decided to get hold of some friends, call in a few favors, see what else I could find out."

"Rangers?"

"That's right." Having been one of them, Nick still had a lot of friends on active duty. "Kyle Whitaker was Delta," he said. "One of the best. He'd been in the service five years when he was diagnosed with schizophrenia. That's the reason he was discharged. Started hearing a voice in his head."

"Jesus."

"I figured that would make your day."

"Lane couldn't figure out how he found her, but a guy with his background probably wouldn't have any trouble."

"Is she using e-mail? Facebook, other social media?"

"She's got a business to run, so yeah."

"There's your answer."

Dylan scrubbed a hand over his face, felt the roughness of the beard he hadn't bothered to shave. "Looks like he tried to kill Lane's dog."

"Fuck, Dylan. He may be escalating."

"We're in Waterside now. Vet says it looks like the dog's going to make it. Finn got out of the yard yesterday. Must have run into Whitaker and the guy wanted to be sure the dog didn't lead us back to him."

"Could be. One more thing. You remember our old friend, the nonexistent Dusty Withers?"

"What about him?"

"Whitaker's best friend in Delta was a guy named Dusty Rawlins. He was killed in action in Afghanistan."

"More good news."

"Listen, bro, I'm not liking this. I'm coming down there, see if I can help."

"Let me talk to the police first. I've got enough info now to at least get their attention. I'll call you later." Dylan signed off before his brother could object.

Nick had his own problems. But Dylan wouldn't hesitate to accept his offer if things continued to slide downhill.

Lane was ready to leave the clinic when the battered blue Toyota rolled up in front of the vet's office. She headed down the sidewalk and slid into the passenger seat.

"How's Finn doing?" Dylan asked.

"He's awake. He was happy to see me." Her eyes filled. "Oh, God, Dylan."

He pulled her across the center console into his arms. "We're going to find this guy. The girl at the rental agency ID'd Whitaker as Dusty Withers. We'll head out to Mad Jack's and talk to the bartender to confirm, but I'm sure it's him."

She felt sick to her stomach. Easing away, she slid back down in her seat. "So he's here."

"Unfortunately, yes."

She took a shaky breath. "There's still no proof he killed Holly."

"He's trespassing and he's been stalking you. That's enough for the cops to bring him in for questioning."

Her insides tightened. She prayed Dylan was right and the police could find Kyle before someone else got hurt.

Dylan reached down and started the engine. The Toyota rolled along the road through town, then turned north toward Mad Jack's. It was already past two. Unfortunately, the bartender, Brian Cresky, wasn't due in for another hour.

Lane sat next to Dylan at one of the rustic wooden tables and they ordered lunch, cheeseburgers and fries for both of them, though Lane mostly toyed with her food. When Brian arrived, Dylan showed him Kyle's photo, and like the girl at the rental car agency, Brian immediately recognized him as the man he'd seen in the bar.

"Has he been in here lately?" Dylan asked.

The bartender shook his head. "Hasn't been around. At least not on my shift. Maybe he caught the ferry and left."

"I don't think so. He hasn't turned in his rental car. You still have my card?"

Brian reached under the counter and came up with Dylan's Eagle Bay Lodge business card. "Got it right here."

Dylan pulled a twenty out of his wallet. "His real name's Kyle Whitaker. If he comes in, call me. It'll be worth a lot more than twenty."

Brian smiled, moving the weird little lip whiskers on his chin. "You got it, man."

From the bar, they drove to the police department and parked in front. Police Chief Wills was in and agreed to see them. Lane took a deep breath as she and Dylan walked into his office.

As tall and imposing as ever, Wills stood up from behind his desk. For the first time, Lane noticed the fishing trophies proudly displayed on the walls.

"Word travels fast," the chief said.

"How's that?" Dylan asked. Wills indicated the chairs in front of his desk, and Lane sat down next to Dylan.

"State troopers are on their way to Eagle Bay with a warrant to search Caleb Wolfe's cabin and his truck."

Dylan's jaw went tight. "Why now? Why not when they first came out?"

"We've had time to do some follow-up, talk to the people at Mad Jack's who saw him with Holly that night. They said the girl was all over him, practically seduced him right there in the bar."

Lane sat forward in her chair. "Caleb went there to tell Holly to leave him alone. They fought about it. Those same people must have seen him leave."

"He's a man, isn't he? He waited outside and took what Holly offered."

"That's not the way it was," Lane said firmly.

"We also interviewed Maggie Ridell again. Apparently Holly told her she was seeing Wolfe. He's denied it from the start. There may be something in his home or car that will tell us the truth." He looked at Dylan. "I figured that's why you were here."

Dylan shook his head. "You're looking in the wrong direction, Frank. Caleb Wolfe didn't kill Holly Kaplan. Did you find anything on Dusty Withers?"

"Only that you were right. Withers doesn't exist."

"His real name is Kyle Whitaker. The girl at Convenient Rental Car identified him as the man calling himself Withers. The bartender at Mad Jack's confirmed it. Whitaker just got out of jail for aggravated assault. He followed Lane up here, has some kind of obsession with her. He's been watching the lodge. Last night, he stabbed her dog, damned near killed him. If you dig deep enough, you'll find he has mental problems. Whitaker's the man who killed Holly."

For the first time, the police chief looked uncertain. "All right, so you've found the guy you've been looking for. Even if he is a stalker—and at the moment I'm not arguing that—what evidence do you have he killed the Kaplan girl?"

Dylan's frustration showed in the hard lines of his face. "Look, we know he was in Mad Jack's—the bartender saw him more than once. We know Holly had a fight with Caleb the night she was killed. Who knows, maybe she left with Whitaker to get even. Or maybe she met up with Whitaker somewhere else and they came back there together. The thing is, if we could find this guy—if we could talk to him—we might be able to figure out what happened to Holly."

"You seem to know a lot about him. Any warrants? Has he broken parole?"

"No warrants and apparently he served his sentence."

The chief leaned back in his chair. "Whether he killed the girl or not, he has no business trespassing on your property." His thick salt-and-pepper eyebrows drew together. "You saw him out there, right? You know for sure it's him?"

"He was out there," Dylan said. "Lane saw him."

The chief's sharp gaze swung to her. "You're sure it was Whitaker? It couldn't be the man's just up here fishing and it has nothing to do with you?"

Lane flicked a glance at Dylan, wishing she could be more certain. "I think it was him. He was kind of far away."

At least she'd seen someone she thought might be him, and they knew for sure he'd been in town.

"All right, we'll take a look at Whitaker. If what you've said about him checks out, I'll put out a BOLO. The problem is if he's the man you say and he wants to stay off the grid, we'll need the state police to find him. I'm not calling them in on a trespassing case. Hell, you can't even be a hundred percent sure it's Whitaker who's out there."

Dylan leaned forward in his chair. "This guy is dangerous, Frank. He was Delta Force. I think he used a Ka-Bar knife on Lane's dog."

Wills's frown deepened. He stood up from behind his desk. "I'll let my men know. As soon as I can free up a couple of officers, I'll send them to the lodge to check things out. But it isn't going to happen until tomorrow at the earliest."

"I appreciate it, Frank." Dylan stuck out a hand and the two men shook.

"I want the right guy for this as much as you do," Chief Wills said. He looked over at Lane. "And I don't want another woman getting killed."

As Dylan guided Lane out of the police station, his cell started ringing. Caleb's number flashed on the screen. Dylan pressed the phone against his ear. "I'm here."

"Cops came out with a warrant," Caleb said, his voice tight and strained. "Searched my cabin, tore it all to hell. Loaded my truck onto a tow and hauled it back to town."

"We just left Frank Wills's office. He told us they were coming."

"Jesus, Dylan, what am I going to do?"

"You're going to stay calm. The police are putting out a BOLO on Whitaker. Once they bring him in, this may all be over. In the meantime, call Peter Keller, bring him up to speed."

"All right. I'll call him, then Paddy, and I'll take a look around, see if we can find any trace of Whitaker."

"Negative on that. Turns out he's Delta. And it looks like he stabbed Finn to keep the dog from tracking him."

"Son of a bitch."

"Wills is going to send out a couple of officers, but probably not until tomorrow. We'll keep watch tonight. Maybe we'll spot him. If he's trespassing, we've got a right to protect ourselves."

"If he's Delta, we aren't going to find him—not unless he wants us to."

It was probably the truth. Delta soldiers were in the same league as SEALs. Being an Army man, Nick would argue they were better. But Whitaker wasn't going to stay in hiding forever. Sooner or later, he was going to come after Lane.

When he did, Dylan meant to stop him.

Chapter Twenty-Nine

It was late afternoon by the time Dylan had refueled at the float dock in Waterside and was ready to get the plane in the air. Lane had called to check on Finn one last time before they left town. He was sleeping peacefully, the doctor said, and his condition was improved.

Lane had asked Dr. Kennedy to keep them updated, and Dylan had promised to bring her back to pick Finn up as soon as he was well enough to go home.

Home. The word stirred an ache in her chest. Home was beginning to feel more and more like being here with Dylan. With Emily and Winnie and Caleb. Eagle Bay was beginning to feel like the place she was meant to be.

It was impossible. She had a home of her own, a business to run. For heaven's sake, she was an interior designer from Beverly Hills!

And as far as she knew, Dylan hadn't the least desire for her to stay.

The plane lifted into the air, the roar of the engine pulling her thoughts back to the present. She watched the dark blue sea falling away beneath them, took in the sharp rise of snow-capped mountains in the distance. She had never seen a more beautiful place.

And yet there was trouble here, trouble she had brought with her.

"I'm worried about Caleb," she said over the hum of the propeller. "You don't think he'll go after Kyle?"

"I don't think so. Caleb's no fool. He knows his limitations. He's not going to do something stupid."

"You think the police will be able to find him?"

"I don't know. Trouble is, they figure Whitaker for a stalker, not a murderer. And in this kind of country it's going to be nearly impossible to figure out where he is."

Lane looked down at the mountains beneath them. They were almost halfway home. She flicked a sideways glance at Dylan. "Since we're already up here—"

"Why don't we do a little searching of our own?" he finished, reading her mind, as he seemed to have a way of doing.

Lane smiled. "That's right. We know he rented a dark green Jeep Wrangler. Maybe we'll spot it."

The wings tipped as Dylan started to descend to a lower altitude and began to change direction. "There're several seasonal owners up here, cabins they only use a few months out of the year. There are always some that are empty."

"Maybe he's broken into one of them and that's where he's staying."

Dylan looked down at the ground passing beneath them. "Trouble is those places aren't that easy to find. Almost no roads up here and the ones that lead to part-time residences get badly overgrown. Worth a try, though."

Dylan descended a little more and began to do a perimeter search of the area on the mainland side of Eagle Bay. When they didn't see anything out of the ordinary, he decreased the circumference of the circle and began again.

Lane figured they were still about eight miles out when the tone of the engine changed. Her gaze shifted from the window to the man at the controls. The lines of his face were set, his jaw hard.

"What's happening?" The engine started coughing, making odd sputtering sounds. "Dylan?"

Instead of answering, he picked up the radio transmitter. "Waterside Airport, this is Dylan Brodie, Nancy Seven Three Five Able Charlie. We're having engine trouble."

Lane's stomach knotted. The radio came to life. "Roger, Brodie. What's your location?"

Lane's fingers gripped the seat as the engine continued to wheeze and sputter and Dylan gave the airport controller their coordinates.

For an instant he turned toward her. "We've got a problem. We're going to land. We'll be okay." His attention returned to the mic. "This is Brodie. We're close to Moose Lake. I'll set her down there. I'll check in once we're in the water."

"Roger that," came the reply. "Good luck."

Dylan sliced her a glance. "Start watching for the lake. We should be almost there."

Lane stared out the window, her heart pounding wildly. For miles ahead, all she could see were trees. The plane hiccupped one last time, sputtered, then went silent. "Oh, my God."

"Watch for the lake," Dylan said firmly as he tried to start the engine again. The plane swooped downward, losing altitude, the air rushing past the wings. Lane trembled. Her mouth was dry, her pulse thundering in her ears. As the airplane rushed toward the tops of the trees, she fought a wave of panic. Swallowing back her fears, she started to pray, then looked ahead and saw it.

"There!" She thrust out a finger. "There's the lake!"

"I got it!" Dylan worked the controls as the plane dropped, fighting to start the engine. It growled but didn't start. Growled again, then suddenly sputtered to life. The propeller picked up speed, giving them a little lift, enough to miss the trees. "Hold tight."

Lane closed her eyes, silently praying they would make it as far as the lake. When she looked again, pine trees were rushing beneath the cabin. One of the pontoons skimmed the very tip of a tree. The plane flew a ways farther then glided out over the water. Dylan eased the nose up and set the pontoons on the surface of the lake.

Lane released the breath she had been holding. Next to her, Dylan worked the controls, and the propeller carried them toward the far end of the lake. It wasn't large. The engine continued to run raggedly, but it was moving the plane toward the distant shoreline.

As if he had planned it, the wake carried them within a few feet of the sand at the edge of the water before the motor fell silent again. The plane settled. The wild ride was over.

Lane slumped against the seat. "We . . . we made it." When she looked over at Dylan, he was grinning.

"What?" he teased. "You didn't trust me?"

She swung at him, hit him solidly in the arm. "This isn't funny."

His smile slid away. He reached for her hand and gave it a squeeze. "I'm sorry I scared you, baby. Sometimes things happen out here we don't expect. I try to keep my options open."

Some of her anger faded. It wasn't his fault the engine

had failed. "You loved it, though," she said, unable to hold back the hint of a smile. "Admit it."

His mouth edged up. "It was a rush. I loved it once we were down and you were safe. I was ninety-five percent sure we'd be okay."

Her russet eyebrows went up. "Ninety-five percent?"

"Well, maybe only ninety."

Lane leaned back in the copilot's seat, the jolt of adrenaline beginning to fade, her heartbeat still not quite slowed to normal. "I'm sorry I hit you. I've never been in a plane crash before."

"Emergency landing," he corrected. "There's a lot of water around. I'm usually not cruising so low. Finding a place to set down isn't as hard as it sounds."

Or at least he didn't want her to be so frightened she would never go up again. She glanced at their surroundings. Miles and miles of tall, forested mountains and rugged granite peaks. Snow lingered at the higher elevations. "So what do we do now?"

"We let everyone know we're safe." Picking up the mic, he radioed the airport, told them they had made a safe landing at Moose Lake and asked the controller to call the Eagle Bay Lodge and tell them what had happened. There was no cell service out here.

"Tell them we'll be spending the night at the lake and walking out tomorrow. I'll get someone up here to fix the plane as soon as we get back to the lodge."

"Roger that." The call ended, and Dylan set the mic back in its holder.

"We're spending the night?"

"Too late to get home before dark. It's only about five miles away. If it weren't such rugged country, it'd be a piece of cake." He glanced off toward the direction of the lodge. "With Whitaker still out there, I don't like the idea of Caleb being there by himself, but there's not much we can do about it tonight."

"Are we sleeping in the plane?"

The sexy grin returned. It did funny things to the pit of her stomach. "I always carry emergency gear. We'll pitch a tent, catch something to eat for supper. You said you've never been camping. Think of it as an adventure."

It was definitely that. This whole trip to Alaska had been an amazing adventure.

Except for Kyle Whitaker. The grim thought reminded her of the man who had followed her. The man who might be a killer.

Dylan swung the door of the plane open and climbed out on the pontoon. Taking a rope out of the baggage compartment, he jumped onto the shore and began securing the plane to a tree near the shoreline.

As soon as he was finished, he came back, helped her out, and carried her to the shore. Then he went back and started unloading his gear. They hauled the equipment up to a nice, flat, sandy spot with good visibility and not a lot of shrubbery around.

She felt a pinch on her arm and slapped away a mosquito. "I hope you've got some insect repellent in that bag."

"Never go anywhere without it." He dug into his big canvas satchel, brought out an aerosol can of OFF!, and sprayed her arms and neck, then her jeans and T-shirt—the white one Dylan had been wearing under his shirt when they'd left the lodge last night. She'd had to borrow it, since hers had been covered with Finn's blood.

"The wind's coming up a little," Dylan said. "Should be enough to keep the mosquitoes away."

The breeze felt good, a little chilly but refreshing. And the mosquitoes were mostly down by the reeds at the edge of the lake.

"I guess you've probably never pitched a tent." Dylan pulled out a cardboard box that said COLEMAN POP-UP on the side, took out a rolled-up green nylon tent.

"This little beauty sleeps four, and it only takes minutes to put up." He told her what to do to help, and it was up in no time. He went back to the plane for sleeping bags. Brought them back and tossed them into the tent.

He flashed a devilish grin. "They zip together."

Lane laughed. "Is that so?"

His grin widened. There was no mistaking what he meant and a little coil of anticipation slipped through her.

"We'll take care of it after supper," he said.

She had never seen this side of him—relaxed, even playful. Away from the pressures of work, out in the forest he loved. He belonged here, she could see. But then, she had never doubted that.

Not since the moment she had first seen him, standing on the deck of a friend's house in Beverly Hills, tall and broad-shouldered, wearing jeans and a red plaid flannel shirt. Maybe she'd fallen a little in love with him right then.

He stood there a moment, staring out at the beautiful, smooth-as-glass, clear, blue mountain lake, his long legs splayed, his features completely relaxed. "You like fried fish, right?"

"Sure." Not that she'd ever had any fish fried outdoors.

He took a deep breath of the pine-scented air. "Then I'd better go get my fishing pole." He smiled, looking like the rugged he-man he was.

In that moment, Lane lost another little piece of her heart to Dylan Brodie.

Supper was over. Emily had gone up to her room to play while Caleb helped Winnie clear the dishes. He was almost finished when a knock sounded at the mudroom door.

Dread spilled through him. Had they come to arrest him? There was nothing to find in his truck, but still . . .

On the other hand, what if it was Kyle Whitaker? Caleb's hunting rifle was in his cabin. No way to get there in time. The shotgun was upstairs, locked in a closet in Dylan's bedroom. The .44 revolver Dylan carried in the woods was in his gear bag on the plane. There were a couple of hunting rifles in the gun safe in the garage. Unfortunately, at the moment he couldn't remember the combination.

Reminding himself it was too soon to panic, he ran over to the window that looked into the side yard. Relief trickled through him. Heading for the mudroom, he pulled open the door, found two boys in their early twenties, with black hair and dark skin, standing on the back porch. Caleb recognized one of them as Alex Kramer, the son of a friend of his in Yeil. Alex had been one of the kids involved in the haunting. His dad hadn't been happy when he'd found out about it.

"Hey, Caleb."

"Alex."

"Jacob Payuk told us about the trouble you've been having. He thought maybe we were the ones who'd been watching the lodge, but we aren't." He gestured to his friend. "This is Jared Deacon. Is Mr. Brodie in?"

"Dylan won't be back till tomorrow. What's going on?"

"We wanted him to know we didn't break our word,"

Jared said. "We figured you'd be trying to catch whoever is out there. We thought maybe you could use our help."

Caleb pulled open the door and stepped back out of the way. "Come on in. Winnie's got some apple pie left in the kitchen if you want some. There's coffee, too."

They flashed each other a glance. "That sounds great," Alex said.

Caleb led them into the kitchen. "This is Winnie, the best cook in Alaska. Winnie, this is Alex and Jared. I told them they could have a piece of your pie."

"Well, of course they can," she said. "With Lane and Dylan stuck up at Moose Lake, they might as well eat it before it goes to waste."

Not that any of Winnie's pie ever got thrown out.

The boys sat down at the long pine table. While Winnie cut slabs of still-warm apple pie and slid them onto plates, Caleb filled mugs with coffee and set them down on the table. He poured one for himself and joined the two boys.

Winnie set a piece of pie down in front of the taller boy. "You're Heather's boyfriend, Alex," she said, referring to the girl who worked for her part-time.

"That's right."

She set another piece of pie on the table in front of Jared and handed each of them a fork. "Heather says you've been working hard researching that no-good Artemus Carmack. How's it coming?"

Alex swallowed a big bite of pie. "There's been a lot of stuff written about him. Mostly in the newspapers. At first it was all good, but it turns out Carmack was a real crook. Scammed a lot of folks in San Francisco out of their money."

"He wound up alone and destitute," Jared added, "living in absolute poverty. He didn't have a friend left in the world."

Winnie made a scoffing sound. "After what he did, it

serves him right." They all knew the story now, how the original owner of the lodge had murdered his wife and daughter, then had two innocent men hanged to cover it up.

"You gonna write about it?" Caleb asked.

"We're working on a paper about Carmack," Jared said, digging into his pie. "We might even get someone to publish it."

"Good for you," Winnie said.

"So what about the guy who's been out there watching the lodge?" Alex asked. "Is he still there?"

"We think so. We think he followed Lane up here. He's got some kind of thing for her."

"Is there something we can do to help you catch him?"

Caleb glanced over at Winnie. He hadn't been able to reach Paddy so he was the only man there. "I appreciate the offer, but it looks like this guy could be really dangerous. He's former Special Forces. We're hoping the police will come out tomorrow. In the meantime, we're all staying close to the house."

"What about tonight?" Jared asked. "Alex's got his deer rifle in the truck. We could take shifts."

It wasn't a bad idea. The boys were no longer teens, and in this country, kids all knew how to handle a weapon. After what Dylan had told him, he'd been planning to stay up all night, but it wouldn't be easy. Having some help would give him a chance to get a little sleep, which would keep him more alert.

"All right. It'd be great if you stayed. Dylan had engine trouble and had to make a forced landing up at Moose Lake. He and Lane are walking out tomorrow, but that still leaves tonight."

"We'll stay."

"Okay, then. I'll take the first three hours. You boys take

the second. Whatever happens, I don't want you going outside. Wake me up if you see anyone out there, or he tries to get into the house."

"We can do that."

"Go get your rifle, and I'll get mine. Hopefully we won't need them, but we don't know what this creep might do. It's better to be safe than sorry."

They all went out the back door and returned with their weapons. Alex carried a .30-30 deer rifle, and Caleb held the .308 Savage he'd been using for years.

"When it's your shift, check all the windows and doors, make sure they're locked." He cast them a meaningful glance. "I'm sure you'll know how to handle that."

Both of them grinned.

"I'll go first," Caleb said. "In the meantime, I'll show you where you can sleep. I'll wake you up in three hours."

"Sounds good."

Caleb took the boys upstairs to the empty bedroom in the family wing they would be sharing. Once they were settled, he made a tour of the house.

The doors were all tightly secured. A couple of windows had been opened to let in the breeze, but he locked them down tight. Winnie had gone to her room; Emily was asleep. It was dark and quiet outside, nothing but the whisper of the wind through the trees.

The best vantage point was Dylan's bedroom. After completing his rounds, Caleb settled himself in a chair at the window, his rifle propped against the wall at his side.

He was grateful the boys were there to help.

It was going to be a damned long night.

Chapter Thirty

Moving silently away from the house, Kyle made his way into the forest. Behind him, the lights of the lodge were going out one by one, but he knew they were still watching.

Moose Lake. He'd heard them talking about the plane, knew Brodie would be spending the night up there, walking out tomorrow. Kyle planned to head for the lake at first light.

He knew where it was. He'd seen it on one of the National Geodetic Survey maps he'd picked up in L.A. He'd studied the map of Eagle Bay and the surrounding landscape. From the start, he'd used it to find his way around.

When the plane hadn't returned by dark, he'd seized the opportunity and headed for the lodge. The big Indian was there with the woman and the child, but all of the workers had left for the weekend.

His mouth edged up. Reaching into the pocket of his camo pants, he pulled out a bright russet silk scarf, the color of Lane's fiery hair. He had taken the scarf from the dresser in her bedroom while the others were eating supper.

In her bathroom, he'd inhaled the floral scent of her

shampoo, the soft fragrance of her perfume. It made him hard just thinking about having her.

He clenched his jaw. It reminded him that she had been sleeping with Brodie instead of him.

His hand tightened into a fist as he walked softly through the forest toward the cabin he had been using.

It isn't her fault, the voice reminded him. Kyle swore softly, knowing the voice was right. If he hadn't been stupid, hadn't lost his temper and let himself be goaded into a fight, Lane would be with him. He just needed to spend some time with her.

It's too late for that, the voice disagreed. *You've already lost her. Get over her. Get on with your life.*

"You're wrong. We were perfect for each other. Lane will realize that once we're together again."

He held the scarf beneath his nose. Brodie was the problem. He had to get Brodie out of the picture.

And the solution had magically come to him.

At first light, he was heading up to Moose Lake. If his luck held, he'd encounter Lane and Brodie at the halfway point as they made their way down to the lodge.

He remembered seeing a stream flowing out of the lake that ran into the bay. He'd take a look at the map again, figure the best way down the mountain, the route the pair would most likely travel, but he figured they would follow the stream.

Too bad Brodie was going to have a terrible accident along the way.

In the morning, Dylan took down the tent, packed up the gear they wouldn't need as they traveled down the mountain, and stashed it aboard the plane. Though he and

Lane had made love and she had slept curled against him, he hadn't slept the way he usually did outdoors.

He was too worried about Whitaker and what might be happening at the lodge.

Dylan picked up his .44, slid it into the holster, and buckled the belt around his waist. Grabbing a couple of energy bars, he stuffed them into his backpack along with a few bottles of water.

For breakfast, they'd eaten MREs—Meals Ready to Eat, prepackaged food he had stocked up on at a sporting goods store and kept in his emergency gear bag.

Sausage gravy and biscuits. Maple oatmeal. Packages of raisins and nuts. He'd made boiled coffee and even found some powdered creamer for Lane. Last night they'd opened a package of pasta with marinara sauce for a side with the five-pound lake trout he'd caught and fried for supper.

Even though he'd been worried about Whitaker, the brief time outdoors had been fun. He hoped Lane had enjoyed it half as much as he had.

He glanced up at the leaden sky overhead. It hadn't rained last night, but dull gray clouds had rolled in off the sea, making the day overcast and grim.

Dylan glanced toward the forest in search of Lane. She had stepped into the trees for a morning bathroom break, but he had warned her not to go too far away. Figuring he had given her enough time and beginning to worry, he started after her.

Up ahead, through the dense growth of pines, he spotted her in his blue flannel shirt, a spare he kept in his gear bag and had loaned her, since they had left the lodge in such a hurry she hadn't brought a change of clothes. Lane had tied the shirt up around her waist, but it still hung like a sack off her shoulders.

Dylan started to smile as he walked toward her. She was watching something in front of her as she slowly backed away. When she raised her arms and started shouting, his adrenaline kicked in and he started to run, pulling his revolver as he raced up the hill.

He stopped when he saw her, standing in front of a black bear, a big one, its small eyes fixed on Lane as if it had just found its next meal.

"Get out of here!" she shouted, backing slowly away. "Leave me alone!" As Dylan moved quietly toward her, she reached down and picked up a heavy stick, swung it a couple of times at the bear, doing exactly what he'd told her. "I said get away!"

Dylan was almost there when the bear went up on its hind legs and let out a nerve-chilling roar. Then it turned and lumbered back into the forest, disappearing out of sight.

Quickly holstering his weapon, he ran on up the hill. "I'm right behind you, honey. He's gone. You're okay."

Lane just stood there, her stick still raised, her legs shaking.

"It's okay, baby, I promise."

She turned toward the sound of his voice. "Did you . . . did you see it?"

He couldn't stop a smile. "I sure did." He reached her, pulled her into his arms, took the stick, and tossed it away. "You were great, baby. I think that ol' bear was more afraid of you than you were of him."

She looked up at him, big green eyes wider than he'd

ever seen them. "It was . . . it was amazing. He was so beautiful."

Of all the things he had expected her to say, that wasn't one of them. *Not as beautiful as you*, he thought. Even in her dirty jeans and a shirt three sizes too big, she was the sexiest woman he had ever seen.

"That was a black bear, right? Not a grizzly?"

He nodded. "Black bear. Big. At least five hundred pounds." As the adrenaline began to wear off, she started shaking all over, and he tightened his hold around her.

"You handled it just right," he said, kissing the top of her head. "Unless you're hunting for food, shooting an animal should be a last resort. I'm proud of you."

She looked up at him, her cheeks pink and her eyes gleaming. "I'm glad I got to see him, but I don't want to see another one anytime soon."

Dylan laughed. "I don't blame you." With her arm in his, he led her back down to their makeshift camp to finish collecting their gear.

"There isn't much of a trail," he said. "Just an over-grown path along the creek. Anyone who comes up to fish usually flies in for the day."

"You said it was only five miles back to the lodge. On a good day, I can do ten on my treadmill. Of course this won't be flat and I won't be watching TV while I'm walking."

He smiled. "The scenery will be better."

Lane took a last glance out at the water. "It looks like a postcard." As if he had scripted it, a big bald eagle soared out over the lake, completing the picture.

"Look! An eagle. Oh, I wish I had my canvas and paints."

He followed her gaze, watching the bird spiral higher and higher, almost said he would bring her back one day so she could paint it. But there wouldn't be time for that.

Slinging his backpack over his shoulders, he slid his arms into the straps. "You ready?"

Lane smiled. "Are you kidding? I just faced down a bear. I can do anything."

Dylan reached down and cupped her face, bent his head, and kissed her. He tried not to think how much he was going to miss her when she was gone.

Caleb yawned. It was still early, but Winnie had been up since dawn and had gotten everyone fed. Alex and Jared were ready to head back to Yeil.

"I really appreciate your help," Caleb said as he walked them out to their pickup, a battered old Ford.

"Call us if Mr. Brodie doesn't get back and you need us again tonight," Alex said.

"I think after the way you pitched in, he'd want you to call him Dylan. With any luck, he'll be back this afternoon. But I've got your cell numbers. I'll call if he doesn't show up before dark."

"Tell Mrs. Henry she makes the best breakfast around," Jared said.

"I'll tell her." Caleb watched as Alex loaded his hunting rifle behind the seat and got into the truck. The engine rumbled to life and they headed up the gravel road back to Yeil. Dylan would be pleased to hear how the boys had volunteered to help keep everyone safe.

It was the weekend. With work on the lodge progressing so well, the crew was off for the next two days. Caleb had finally reached Paddy O'Ryan, filled him in, and asked him to come over. With Whitaker out there and Dylan still missing, he liked having a capable man like Paddy around.

He was headed back to the house when his phone

started ringing. Caleb recognized Jenny's number, and a warm feeling expanded in his chest.

"Hi, honey."

"Hi, Caleb. I just called to make sure you're okay."

He felt better just hearing her voice. "I'm all right. They searched my cabin, towed my truck off to search for evidence. There's nothing to find so I'm not worried about that."

"Would it be okay if . . . if I drove out to see you?"

It surprised him how much he wanted that. "I'd love to see you, honey, but . . . there's a problem. There's a guy. He may be the one who killed Holly. He's been out here watching the lodge. Until we figure a way to catch him, it isn't safe for you to come out."

"Oh, Caleb! Now I'm even more worried."

"I'm a little worried myself. We're hoping the police will be able to help. They should be out sometime today."

"Will you call me, Caleb? I need to know you're safe."

His heart squeezed. He couldn't remember the last time a woman had really cared about him. It sure as hell hadn't been Holly.

"I'll call you, honey. I promise." Caleb hung up the phone. At the sound of a vehicle coming up the road, he turned and looked in that direction. A dark brown rental car pulled into the parking area and the engine went still.

The door cracked open and a familiar tall man with black hair and a lean, powerful build got out, hauled a duffel out of the backseat, settled it on a broad shoulder, and started walking toward him.

He had the same blue eyes and hard jaw as his brother, but his features were less rugged and he was even better-looking.

Caleb felt a rush of relief as Nick Brodie strode toward the lodge.

* * *

Nick set the duffel he was carrying down at his feet. "Hey, Caleb."

"Hey, Nick. Man, I'm glad to see you."

Nick shook Caleb's hand. "What's up? Besides the fact you're smack in the middle of a murder investigation."

"Yeah, and the murderer might be camping on our doorstep."

Nick frowned. He had told himself his brother didn't need him, that the cops would eventually get everything straightened out, but the bad feeling he'd been having wouldn't go away.

He glanced toward the house. "Is my brother around?"

Caleb looked past him toward the forests behind the lodge. "Last night, Dylan had engine trouble on his way back from town. He set down in Moose Lake. He and Lane spent the night up there. They're hiking down the mountain today, probably on their way back by now."

Nick felt a sliver of uneasiness. According to Dylan, Kyle Whitaker had come to Alaska because of Lane. He was obsessed with her. According to Dylan, he had stabbed Lane's dog, probably to keep from being tracked. The guy was Delta. He was dangerous. He wanted Lane Bishop and Dylan was the only man standing in his way.

"How'd you get here?" Caleb asked.

"Flew Anchorage to Juneau last night. Since there wasn't an early commercial flight from there to Waterside, I flew private this morning. I had a rental car waiting, and here I am."

"Come on in. There's coffee in the kitchen. If you're hungry, you can probably get Winnie to fix you something to eat."

Nick looked off toward the mountains. "Listen, Caleb, I'm going to take a look around, see what I can find. I'll be back in a few minutes."

"Want me to go with you?"

Nick shook his head. "You go on in." He liked to work alone, at least at first, get into the perpetrator's head. If this guy was a killer, he might have left something behind. Hell, there was a good chance he was still out there.

Reaching down, he unzipped the duffel, took out his Glock 21, .45 caliber, and clipped the holster to his belt.

"Where's Emily?"

"She's in the house with Winnie."

"Good. Keep them there. Anyone else around?"

"Paddy O'Ryan's on his way, but he isn't here yet."

Nick nodded. "Like I said, I'll be back in awhile."

"I'll take your bag, put it in one of the empty bedrooms upstairs. Be careful."

Nick smiled darkly. If he wasn't a careful man, he'd have been dead long before now.

Nick surveyed the area outside the lodge, the mountains and the forests surrounding it. He'd been there before, spent two weeks with Dylan when he'd first bought the place.

There was an old cemetery up on the hill, he recalled. Be a good place for surveillance. Another hill rose to the south, above a trail that led to a stream coming down out of the mountains.

Nick checked the trail first, easier access, less chance of being spotted. It didn't take him long to find the place in the grass where someone had been lying, but it didn't look like it had been used lately.

He headed up the hill toward the cemetery. It took a while, but he finally found a track, hard as hell to spot. He figured the guy had blurred the print with a rag or maybe just leaves or grass.

He found two more blurred tracks, but they disappeared into some rocks above the cemetery.

Unease slid through him. The tracks looked fresh, maybe just a few hours old. He moved quietly around the area, but couldn't pick up the trail and saw no more sign of anyone.

Nick headed back down the hill. Worry tightened the muscles at the back of his neck. Every warning bell in his head was ringing, telling him he needed to reach his brother, that Lane was the objective but Dylan was the target.

He circled the lodge, following a hunch. Under one of the windows in the guest wing, he found another fairly fresh print.

Examining the window, he saw that the lock had been jimmied. It was tightly closed now, but Nick figured the perp had been inside the lodge. Probably last night.

Which meant he could very well know that Dylan and Lane were up at Moose Lake.

He headed for the back door, found Caleb waiting.

"Paddy's here," Caleb said. "You find anything?"

"Looks like the guy was in the house. Could have been there last night."

"Son of a bitch. How'd the bastard get in?"

"He knows how, believe me. I found a couple of tracks up near the cemetery. They're fresh. I have a feeling he's headed up to the lake. You're the best tracker I know. We need to find him before he finds Lane and Dylan."

"Paddy can stay with Emily and Winnie. I'll get my rifle."

"Get your sidearm, too."

Caleb nodded and headed off to collect his weapons

while Nick went upstairs and found his duffel. He had a concealed carry permit. He'd brought his rifle as well as his Glock .45. He loaded the rifle, stuffed ammo into the pockets of his camo vest, and slipped it on, shoved his cell phone into another pocket.

Ten minutes later, he had talked to Paddy, warned him to stay in the house and stay alert, though he figured it was Dylan and his lady who were in the crosshairs.

With Caleb at his side, Nick headed up to the cemetery, stopping at the place he had found the boot print. Caleb knelt in the grass, pressed his finger to the ground to test the size and depth.

"He's tall," Caleb said. "Over six feet, maybe a few pounds lighter than I am. Got his boots wrapped with something."

"I figured."

Caleb started prowling, looking for the next track. Didn't find it where it should have been.

"Here." He pointed to another distorted print. "He's stepping on rocks to keep from leaving a trail. Stepped here, though." He found another track a little farther up the hill.

"Where's he going?" Nick asked, but he could already hear the rush of running water.

"Upstream," Caleb said. "That's the way Dylan will be coming down."

"Let's go."

Chapter Thirty-One

"How you holding up?" Dylan asked.

Lane shoved an overhanging branch out of the way. "I'm doing okay." She wiped the perspiration off her forehead. "This definitely isn't like being on a treadmill."

"It's rough country. Even traveling downhill, I knew it wouldn't be easy. I probably should have found someone to fly in and pick us up."

Lane set her hands on her hips. "Why, because of me? You wouldn't do that if you were by yourself."

"No, but you didn't sign on for this kind of duty when you agreed to come up here."

"I came to help you with the lodge, yes, but I also wanted to see Alaska. I'm seeing it for real. If it weren't for Kyle Whitaker . . ." She broke off, shook her head.

"If it weren't for Whitaker, what?"

"I'd really be enjoying myself."

He cast her a glance. "Most people do this time of year."

There it was, the subtle reminder that she was just a tourist, that she could never be happy actually living up here year-round. Living up here with him.

Maybe he was right. Maybe she'd be as miserable as

Mariah had been. The thought turned her mood as dark as the cloudy day.

They trekked in silence for a while, climbing over downed trees, making their way around granite outcroppings. The grass was deep and boggy in places, the trail along the creek almost nonexistent. But the sound of the water rushing over the rocks in the streambed kept them heading downhill.

An hour passed, then another. "Let's take a break," Dylan said, stopping next to a fallen pine tree, the perfect spot for them to sit.

He unslung his backpack, reached in and grabbed a bottle of water, and passed it over to her. "Better stay hydrated."

She nodded, took a long swallow, and passed the bottle back to him. She watched him as he drank, his strong throat moving up and down, and for some crazy reason it turned her on. Desire slipped through her like liquid heat, and she fought to hold back a smile.

"What?" Dylan asked.

"Nothing." She shook her head. "It was nothing."

Those amazing blue eyes fixed on her face. "Good idea," he said, clearly reading her thoughts, and he hauled her into his arms. Lane laughed as he bent his head and kissed her, began to work the buttons on her borrowed flannel shirt.

Grinning, she pushed him away, started undoing the buttons herself. Just as Dylan ducked his head to kiss her, a gunshot sounded, echoing like thunder across the canyon. A wood chip flew off the log. Lane screamed as Dylan shoved her to the ground and came down on top of her, forcing her flat on the earth behind the fallen pine. Her heart was pounding so loud she could hear it.

Another three shots rang out, two of them thudding into the log, another pinging off a rock just inches away.

"It's him," he said as he eased himself off her, staying low, both of them on their bellies behind the downed tree.

"Maybe . . . maybe it's a hunter."

"It's him. He wants me out of the way so he can get to you."

She squeezed her eyes shut, praying Dylan was wrong, knowing he was right.

The gun Dylan had brought was in his hand. Moving out of sight behind a broken limb, he scanned the hillside where the shots had come from.

"Can you see him?" Lane whispered.

"No." He moved farther down the log, pulled off two shots that echoed up the canyon. Waited. But there was no return fire.

"What . . . what are we going to do?"

Dylan returned to his position beside her, stared back up the hill. "That was a deer rifle, nothing fancy. He probably stole it somewhere. Hard to get a gun on an airplane. The point is, he isn't that well armed. If I can get around behind him—"

"No!" Lane gripped his shoulder. She whirled in the direction the shot had come from. "Kyle, is that you? If it is, please don't kill Dylan!"

"Dammit, Lane!"

They waited what seemed an eternity, but no answer came.

"Maybe now that he knows we know who it is, he'll back off," Lane said.

"Maybe." Dylan's gaze scanned the forest across the creek and the thick pines on the other side of the fallen tree where they had taken cover. "I can't go after him. I can't leave you here by yourself—not when it's you he wants." He studied the landscape. "If we move away from the trail, stay hidden in the trees, we can make it the rest of the way down the mountain."

He reached over and unfastened the last few buttons on her blue flannel shirt, letting it fall open. "As long as you're wearing this, he can spot you a mile away." His own shirt was brown.

While Lane took off the shirt, Dylan opened his pack and pulled out a long-sleeved black T-shirt. "Put this on."

Stomach churning, she pulled on the T-shirt, took the black wool cap he gave her and stuffed her red hair out of sight underneath. At least they wouldn't stand out in the woods.

"You ready?"

She nodded, but she wasn't ready at all.

"I'll go first. I don't think he wants to hurt you, but we can't know for sure. I'll see if I can draw his fire."

As he started forward, she gripped his arm. "Isn't there some other way? If we don't get down the mountain, Caleb will come looking for us. Maybe we ought to—"

His hard kiss cut off her words. Gun in hand, Dylan darted toward the trees.

Stupid, Kyle. Really stupid. The voice could be brutal. Kyle knew he deserved it.

"I didn't kill him, all right?" He'd wanted to, though. When he'd seen Brodie touch her, kiss her, known he was going to take her right there, all his well-laid plans had gone up in smoke.

Moving fast but silently, Kyle began making his way back down the mountain. If Brodie had died in some kind of freak accident—beneath falling rocks, sliding off a cliff—Lane would never have known he was the one who had done it. She would have let him comfort her, let him take care of her while she grieved.

But killing Brodie outright would make her hate him. *Please don't kill Dylan*, she'd begged.

Until that moment, he hadn't realized they'd discovered he was there.

It didn't change anything. In fact, his little mishap might turn out to be a blessing. With the threat of him lying in wait for them, they would have to travel with utmost care, avoiding any place that would put them out in the open.

Brodie would do everything in his power to stay out of Kyle's gun sights—only Kyle wouldn't be there.

He almost smiled. A new plan was forming in his head, something he had considered a couple of times and discarded. But now the wheels had been set in motion and the new plan was looking better all the time.

Kyle would be back down the mountain hours before Lane and Brodie could make it, as they were forced to travel slowly, with extreme caution.

He chuckled, but the sound came out harsh and grim. When they got back, they were in for a big surprise.

Lane had never been more scared in her life. Not even when she'd thought the plane was going to crash. Not even when she'd faced a bear. They were quietly inching along, moving deep in the forest, climbing over downed trees and boulders, always moving from cover to cover.

So far there had been no sign of Kyle. "Maybe he gave up and left," she said. "Maybe when I called his name, he realized he couldn't get away with killing us."

"He's not trying to kill you, love. He wants me out of the way so he can get to you."

A sliver of fear ran through her.

Dylan reached out and cupped her cheek. "I'm not going to let him have you."

Lane leaned into his hand. She wanted to tell him she loved him. In case something happened, she wanted him to know. She swallowed, started to speak, but he was already moving, urging her toward the next deep cover.

They reached it safely. No shots, no sounds of movement in the forest.

"I don't hear anything," Dylan said.

"He's a soldier. Special Forces, remember? He wouldn't make noise."

"That's not the kind of sound I'm thinking about. No squirrels chattering a warning. No bird cries—not until they hear us coming. They aren't signaling that someone's moving ahead of us."

"Maybe he's circled around, or climbing above us to get a better shot. Oh, God, maybe he's coming up behind us."

Dylan's sharp gaze searched the forest. "Could be. Wherever he is, I don't believe he's given up. We've got to assume he's still out there." He took her hand. "Stay low and follow me."

Kyle was making good time. The trail along the stream was getting easier, the ground flattening out as he got closer to the sea. He was moving fast, making plans and revising them—when he spotted two men coming up the trail.

The big Indian, Caleb Wolfe, and another man tall and

dark moved quietly through the forest. Kyle slipped off the trail into deep cover to watch them.

The Indian was a tracker. Looked like a good one. The other guy moved silently, with a familiar sort of ease, his gaze always searching, watching for predators.

Kyle could recognize ex-military a mile away. Careful to stay low and out of sight, he waited for the men to pass along the trail. They were headed to the lake, he figured, making their way toward Brodie and Lane.

They were probably worried about them, anxious to reach them, make sure they got safely back to the lodge.

His mouth edged up. He couldn't have planned it better if he'd tried. Now Wolfe was out of the way, making it easy for him to accomplish his goal.

Leaving his position, he circled away from them, moving farther down the hill. Once it was safe, he cut back and took the easier path, the shortest route down the mountain.

It was all coming together.

It wouldn't be long now before all of this was over and he and Lane were on their way.

"We've lost his trail," Caleb said, his gaze going up the mountain toward the lake.

"Doesn't matter. We know where he's going. We know Lane and Dylan are headed this way." On a slim chance, he pulled out his cell and checked the bars. No service here or anywhere farther up. No way to reach them.

They continued up the trail, had just about made it to the halfway point when Caleb stopped. "Listen. You hear that?"

The forest creatures were talking, signaling each other.

Someone was moving through the forest off the trail in the dense thickness of the trees and shrubs below them.

"Could be them," Nick said.

"Could be him," said Caleb.

"Let's get out of sight. We'll wait here, see who shows up for the party."

They took a position on the hillside, hidden among the rocks, foliage, and pines where they could look down into the heavy growth of trees toward whoever was moving their way.

It went quiet again. Every once in awhile, Nick could hear the rustle of shrubbery, the faint disturbance of the grass. A branch moved. Someone slipped quietly through the shadows.

A second someone followed.

"It's them," Nick said, though he waited a few more moments to be sure.

"Why aren't they using the trail?"

"Let's find out." Cupping his hands around his mouth, he made the cawing sound of a raven. Two short and one long. Sounds he and his brothers had used to signal each other as kids.

The forest went silent. Then a return. Two short raven calls and a long.

"It's them." Grinning with relief, Nick started moving toward the sound, Caleb close behind him. They kept low. They'd followed Whitaker in this direction. They'd lost his trail, but that didn't mean he wasn't out there.

He caught up with his brother as he and the woman he recognized from her Facebook photo as Lane Bishop stepped out from behind the thick trunk of a tree.

"Man, am I glad to see you two," Dylan said, clasping him in a big bear hug.

"You okay?" Nick asked.

"Whitaker took a few shots at us." He turned to the woman, a redhead even more beautiful than Mariah. "Lane, this is my brother Nick."

"Nice to meet you," she said with a smile. "Thanks for coming to help us. You, too, Caleb."

Nick glanced up the mountain. "Whitaker's still out there. We'd better get going."

As they started down the hill, careful to stay under cover, he heard Lane speaking to Caleb, thanking him again for his help. Nick didn't think Mariah would have bothered.

Still, he wondered if his brother was making the same mistake he'd made before, falling for a beautiful woman who would make a miserable wife.

At the moment, Nick figured that was the least of Dylan's worries.

"I'll scout ahead," Nick said. "Stay low and out of sight. I'll be close by if you need me."

Dylan nodded and they headed off down the mountain.

Chapter Thirty-Two

Kyle surveyed the lodge, then moved closer, circled the structure, and got a glimpse through the windows of what was happening inside. The ruddy-faced, red-haired man he had seen there working was in the kitchen with the woman and child.

From what he could tell, the crew was gone and there was no one else around.

Kyle headed for the guest wing. In less than five minutes, he was inside the house. No one up here used alarm systems. It was almost too easy.

The construction crew had left their gear. He located a roll of duct tape, stuck it into the pocket of his camo pants. Reaching into his jacket, he pulled out a handful of the plastic ties he always carried, handy for solving any number of problems, then headed down the hall.

Slipping silently through the mammoth living room, he positioned himself outside the door between the formal dining area and the kitchen.

"Anyone hungry?" the older woman asked. "How about you, Paddy? I've got some homemade chocolate chip cookies. Be nice with a glass of ice cold milk."

"That sounds great, Winnie."

He could hear the woman, Winnie, moving off toward the refrigerator. As she pulled open the door, Kyle purposely bumped a table, knocking over a small pottery vase sitting on top.

"What was that?" Paddy asked.

"I don't know," said Winnie.

"I'd better go see."

Pressing himself back against the wall, Kyle waited. The minute the burly man walked through the door, he stepped behind him. Using the side of his hand, he took him out with a hard chop to the back of his neck. Kyle caught him as he went down, dragged him out of the doorway, and used a plastic tie and piece of duct tape to keep him quiet and out of the way.

"Paddy?" Winnie called out. "Is everything okay?"

Kyle stepped into the doorway. "Everything's just fine." The woman shrieked at the sound of his voice. "It'll stay that way if you do exactly what I tell you."

The kid opened her mouth, but no sound came out. He'd never heard her say a word.

"What do you want?" Winnie asked, trembling, her bosom rising and falling with each breath. "What did you do to Paddy?"

"Your friend is fine . . . or he will be as soon as he wakes up." He smiled. "But since you asked, what I want is some of those chocolate chip cookies."

Winnie cast a worried glance at the little girl, hurried over to the jar, and pulled out a handful of cookies. They smelled delicious. She set them on the table in front of him. "Take them and go. Leave us alone."

Kyle grabbed a cookie and stuffed it into his mouth.

Damn, it was as good as it smelled. He took the rest and crammed them into a pocket in his jacket.

"I'm going to need the kid to go with me. Emily, right? I've heard you talking to her."

"You . . . you were in the house?"

"Sure. I've been in a lot of times. Those two college boys made it easy. I just went in through that little door they were using. Harder coming in through a window, but not much. You guys ought to get an alarm system."

"I want you to leave," Winnie said. By now the girl was clutching her around the waist, hanging on and looking up at him with big, blue terrified eyes.

He wasn't much of a kid person. He wished he didn't have to take her, but he needed to move things along, and he knew Lane would come after the child.

"I'll leave," he said. "But Emily goes with me."

Winnie pulled the kid tighter against her. "You aren't taking her. You'll have to kill me first."

The ringing started in his head. "Don't say that. I'm not a killer." The voice kept clamoring, saying something, but he couldn't make out what it was. "It was an accident, okay? I didn't mean to hurt her. It was just a game."

Winnie looked like she was going to faint. She straightened, and he could tell she was fighting to keep herself together.

"Get out of the house," she said. "Nick and Caleb will be back any minute. Nick's a policeman. You'd better get out while you can."

The ringing grew louder, making it hard for him to think. *If you're going to do this, you'd better get moving*, the voice said.

"They're on their way up to the lake. I'll be long gone before they get back. Now give me the girl." Emily shrunk back against the heavyset woman. She might not be able to talk, but she understood what he meant to do.

"I don't want to hurt you," he said to her.

The kid started wheezing, trying to say something. Kyle ignored her and started for the woman. She shoved the girl behind her, grabbed a big iron skillet off the stove and swung it as hard as she could. "Run, Emily!"

Kyle ducked the blow meant for his head, but it crashed against his shoulder. It hurt, dammit. But not enough to stop him. He caught the kid as she rushed for the door, hauled her back into the room, turned, and slammed a fist into the woman's jaw. She went down like a sack of wheat.

Now you've done it, the voice said.

The kid shrieked and started making that wheezing sound again, trying to say something as she backed away from him into a corner. She was crying now and the voice got louder.

You're in it now, aren't you, Kyle? You need to leave. You need to get out of here before they come back and catch you.

He turned his wrath on the girl. "Shut up! You hear me? Just shut the hell up!" She whimpered and he forced himself under control. "Look, I'm not gonna hurt you, okay? I didn't want to hurt your friends. I just need to talk to Lane. She won't come unless I take you with me. Understand?"

She shook her head no, but he could see she understood perfectly. "Come on. I need to get you back to the cabin. We'll wait for Lane there. I'll let you go as soon as she comes to get you. Okay?"

The kid shook her head again. With a sigh of frustration, he grabbed her wrists, forced them together in front of her, and bound them with a plastic tie. He probably didn't need the duct tape, since she couldn't talk anyway, but he didn't want to hear those wheezing noises.

Hoisting the kid over his shoulder, he headed for the door. She struggled for a moment, then went still. Guess she figured there was no way she was going to get away from him.

And she was absolutely right.

Dylan didn't lead Lane and Caleb out of the cover of the forest until he spotted Nick next to the old picket fence around the cemetery.

"No sign of him," his brother said. "He must have taken off after he took those shots."

"Gonna be hell trying to find him," Dylan said as they moved closer to the lodge. "We need to get the state troopers in here." He started to pull out his cell, paused when he felt Nick's hand on his arm, saw him motion for them to move into the shadows next to one of the cabins.

"What is it?" Dylan asked softly, once all of them were out of sight.

"I'm not sure. Something doesn't feel right. Seems a little too quiet."

The hair went up on the back of Dylan's neck. He'd learned to trust his brother's instincts. And his own.

He pulled out his cell. "My phone should be working. Let's call." Dylan punched the lodge number. Four rings and no one picked up. He shook his head and closed the phone, a hard knot forming in his stomach.

"Oh, God," Lane said.

"Stay here while I take a look." Nick pulled his weapon. Dylan pulled his .44. "I'm with you," he said. "Stay with Lane," he told Caleb. Together they moved off toward the house.

At the mudroom entrance, Dylan used his key to unlock the door, trying to make as little noise as possible. Gun in hand, Nick turned the knob and shoved the door open. He waited a second, then slipped inside. Dylan moved in behind him, his pistol in a two-handed grip.

Working together as they moved down the hall, they cleared the office, went into Winnie's rooms and cleared them, then headed for the kitchen. Dylan spotted Winnie, bound and gagged and lying on the floor. Her eyes filled when she saw him.

Dylan's stomach clenched. While Nick kept watch, he knelt beside her and pulled off the gag. "Where's Emily?"

"She's gone," the older woman said tearfully, a near hysterical note in her voice. "He took her. He wants Lane to come and get her."

Nick found Paddy in the dining room. He was awake, also bound and gagged. As soon as both of them were free, Dylan signaled to Lane and Caleb that it was safe to come into the house.

"He's got Emily," Dylan told them as they walked into the kitchen. "He wants to trade her for Lane."

"Oh, God," Lane said, sagging down on the bench at the long table next to Winnie. Caleb looked sick.

Dylan turned to Nick. "Do we bring in the police or go after him ourselves?" He trusted his brothers with his life, trusted Nick to know the best way to help his daughter.

Nick raked a hand through his wavy black hair. "At the moment, we don't know where Whitaker's taken her. The troopers will bring in dogs and choppers. Whitaker has a history of mental illness. We can't be sure what he might do."

"He killed Holly Kaplan." Winnie sniffed back tears. "He told me it was an accident." She started crying. "Now he's got our little girl."

"We'll get her back," Dylan vowed, so furious he could barely force out the words. "I promise you." He'd been certain Whitaker had murdered Holly. He was only a little surprised the man had admitted it. "He's got to call. He expects Lane to come to him. Once he gets where he's going, he'll call."

Lane rose from the bench. "When he calls, I've got to talk to him. I'll tell him I'm coming. That'll keep Emily safe."

"That's a good idea," Dylan said. "As long as you understand you aren't really going anywhere near him."

Lane's chin went up. "That's where you're wrong. I brought this down on all of you. I'm the one who's going to fix it."

"Not a chance," Dylan said.

"I'm going," Lane said. "There's no way I'm letting him hurt that little girl."

The room fell silent.

"We'll figure it out," Nick said gently. "Once he calls, we'll decide what to do. Let's see how it all plays out."

They sat nervously staring at the three phones lying on the kitchen table. The lodge phone, Lane's next to it, Dylan's next to hers. They had no idea which number Kyle would call.

An hour slid past. "I'll make a check of the house," Paddy said, just for something to do. Winnie busied herself brewing a fresh pot of coffee while Lane paced the kitchen floor. Dear God, where was Emily? Where had Kyle taken her?

Nausea rolled through her and she trembled. With a last glance at Dylan's grim features, she walked out of the kitchen, through the dining area, across the great hall to the entry. She opened the front door, left it cracked enough so she could hear the phone, and walked out onto the porch.

The wind was blowing, whipping a cold breeze across the bay. The sun had disappeared behind the clouds, leaving the sky a sullen gray.

Fear gripped her. This was all her fault. Kyle was here because of her. He had killed a woman, and now he had Dylan's little girl.

Her chest felt so tight she could barely breathe. Moving to the edge of the porch, she forced in a lungful of air. She didn't hear Dylan approach, didn't know he was behind her until he gently caught her shoulders and turned her into his arms. Fighting back a sob, Lane clung to him. "I'm so sorry," she said. "So sorry."

His hold tightened around her. "This isn't your fault, Lane. None of it." He brushed a finger along her cheek. "We're going to get her back. I swear it."

But there was no way he could know that for sure.

She glanced up at a sound, realized the phone had started ringing. Both of them raced back into the lodge and ran for the kitchen.

It was Lane's cell phone, with an incoming call from a number she didn't recognize. She grabbed it and pressed the phone against her ear. "Kyle, is that you?"

"Hello, Lane. I've missed you, sweetheart."

A chill slid down her spine. She held the phone so both

Dylan and Nick could hear the conversation. "Where are you, Kyle? Where have you taken Emily?"

"I didn't want to take her. I just need to talk to you."

"Okay. Where are you? Where's Emily?"

"I'll tell you where we are if you promise to come. You haven't called the police, have you?"

"No. I-I wouldn't do that. Winnie told me you just wanted to see me, talk things out."

"That's right. I would have called sooner, but you were with Brodie. And . . . some problems came up."

She knew what those problems were. Finding a way to keep from getting caught after he'd murdered Holly. "Is . . . is Emily all right?"

"She's fine. She wants to go home. I need to see you, Lane. We need to talk. Once we do, you'll see what a perfect match we are. We can go away together."

Nick started nodding, telling her to agree. She moistened her lips, which felt cold and numb. "Talking sounds good. Where are you? How will I find you?"

"Are you sure you won't call the cops?"

"I won't call them. I don't want Emily getting hurt."

"I don't want that, either. But you have to come alone. I'll be watching, making sure no one follows you. I'll know if you're trying to trick me."

"I won't trick you. Dylan wants his daughter safely returned. He'll let me come by myself."

There was silence on the other end of the line. He was trying to decide whether or not to believe her. She closed her eyes, whispered a little prayer.

"There's a cabin," he finally said. "It's at the end of a dirt lane south of Yeil. The turnoff's overgrown, nearly impossible to spot. It's exactly three-point-one miles north of the lodge. Watch your speedometer. Make the turn, then drive to the end of the road. It's another two miles."

"Okay, I've got it."

"I'll see you soon, sweetheart." Kyle hung up the phone. Lane's knees were shaking badly. Dylan eased her over to the table and back down on the bench.

She took a shuddering breath. "You both heard him. I've got to go by myself."

"Bullshit," Dylan said.

"There's no way around it, Dylan," Nick said. "Lane's got to go. You know it and so do I."

Dylan's jaw was so tight it looked painful. He started to speak, but Nick's words cut him off.

"She's got to go, but she won't be alone. We'll be with her. All three of us."

"Count me in," Paddy said. "I'd love to give that bastard a little payback."

Lane almost smiled.

"You aren't up to it yet," Dylan said. "Besides, I need you to stay here with Winnie. If the son of a bitch comes back, this time you'll be ready for him." It was a kindness, but it worked.

"All right," Paddy reluctantly agreed.

Lane looked at her watch. "He's expecting me. I need to get going."

"All right," Nick said. "Here's what we're going to do."

Chapter Thirty-Three

Dylan didn't like it. Not one bit. He didn't want to put Lane in danger. But Nick was right. Lane was the key to bringing Emily out safely.

Rifle slung across his back, he moved through the forest at a good, fast clip. The first few miles, he, Nick, and Caleb had ridden beneath a tarp in the bed of his pickup while Lane drove toward the turnoff. They climbed out a mile before they reached the cabin, split up, and headed at a jog to the rendezvous point.

Ironically, he figured that as close as the cabin was to the lodge, they might have spotted it from the plane. Instead, the engine failure had brought them down at Moose Lake. If he hadn't just moved into the area a few months back, he might have known the cabin was there.

He checked his watch, but didn't slow. He knew his way around a forest, knew how to make the best time. It wasn't much farther. The plan was to take up positions around the house, Nick covering the back, he and Caleb on both sides of the road near the front, where they could watch the front door.

Each of them carried one of the handheld Motorola radios he used on hunting and fishing trips. Their range was only a couple of miles, but once they reached the cabin, they'd be close enough to stay in contact.

He was very close now. Dylan had located the cabin on the Internet and checked it out on Google Earth. He slowed, carefully placed each footstep as quietly as he could. Through the woods, he could hear the pickup rolling slowly down the road, knew Whitaker would be positioned somewhere he could watch Lane's approach. He would want to make sure she'd come alone.

Dylan pushed the TALK button on the radio. "I can see the cabin. Truck's almost there. I'm moving into position. Over."

"Roger that," Caleb said, "I'm almost there."

"I'm in position on the hill at the back," Nick said. "Got the back door in my sights." The radio fell silent.

Dylan moved closer, staying low and deep in the foliage around the cabin. It was made of logs, was heavily overgrown, and had obviously not been in use for the past few years. That wasn't uncommon up here.

As he settled into a spot where he could see the front door beneath the porch roof, he unslung his rifle, belly-crawled up behind a boulder, and settled in to wait.

Using his binoculars, he scanned the area around the house, spotted Lane behind the wheel of his truck, bouncing along the rutted road the last few yards to the house. As planned, she honked her horn a couple of times, and a movement in the window caught his eye.

"There you are," he said, catching a glimpse of Whitaker inside the house. Eager to see Lane, Whitaker hadn't noticed the men taking up positions around the cabin.

The distraction, the first part of the plan, had worked.

Dylan settled his rifle in a notch at the top of a granite boulder. He was ready as the truck braked to a stop in front of the house.

Lane rolled down the window and turned off the engine. "I'm here, Kyle! Are you in there?"

The front door opened a crack. "Come inside, Lane."

"I'm not coming in till you let Emily come out. She can wait in the truck while we talk."

"You come in. The girl comes out when you get inside the cabin."

Dylan's muscles tensed. He had warned her—under absolutely no circumstances was she to go into the house.

"I'm not doing that, Kyle. I need to be sure Emily is safe. Then we can talk."

Silence fell. A few minutes later, the door swung open, and Kyle walked out with Emily in front of him, using her as a human shield. A powerful arm wrapped around her neck, and Dylan fought down an image of Holly Kaplan, strangled and lying dead in the grass outside Mad Jack's Saloon.

"You need to come in, Lane. I don't want to hurt her, but you know I can. All I want to do is talk."

Dylan swore as the pickup door swung open and Lane climbed down from the driver's side of the truck. "I'll come to you, Kyle. But you have to let Emily go. She can wait for me in the truck, okay?"

Whitaker seemed uncertain. He turned his head one way and then another. His mouth was moving. He seemed to be talking to someone other than Lane, but there was no one there.

"Okay," he finally said, returning his attention to Lane. "You come inside and the kid can wait in the truck."

Dylan's pulse pounded as he watched Lane slowly approach the porch.

"Let her go, Kyle," she said softly. "Then I'll come inside."

Lying flat on the ground, the barrel of his Weatherby steadied on top of the boulder, Dylan watched through his scope as Lane approached the porch. She was directly in his line of fire. On the other side of the road, Caleb wouldn't have a clear shot, either. Dylan swore a silent oath.

Lane moved slowly. "She's scared, Kyle. Please let her go." She turned to Emily. "Go get in the truck, honey. Kyle and I need to talk. I'll drive you back home when we're finished, okay?"

"N-n-n-no. D-d-d-don't. G-g-g-go."

Shock rolled through Dylan at the sound of his daughter's voice. Lane grabbed the child, pulled her out of Kyle's arms. "Get in the truck, Emily!" She shoved the girl in that direction even as Kyle was trying to haul Lane into the house. Instead of running away, Emily turned and ran after them, pushing at Kyle, trying to keep him from dragging Lane inside.

Dylan's finger tightened on the trigger. His heart was racing, trying to beat through his chest. No way he could fire without a clear shot.

"Get in the truck!" Lane shouted, but it was too late. Kyle hauled them both inside and slammed the door.

Dylan's chest clamped down in rage and fear. Emily and Lane were in there, at the mercy of a killer. He wanted to go down and tear the goddamned door off its hinges, shoot Whitaker where he stood.

He took a deep breath, forced himself under control. His mind shot back to his daughter. The first words Emily had said in three years had been forced out of her mouth by fear for Lane.

Renewed anger rolled through him. Through the rifle scope, he sighted through the cabin window. He could see Lane and Emily on the sofa. Kyle was somewhere out of view. At least they were okay for the moment.

Dylan brought up his radio, pressed the TALK button. "Plan A's a bust," he said to Nick. "They're both inside."

Nick's deep voice crackled through the speaker. "I can't see anyone moving in the windows at the back of the house. Time for plan B."

Dylan had known his brother would have one. It was what a Ranger did when plan A went south and turned into a goat fuck.

Dylan pushed the TALK button. "He still doesn't know we're here. Over."

"We need to move in," Nick replied, "find out what's going on in there. Caleb, you there?"

"I'm here."

"Keep your rifle on the door. If you get a clear shot, take him out, but don't risk hitting Lane or Emily."

"Copy that. Over."

"Dylan, you move around, come in on the side where he can't see you. Try to find out what's going on in there. I need two minutes to reach the back door. The first chance we get, we go in."

"On my way." Moving toward the side of the house where he would be out of sight, Dylan headed for the cabin.

Lane sat on the sofa, an arm around Emily's small shoulders. She could feel the child shaking. "Everything's going to be okay," she said softly.

"H-h-he . . . h-h-h-hurt . . . W-W-W-Winnie."

"Winnie and Paddy are okay," Lane said, not wanting to make a big deal out of the fact the little girl was talking, afraid if she did, Emily would stop. "They're waiting for us back at the lodge."

"Shut that kid up. I brought you here so we could talk."

Lane looked up at him. "Why don't I take her outside, put her in the truck? Then we can talk."

Kyle just shook his head. She had forgotten how good-looking he was. Dark hair, hard jaw. His slightly Roman nose didn't detract from his long-lashed brown eyes or the fullness of his lips. A woman would have to be dead not to notice his powerful build.

But the attraction she'd felt had been purely physical. It hadn't taken her long to sense that something was off about him. The way he'd get confused. The way he would look up and say something. As if he were talking to someone who wasn't really there.

He was doing that now. Forming words, then shaking his head.

"Let me take her out to the truck," Lane pressed.

"No!" He walked over to the couch and grabbed Emily's arm, started dragging her toward the tiny bedroom at the back of the cabin.

Lane came up off the sofa. "Kyle, don't! You'll hurt her! I'll never forgive you if you hurt Emily!"

He let go of the little girl's arm, and Emily raced back to her, her face sheet-white against the frame of her glossy dark hair. Lane bent and caught her in her arms.

"It's okay, honey. Kyle isn't going to hurt you."

"Take her into the bedroom and close the door. Tell her to stay there until we're finished."

At least she'd be out of harm's way as much as possible.

"All right." Lifting the child against her hip, Lane carried Emily into the bedroom. "Your daddy's outside," she whispered against the child's ear as she walked through the bedroom door. "Stay quiet. Get out if you can."

Emily faintly nodded.

"Hurry up!" Kyle said.

Lane set Emily on her feet, turned, and walked out of the bedroom, closing the door behind her.

She pasted on a smile. "That's better. Now we'll have a chance to talk. You came all the way up here to see me. What was it you wanted to say?"

Kyle looked relieved. Lane forced herself not to flinch when he took her hand and led her over to the sofa.

Nick was standing at the back door of the cabin when he saw the screen moving at the bedroom window. The screen fell off and Emily's head popped out as she climbed over the sill. Relief trickled through him. *One down, one to go.*

The minute she spotted him, the little girl ran toward him. Lowering his weapon, Nick caught her against his side.

"U-U-Uncle N-N-Nick," she whispered. "L-L-Lane's in-in—"

"I know, sweetie." Keeping his voice soft and low, he tried not to show his surprise that she was speaking. "We're going to get her out." He pressed the TALK button. "I've got Em."

"Thank God." There was a moment of relief in Dylan's voice; then the tension returned. "I'm moving beneath the front window."

Nick turned to the child. "Go up the hill. Get behind a rock and don't come out until we come get you."

She nodded, raced away. He watched till she disappeared behind a boulder. "Em's safe. I'm at the back door."

"Give me a minute. I'll see if I can get a fix on where they are."

Lane sat on the sofa next to Kyle. He had positioned himself on the other side of her, away from the window. No way anyone who might be out there could get a shot. The man was no fool.

"You remember when we were dating?" he asked, flashing her a smile, the one that had convinced her to go out with him. "How we always got along so well? Remember how you said we were a perfect match?"

"You said that, Kyle."

He frowned. "Maybe. Maybe I did. But it's true, right? We were perfect together. If I hadn't got in that fight, we'd still be together, right?"

"I don't know, Kyle. That was a while back."

He glanced toward the bedroom door. "You like kids, right? Maybe a few years down the road, we could have a couple. I mean, if that was what you wanted. Not right away, though. We need time to get to know each other."

Lane wished she could look out the window, try to spot Dylan, but she would have to turn around to do it and she might give him away.

". . . so what do you think?"

Oh, God, she'd lost track of the conversation. "About . . . about having kids?"

"No, dammit, about leaving together. I've got tickets for the ferry. It's due in Waterside tomorrow. We can drive in tonight, be there when it leaves in the morning."

It wasn't logical. There was an abducted child in the bedroom and he had murdered a woman.

"I'd need to get my things," she said, stalling for time. "I'd have to go back to the lodge and get them."

Kyle shook his head. "No way I'm letting you go back to Brodie." His features tightened until he didn't look handsome at all. "You fucked him, didn't you? You fucked him six ways to Sunday."

Fear slipped through her. "I didn't know you cared that much, Kyle. I didn't know the way you felt."

He relaxed a little, released a breath. "It's all right, I forgive you. I was mostly to blame. I shouldn't have got in that fight."

Her mouth felt dry. She glanced across the room to the tiny kitchen. "Is that coffee I smell?"

He smiled. "I made a pot before you came. I remembered you always liked coffee."

"It smells really good." She rose from the sofa, hoping to distract him. "Do you mind if I get myself a cup?"

Dylan, Nick, and Caleb were out there waiting for a chance to get inside the house. She prayed Emily would stay in the bedroom, or that she had gone out the window.

Unfortunately, Kyle rose, too, took Lane's hand, and led her over to the kitchen counter. "I'll get the cups."

Taking down a pair of mugs, he set them on the counter and filled them with hot black coffee. Steam rose from the top of the mug.

Over Kyle's shoulder, Lane caught a glimpse of Dylan next to the window. He quickly moved out of sight beside the front door. Lane's heart was pounding. This was the chance she had been praying for. She picked up the mug, blew on the top, pretending to cool it. When Dylan came into her line of vision again, Lane tossed the scalding coffee into Kyle's face and bolted for the front door.

Everything happened at once. Kyle knocked her down and threw himself on top of her. Dylan crashed through the front door, and Nick kicked the back door open. Lane struggled, but Kyle was a powerful man and he was straddling her, pinning her to the floor.

"Don't move!" Dylan commanded. His revolver, and Nick's big semiautomatic were pointed straight at Kyle's head.

"Move back or I kill her!" Kyle shouted. Lane swallowed, felt the cold steel blade of a knife pressed into her throat. She looked up at him, into eyes that had changed from those of a would-be lover to the eyes of a killer.

"Take it easy," Dylan said, lowering his weapon a fraction. Nick shifted position, the barrel of his gun aimed in a way that Whitaker would take the bullet and it wouldn't hit Lane. "Nobody needs to get hurt."

Lane stared up at Kyle, his face red and beginning to blister, coffee running down his cheeks. "Why did you do that, Lane? I thought you cared about me."

"Get off her, Whitaker," Nick warned.

"You need to think this through," Dylan said, shifting his own position a little. "Killing Holly was an accident. Accidents happen. You kill Lane, you'll be a murderer."

"I'm not a murderer," Kyle said, but the blade didn't waver.

"Let Lane go and we'll work this out," Nick said. "You don't really want to hurt her and she doesn't want you to get hurt, either."

Kyle's gaze remained on her face. "What'll I do without you?" he asked, and in that moment, Lane read his thoughts. She'd been the focus of his life for months. Without her, he had no goals, no idea what to do with himself. He was going to die and take her with him.

Kyle's hand tightened on the knife and Lane screamed at the echo of gunfire. Two bullets from Nick's gun, and two from Dylan's, slammed into Kyle's body. The knife fell away and he slumped sideways onto the floor.

In an instant, the weight of his body was completely gone and she was being hauled up into Dylan's arms. Shaking and crying, she clung to him, held on to him for dear life.

"It's okay, baby. It's over."

Lane trembled, then remembered the little girl in the bedroom. "Emily!" She tried to break free, but Dylan's hold only tightened.

"Em's safe. She climbed out the bedroom window."

Lane started crying. "I was so scared for her." Terrified that she would be the cause of the little girl's death. Horrified to think what her loss would have done to Dylan. To her.

Dylan slid an arm around her waist and started leading her toward the door. "Come on, baby. Let's get out of here."

Lane swallowed, felt a moment of pity for the man whose life had ended so badly. Leaning against Dylan, she let him guide her out the door.

Dylan led Lane outside and spotted Caleb coming down from his position on the hill. As he reached the cabin, he saw Kyle lying on the floor inside. "I guess it's finally over."

"Over for all of us." Lane was safe and Caleb's name would be cleared. At the bottom of the steps, she glanced back toward the house.

"I think . . . I think he wanted you to shoot him."

Nick walked down the stairs behind them. "Suicide by cop," he said. "I think you might be right, Lane. We'll never really know."

"Whatever happened, it wasn't because of you," Dylan said firmly. "Life isn't always fair. Whitaker got a rotten deal, but a lot of people have problems. He could have made different choices. Instead, he killed a woman, nearly killed you, too."

They rounded the house to the back, spotted Emily's dark head where she peered over the top of a big granite boulder. With a sob, she raced toward them down the hill.

"She's talking, Dylan," Lane said. "Did you hear her?"

"She told me Lane was inside," Nick said, "wanted me to go in and help her. Maybe something good came out of this after all."

Dylan ran to meet his daughter, caught her up in his arms. "I've got you, honey. Lane's safe and everyone's okay."

Emily buried her head in his shoulder. "I w-was so s-scared, D-daddy."

Dylan's eyes slid closed. He swallowed past the tightness in his throat and hugged his little girl. "I've got you now. You don't ever have to be afraid again."

Chapter Thirty-Four

Amazing how quickly the past few days had gone by. After the shooting, Dylan had phoned the Alaska State Troopers; then all of them had waited outside the cabin for the police chopper to arrive.

With the deep forest and heavy foliage, the helicopter had to land a mile away. The troopers found the overgrown road and walked in on foot. Other officers and the coroner drove in by road, making the time-consuming journey from Waterside.

By the next day, things had settled down. Nick returned to Fish Lake, the rural town he lived in north of Anchorage, and got busy doing less than nothing again. Dylan hoped that would soon change.

Rafe called, ranting at him and Nick for not keeping him in the loop. His older brother had been worried, he'd finally admitted, which wasn't easy for Rafe to admit, since he wasn't exactly the touchy-feely type. But then none of them really were.

The mechanic in Waterside had flown into Moose Lake to make engine repairs on the plane. Dylan and Caleb had hiked in to meet him, then flown the plane back to Eagle Bay.

Caleb had been cleared of all charges. In Whitaker's rented Jeep, they'd found a charm off Holly's silver chain, along with a scarf belonging to Lane that Kyle had taken from the lodge. It still sent a shudder down Dylan's spine to think of the guy prowling around inside the house.

Finn was home and healing very well, a huge relief to Lane and Emily.

For the last few days, Caleb had been in Waterside, spending time with Jenny. He seemed really happy. Dylan hoped things worked out for the two of them.

Emily was talking, but she still didn't say very much. Though the dam had been breached, Dylan could see that whatever barrier stood between them remained, making their brief conversations stilted and uncomfortable.

Things would get better, he told himself, hoping he could find a way to make that happen.

But added to that disappointment, things had begun to deteriorate between him and Lane. In the few days since the shooting, she'd been sleeping in her own room instead of beside him in his. He wasn't sure if she was trying to recover from seeing a man killed in front of her, or if she was distancing herself, preparing herself to leave.

He found out that night after supper when her familiar soft rap came at his door. Barefoot and wearing just his jeans, he pulled the door open, found Lane standing in the hall, her pink fleece robe belted around her, the collar turned up and her hands shoved into her pockets.

His heart jerked. At the same time desire slid through him. He wanted to drag her inside and off to his bed. He wanted to ravish her.

He wanted to tell her he had fallen in love with her, that he never wanted her to leave.

He wouldn't. He couldn't do that to Emily. Or to himself.

"Could we . . . could we talk?"

"Sure." He forced himself to step back to let her pass. "Come on in." She wanted to talk. He could see by her face it wasn't going to be good.

They sat down on the sofa in front of the empty hearth. He wished there was a fire. "You feeling any better?"

"A little. I know there was nothing anyone could have done to change what happened."

"Only Kyle."

"I've thought a lot about it. In a way, maybe it was for the best. I don't think Kyle was the kind of man who could stand being locked up in a mental facility, and that's what would have happened to him."

He took her hand, brought it to his lips. "I wish it could have been different."

"I wish a lot of things could be different." She glanced down at their linked hands, eased hers free. "I've decided to go back early, Dylan. Everything's been ordered. Some of it isn't here yet, but it's on its way. I think it would be better for all of us if I left now instead of waiting."

His chest clamped down. He didn't want her to leave. He wanted her to stay so much, he had to clench his jaw to keep from saying the words. It wouldn't work. Both of them knew it. Had known it from the start.

"I know you have your own life to live."

She nodded. "I've got a flight out day after tomorrow. That'll give me time to pack my samples and get them ready to ship. And say good-bye to everyone."

He swallowed, ignored the tightness in his throat. "All right."

She reached up and touched his cheek. "There's so much I want to say."

"You don't have to say anything. We knew how this would end when you came up here."

Her eyes filled. "Maybe I did. I guess I did. Doesn't make it any easier."

"No, it doesn't."

"Make love to me, Dylan. I need you."

He needed her, too. Maybe had known it deep down the first time he'd seen her.

Kissing her softly, he scooped her into his arms and carried her into the bedroom. There was nothing beneath her robe, he discovered as he settled her in the middle of his bed and stripped the fluffy pink fleece away, let his gaze roam over her long legs, slender waist, and pretty, upturned breasts.

"I'll always remember these weeks we've been to-gether," he said.

"I couldn't forget, even if I tried."

He kissed her, left her long enough to slide out of his jeans, then came down beside her on the bed. He spent long moments just looking at her, memorizing the lines of her face, her supple, slender curves. She was so beautiful.

But it was a deeper sort of beauty than he had noticed when he had first seen her. There was a kindness in Lane that made her lovelier than he'd first realized. A boldness of spirit and a giving heart.

He kissed her softly, looped strands of fiery hair behind her ear. He kissed the corners of her mouth, her bottom lip, her eyes, her nose, took her mouth again. His chest was aching. He had never really understood how painful it could be to love someone.

He understood it now.

They made love slowly, deeply. A different sort of love-making from before. They climbed the pinnacle together, bodies joined, breathing as one, and his heart filled with love and pain.

He wanted to tell her. Knew it wouldn't be fair.

He thought that she might love him, too, but it didn't matter. Couldn't matter. As they spiraled down, the world tried to intrude, but he refused to let it.

"Sleep with me tonight," he said.

"Dylan . . ."

"Please, love. Tonight's all we have."

She nodded. He ignored the tears in her eyes as he curled her against him. He'd let her sleep for a while, then make love to her again.

For him, there would be no sleep. He wanted to hold off the dawn, wanted to postpone those final hours, knowing the rest of his life would be without her.

In the office the following morning, Lane continued packing, getting ready to leave on the flight out tomorrow. She had gone to Dylan last night, unable to bear staying away a moment more. Making love with him had been her final good-bye. Both of them knew it. Both of them felt the pain.

Her own was deeper than she could have imagined. She couldn't face it again tonight. Tonight she would sleep alone, be ready to travel first thing in the morning.

Caleb was driving her to Waterside. She was taking one of the small commercial planes to Ketchikan, catching a flight to Seattle, and heading back to Los Angeles from there. When she'd told Dylan her plan, he hadn't tried to dissuade her.

Another good-bye would be painful for him, too.

She thought about their last night together. As she had stood in the hall outside his door, she had thought about telling him the truth, telling him she loved him and wanted to stay. But the moment she had seen his face, she had known it would be useless.

Dylan didn't believe she could be happy living in the harsh environment of Alaska. Her unhappiness would make him and his daughter unhappy, too. Nothing she could say was going to change his mind.

She tossed a stack of carpet samples into the shipping box and closed it up, sealed it with packing tape, and set the box aside. She worked for another half hour, getting things labeled and organized.

She was almost done when she looked up and saw Winnie standing in the doorway. Lane managed to muster a smile. "I'm glad you're here. I was coming to say good-bye."

Winnie walked forward, wrapped Lane in her chubby arms. "We're all going to miss you."

She just nodded, fought not to cry. "I'll miss all of you, too."

"Especially Dylan," Winnie said, easing her hold and stepping back to see Lane's face.

Lane glanced away.

"I know you love him. Why don't you tell him?"

She shook her head, wiped a stray tear off her cheek. "You know the way he feels. He's sure I'd leave him and Emily, just like Mariah."

"But you wouldn't, would you?"

She wiped another tear. "No." She turned, walked past Winnie, then stopped and turned back at the door. "I've got to go upstairs and finish packing. Thank you for everything."

Winnie said nothing. Lane saw her brushing away tears of her own.

Upstairs, she walked past the suitcase lying open on her bed, and moved over to the window. On the other side of the glass, beautiful forested hillsides surrounded the lodge. Jagged granite peaks glinted white with snow.

She remembered her last plane ride, the engine failure, camping with Dylan beside the lake, making love in a tent, watching him grin as she praised the taste of the fish he had caught and fried. She remembered the bear she had confronted, standing up to it and driving it away. She remembered the long trek through the woods, dodging gunfire.

She was stronger than Dylan believed. She'd be stronger still with a man by her side who loved her. She thought about telling him that.

But Dylan wouldn't believe her.

Lane packed the rest of her clothes, then closed her suitcase. Tomorrow she was going home.

Dylan walked out the front door, onto the porch that overlooked Eagle Bay. It was beautiful here, with the changing blues and grays of the sea and sky overhead, the mountains reflected in the water. As far as he was concerned, the most beautiful place in the world. The wild forest creatures added life to the landscape around him, moose and bear, squirrels and birds, the fish he watched jump in the bay.

Alaska was in his blood. It was part of his DNA. He wouldn't be happy anywhere else, and he was smart enough to know it. And he knew that Lane understood.

It was something else he admired about her.

He turned at the sound of small footsteps behind him, saw Emily hurrying toward him across the porch.

He managed to smile. "Hi, honey. What are you doing out here?"

She looked up at him with solemn blue eyes, a lighter shade than his own. "Lane's l-leaving, Daddy." A rusty note remained in her voice, but every day she sounded better.

"I know, sweetheart. She has to go back to L.A."

"Don't d-do it, Daddy. Don't s-send Lane away."

His heart squeezed. He wasn't sending her away, and yet it felt as if that was exactly what he was doing.

"She wouldn't like it here, honey. Sooner or later, she'd want to go back home."

"No, s-she wouldn't. Lane is-isn't like Mama. She wouldn't run off and leave us."

"Listen to me, honey—"

"Mama d-didn't love us, Daddy. She s-said so. She told me the n-night she ran away."

Dylan frowned as he knelt in front of his daughter. "You saw your mother that night?"

She nodded, looked as if she was fighting not to cry. "I f-followed her outside. There was a man there w-waiting in his car. I b-begged her not to go. I asked her to t-take me with her, but she wouldn't. She said she never wanted a kid. She didn't want me. She said she would be happier somewhere else."

Emily started crying, and Dylan pulled her into his arms. "It's all right, honey. That was a long time ago."

"It was my f-fault she left. And then she got killed."

Dylan's arms tightened around her. "It wasn't your fault. It was mine. Your mother never wanted to live in Alaska. She hated it here. That's the reason she left."

She looked up at him, her pink cheeks streaked with tears. "Mama didn't love us enough."

"No, she didn't."

"But Lane does. I k-know she does. Lane loves us enough to stay."

He looked over the little girl's shoulder, saw Lane standing on the porch next to Finn.

"Yes, I do," Lane said, her green eyes shimmering with tears. "I love you both with all my heart, and I'd never leave you."

Dylan set Emily on her feet. His chest was squeezing. Finn woofed, and Emily ran over and threw her arms around the big dog's neck.

Dylan walked toward Lane.

"I want to stay," she said softly when he reached her. "I love you, Dylan. It doesn't matter where I live as long as I'm with you."

He drew her against him, buried his face in her hair. "I don't want you to leave. I don't ever want you to leave. I love you, Lane. It's killing me to let you go."

She looked up at him, her eyes brimming with tears. "Then ask me to stay."

A shuddering breath whispered out. Hope was clawing its way into his chest. "What about your job? You have a house, a business to run in L.A."

"I'm a painter. Painting is what I love to do. Since I've been here, I've figured that out. I'm good at it, Dylan. I think I could sell my work in the galleries up here."

"You're better than good. You're amazing."

"Haley is running the business and doing a really great job. I'd still have an interest."

"Do you really think you could be happy here?"

"As long as you loved me, I could be happy just sitting on the front porch looking out at the sea."

He crushed her against him. "I love you, Lane. I've never loved anyone this way." He drew back to look at her. "You wouldn't be lonely. We'd have plenty of guests staying at the lodge. Well, not in winter, but—"

"I don't care."

He started smiling. "You should see it here when it snows. Big white flakes falling, weighing down the branches of the trees. The ice in the creek sparkles like diamonds. It's like living in one of those crystal snow globes."

"You can show me. You can make me see it through your eyes."

Something unfurled in his chest. "I love you. Will you marry me?"

Lane threw her arms around his neck. "I thought you'd never ask."

Emily took off running for the house. "They're getting married!" she shouted, racing in to tell Caleb and Winnie. "Daddy and Lane are getting married!" Finn rushed after her, and the two disappeared into the lodge.

Dylan looked down at Lane. "I should have seen it. I should have realized you were the one. I should have figured it out when you scared away that bear."

Lane laughed. She was crying when he kissed her. But they were happy tears.

His own joy came from a place he'd closed off a long

time ago. Lane had opened the door to that dark, lonely place inside him.

He found himself smiling. He had given her the chance to go back. Now he'd never let her go.

Dylan bent his head and kissed her.

Epilogue

The Eagle Bay Lodge was officially open, with more than half the rooms filled with sportsmen, some with their wives. Dylan and Lane were officially engaged. They planned to marry next summer, when family and friends could join them. They were both excited, but not in a rush. For the moment, they were just happy to be enjoying their lives, and for Lane, the adventure of living in Alaska.

Dylan had been wrong about that. Lane loved it here.

"I might not have been born here," she would say with a grin. "But I got here as quick as I could."

Emily was talking a mile a minute now. Dylan smiled to think he couldn't seem to shut her up. She had blamed herself for her mother's death and kept her misplaced guilt locked inside.

She was free of that now.

Lane was painting. Every time she hung one of her landscapes in the great hall, one of the guests wanted to buy it. She was a terrific artist. But he had known that from the start.

"Dylan!" Waving a newspaper, she ran toward him down the grassy slope in front of the float dock, where he was working on the plane, making a few little adjustments to the engine.

Tossing down his wrench, he started up the gangway, caught her in his arms, and twirled her around, nuzzling his face in her hair.

"What is it, love?"

She shoved the newspaper in front of him. "I got an e-mail from the boys in Yeil, Alex and Jared. They did it, Dylan."

"All right, I'll bite. What'd they do?"

"I printed the article they sent me. It was in the *San Francisco Chronicle*. Alex and Jared went down to San Francisco. Remember, that's where Artemus Carmack lived?"

"I remember."

"Apparently his wife's family lived there, too. It's where he and Olivia met. When Artemus went broke, Olivia's parents bought his mansion in Pacific Heights. Descendants of the family still own the house. A few years back, one of them found his journal among some old papers in the library."

"You mean the fool admitted to committing the murders?"

"Can you believe it? When Alex and Jared went to the house to talk to them, Olivia's family gave them the journal. The family had read them, but in those days reputation was more important than justice. Still, secretly they hated that the man who'd killed Olivia and little Mary had gotten away with murder. At last the day had come to see the truth exposed."

Dylan looked down at the printed piece of paper. "That's what's in the article?"

She nodded. "The article is also about us, Dylan, and the Eagle Bay Lodge. How we urged the boys in Yeil to prove what really happened. The paper is going to do a series about Carmack, once one of San Francisco's most prominent citizens. They're going to tell the truth about what happened to Olivia and her little girl."

He felt a trickle of unease. "They gonna say the lodge is full of ghosts?"

"According to Alex and Jared, since there never really were any ghosts, they're leaving that part out."

"In that case, maybe it'll be good for business."

"That's what I was thinking when I agreed to let them come up and do a photo shoot."

He grinned. "Maybe it'll also be good for your budding career as an artist."

She laughed. "Could be." She looked past him out at the bay. "You know, I never told you this, but remember the day you flew me up here? That funny dream I had about the raven?"

"What about it?"

"We didn't fly over the cemetery that day."

He glanced away, feeling a little guilty. "Yeah, I know. I just didn't want any more trouble." He looked down at her. "I wonder why you had that dream."

Lane turned and gazed back up the hill in the direction of the old cemetery, where the raven totem stood guard over the villagers who were buried there. "I don't know. I guess some things can never be explained."

But Dylan figured the dream she'd had was just one more sign that Lane belonged there. As they walked back up the hill toward the lodge, he smiled.

Author's Note

I hope you enjoyed Dylan and Lane in *Against the Wild*. It's the first of three novels about the Brodie brothers of Alaska, romantic, high-action adventures I'm hoping will keep you entertained.

You've met Dylan's brother, Nick Brodie, a former police detective with a serious case of burnout. In *Against the Sky*, you'll meet Samantha Hollis, owner of the Perfect Pup dog-grooming salon, a woman from California who is definitely in for trouble with both Nick and Alaska.

Trouble that involves solving a murder and puts both their lives in danger.

I hope you'll watch for *Against the Sky*, then Rafe Brodie's story, *Against the Tide*. Till then, very best wishes and happy reading.

Kat

Please read on for a preview of *Against the Sky*, available now!

Nick helped Samantha into his black Ford Explorer for the drive down the hill to his house. It had started to rain. This late in September, rainy days were a given.

"What do you think really happened to Jimmy?" she asked. "A fistfight with a schoolmate wouldn't explain why he didn't come home all day."

"Maybe he was afraid of what his aunt would say when she saw his battered face, but it's hard to believe. Jimmy's usually the kind of kid who tackles trouble head-on."

"Then what else could it be?"

Nick shook his head. "Worrying his aunt that way was really out of character." He ran a hand over the late-night beard along his jaw. "I don't know, it seemed like he was trying to brazen it out, putting up a tough front, but I got a feeling he was scared."

"Of his aunt?"

Nick shook his head. "No." He sighed. "Hell, he's a kid. Maybe I was reading the whole thing wrong. I'll talk to him in the morning, see if I can get him to open up." He looked over at Samantha as he pulled into the driveway. "I've got a microwave. How about we heat up some of that chicken you cooked before we had to go looking for a runaway kid?"

"Good idea. I'm really hungry."

"Me, too." But the kind of hunger he was feeling had nothing to do with food and everything to do with Samantha Hollis. He tried not to remember the last time they had been together, the softness of her lips, her small, feminine curves, her sweet cries of passion as she'd moved beneath him.

He tried to prevent it, but by the time he pulled the car into the garage, turned off the engine, and helped Samantha down from the SUV, he was hard as a frigging stone.

Samantha smiled as he led her into the kitchen. "I imagine after all the excitement, we'll both get a good night's sleep."

He cast her a thunderous look. "You really think so? Because I'll be lying there half the night aching for you, wishing you were in my bed instead of your own."

Her eyes widened. "But you said—"

"I know what I said. I said you'd be safe if you came to Alaska, and I won't break my word. Doesn't mean I don't want you." He leaned over and very softly kissed her, felt his arousal stirring beneath his jeans. Samantha returned the kiss, making him harder still. Then she pulled away.

"I-I'd better get the chicken out of the fridge and into the microwave." She started walking toward the refrigerator, stopped, and turned back. "I'm glad your friend Jimmy is safe."

"Yeah, at least for now." It took superhuman effort to force his mind off sex and onto the conversation he needed to have with the boy in the morning. The kid was important to him. The boy's father had just died, and Jimmy was convinced it was murder. It was crazy, but after what had happened tonight, it was clear that something was wrong. Nick needed to find out what the hell was going on.

Samantha couldn't sleep. Nick had said he'd be lying in bed aching for her, wishing she were there beside him. She hadn't thought she would be the one aching, unable to sleep.

How could she have forgotten the magnetic pull of the man? The aura of masculinity that had so effortlessly seduced her before?

Just looking at that lean-muscled body as he walked around the house made her want him, those long, purposeful strides that had attracted her from the moment she had seen him in the hotel. And those amazing eyes, the most arresting shade of blue she had ever seen. Eyes that should have been cool, but instead seemed to burn with an inner heat.

Nick was the kind of man who touched easily and without conscious thought, the kind who made a woman feel protected and desired. She remembered the feel of his hard body pressing her down in the mattress, his muscles flexing as he took her, the pleasure he had given her. She remembered every moment she had spent with Nick.

She wanted Nick Brodie, had from the moment he had rescued her from a stranger's unwanted advances.

But now there was more at stake. So much more. She needed to know him, trust him. She needed time to be certain he was the kind of man he seemed.

She heard movement in the bedroom next to hers.

Nick was awake, just as he'd said. How long could she resist the urge to go to him, to offer him her body as she had done before?

With a sigh, Samantha plumped her pillow, put it over her head, and tried not to wish Nick would storm through the door and demand a place in her bed.